Paint the Moon

Katia Rose

Copyright © 2025 by Katia Rose

All rights reserved.

No part of this book may be reproduced in any form or by any electronic or mechanical means, including information storage and retrieval systems, without written permission from the author, except for the use of brief quotations in a book review.

The following is a work of fiction. Names, characters, businesses, places, events, locales, and incidents are either the products of the author's imagination or are used in a fictitious manner. Any resemblance to actual persons, living or dead (or lingering between those two states), or actual events is purely coincidental.

This book has been licensed for your personal enjoyment only. Please respect the author's work.

Chapter 1

Natalie

My great-aunt owned way too many porcelain dolls.

From the top shelf of the closet, four pairs of glazed eyes stare down at me, their vacant expressions framed by Shirley Temple ringlets and frilly lace bonnets. The shadows of the closet give the dolls' pink rosebud mouths a menacing aura, like they might just curl back their lips to reveal six-inch fangs ready to puncture my jugular.

"You guys!" I yell as I take a step back from the closet door. "I found more!"

"No fucking way!" Jacinthe calls out, her voice muffled by the walls of the guest bedrooms we're working on clearing out. "Did she have them in every fucking room of the house?"

I hear a door slam, and then Jacinthe's typical stomping gait moves down the hallway towards me, the creaking floors of my aunt's ancient house echoing in her wake.

Stealth has never been my best friend's strong suit. I might as well have an enraged baby elephant barreling towards me, not a five-foot-two French Canadian butch lesbian with a passion for expletives.

"*Tabarnak!*" she groans after sidling up beside me. "In the closet? That's creepy as hell, man."

"Maybe we should check under the floorboards too," a voice says from behind us.

We both whip around to find Maddie leaning against the doorframe, the gloomy winter light outside reflecting against her thick glasses and making her sudden appearance seem even more specter-like.

I shudder as I glance down at the wide oak floorboards beneath my feet. "Don't even say that."

"And stop sneaking up on us," Jacinthe snaps at her younger cousin. "This place is already creepy as shit without you popping up out of nowhere, *petit fantôme*."

Maddie earned the nickname 'little ghost' when she was just a toddler with giant, dark brown eyes always watching everyone behind her glasses. Even at twenty-three, she hasn't lost the ability to slip into a room without a sound, but she's grown to give as good as she gets when people make fun of her unnerving tendencies.

"Maybe if you didn't stomp around like a tranquilized horse, you'd actually hear me coming, *bête*."

Jacinthe squares up, and I step between them on instinct, as ready to ward off a battle between the two cousins now as I was in our elementary school days.

"*C'est toi la bête!*" Jacinthe snaps, shaking her head and blowing out a heavy breath through pursed lips.

The whinnying sound does not help with denying the tranquilized horse allegations.

"You're both beasts in your own special ways," I say. "Now stop acting like children and help me get these dolls out of the closet before the sun sets. I don't want to find out what happens to them at night."

Maddie slinks off and returns with a stool a few seconds later. I climb up and pass the dolls down to Jacinthe one by one. She gives them to Maddie to pile up with the other dolls in the next room over, which has become the collection point for the several dozen porcelain dolls my great-aunt Manon had displayed throughout her six-bedroom home.

Technically, it's my six-bedroom home now.

Tante Manon passed away almost three months ago, but I still haven't wrapped my brain around the reality that out of every relative she could have picked to bestow her legacy upon, she chose me.

My cantankerous aunt who seemed to despise every human being on the planet—especially the ones related to her—left me the remainder of her sizeable life's savings and the deed to her house, which just so happens to be one of the oldest and largest properties in the historic town of La Cloche.

Three months ago, I was subsiding on ramen noodles in the tiny apartment above my mom's shop. I'm still officially living there, but now I also own a bigger plot of land than my parents.

"You know, I think this is the first day none of your wacko relatives have shown up to bother us," Jacinthe says as she takes the last doll out of my hands.

We find Maddie rearranging the pile of dolls so the new arrivals will fit on the double mattress kitted out with a floral duvet and frilly bed skirt. The mass of tiny porcelain bodies looks like some kind of gruesome sacrifice.

"I almost wish they had," I say to Jacinthe. "Maybe they could have at least taken some of these away."

My family was as shocked as I was by the contents of

Manon's will, and it seemed like every distant relative from the far reaches of Québec showed up in La Cloche to dispute the legitimacy of the documents. I can't remember how many lawyers I spoke to over the blur of the last few months. My dad even caught a private investigator trying to climb through a window when he came over to check on the house before the process was finalized.

"We should go stick these in all their windows at night," Jacinthe says as she drops the doll in her hands onto the middle of the pile. "That will teach them to mess with you."

Maddie straightens the doll out to align with the carefully organized rows of bodies she's made.

"You know, that's not a bad idea," she says. "I still don't get why they've been so awful to you, Natalie. If they wanted the house that bad, they should have spent some time with Manon before she, you know, died."

She winces like she regrets being so blunt, but I just shrug.

"It's not like I spent time with *Tante* Manon either. I barely saw her outside of Christmas and Easter dinners."

"Yeah," Jacinthe says with a pointed look at the bed, "because she was fucking terrifying."

"Jass!"

Maddie shoots daggers at her cousin, and Jacinthe gives her a confused look before her eyebrows shoot up with comprehension.

"Right, right. *Ben*, not to speak ill of the dead, *là*," she says with her best attempt at tact. "She was your aunt. I didn't—"

"It's fine."

I wave her off, barely holding back a grin. Jacinthe definitely did not miss a calling as a grief counselor, but in the storm of the past couple months, the bluntness I know

Paint the Moon

and love her for has been a rock to cling to and keep me steady.

She pushes the dark, choppy layers of her chin-length hair out of her face, chewing on her lip like she's not sure if she's supposed to continue with the chagrined routine.

"She *was* terrifying," I say. "Remember how we used to joke that she'd chop our legs off if she caught us running around her yard? I mean, even now, I'm still nervous every time I walk through the gate. Plus, I'm pretty sure she never spoke more than five sentences to me in her life. I was convinced she didn't even bother remembering my name, but then..."

Then there it was in the will.

My name.

Just my name.

"They have a point."

Maddie and Jacinthe both tilt their heads at the exact same angle, in one of the rare displays that make them look like sisters and not just cousins.

"All those relatives," I add. "They keep saying I don't deserve this, and they're right."

I drop my gaze to the floor as a rush of heat floods my cheeks, and I hope the thick mass of my hair is enough to hide it. I tilt my chin down to make my hair slide even farther forward as I stare at the splatters of teal and crimson paint flecked across the tips of the sneakers I changed into after kicking off my winter boots at the front door.

I usually only wear these shoes in the studio. I remember exactly what piece I was working on that left the teal and crimson layered on top of dozens more flecks of acrylics.

I remember staying up until two in the morning on a random Monday, brush in one hand and my usual mug of tea in the other, a Maggie Rogers album crooning out of my speaker, the whole rest of the world soft and asleep while I coaxed new life out of my canvas.

It was the last piece I finished before my exhibition, and I poured all the love of a mother spoiling her youngest child into every stroke of paint. I thought it was one of my best in years. I made sure it had a prime spot, dead center on its own wall in the middle of the gallery.

It didn't sell.

Nothing in my exhibition sold.

"I mean, why me?" I say, gaze still pinned to my shoes. "She could have picked my brother, my parents, literally any random relative who's crawled out of the woodwork since she died. What does a single, childless, twenty-six year-old failed painter need a six-bedroom house for? It doesn't make sense. I should give it up. I should just hand it over to someone else like they're all asking me to. I don't deserve it. I'm not good enough."

My voice cracks, and I curl my fists even tighter.

This isn't me.

I don't cry.

When I feel the urge to cry, I paint about it, but I haven't touched a brush since I came back to La Cloche after the exhibition that concluded my six month artist in residence position in Thunder Bay. I don't know how else to get everything out: the shame, the guilt, the whispering voices reminding me that I got picked for a once in a lifetime opportunity out of hundreds of other applicants, and I blew it.

I want to splatter inky black across crisp white canvas. I want to grab a scalpel and carve violent gouges through viscous globs. I want to dig my nails straight into the paint, but I can't, not anymore, and so the feelings curdle within me, like brushes left to soak for so long they get moldy and covered in goo.

I jump when Maddie claps her hand down on my shoulder.

"You are *not* a failed painter," she says, squeezing me until I have no choice but to look up and meet her gaze.

Her giant brown eyes don't blink at all behind her glasses as she stares me down.

"You're an artist, Natalie. You always have been, and you always will be. One show doesn't define who you are."

"*C'est vrai, ma belle,*" Jacinthe agrees with a nod. "Who says those fuckers in Thunder Bay have any taste anyways? Who names a city Thunder Bay? It sounds like something out of a dumb superhero movie. Way too dramatic."

I huff a laugh.

"I mean, *our* town is named after a giant bell."

Jacinthe crosses her arms. "Damn right it is, which means we're better. They don't have a cool bell in Thunder Bay. They just have, uh..."

"Thunder?" Maddie suggests.

Jacinthe bobs her head, her eyes sparking with righteous zeal. "Right. Yeah. Just some dumb old thunder, and, like...a bay."

This time, I tip my head back and laugh for real.

"Thunder and a bay," I choke out. "Wow, Jass. Wow."

She glares at me, but the corners of her mouth can't keep from quirking up.

"Damn, it's almost dark now," Maddie says, gliding over to the window. "When did that happen?"

The grey light of the cloudy March day has shifted into the gloom of dusk. An eerie mist is rising off the couple feet of snow still coating the ground.

Jacinthe takes one glance out the window and then spins on her heels.

"I'm getting the hell out of here before these dolls come to life and try to suck my blood."

Maddie and I can't argue with that. We're right behind her as she trudges down the creaking staircase and heads for our boots and coats piled by the front door. We decide to head into town for some hard-earned pizza and beer. Once we're suited up and standing on the wrap-around porch outside, I fish the tarnished silver key out of my purse to lock up.

The click of the bolt sliding into place echoes in my ears even after we're slipping our way along the icy path across the front lawn to our cars.

Chapter 2

Natalie

On a Tuesday night in March, La Cloche might as well be a ghost town. The holiday crowds are long gone, the height of ski season at Mont-Tremblant has passed, and the icy, fog-filled country roads keep all but the most intrepid scenery seekers from venturing off the highway.

The streetlights splash a golden glow across the congealing snow banks lining the sidewalks and cast shadows in the darkened windows of the colourful storefronts. After I choose from one of the many empty parking spots and get out to meet Maddie and Jacinthe, we walk past a selection of artists' shops and studios on our way to Mack's Bistro.

La Cloche is known for being a bit of a hippie haven. A town this small really shouldn't be able to support an organic health food store specializing in natural remedies, but that's the business my mom has been running my entire life, right alongside all the sculptors, jewelers, florists, antiques curators, tarot readers, and ecstatic dance facilitators who call La Cloche home.

There are plenty of painters too. The old-fashioned iron lampposts lining the street are hung with banners displaying pieces by local artists. They change them to match the seasons. We pass right under a fluttering landscape of mine that gets hung up every winter.

My shoulders tense, and I keep my eyes glued to the sidewalk while I fight the urge to rip the banner from its post.

"*Regarde*. The church looks really pretty tonight."

We've reached Mack's. I lift my gaze to look over where Maddie is pointing out the small, white church down where the main street, Rue Principale, forks in two.

Technically, it's not an active church anymore. In true hippie fashion, it's been repurposed as a non-denominational community center, but the towering steeple still houses the town's namesake: the oldest church bell in Canada, brought over from France itself.

Tonight, the solar-powered lanterns strung along the churchyard's white picket fence give an almost fairytale-like effect in the darkness of the evening. Combined with the stillness of the empty street and the whispering breeze in the chilly air, you can almost imagine someone has cast a spell on the town, lulling this place into the peace of an enchanted sleep.

My shoulders relax, and I let out a quiet sigh.

No matter how ugly the rest of my life might get, La Cloche always finds a way to show me something beautiful.

The moment slips away when Jacinthe pulls the door of Mack's Bistro open and the sound of classic rock spills into the street. The scent of fried food and wood-panelled walls hits my nose as we step into the blast of warm air from the heater.

Paint the Moon

Mack's is a staple of La Cloche nightlife during tourist season. Turns out there's only so much sightseeing you can do before the urge to eat a grease-soaked dinner and down a pint wins out over the more health-conscious options in town. Tonight, however, there are only a couple locals milling around the brown vinyl booths and dark wood bar.

Mack himself comes out from the back at the sound of the door opening, bald head shining and a worn apron thrown on over his t-shirt and jeans. His eyes narrow when he spots us.

"Not you three," he grumbles.

Jacinthe's face splits into a mischievous grin.

"*Câlice*, Mack," she drawls as she clomps over to give him a pat on the shoulder. "Is that how you talk to your customers?"

He crosses his arms and glares at her. "You are not a customer. You are the spawn of Satan."

Getting a part-time job at Mack's is a rite of passage for the youth of La Cloche. Jacinthe and I did our time together during ski season when we were seventeen. Mack made the mistake of letting her be a line cook, a role in which her quick temper and passion for expletives allowed her to flourish into the French Canadian equivalent of Gordon Ramsay, sans any actual cooking knowledge.

Mack's nerves never quite recovered.

Jacinthe tuts at him as she makes her way over to our favourite booth. Maddie and I follow, and we put in an order for a round of beers and an extra-large cheese pizza.

I slip away to the washroom after devouring my first slice within minutes of our dinner arriving. When I come back, I find Jacinthe and Maddie arguing at each other from across the booth.

"It's a good idea!" Jacinthe says as I slide into my spot beside her.

Maddie tips her beer glass towards me. "Well, why don't you see what Natalie thinks?"

"Thinks about what?" I ask.

"We were just talking," Maddie says, her voice a little too measured to sound natural, "about what you might do with the house. You know, once we've got it all cleaned out."

The back of my neck tingles, my muscles tensing up like an invisible threat has slipped into the room. It's the same feeling that's come over me every time I've thought about the future since getting back to La Cloche.

"I, um, haven't really thought about that."

I hate the way my voice shakes. I hate the way I can't keep even my vocal cords under control these days. My throat swells shut, and the pizza that looked so delicious just seconds ago now makes my stomach churn.

"What about the inn?"

Jass raises an eyebrow like I'm supposed to know what she's talking about, but I just squint at her.

"Huh?"

Maddie clears her throat, and I notice her shooting daggers at her cousin, but Jacinthe doesn't back down.

"You know. Remember when we all worked at the hotel that one summer, and we decided we should run our own inn together when we grew up?"

A hazy memory of one of my teenage summers surfaces, tinged with the scent of cleaning products and sweat. The three of us spent a few months on the housekeeping team at a small hotel in Mont-Tremblant, where our infuriating manager fueled many a long discussion about how much better we could run our own hotel in La Cloche.

We got pretty serious about it, even going as far as

drawing up a business plan, but our enthusiasm faded once school started in the fall, just like it always did for the many harebrained money-making schemes we'd dream up together when we were younger.

"What about it?" I ask.

Jacinthe rolls her eyes like I'm really testing her patience. *"Voyons.* The house. Manon's house. What if you made it into an inn?"

A squawk bursts out of me. I look to Maddie for confirmation that this is insane, even for Jacinthe, but all she does is take a sip of beer, her eyes pensive behind her thick glasses.

"You're in on this too?" I demand.

She shrugs. "Jacinthe brought it up, but you have to admit, it actually makes a lot of sense."

It does not make sense.

It's only been a few months since the culminating moment of my art career ended in utter failure. Apparently, I don't even know how to do the one thing I planned on dedicating my whole life to, never mind chasing after a literal teenage dream I haven't thought about in years.

Still, something about the idea has me blinking at Maddie like she's an oracle into an alternate universe.

I can see it: the house painted in a fresh coat of white, the bland grey shutters replaced with a brilliant emerald green, a few sofas and maybe even a hammock set out on the porch. I can see guests sipping their morning coffee out there, watching the mist clear from the woods as the first bird songs of the day ring out through the quiet air.

I can see it all the way I used to see paintings in my mind: the colours I'd mix together, the brushes I'd choose to bring every detail to life.

"Fuck yeah!"

Jacinthe's voice makes me jump like she's snuck up behind me. I blink to bring the room around us back into focus, the wood panelling and worn-out floorboards replacing the visions in my mind.

I realize my hands are shaking. I shove them under my thighs.

"Let's make a hotel!" Jass urges.

I force myself to grin, rolling my shoulders back to shake off the eerie sensations.

We're just joking around. We're just having a fun, beer-fueled conversation.

"Let's?" I say. "Oh, so we're doing this together?"

"Duh," she answers. "As if you could do it without us. We're a dream team! We're like the perfect business partners. Remember when we ran that lemonade stand together?"

Maddie and I burst out laughing.

"Yeah, when we were like, ten," I say.

Jass waves her beer at us. "Doesn't matter. It was the shit. We made so much money, and we're still the perfect combination: Maddie does all the math and money stuff, Natalie does all the artistic marketing stuff, and I do all the talking."

All three of us laugh at that.

I can still feel the vision of the house tugging at the corners of my mind, fighting to slide into focus, but I dig my nails into the smooth vinyl underneath me to keep me grounded in the here and now.

I'm not letting myself get swept up in an illusion of what could be.

Not again.

"We could call it the Lemonade Inn," I say, keeping my voice breezy. "We could paint the whole house bright yellow as an homage to our first business venture together."

Jacinthe snaps her fingers. "*Parfait*! I like it. We could plant some lemon trees in the yard."

Maddie grimaces. "Lemon trees don't grow in Canada."

I shake my head. "Anything is possible at the Lemonade Inn."

Jacinthe and I high-five. Maddie groans as we make another half dozen lemon-themed jokes about this theoretical inn, but she still joins in when we expand our horizons to other suggestions.

Jacinthe says we could team up for promotions with the trail riding company her family runs during the summer. I say we could go all out and provide every guest with their own personal pony for the duration of their stay.

"We could get a sleigh for the winter!" Jass adds. "I would look so sexy driving a sleigh."

"That's actually not a bad idea," Maddie says. "The tourists would eat that up. Oh, we could make a skating rink too! And put a bunch of twinkle lights and candles around it. It'd be perfect for Valentine's Day vacations."

"We could make a special sex dungeon suite in the creepy basement," I say with an eyebrow wag, "for the adventurous couples."

Maddie does not deign to respond to that and instead pulls her phone out.

"We'd probably need, like, an interior designer, right?" she says as she types something.

"I guess, yeah," I say before suspicion takes hold. "Wait. What are you doing?'

"I'm looking for one. Oh, wow, this is pretty! Look at this place. They've done lots of boutique hotels."

She slides her phone across the table, and I see she's

pulled up the website of some firm called Leung Designs. A gallery of their work shows a chic but cozy lobby complete with a moody, Hemingway-esque bar area with vintage brass accents I can totally see the tourists of La Cloche going crazy for.

"That is nice," I say, "but—"

Before I can protest any further, Maddie snatches the phone back and keeps scrolling, the glare of the screen reflecting in her glasses.

"Oh, look! They do free consultations. They'll even do one on site if you're close enough to Montreal. Hmm, we're probably too far. I should still send a request anyway. Their work looks really good."

I shake my head. "Maddie, don't."

She's already typing again. My pulse speeds up, and my voice comes out way sharper than I intend.

"Maddie. *No.*"

She looks up, her big eyes flaring even wider at the venom in my tone. Even Jacinthe looks taken aback.

"I'm sorry." I pause and force myself to blow out a long breath, ignoring the way my heartbeat is still hammering in my ears. "Look, this has been a fun conversation, but we all know I'm probably just going to sell the house, right?"

They blink at me with way more shock than I was expecting. Jacinthe's jaw has dropped open, and Maddie's forehead wrinkles.

"You are?"

They're both looking at me like I just kicked a puppy, and I have no idea why.

"I mean...yes? That's really the only logical thing to do."

I didn't even think it needed to be said out loud. I'm not going to live in a six-bedroom house all by myself, and it's not like there's even a hint of a serious girlfriend for me

Paint the Moon

here in La Cloche. I don't exactly relish the thought of becoming a landlord, so selling seems like the only way to go.

Jacinthe clears her throat and gestures at the stack of notes Maddie has scribbled. "This seems pretty logical to me."

I can't keep myself from scoffing. "We're just tipsy and getting carried away with ourselves. This is not a real idea, right?"

Again, they glance at each other with way more disappointment than I was bracing for.

"Oh," Maddie mumbles.

I look back and forth between them, waiting for the other shoe to drop.

"What?" I ask after a moment of silence ticks by.

"It's just...do you really want to sell it?"

Something about Maddie's quiet, almost pained tone makes me pause and think.

I keep calling the place Manon's house, but there's a part of me—a very small, submerged part like a seed buried in deep, dark soil—that's begun to think of it as mine too.

I'd be ripping that seed out if I sold the house.

"There's no reason for me to have it," I say.

Maddie tilts her head just enough to catch Jacinthe's eye, the two of them sharing another glance I can't read.

Annoyance flares in me like a match lighting up.

"Why do you keep looking at each other like that?" I snap.

I regret the words as soon as I say them, but I can't bring myself to take them back.

"It just seems like...*ben*, like the house is...good for you, *là*."

Even Jacinthe has lowered her voice now, like she's

approaching a wild animal caught in a trap. Her soothing tone just makes my blood boil even hotter.

"Good for me?"

She shrugs and gives Maddie a pleading look like she's calling in backup.

"We know you're going through a tough time," Maddie says after chewing on her lip for a moment.

I open my mouth to protest.

"Even if you don't want to talk about it," she interrupts with a pointed look, "and having the house to work on...it's kind of been like having the old Natalie back."

Her words hit me like a punch to the sternum, caving my chest in.

They feel sorry for me.

That's what those looks between them are for. They pity me. I've become this fragile thing they have to tiptoe around.

"Well, I'm not the old Natalie anymore," I mutter. "I'm sorry if that's an inconvenience to you."

Maddie's cheeks go pale. "I didn't mean it like that. I just—"

"I know. I know."

I dig my nails even harder into the booth's cushion.

I don't want to be this person. I can't go back to the old Natalie, but I don't know who this new Natalie is, and I'm not sure I like her.

If I were Maddie and Jacinthe, I definitely wouldn't like me right now.

I can't lose them too.

I might have lost the vision of my future I'd been chasing for years, but I can't let myself lose the best friends I have right here in the present just because I can't pull my shit together.

"I know you guys are worried," I say, staring down at the reflections of the bar lights in the polished wood table top. "I appreciate that. I really do, but I just...I need time to figure things out, okay? If art isn't going to work out for me, then—"

Jacinthe lets out a grumble that verges on snarling. "One *maudit* show full of idiots doesn't mean that—"

"It wasn't just a show."

I'm back to snapping at her again, but I'm sick of everyone saying it was just one show and that it doesn't define me.

It was *the* show. I spent half a year working on that exhibition and a lifetime building the skills to do it. I pinned everything on that artist in residence position. It was supposed to put me on the map. The entire Canadian art world would be looking at me. Critics from the other side of the country were flown in just to write about my work.

I pushed myself harder than I ever have before, letting go of my old techniques and subject matter to show them I could be more than just a small town prodigy, more than just a girl selling prints in the back of her mom's shop. It was my chance to be *bigger*, and I blew it. Not only did I fail to sell a single thing, but I failed to get even one positive review.

No one prepares you for the moment you find out the one thing everyone has always told you you're good at isn't good enough.

My eyes sting, and I push myself to my feet.

"I don't want to get into this tonight, okay?" I say, blinking hard. "I'm sorry I'm being weird and rude. I'm just tired. I think I should call it a night."

Maddie leans closer, reaching for my arm. "Natalie..."

I shake my head. "I'm okay."

I say goodnight, and after a few pleas and protests, they do the same. Once I'm back out on the sidewalk, I suck in a deep gulp of the chilly night air.

I glance over at the church, but even with the string lights still twinkling along the fence, the scene doesn't look peaceful and enchanted anymore.

It just looks empty. The whole town looks so empty and cold.

Chapter 3

Brooke

"Another day, another dollar."

Layla grabs her mug just as the coffee machine finishes dispensing a stream of hot liquid, and we cheers before downing our first sips of caffeine.

She joins me in leaning against the counter of the office's cramped break room. Her white mug is printed with the words 'World's Best Receptionist.' It was a Christmas gift from me a couple years ago, and despite the already rocky start to this day, the sight of her using it makes me grin.

"Another day, another complete failure on the part of my landlord to keep my apartment from flooding," I say before taking a few more gulps of coffee.

Layla's eyebrows shoot up. "He still hasn't fixed that?"

"He says he's *getting around* to it."

I put the words in air quotes. I've sent a half dozen messages about the mysterious bulge in my bathroom ceiling that seems to grow bigger every time I shower, but apparently that isn't a huge priority in Landlord World.

It's not the first time this week I've felt like a low priority. The whole reason I'm huddled up here in the break room with Layla instead of getting started at my desk is the lingering memory of just how low a priority my boss proved me to be only yesterday.

"I really hope Eric doesn't come in today," I say. "I swear to god, if he makes one of his stupid jokes at me, I'm going to scream."

Layla shuffles closer and pats my arm. "I know, babe. Keep chugging that coffee. It will give you strength."

I only manage another sip before a tirade comes bursting out of me with the same force I imagine is going to explode my bathroom ceiling any day now.

"Can you believe he said we'd circle back to discussing a promotion *next year*? It's March! Meanwhile, I'm basically already doing the work of a project manager anyway. It's insane that I even have to ask him for the job title."

My voice has gotten loud enough that I cast a wary glance at the glass door to the rest of the office, but we're here early enough that only a couple of my fellow interior designers are getting set up at their desks.

Layla raises her mug in agreement. "You're so right. What the hell is his problem? This place would be nothing without you!"

Her encouragement doesn't help extinguish the flames lighting up inside me. If anything, they just burn even brighter as I think back on the humiliation of yesterday's meeting with Eric.

"But did I say any of that to him?" I ask. "No, I didn't. That's the worst part, Layla. I just...sat there. I lost sleep for weeks leading up to that meeting I called with him. I've sunk so much time into this firm, hoping it would all pay off someday. That's how it's supposed to work, right? Eric took a chance hiring me right out of design school, and I've spent years doing everything I can to prove I deserved it. Eventually, it *has* to be enough. I was going to tell Eric just that, but when he shot me down, I just...choked."

The flames burn down into searing embers, leaving my throat coated in ash.

Layla pats my arm again. "It's not your fault."

I shrug, keeping my gaze pinned to the ugly green linoleum tiles under our feet. You'd think as an interior design firm, we could put some money towards a more stylish staff room, but it's not like Eric ever comes in here to hang out with his staff.

"It kind of is."

"No, it's not. You've worked here for years. You've consistently done amazing stuff for this company, and you'd expect your boss to at least show an interest in hearing you out. Of course it threw you off when he dismissed you like that. Anybody would have been flabbergasted."

I chuckle. "That's a good word for it. My flabber sure was gasted."

Layla indulges me with a chuckle of her own, and we both take another sip of our drinks.

"Ugh," I groan. "I just want this day to be over, and it hasn't even started yet."

She bumps me with her hip. "Hey. At least you look cute. We're totally twinning today."

She's wearing a tweed pinafore-style dress over a grey turtleneck and some black tights, her auburn hair pinned up in her usual chic bun. I've paired a tweed skirt with a blouse and some fleece-lined tights to combat the lingering chill of Montreal's brutal winter.

"We do look cute," I say, grinning in spite of myself. "Thanks for listening."

"Of course. I'm always here for you. I can even accidentally spill coffee all over Eric when I'm delivering his mail today if you want."

"Don't tempt me," I warn, relishing the mental image. "Shall we go out and face the music?"

Layla takes a few languid steps toward the break room door and sweeps it open with a flourish. "If we must."

The office is mostly open concept, with a reception desk presiding over a dozen desks and swivel chairs. Eric has his own office at the back next to a glass-walled conference room with the typical large table and projector screen. Layla heads for the reception desk, and I collapse into my swivel chair before pulling my laptop out of my bag.

I plug into my monitor and keyboard before I pull up the files for the latest project I've been added to—the project I will *not* be promoted to managing, despite the fact that I've been working here since Leung Designs was just a handful of desks in a creepy warehouse.

I pop my earbuds in and put on some coffee shop jazz as I wait for the files to load. Layla calls me an old man for it, but there really is nothing like smooth jazz for getting in the workday flow.

Eric Leung himself strides in a few minutes later, a camel coat slung over his arm and an obnoxiously large silver watch flashing on his wrist. He waves to the office at large before doing a lap to stop in at everyone's desks for a quick check-in, which would seem like the behavior of an attentive and caring boss if I didn't know it was just an opportunity to start his day off with some nitpicking.

"Brooke! You done playing DJ?"

He rounds the corner to my desk and chuckles as his gaze flicks between me and my laptop screen.

"Huh?"

Paint the Moon

I follow the direction of his stare and see I've re-opened my search for 'relaxing coffee shop jazz tunes,' since my first pick wasn't quite the vibe I wanted.

"Oh, I—"

Eric taps his watch. "Tick-tock, Brooke. It's past nine now. You think we could pick up the pace on selecting the" —he pauses to squint at my screen—"jazz tunes?"

I grind my molars to keep my jaw from dropping open.

There is no way he doesn't see the irony in the fact that he strolled in at a quarter past nine just to mock my taste in music.

We stare each other down for another few seconds before his face splits into a satisfied smirk.

"Got ya!" he crows. "Pulled another fast one on Brooke."

I blink at him, and for a second, I consider screaming, just like I told Layla I would.

Instead, I force the corners of my mouth up.

"You sure did, Eric."

My face aches with the effort of maintaining what I'm sure is a demonic-looking grin, but Eric doesn't seem to notice. He just raps the corner of my desk with his knuckles and chuckles to himself.

"Hey, listen," he adds, "can you stop by my office in about five minutes? I have something I want to run past you."

I'm too surprised by the request to answer right away, but that doesn't seem to matter. He's already headed to his office by the time I manage to mumble my agreement. I wait until exactly five minutes are up, and then I leap out of my chair and take a few hurried steps over to his office door.

The sooner I get this over with, the better.

Inside, the decor is made up of minimalistic shades of

white and light wood. Eric invites me to take a seat on the wooden chair pulled up in front of his desk.

"I have a consultation I'd like you to do," he says before I've even gotten off my feet.

I press my lips together as my face begins to heat up.

Consultations are done by project managers. I've filled in a time or two when needed—yet more evidence in favor of my promotion—but it's technically above my pay grade.

I grip the edge of the chair hard, my fingertips curling around the wood.

Eric has asked me for some pretty insane requests during my years with the company, but asking me to cover someone else's consultation the day after he turned down my request for a promotion is something else.

"Brooke?"

I blink and find him squinting at me, and I realize I must have missed whatever else he said. I mumble an apology.

"I said, if the client signs on, I'm giving you project manager."

The floor tilts under my chair.

"Excuse me?"

He continues on like he hasn't just shifted this whole office on its axis.

"It's a small project. We just got the inquiry a couple days ago, and I think you'd be a great fit."

He starts to launch into a description of the project, but I'm so stunned I cut him off.

"You want me to be project manager?"

"Yes, Brooke. That's what I said. You spacing out on me?"

He chuckles, that irritating grin sliding back into place on his face. I squeeze the chair even harder.

Paint the Moon

"It's just, yesterday—"

"Well, today is a new day. Now, let me tell you about the job."

He shifts to face his laptop and clicks around for a few seconds before he begins talking again.

I can't hear a word he says.

My ears are filled with a strange rushing sound, and gravity still seems to be playing tricks on the floor. Even the walls look like they're moving.

There's no way this is real.

I squeeze my eyes shut for a second as the vertigo threatens to progress into nausea.

"It's farther out of the city than we'd normally be interested in," Eric is saying when I manage to tune in again, "but since that restaurant client dropped us last quarter, I need something small to squeeze in and make up for it. I offered to send someone out to the site as a courtesy. It's a bit of a drive, but you'll get a travel stipend. I figured you wouldn't mind a little inconvenience like that."

Of course he figured that.

"How far is it?" I ask.

"Oh, just a couple hours. It's in some small town up past Mont-Tremblant. It's called, uh…"

Eric's eyes dart around the screen as he scrolls through his messages for a few seconds.

The rushing sound fills my ears again. My heart beats so fast I can feel it thumping under my blouse.

The nausea returns. My mouth goes dry.

Up past Mont-Tremblant.

I don't go up past Mont-Tremblant.

I don't go anywhere near there.

Not anymore.

"La Cloche."

The words clang in the air like the church bell the town is named for. I swallow the urge to ask him to repeat himself.

I know what he said.

"Brooke?"

I slump forward, catching my head in my hands. I watch the carpet spin.

"Brooke, are you okay?"

I shake my head.

"I feel sick."

The next few seconds are a blur. I must manage to sit up, because the next thing I know, I'm sprinting out of Eric's office. I see Layla's head lift over at the reception desk, her eyes flaring wide as soon as she spots me.

She jumps to her feet and comes barrelling in after me as I lunge for the privacy of the break room.

"Hey!" she calls out as the door slams shut behind her. "Oh my god, Brooke, what's the matter?"

I'm standing with both my hands splayed on the counter, head bowed as I gasp for air.

"He...he..."

"It's okay." She sidles up next to me, her hands fluttering around like she can't decide what to do. "What is it? Talk to me."

"He...he wants to make me project manager," I spit out. "He just offered me the job for a new client."

She freezes.

"What?"

"It's some sort of hotel? I wasn't really listening. I...I..."

I give up trying to talk and focus on getting more oxygen instead.

It feels like the room doesn't have any air left.

"Wait," Layla says. "Is this that house someone wants to

convert into an inn? I remember forwarding that to Eric. I didn't think we'd take it. Wait, he offered you project manager? Brooke, that's huge! That's, like, exactly what you wanted!"

She tilts her head to catch my eye, her expression a mix of elation and confusion.

"You don't look excited. Why don't you look excited?"

"It's... It's..."

My throat feels like it's closing up. I grab the edge of the counter as my knees begin to wobble.

"You're in shock," Layla says, nodding like she's administered an official diagnosis. "Here. Come on. Sit down for a second."

She grabs my arm and guides me over to one of the black leather chairs surrounding the break room's glass table. The top is forever coated in coffee stains, but I don't pay them any mind as I hunch forward to drop my head in my hands.

I listen to the sound of Layla's footsteps and the gurgle of the sink as she fills up a glass of water. She sets it down beside me and then takes a seat in the chair next to mine.

"It is pretty shocking," she says, her voice low and measured, like she's visiting a hospital room. "I know he literally just turned down your request for a promotion. Anyone would have a bit of whiplash, but, Brooke, this is a good thing! This is what you wanted! You finally get a chance to show him what an incredible project manager you're going to be."

I let out a low moan and lift my head. Layla leans closer and gives me a pat on the arm.

"Yeah, it's not the most high-profile project ever," she says, sounding more like a coach giving a pep talk now, "and sure, it's a bit out of the way, but—"

"It's in La Cloche."

My own voice is more of a croak, the name of the town coming out like the ragged caw of a crow.

Layla fights to keep the encouraging grin on her face.

"Right. Yeah. Like I said, not the most glamorous of jobs, but you love small towns! Remember when you dragged me off on that weekend trip to Saint-Sauveur? You were in heaven! I've never seen you like that. This La Cloche place is probably so charming, and you—"

"Layla." I strain my vocal cords to repeat the words with more urgency this time. "It's in *La Cloche*. It's...it's *his* town. It's the town where I was supposed to get married."

More than married, really. It's the town where I was supposed to live. It's the town where I imagined myself having a family, growing old, maybe even starting up my own interior design firm somewhere along the way.

That was back when I believed there was somewhere life really could look like a fairytale, somewhere soft and eternal. Unchanging. Just like an ivy-covered house in the woods, with candles in the windows and smoke curling out of the chimney. Maybe a cat pacing the wraparound porch.

I thought I could find something to call my forever, something no one could ever take away.

"Oh." Layla raises a hand to her mouth, her eyes so wide she looks like a cartoon character. The colour has drained from her face. "No way."

"Yes way."

Her forehead wrinkles, her eyebrows bunching up. "You're sure?"

I can't hold back an exasperated scoff as I release the water glass and rake my hands through my hair, destroying the careful work I put in with my blow-dryer this morning.

"Of course I'm sure, Layla!"

"I'm sorry, I'm sorry. It's just...that's a hell of a coincidence."

I sigh and force myself to stop attacking my hair. "You're telling me."

I slump forwards, resting my head in my hands again and staring down at the congealed coffee rings on the table.

"I can't believe this is happening," I say, my voice muffled by my crumpled posture. "The chance to finally make some progress here falls into my lap, and I have to turn it down."

Layla sucks in a breath. "Whoa whoa whoa. Who said anything about turning it down?"

I snap my head up to gawk at her.

"I can't just show up there, Layla. I've never been back. Not in six whole years. I told myself I wouldn't *ever* go back. That part of my life is done. That part of *me* is done. I'll have to make up some excuse for Eric to tell him I can't do it. I'm sure everyone else already did."

She squints at me. "What do you mean?"

I ball my hands into fists and rest my chin on my knuckles.

"Oh, come on. He didn't actually pick me because he thinks I'm the perfect fit. He asked me because no one else will do it. No one's going to want to waste their time on a country inn when they could be building up their resumes with the latest downtown boutique hotels. That's why he gave me manager on this."

Layla's expression hardens. She sits up straighter in her chair and crosses her arms over her chest.

"Even if that's true, *I* know you're the perfect fit for a job like this. This is exactly your style. All your work is amazing, of course, but you shine with that charming chalet kind of vibe. Remember that restaurant you basically did all by yourself out in Saint-Jérôme? That was stunning!"

Her posture relaxes, but her eyes are still burning bright with the urge to defend my worth—even when she's defending me from myself.

A pang of gratitude hits me in the chest.

"Thank you," I murmur. "You're a really good friend."

She smiles and reaches over to stroke the sleeve of my blouse before giving my arm a quick squeeze. Some of the tight muscles in my shoulders loosen.

"Ugh, if it was anywhere else..."

If it was anywhere else, it really would be the perfect job for me, second-hand offering or not. I knew Leung Designs had its sights set on becoming a cutting edge, urban contemporary firm when I started here. I told myself if I was staying in Montreal after the wedding fell through, I'd commit to going as far as I can in the city, but Layla is right. Nothing gets me more excited to come into work or keeps me at my desk later at night than working on an older building, immersing myself in its quirks and details, turning them over in my mind like puzzle pieces as I meld the old with the new.

Some designers look at the kinds of buildings I love and shudder. They see nothing but roadblocks and complications, but I know that if you look hard enough and listen long enough, every building has a story to tell. There's always a thread, a narrative you can follow through the decades to find out exactly what the place wants to say, and once you know that, you earn the honor of writing that building's next chapter.

Layla clears her throat, the sudden noise in the quiet room making me jump.

"May I speak frankly?"

I squint at her and nod, the tension returning to my shoulders. "Okay."

"You said you haven't been back in six years, right?"

I nod again.

"And based on that time we drunkenly stalked that asshole's Instagram a couple years ago, he doesn't even live there anymore, right?"

Apparently, my ex-fiancé bought a condo in Saint-Jovite just a couple years after we were supposed to get married.

Funny how he could commit to a mortgage but not to me.

A muscle in my jaw ticks. I nod again.

"Uh-huh."

"It's been over half a decade," Layla continues. "You'd just be there for a job. You'd barely be there at all. Sure, as manager, you'd be on site a little more than usual, but given the distance, I'm sure you could justify only going out there when it's absolutely necessary. I'll use my receptionist powers to back you up. It'll be a handful of meetings, tops."

When she says it like that, it's hard not to admit she has a point.

Over half a decade.

Part of me feels stupid for hesitating at all. I've had six years to get over it. I *am* over it. I'm a completely different person now. I have completely different goals and a completely different life.

It's not like that's all going to crumble to pieces the second my feet touch the tourist-trod soil of La Cloche.

It's just a town.

I open my mouth to tell Layla she's right, that I can handle a few meetings, that it's really no problem at all, but I can't get the words out.

Instead, I find myself mumbling, "I don't know…"

Layla leans over and grips my arm again.

"You deserve to take this job. Eric's an absolute clown for dangling project manager over your head for so many years. I'd hate to see you miss out on the chance to finally show him what an idiot he's been just because some random dude was also an idiot six years ago."

I blink my eyes hard, willing the heat pricking their corners to go away.

She's wrong.

Or at least, she's not totally right.

I was an idiot too. I was an idiot for believing in something as immature as a happily ever after.

"You're my best friend. I want the best for you," Layla urges. "Always. If this turns out to be a mistake, I'll help you find a way out of it. I promise. But for now...it's just a consultation, right?"

I bob my head. "Yeah. Yeah, that's true."

The consultation would take an hour or two tops, and I'd get a travel stipend since it's so far out of the city. Getting paid to take a long drive through the Laurentian Mountains doesn't sound so bad.

The drive was one of my favourite parts of going out to visit La Cloche. At this time of year, all the tree branches look like they're encased in crystal. They turn into glowing fairy wands when the late afternoon sun catches on the melting ice coating the boughs.

Layla can tell she's on the verge of a breakthrough. She jabs a finger at me, her grin getting wider.

"You're thinking about doing it. I can tell."

I shrug, not ready to give in yet. "I'm thinking..."

I trail off as I realize maybe it's best not to think at all.

I either take this shot, or I'm back to working way too hard for way too little.

Eric telling me what a great job I do isn't going to get me any farther in this industry. Having project manager on my resume is.

"I'm thinking it is just a consultation, right? I can handle a consultation. You're right. I can't miss out on this just because of...some guy."

In the back of my head, a voice pipes up to try and tell me the life I wanted in La Cloche was about way more than just a guy, but I raise my own voice loud enough to drown it out.

"I can do it. I can handle going back to La Cloche."

Chapter 4

Brooke

I belt out the words to an Indigo Girls song, reaching for the volume knob as I round a bend in the road just a little too fast.

My heart leaps into my throat as my hatchback's tires squeal in protest, but all that comes out of my mouth is an exhilarated whoop.

I'm in paradise.

The sunlight is hitting the icy tree branches just like I remembered: the soft golden rays of midmorning making them glint and glimmer like magic wands as water droplets pitter-patter down to form rivulets in the thin layer of snow on the forest floor.

Everything shines. Everything glows. The mountains are lit up with the promise of spring's approach, and even though it's several degrees colder out here than back in the city, I have the windows cracked to let the pine-scented air fill my lungs while I wind my way along the twisty two-lane highway.

I do slow down a little, pumping the brakes and watching out for the turn-off that will take me to La Cloche.

Paint the Moon

The cell signal has been patchy, and I gave up on my GPS almost an hour ago. Once you get out of Montreal, it's basically a straight shot up the 117. You just have to make sure you don't miss the turn.

I remember *him* pointing it out to me every single time: the red barn on the hill that stands like a welcome sign, and just past the pasture below it, the sudden juncture with an actual green highway sign pointing the way into town.

I drive for a couple more minutes until I see the barn.

My breath lodges in my throat.

I slow down even more, easing the car into a crawl down the hill. I'm on autopilot as I flick on my turn signal and cut across the road. I can barely feel the steering wheel spin in my hands, and then suddenly, I'm headed straight for it.

La Cloche.

The woods on either side of me begin to thin, giving way to the first few houses: small stone buildings nestled in the folds of sprawling, tree-dotted properties. I spot someone careening around on a snowmobile, the buzz of the engine loud enough to hear above my music. I smell the smoky-sweet scent of a bonfire.

As I drive closer to town, the properties begin to get smaller. The road narrows. There's less snow here. I even spot a couple clumps of mud bubbling up from the frigid ground.

There are streetlights now, and a sidewalk, and a couple other cars on the road.

I keep driving, and then there it is, rising like an ivory tower: the steeple of the church that houses the town's namesake. Under the green shingled roof of that white clapboard steeple rests the oldest church bell in Canada.

It's also the church where I was supposed to get married.

Technically, it's not even a church anymore. It was repurposed as a community center decades ago, but they still do weddings, and they were supposed to do mine.

I waited in the foyer of that church for two hours, phone pressed to my ear. I chewed on my lip until all my lipstick wore off. I called and called and called. Everyone did.

He didn't answer, and by the time he showed up, I already knew it was over. He didn't even have to say it, but he still did.

I just can't give you what you want, Brooke. I can't be the guy you need.

My car's engine cuts out, and I jolt with alarm before realizing I'm the one who shut it off.

I parked the car without even realizing it. I'm on a side street just off the main road, where I'm supposed to be meeting the client at a coffee shop in less than ten minutes.

I drop my keys into my purse on the passenger seat and then grip the steering wheel so tight my knuckles go white.

I close my eyes and force myself to take a deep breath.

Over half a decade.

That all happened more than half a decade ago. It might as well have happened to a different person altogether.

I'm not even in my twenties anymore. I'm a thirty year-old woman with an established career. I live in a nice apartment in a great part of Montreal. I have friends. I go on dates, and maybe those dates haven't ever turned into much, but I also have an adorable corgi to go home and cuddle on the couch with every night, and really, what else do you need?

In one fluid motion, I open my eyes, whip my seatbelt off, and fling the car door open to step out onto the street.

I hustle over to Rue Principale as fast as my heeled leather boots will allow, my eyes peeled for the café. The name wasn't familiar, so I'm pretty sure it's a new establishment. Luckily, it only takes a couple minutes of searching before I spot the sign for Café Cloche.

Not exactly the most original choice in names, but I suppose it's on theme.

Inside, I'm greeted by a blast of warm air and the sweet scent of pastries and steamed milk. The walls are a lush terracotta brown and covered in colourful artwork in dark wooden frames. Black tables and chairs fill most of the space, along with a couple rattan indoor swings suspended from the ceiling by the front window.

My mind snaps straight into design mode, analyzing the most likely flow of foot traffic and spitting out a few optimized solutions for an improved seating layout.

I scan the room before spotting a woman getting up from a table to walk over to me.

She's much younger than I expected. She can't be any older than her early twenties. She's wearing dark leggings under a slouchy grey sweater, and most of her face is taken up by a pair of thick-framed glasses.

Even without them, I'm pretty sure she'd have some of the biggest eyes I've ever seen, like a real-life Pixar character.

She also looks familiar enough to have the hairs on the back of my neck standing on end, but I can't quite place her. I plaster on my most professional smile and take a step forward anyway.

"Madeleine?"

She extends her hand. "Maddie. Hi. You must be Brooke. Thank you so much for coming all the way out here."

We finish shaking hands, and she gestures over to where she was sitting.

"I got us a table. I figured you'd probably want to order for yourself."

After I've set my things down and gone up to the counter to order a latte, I turn around and find her squinting at me. She replaces the look with an apologetic smile as soon as she catches me staring.

"Sorry," she says as I sit down across from her. "I just have to ask: have we met somewhere? You look really familiar."

My skin starts to feel clammy and hot all at once. I tug at the neck of my sweater.

"Oh. I've, um, been on holiday in La Cloche before. Maybe it's that?"

She purses her lips and then nods. "It must be. I've worked enough random part-time jobs in this town that I'm sure we would have crossed paths if you were here during tourist season."

She chuckles, and I do my best to sound amused rather than petrified as I laugh along with her.

"So," I say, reaching for my bag to give me a distraction, "should we get started?"

"Oh, actually, is it okay if we wait for someone else? She's running a little late."

I look back up at her as I tug my laptop out of its case. "Of course."

Maddie is quiet as I get the laptop running, and I notice she's shifting in her seat.

"Is she your business partner?" I ask after another few seconds tick by.

"She...yeah." She bobs her head a few times. "Yes, she is. She's actually the one who owns the house."

"Oh, I see."

Acoustic guitar music drifts through the café's speakers,

Paint the Moon

along with the chatter of the handful of other occupied tables. Maddie is fidgeting even more now, casting nervous glances at her blank phone screen where it sits on the table.

"How is your latte?" she blurts.

I realize I haven't had a chance to take a sip yet and lift the mug to my lips.

"It's very nice," I say after swallowing.

It really is: rich and creamy with a sprinkle of cinnamon I had added at the barista's suggestion.

Maddie nods, her glasses slipping down her nose. "They make great coffee here. Best in town, and I've lived here all my life, so you can trust my opinion."

She's practically vibrating, like she's on her fourth or fifth coffee of the day. Her eyes dart around the room, glancing over my shoulder towards the street outside and then back down at her phone before repeating the same rapid sequence.

I don't think I've ever seen someone so nervous about an interior design consultation.

Despite my own nerves about being recognized—and about this entire situation in general—a surge of concern makes me lean over the table and drop my voice.

"Are you o—"

Maddie's phone lights up before I can finish asking if she's all right. She lunges for it like it's a lifeline.

"Oh, she's almost here!"

She sets the phone back down, looking over at the windows one final time before she also leans closer to me. Her shoulders rise and fall as she takes a deep breath, those giant eyes finally fixed on me.

"So, um, this is a little unorthodox, but I feel like I should let you know...she doesn't actually know you're here with me."

I tilt my head and squint at her.

"This is, um, a surprise meeting," she adds.

I have no idea what I'm supposed to say to that. I don't even know what that's supposed to mean.

Maddie starts speaking so fast I can barely keep up.

"You see, I didn't think your firm would actually be interested in a project like this, especially when it's so far outside the city. I really only got in touch out of, um, curiosity, but then I was told someone would be happy to come hear about the job, and I just thought, why not, right?"

Her lips lift in a frantic smile that I think is meant to reassure me.

It does not.

"But the property owner..." I say, turning her words over in my mind, "your business partner...she doesn't know?"

Maddie winces. "She's, um...a little hesitant. About the business. She just inherited the property a couple months ago, and the inn idea is still pretty new, and I thought maybe having a professional's opinion about the house's potential and what we'd need to do to get it ready would help."

This is officially the weirdest consultation I've ever been to.

"I see," I offer, even though I do not see. Not at all.

"We are very serious about it, though!" Maddie urges. "I don't want you to think this is some kind of joke. I'm really grateful to you for coming out here, and I want to respect your time. I just...I haven't had a chance to give her all the details yet, and—"

She cuts herself off as the bell above the door tinkles. I hear footsteps cross the room, and a woman's voice calls out a cheery hello from a few feet behind me.

I twist in my seat.

The floor drops out from under my chair.

I'm falling.

I'm falling straight back through the years to the last time I saw the woman in front of me.

She was at the church, of course. I remember her pacing the foyer, her face a raging storm cloud as she bashed out a few messages on her phone before disappearing out the front door.

She left to go find her brother.

The groom.

Today, she freezes just a couple steps from my chair, her whole body going rigid.

She's wearing a khaki bomber jacket and baggy jeans instead of a cocktail dress, but her hair is the same wild mass of golden-brown waves, her severe features still as striking as I remember. I watch her expression shift from confusion to shock to a glinting spark of something I can't quite place.

"Brooke?" she says, my name a question, like she needs confirmation this is real.

"Natalie."

I give her the confirmation. I give it to myself too, letting the syllables on my lips seal my fate.

My new client is my ex-fiancé's little sister.

I watch Natalie's gaze shift from me to the chair behind me. She fixes a sharp glare on her friend.

"Maddie, what the hell is going on?"

Chapter 5

Natalie

"I had no idea she was Jonas's ex!"

I plant my hands on my hips and gawk at Maddie.

"That still doesn't explain why you're having coffee with her!"

We're standing on the slush-covered sidewalk outside Café Cloche, and I can't resist letting my eyes dart over to the steamed-up window, where I can just make out the shape of Brooke's blonde head facing away from us at the back of the room.

It has to be close to seven years since the last time I saw her.

"Well, the idea was for us all to have coffee together," Maddie says.

"Yes, but why?" I demand.

"I'm trying to tell you why!"

Her face is pale and creased with agitation, her hands balled up in her sleeves as she shifts her weight from foot to foot.

I can't remember the last time I saw her this nervous. I

blow out a heavy breath and force myself into silence so she can speak.

"You remember how we looked at that interior design firm last week, on that night we got pizza at Mack's?"

A wave of apprehension makes my jaw clench, but all I do is nod.

"Well, after you left, Jass and I stuck around for another drink, and then one drink turned into two, and then...I ended up sending the firm a message."

I try to stay quiet. I really do. I cross my arms over my chest and hold my breath, but I only manage to hold my words back for a couple seconds before they're hurling out of me loud enough to make a shopkeeper glance at us from where he's cleaning his windows across the street.

"You drunk emailed an interior design firm? About *my* house? Maddie, what the hell? I specifically remember telling you *not* to do that."

"I know, I know." Her face gets even paler, her expression pained. "I'm really sorry. We shouldn't have done it. I wasn't going to let it go any farther than that, but they responded and said they actually would be interested in the job and that they'd even send someone out here for a free consultation. It really seemed like you were having fun talking about the idea at Mack's, and I just thought...I thought..."

She drops her gaze to the slushy pavement between us, her shoulders curling inward.

I want to tell her everything is okay, but the fact that my brother's ex-fiancée is sitting in a café waiting for us is so far from okay I can't even bring myself to lie about it.

"Yeah, it *was* fun," I say, fighting to keep my voice even, "because we were just joking around. It wasn't *real*. It's not exactly fun for you to go behind my back and bring in a professional to ambush me with."

She nods, still not meeting my eyes. "I know. It was stupid of me. I thought maybe once you saw a professional was taking the idea seriously, maybe you'd get more on board."

"Why?"

She opens her mouth to answer, but I cut her off after realizing my question wasn't specific enough.

"Why do you and Jacinthe care so much about this?"

She looks up at me, her bottom lip quivering. "Because we care about you."

I cross my arms and take a step back, the urge to hug her warring with the urge to yell at her and then get Jacinthe on the phone to yell at them both for good measure.

They both need a long lecture about releasing this idea that my dead aunt's house is the key to my future happiness.

We don't have time for a long lecture, though. We've already abandoned Brooke for long enough I'm surprised she hasn't given up on this insane meeting and fled the town.

"I'm sorry," Maddie says. "I wanted to tell you in advance so I could cancel the consultation if that's what you wanted, but I got the days mixed up, and then she was already on her way here, and I thought I could at least get you to come to the café early so we could figure things out, but then that didn't work out either, and...well, honestly I can't believe she's Jonas's ex. Like, *tabarnak*. There was no way to see that one coming, but still, I really fucked this up, and...I'm so sorry."

I watch her continue to shuffle around on the sidewalk like she's bracing for me to punch her, and I decide it's time to cut the poor girl a break.

Paint the Moon

She did try to get me to show up earlier for this coffee date, and the fact that Maddie—one of the most precise people I've ever met—got her dates mixed up just shows how stressed and overworked she is at her internship.

Before I can say anything else, she spins on her heels and reaches for the café's door.

"I'll go in there and tell her this isn't going to work out and that it's completely my fault."

I grab her arm. "Maddie, wait."

She looks over her shoulder, her fingers still wrapped around the handle and her lips pressed tight together with nerves.

I take yet another patience-summoning deep breath.

"Brooke came all this way, and...well, my brother literally left this woman at the altar. The least I could do is have coffee with her, right?"

Maddie gawks at me, her expression so stunned I can't help grinning as I follow her into the cafe. Brooke turns at the sound of our footsteps, her eyes locking with mine as I walk up to the table.

She's even prettier than I remembered.

I was only eighteen when she met my brother, and I spent most of the two years their relationship lasted travelling around Australia and New Zealand during my college dropout phase. I only met Brooke a couple times before the wedding.

That was enough for her to make an impression. With a face like that, one glance is enough for her to make an impression.

It's beyond cheesy, but as I stare at her now, I can't help thinking the exact same thing I thought when I came home for the holidays and met her for the first time.

She looks like a Christmas angel.

Bright blonde hair that gleams like spun silver in the shadows and gold filaments in the light. Eyes like sea glass, glinting with swirled shades of blue and green. Petal pink blush staining her cheeks the same shade as her lipstick.

"You're back."

Her voice jolts me back to the present, and my skin starts to heat up under the neck of my jacket as I wonder just how long I was staring at her.

There's a slight curve to her lips, one of her eyebrows arching up, like she's still deciding whether to be amused or exasperated by this situation.

I'm right there with her.

"I'm back," I say, grabbing a chair from the nearest table and hauling it over while Maddie drops into her seat.

"Sorry for the delay," I say. "There was, um, a slight miscommunication between me and Maddie."

Brooke presses her lips together, and I wonder if she's trying not to laugh.

We must look absolutely ridiculous to her. Here she is in her slick city woman clothes, all professionalism in grey wool pants and a silky cream blouse, the scent of vanilla drifting off her skin. Meanwhile, I'm in a flannel and jeans with my mane barely tamed into a ponytail, trying to pretend like I have any idea what's going on.

"So, what do you need to know?" I ask, doing my best to sound even slightly competent. "About the house?"

She nods, her expression smoothing into a mask as serenely professional as her outfit. She folds her hands on the table in front of her, and I can't keep my gaze from darting down to her fingers.

No rings.

Just a subtle French manicure on her nails and a silver bracelet circling her wrist.

"Today's consultation is a chance for me to get to know more about your vision and needs for the space, and for you to hear more about what Leung Designs offers and the services we can help with."

I snap my attention away from her hands and focus on what she's saying.

"We specialize in bespoke commercial spaces, with an emphasis on hotels and restaurants. We've worked on some of the most sought-after boutique hotels in the greater Montreal area, and we're all about taking a personalized, collaborative approach with our clients to make sure the final product is as unique as you and your business."

That would be great if we actually had a business.

The more she says, the more my skin flushes with embarrassment. I don't have a vision to share with her—unless you count the mental image of Jacinthe driving a sleigh through the grounds of the Lemonade Inn.

Brooke is only four years older than me, but I feel like a child as I lean in closer to see the gallery of projects she scrolls through on her laptop screen.

"Wow," Maddie gushes. "These are stunning. Did you design all these yourself?"

Brooke's mask wavers for a second, so quick I almost miss the shadow that crosses her features before she hides it with a smile.

"I was part of the team for all of these, yes," she says. "I've been with Leung Designs for almost six years."

That would mean she started there not long after her breakup with Jonas.

She shows us a few more images, but I end up staring at her out of the corner of my eye instead.

As far as I know, she and my brother haven't spoken at all since a couple days after the wedding. She took all her stuff, moved out of the apartment they shared in Montreal, and that was that. He'd been living in the city while doing some construction training courses. They only had that apartment for less than a year before the wedding—or rather, the *not* wedding.

I can't reconcile this polished career woman with the kind of person who'd get swept up in a whirlwind engagement with Jonas, of all people.

I love my goof of a big brother, but 'responsible' has never been one of his top qualities.

"By the way, would you like to order a coffee or anything? I really don't mind waiting."

I realize I've once again been caught staring at Brooke while I drift through the past.

I clear my throat. "Oh, uh, right, yeah. Thanks. I will get something."

I stumble through the process of ordering an Americano and then come back clutching my warm mug while I tell myself to get a grip.

Maddie is still ooh-ing and ah-ing over the gallery images when I sit back down. The pictures are stunning. A lot of the projects have a retro but sleek, almost jazz club style to them that I can totally imagine the artsy, antique hunter crowds of La Cloche going nuts for.

Brooke continues with her pitch after getting a nod from me.

"As an interior design firm, our main goal is to create a space that fits the functional needs of your project and streamlines both staff and customer experiences, all while showcasing your unique style and brand. We'd analyze the existing structures and layouts, consult with you as we come up with our complete plan of action, and coordinate with any additional professionals needed such as architects and contractors. We can also help with things like acquiring permits. Basically, we want to make life as easy as possible for you while still allowing you to be as involved with the process as you'd like."

My head spins as I try to keep up with her.

Permits. Contractors. Branding.

I don't know the first thing about any of those topics, and they must be just the tip of the iceberg.

"I feel like a bit of an idiot," I blurt. "I didn't realize interior designers did this much."

Brooke gives me a smile that's slightly strained.

"That's a common misconception. A lot of people confuse interior designers with interior decorators. We do help with things like creating an overall style for the space, but that's only one part of the process. In a nutshell, we're the people who figure out where your walls should go, not just what colour they should be."

She sits up a little straighter in her chair, her chin lifting, and the cool confidence in her tone would be intimidating if it weren't so sexy.

Sexy?

I always thought she was pretty, sure, but it's not like I ever gave myself the chance to think of my brother's fiancée as *sexy*.

Still, I can't help noticing how the six years since I last saw her have added an undeniable poise to the way she carries herself. She's the kind of person who probably makes a whole room go quiet when she walks in, and it's not just because she's beautiful. It's because everything about her declares that she's *someone*.

That is sexy.

It's also the kind of thing I wish people thought of me. It's the kind of thing I wish I thought of myself.

Before I get the chance to stray too far down that trail of thought, Brooke's cheeks flush a more vibrant shade of pink, her posture slumping as she huffs an embarrassed laugh.

"God, that made me sound really elitist, didn't it?" she says. "It's not that I don't have a huge respect for decorators. It's just that most people assume my job is something it's not."

She starts clicking through a few windows on her laptop, not looking at either of us, and I'm hit with the urge to reassure her.

"That would be frustrating," I say. "Thank you for explaining it to me."

She looks back up and smiles again, her eyes warm and genuine this time.

My pulse speeds up.

"So," she says, breaking our eye contact to smile at Maddie too, "tell me about your brand."

"We're...developing that," Maddie says when I don't offer up an answer.

I wish I had more to add, but 'developing' is about ten steps ahead of where we are.

"That's okay," Brooke says, her tone way more patient than we deserve. "Everyone starts somewhere. How about you tell me more about the property?"

I seize the opportunity to talk about something I actually have information on and begin blurting every detail that comes to mind.

"I haven't had it for very long. It was my great-aunt's house. She passed away a few months ago and left it to me."

Brooke's forehead creases. "I'm sorry for your loss."

"Thanks." I shrug. "We weren't close or anything. Nobody can even figure out why she gave it to me, but yeah, I've got a

Paint the Moon

house now. It's six bedrooms with two acres of property and a barn out back. There's a small pond too. It's a beautiful yard, actually. It's just in need of a lot of TLC. My aunt lived there alone for decades, so the whole place needs fixing up."

Brooke nods a couple times and then takes a sip of her drink. I realize I'm making it sound like the place is a complete dump and rush to backtrack.

"I mean, it's not falling apart or anything. It's mostly just surface-level stuff, as far as I can tell. You'd probably know better than me."

I let out a nervous chuckle, and she indulges me by joining in.

"We can definitely arrange for the TLC. I have some contacts in landscaping as well, if you want a referral. There's a lot you could do with a property that big."

My mind spins. That's a whole separate company I'd need to hire. I have no idea how much Brooke's firm even cost.

"Um, yeah," I mumble. "I guess we would need landscapers."

An awkward silence follows as Brooke's gaze darts between the two of us and her laptop screen a few times.

She's probably got a whole list of questions she's now reconsidering, given how we can't give her a single straight answer.

She might even be working up the courage to excuse herself and walk out.

The silence stretches on, broken only by the soft acoustic guitar chords drifting from the speakers and the rattle of dishes echoing out from the cafe's back room.

"We could go see the house."

Brooke and I both shift our attention to Maddie.

"That was the plan—to stop by, right?" she says, looking at Brooke. "Once we discussed things here first."

"I would love to see it," Brooke chimes. "That's a great idea."

Maddie hops to her feet, and the two of them start pulling their coats on. They're headed for the door by the time I manage to snap myself into action.

"Right," I mutter as I follow them out. "Let's go see my house."

Chapter 6
Brooke

Natalie sits beside me in the passenger seat and directs me along the five minute route to the house. Maddie is perched behind us in the back, but she stays so quiet I almost forget there's anyone else in the car.

Natalie Sinclair.

We were barely ever more than strangers, but seeing her now still feels like getting a glimpse into an alternate universe.

We wouldn't be strangers there. I would have had time to get to know her. Years of holidays together. Family dinners. Constantly bumping into each other around town. Maybe we would have even become friends.

I watch her from the corner of my eye as she tells me where to turn at the next intersection. She has a strong, almost regal profile, even with a few stray locks of frizzy hair falling into her eyes.

I probably could have made a better effort to get to know her back then, even though we only had a few chances to meet before the wedding date, but something always held me back.

Natalie just seemed so *cool*, so effortless and natural, like she truly didn't care what anyone thought. She'd lounge around in paint-splattered overalls, reading books I'd never heard of or sharing stories about parts of the world I'd never seen.

To this day, I've never travelled on my own, and she flew across the globe by herself on a whim with no plans or commitments in mind, just a thirst for inspiration and a surge of wanderlust spurring her on.

I remember feeling so boring in comparison, like my life goals were all mapped in black and white while hers swirled in a Technicolor tapestry.

"It's just up there. The one with the black iron fence."

She points through the windshield, and I get my first glimpse of the property. I never got the chance to attend a family dinner at the infamous *Tante* Manon's place, and my ex's descriptions of the childhood terror she inflicted on him didn't make me think I was missing much, but by the time I roll the car to a stop in front of the gate, I can't hold back a gasp.

The house is perfect.

It's more than brochure-worthy. It's a fairytale come to life.

Sprawling gabled roofs edged with woodwork so intricate it looks like piped frosting. Old-fashioned shutters on the windows. A wraparound porch with wide floorboards and ornate wooden posts. There's even a tiny stained glass panel over the large front door, and I can see the withered remains of vines that must burst with vibrant green all summer long clinging to the white walls.

Paint the Moon

Two large evergreen trees flank the building, standing like sleepy giants with their branches stretching out wide.

"Wow," I murmur, after blinking at the scene through the car window for what feels like several minutes.

"It's stunning, isn't it?" Maddie says from behind me. "You can see how it would make a beautiful inn."

All I can do is stare.

This is exactly the kind of house I used to dream of living in.

Sure, six bedrooms is a little much, but it's got everything I used to want: the cozy porch, the sprawling yard, the towering old trees just begging for some Christmas lights.

It's long past the holidays, but I can still picture candles burning in the windows and smoke curling out of the ash-stained chimney.

The chimney could use a scrubbing. Really, the whole place could. Natalie wasn't lying about the TLC. The walls need a fresh coat of white, and a few of the shutters should be replaced. The spiky iron fence looks like something out of a haunted mansion attraction and should probably be removed entirely.

My brain buzzes with a thousand ideas for renovations, and I haven't even set foot inside.

"Shall we?"

Natalie slips her seatbelt off and then climbs out into the road. I shut the engine off and follow suit. There's a large gate with a snow-dusted driveway behind it, but the thick chains locking it shut look like they haven't budged in a while. Natalie unlocks a smaller gate instead, revealing a narrow footpath that runs straight to the front door.

"Careful," she warns as she holds it open for me and Maddie. "I keep forgetting to buy salt, so the whole yard is a death trap."

She's not exaggerating. We wobble and slide our way along the icy ground until we reach the wide steps up to the porch.

They groan under our feet, and as I stare at the thick black door that seems to loom over us, a shiver runs up my spine.

"Your aunt really lived here all alone?"

It's not exactly an appropriate thing to ask a potential client, especially when I can't keep the incredulity out of my tone, but the thought of a solitary old lady wandering the halls of a house this big for decades has creepy factor written all over it.

"Yeah, she wasn't, um...very social," Natalie says as she digs through her jacket pockets before pulling out a lone key without a ring.

She twists it in the lock, and the door opens with a keening creak that makes the hairs on the back of my neck stand up. The overcast winter day does nothing to illuminate the empty house. Beyond Natalie, all I can see are shadowy outlines of the entryway and the dark depths of a hallway receding into the distance.

Maybe I was too quick to admire the place.

"Here's hoping I actually paid the electricity," Natalie says as she heads for the closest light switch. "It's been a nightmare trying to sort out all the bills."

There's a half second's delay after she flips the switch, but then a globe light above her head flickers on.

"Aha!" she crows. "Let there be light!"

"*Câlice*. It's creepy when it's dark in here," Maddie mutters as she follows Natalie inside.

Natalie hunts around for more light switches, and soon the hallway and adjoining living room are illuminated as well.

Paint the Moon

The spectral effect fades away, and I'm left in awe of the original dark wood trim and arched entryways. The hardwood floors are immaculate, probably due to the kitschy old lady rugs covering most of their surface.

"This is a gorgeous home," I say, following Natalie through into the living room, where a river rock fireplace literally steals my breath away.

Natalie notices my eyes bulging and chuckles.

"You like it?" she asks, striding over and giving the mantle a pat like it's a prized cow.

"I love it."

I can't hide the breathy sincerity in my tone. My throat feels tight, and my chest is welling up with a feeling I don't have a name for.

"Brooke?" Natalie frowns and steps closer to me. "Are you all right?"

I bob my head, but my voice still comes out shaky.

"Oh. Yes. Sorry, it's just...I don't see houses like this very often."

We don't work on places like this in Montreal. There are no places like this in Montreal.

The last time I was inside a house with a fireplace like that was at my grandma's place, back out in New Brunswick.

Back before we left.

Hers wasn't as grand as this one, sure, but it had the same river rock facade, like a fairy cottage in the woods. I remember tracing my fingers along the ridges between the smooth stones, my socked feet dancing along the warm tiles in front of the fire.

"Do you want to sit down?"

Natalie gestures at one of the tufted couches arranged around a rose-patterned rug.

"Oh, that's all right," I say, giving my head a shake. "We can complete the tour."

A cough from behind me makes me jump, and I spin around. I completely forgot Maddie was in the room.

"I'm getting a work call," she says, holding up her vibrating phone. "You two go on. I'll catch up."

Natalie guides me back out to the hallway. The echoes of Maddie's conversation follow us until we reach the kitchen.

"I can't believe they're calling her again," Natalie mutters as she turns more lights on. "It's supposed to be her day off."

"Does she have a stressful job?" I ask as I observe the kitchen.

The room is more dated than what I've seen so far, with battered cupboards and dingy countertops. They'd need a total remodel and an expansion if they're planning on running any kind of food service at the inn.

"Oh, sorry, I'm just grumbling," Natalie says as she wipes some dust off one of the countertops. "She's interning to become a financial risk analyst. They're literally paying her minimum wage, and they still think they can get her to come in for extra hours off the clock. She'll do it, too. It's her first real job out of school, so she feels like she doesn't have a choice. It just makes me so mad to see people taking advantage of her."

"Bosses suck," I say, with just a little too much vehemence.

Natalie chuckles and leans against the counter. "You speaking from experience?"

I step over to an antique wooden buffet facing the counter and mirror her pose.

"I'm speaking as a representative of Leung Designs, so really, I shouldn't be speaking about this at all."

Her grin gets even wider, and she mimes zipping her mouth shut and turning a key.

"Your employment-related resentment is safe with me."

I should be mortified, but instead, I just laugh.

"You seem pretty protective of Maddie," I say, grasping for a subject change. "That's sweet. How long have you been friends?"

"Since we were toddlers," she answers. "Well, technically we weren't toddlers at the same time. She's the cousin of my best friend, but we all became best friends as we got older. Maddie is four years younger than me and Jacinthe, so I guess I still sometimes think of her like a little sibling, since I never had one of my own."

She freezes as the words leave her mouth, her eyes widening as her jaw clamps shut.

My spine stiffens, and we both stay quiet as tension seems to crackle through the room, like old electrical wires sparking and sizzling.

I know we're both thinking about the sibling she *does* have.

The one I was supposed to marry.

"He doesn't live here anymore."

Natalie's voice cuts through the silence, all the lightness gone from her tone. Her face flushes, and she stares down at the tips of her shoes, opening and closing her mouth a few times before she looks back up.

"Sorry. I don't know why I said that. I guess I was just thinking that this must all be so weird for you, being in this town, seeing...me... I mean, shit, it's really weird for me too, and you're the one who...um..."

Her cheeks and neck are a splotchy red now. She shoves her hair out of her face and coughs.

"I just thought you might want to know Jonas doesn't live in La Cloche anymore. He moved to Saint-Jovite a while back."

A sound somewhere between a grunt and a snort tries to burst out of me, and I put all my concentration into swallowing it back down.

Saint-Jovite is less than a half hour down the highway. It's not like he fled the country, and I already learned about his move a couple years ago during that bout of drunken Instagram stalking I really should have let Layla talk me out of.

Still, the fact that Natalie wants to make this a little easier for me makes my chest bloom with warmth.

"I see."

I don't know what else to say.

This is supposed to be the job that puts me on the map. This is supposed to be my chance to prove all the years I've put in at Leung Designs haven't been for nothing. This is supposed to be the project that changes everything.

It is *not* supposed to include getting flustered over a conversation with my ex-fiancé's sister.

I straighten up and step back over to the kitchen's arched entry.

"Should we continue with the tour?"

Natalie looks startled for a moment before she nods.

"Right. Yeah. Of course."

She takes me through the rest of the ground floor, which includes a dining room, a walk-in pantry, and a study. I make a few mental calculations about which walls are likely to be load-bearing and how we might reconfigure the space to create a lobby area as well as an industrial kitchen big

Paint the Moon

enough to handle at least six hotel rooms' worth of daily breakfasts.

I still don't know if a bed and breakfast is the plan, but if our chat in the coffee shop is anything to go by, neither does Natalie.

"Is there a basement?" I ask when we reach the staircase up to the second floor.

"Yes, but it's more of a dungeon, by which I mean it's not finished and has no functional lighting. I have no idea what the hell could be lurking down there."

I chuckle. "All right. Might have to save that for a phase two renovation if you want to get this place open as soon as possible."

We head up the staircase, the thick runner carpet muffling the creaks and groans of the steps. Natalie shows me through the bedrooms. Most of them are cluttered with cardboard boxes and bulging trash bags. The beds have all been stripped of their sheets and pillows.

"Excuse the mess," Natalie says. "We've been working on clearing my aunt's stuff out. Turns out one small lady can amass a lot of stuff over the span of several decades."

I walk over to run my finger along the dust-coated brass footboard of the bed. With a little polish and a good scrubbing, it could be a stunning piece of furniture.

"She kept all the bedrooms furnished? Did she have a lot of guests?"

I turn to find Natalie leaning against the doorframe, bracing one of her forearms above her head and toying with the end of her ponytail.

She's a few inches taller than me. I'd have to lift up on my tiptoes for us to stand eye to eye.

For a second, I picture doing it. I imagine striding over until we're nearly chest to chest and then shifting onto the balls of my feet so I can look straight into her steely blue eyes.

I noticed them at the cafe. They're nothing like *his* warm brown. Not much about her is like him at all. There's an intensity to her, a gravity, like she's a planet that will pull you into orbit if you get too close.

"She didn't."

Natalie shifts her position, her voice breaking the stillness of the moment.

I take a fumbling step backwards, my calves bumping against the edge of the bed before I can steady myself.

"She mostly kept to herself. She, uh, didn't really like people."

I nod and reach for the brass knob of the bedpost, smoothing my thumb over its surface like I'm stroking a crystal ball. I stare into the bulbous reflection of the spackled ceiling so I don't have to meet Natalie's gaze.

I feel a little dizzy, and I wonder if I should have grabbed a snack at the cafe.

"She lived in a really big house, for someone who didn't like company."

"Her husband bought it."

Curiosity makes me turn my head to give her a questioning look. I didn't know there was a husband.

"He died a few years after they got married," Natalie explains. "Car accident. I think *Tante* Manon was still in her twenties at the time."

I shudder as I imagine everything the poor woman might have imagined filling these empty rooms with—children, laughter, memories—only to have her dreams all ripped away in a few seconds.

"That's awful. She was alone ever since?"

Natalie's voice has gone quiet. "Yeah, she was."

Paint the Moon

She pushes off the doorframe and wraps her arms around her stomach, her expression pinched.

I move closer.

"Are you okay?"

She jerks her chin in a nod, her gaze pinned to the floor.

"I guess I just never really thought about what that meant. You couldn't do much on your own as a woman back then, especially in a remote small town in Québec. La Cloche only turned into an artsy hippie town back in the seventies. It was dying out for decades before that."

I remember her brother explaining the history to me. The hippies wandered in from other parts of the country and brought tourist dollars along with them—enough tourist dollars to buy up the failing church housing the famous bell. They revived the town and gave it a whole new industry, but the tension between the French-speaking locals and the English-speaking outsiders has never quite faded away, despite a couple generations of intermingling.

"And *Tante* Manon, she was just...here," Natalie continues. "For all that time. She could have sold the house and left. Started over. Found a new husband or something."

Natalie said she didn't know her aunt very well, but the tremor in her voice tells me otherwise, like maybe there's something about her aunt's story that strikes her deeper than she's ever realized.

Or maybe I'm reading into things.

Maybe I'm just caught up in the past—her past, my past, the past of this house.

Suddenly, the weight of all those memories feels like a heavy blanket blocking out the present and shrouding us here in a moment where time loses its hold.

"Maybe she felt like this would always be her home."

"Yeah." Natalie nods again, still not looking at me.

"Yeah, that makes sense. I mean, I'm still in La Cloche too, aren't I? Maybe some people are just meant to play small."

I blink at her, tilting my head as I watch a wry, bitter smile twist her lips before it fades away.

"What?"

I don't mean to ask the question out loud, but it's blaring in my mind again and again.

How could someone like Natalie Sinclair ever think she's playing small?

I've only met her a handful of times, and I can't imagine anyone calling a life like hers small.

"I'm sorry." She shakes her head and lets her arms drop to her sides. "I shouldn't have gotten into that. I'm just rambling. You're not here to listen to me ramble. You're here for a job."

She lifts her head, and all the vulnerability of the past few minutes is gone. The thick blanket cutting off the rest of the world is flung away, and reality rushes back in to fill the space.

We finish up the tour. We've seen most of the top floor by now. Natalie skips the last couple bedrooms and leads us back downstairs.

Once again, I almost jump out of my skin when I'm reminded we're not alone in the house. Maddie steps out from around the corner to meet us in the foyer.

"Well, I think that's everything," Natalie says, stuffing her hands into the pockets of her jeans.

"Did you want to show her the barn?" Maddie asks.

Natalie shakes her head. "No."

Her voice comes out loud enough to echo against the walls. I jolt with surprise and glance at Maddie. She looks just as startled as I do.

"It's just, uh, a huge mess out there," Natalie says, a

forced lightness in her tone. "I, uh, haven't been to check on it in a while."

Maddie is still giving her a weird look.

"Besides," Natalie adds. "We've taken up enough of your time. You probably want to get on the road. Thank you for coming all the way out here."

I nod and clear my throat, my mind whirring as I fight to remember everything I'm supposed to say at the end of a consultation.

"Well, before I go, did you have any questions?"

Maddie gives Natalie a pointed look and a not-so-subtle jab with her elbow. I cover my mouth and pretend to cough to hide my grin. They really do look like two siblings arguing.

Some sort of silent message passes between them that makes Natalie's eyes widen with realization.

"Oh wait." She turns to me. "I guess I should ask how much you cost?"

I cough for real this time.

Natalie's cheeks go red.

"Uh, I mean, uh, how much the firm costs, that is. How much it would cost to hire you. The firm. The, uh...well, what is the rate of pay?"

She sounds like she's on the verge of choking, and her face is more flushed than ever. It's actually pretty cute.

Cute?

I've never called a client cute before, not even in my own head.

The reminder that she's a client—or rather, that I desperately need her to become a client—cuts through my thoughts like a golden arrow, shooting straight through the chaos of this meeting to guide me to my goal.

"I can prepare a more formal estimate based on the

various factors we've discussed so far," I say, falling into the well-practiced tone of confidence mixed with light reassurance that I've developed for talking about money, "but just based on the size of the house and the amount of guests you're planning to lodge..."

I give her a number, and even though she keeps her expression steeled, I notice all the blood that's rushed to her face drain away.

I turn up the dial on the reassurance.

"Like I said, I'll send you over a more formal estimate and some additional information once I'm back in the office."

Maddie steps forward. "That's great. Thank you so much. I'll go get your coat."

She disappears to where we left our jackets in the living room.

Natalie stays quiet.

"So, I guess I'll go?" I say after a moment. "Unless you need a ride back into town. I—"

"That's fine."

Her voice still has a veneer of politeness, but she's got a thousand-yard stare that seems to look straight through me, like I'm already gone.

Chapter 7
Natalie

"I can't hire her, Maddie!"

I pace in front of the cold, empty fireplace while Maddie watches me with her arms crossed over her chest. She's just come back inside after seeing Brooke off.

"Why not? She's amazing!"

"*Why not?*" I spare her a disbelieving glance as I pass in front of her. "Even if we're completely ignoring the fact that she's my brother's ex-fiancée, did you hear how much money it would cost?"

"It's actually less than I was expecting."

I freeze mid-step.

"What?" I demand, my eyes bulging. "That's, like, more dollars than I have ever contemplated in my life."

She shrugs—literally shrugs, like we're mafia bosses coolly contemplating the salary of our new assassin.

"You own one of the most expensive properties in La Cloche. You're a rich bitch now."

I keep gawking at her. "Not *that* rich."

"We could easily acquire a business loan for this."

"A *loan?*"

I sound like a parrot repeating everything she says with deranged emphasis, but I can't get any more words out.

"Yes." She drops into the nearest overstuffed armchair and crosses her legs. "We'd have very little competition and very high demand. There are only a couple hotels within a half hour drive of La Cloche and a few short-term rental properties in town. People are always saying we need something like an inn. We get all the drive-through tourists from Mont-Tremblant, but there's nowhere for them to stay if they want to spend the night. We could fill that gap."

I half-expect her to whip out a slideshow presentation to prove her point. She sounds like she's repeating a script.

"How much have you thought about this?"

She shrugs again. "I've literally spent years training in how to assess financial risk. Plus, with interning going as bad as it has been, it's nice to daydream about working on something where people would see me as more than just the coffee and errands girl."

Her face falls, and when she speaks again, there's a somber note to her voice.

"Jacinthe has been thinking about it too. You know they're probably going to end up downsizing the farm."

Dread shoots up my spine.

"She said that?"

With Jacinthe's mom's health doing so poorly, I've been bracing for them to have to sell off some of their land and horses, but Jacinthe has always been the first person to claim that won't be necessary, with plenty of vehement swearing to emphasize her refusal to accept the possibility.

"No, but...you and I know it," Maddie murmurs. She sighs before re-crossing her legs and sitting up straighter. "I'm just saying, if there were ever a time in our lives to take on a project like this, now would be it."

Paint the Moon

Her eyes are blazing, her jaw set in a determined line, and it hits me then that this idea we've schemed up together isn't just about helping me.

Still, I can't just blow off reality. We're not talking about starting a girl band or a punk rock quilting club or a pop-up shop in the community center—all things the three of us tried doing together at some point in our childhoods.

This is way beyond the scale of any of that.

I take a seat on the couch a couple feet from her chair and try to keep my voice as gentle as I can.

"It's not just some project, Maddie. It's...huge. There's so much I haven't even thought of. Let's face it. We don't know anything about this stuff."

She shakes her head, the stubborn set of her jaw making her look just like her cousin.

"We do, though. We've all worked pretty much every tourism job there is in La Cloche. We know this town. We know why people come here and what kind of experiences they want to have, and we...we *love* it here. It's our home. That's exactly what we'd be doing running an inn: giving people a chance to call La Cloche home for a while."

Her words are an echo of what Brooke said upstairs, about Manon.

Maybe she felt like this would always be her home.

I don't have to stay here. If I sold the house and combined that with the inheritance money, I could live pretty much anywhere in the world, at least for a while.

I *have* lived in other parts of the world, but I came back.

I always came back. This is my home. These quiet streets and the forests around them, the winding streams and rolling mountains, the scenes I've painted again and again and again like a one-trick pony.

I chose to come back here—or at least, I thought it was a choice.

Lately, I've been wondering if it's the only option I'm truly cut out for. The Canadian art world sure seemed to think so.

Maddie watches me for a few moments, blinking from behind her glasses like a *petit fantôme*.

"*Voyons*," she says, breaking the silence to stretch her arms above her head. "It's not like we're opening a Hilton. It's six bedrooms. How hard could it be?"

I have to laugh at that.

"You know nothing good ever happens after someone asks that question."

"*D'accord*."

She makes a show out of leaning over to knock her knuckles against the wooden side table, warding off the invitation to doom and chaos.

"So say we scrap the idea." She sweeps her hand out like she's erasing a chalkboard. "You sell the house. Some random hotshot couple from the city snaps it up. They tear the place up, make it all modern and weird. They tear the barn down. They cut down the trees to put in a pool. They ruin everything, and you never step foot in the house again in your life."

She waits, and sure enough, I can't keep myself from wincing at the thought of those beautiful old balsam firs reduced to a pile of woodchips.

That might not happen, but any new owners would definitely demolish the barn—the place I used to sneak out and explore when I was supposed to be playing quietly in the office during social hour after stuffy holiday dinners with *Tante* Manon.

Jonas was always too scared to dash across the yard with

me, so I'd go by myself. The barn was my haven, my secret playground, shimmering with gossamer spider webs and always filled with the gentle cooing of pigeons in the rafters.

Even then, the building was neglected. Now, it's so derelict they'd flatten it without a second thought.

"I..."

I try to tell Maddie it doesn't matter, that it's just a house, a house I've never even lived in, but I can't get the words out.

"I know you're hurting, *ma chère*."

The endearment is sweeter than anything I'd usually hear from a friend, the words like a warm hug I didn't know I needed. I slump against the back of the couch, blinking hard as my throat gets tight.

Maddie shuffles closer. "I know you don't want to talk about what you're going through, but that doesn't mean Jacinthe and I don't care. If you don't want to build an inn, that's fine. It's not really about that. It's about making sure you give yourself some time."

I search her face like she's got all the answers hidden behind those thick lenses, somewhere in her super computer of a brain.

"Time for what?"

"Time to find...Natalie."

My spine stiffens. I already told her and Jacinthe they can't just will me into pretending I never went to Thunder Bay at all.

"I know you're not the old you," she adds, like she can read my thoughts. "I wouldn't want you to be. People are supposed to change. I just...I don't want to see you give up on the new you before you've given her a chance."

The new me.

The new me doesn't seem to be capable of much. I can't

paint. I'm picking up shifts at my mom's store that she's only giving me out of pity. I can barely cover my rent.

There's my staggering new inheritance, of course, but that's dumped into a savings account I'm too scared to even look at.

I prop my elbows on my knees and drop my head into my hands, sucking in a couple shaky breaths. Maddie gets up to come sit beside me on the couch, rubbing my shoulder as she asks if I'm all right.

"I'm fine. I...I think I just need some time alone. You know, to think."

"Okay," she says after a moment. She leans over to smack a kiss on the top of my head. "*Bisous.* Call me or Jass if you need anything."

I stay hunched in the same position, listening to the sound of the front door swing shut, followed by the creaking of the porch. I sit there for so long I'm sure Maddie has walked all the way back into town by the time I get to my feet.

I should probably go get my car. I was going to load it up with a few boxes to drop at some thrift stores in Saint-Jovite. We've already exhausted the good graces of the local thrift shop with our pleas that they take yet more of Manon's clothes and knickknacks.

Instead of doing any of that, I grab my boots and coat, and then I walk through the empty house until I reach the back door in the kitchen.

The barn waits like an old friend: a little haggard and worn from the years, but still sitting exactly where you'd expect to find them.

I slide my boots on and then cross the snowy yard. The barn is painted the same faded white as the house. Tall stalks of dead, yellowed grass cluster around the foundation

Paint the Moon

and nearly obscure the door. The roof's shingles are peeling and spotted with lichen.

I swat the weeds away when I reach the wooden door. No one has even bothered to padlock it.

The hinges have frozen, and it takes a few strong yanks before they give way with a loud snap. The door creaks, a keening cry that echoes through the empty space inside.

With its two-storey ceilings arching up into the rafters, the barn feels cavernous, almost cathedral-like in the quiet of the early afternoon. Most of the stalls have been ripped out, leaving the majority of the concrete floor bare. A dusty workbench covered with a few rusting, old-fashioned tools sits against one of the walls. A wheelbarrow with a deflated tire is lying upside down on the ground.

There haven't been any animals in here for decades, but the musty scent of hay and straw bedding still hangs in the air.

None of that would have kept me interested for more than an afternoon as a kid.

It was the light that kept me coming back.

High above my head, the walls are lined with big square windows interspersed between the rafter beams. Soft winter daylight floods inside, catching on spider webs and turning them into shimmering mandalas. The frost clinging to the walls gleams and sparkles like the whole barn is lined with quicksilver.

I don't know who made this barn. I don't know if they even realized what they were doing, but somehow, they created the most glorious light I've ever seen inside a building.

I used to sit on the cold, hard concrete, knees pulled up to my chest under my Easter dress, and stare, mesmerized, at each shift of the sunrays.

It didn't matter what time of day I came out here: golden mornings before church, azure afternoons during brunch, inky twilight evenings after dinner. There was always so much light, always changing, always morphing into something new, leaving me with nothing but ephemeral moments of awe.

This is the place I realized I wanted to be a painter.

I wanted to splash that light across a canvas, pin it down, capture it like a lightning bug in a jar. I wanted people to look at what I made and *feel*—feel that same overwhelming wonder that made my tiny body tremble with the awareness that nature is so much more ancient and expansive than I could ever comprehend.

Today, my breath clouds in front of my face, the light sifting through the condensation as I lower myself to the floor.

I tug my jacket down to protect the seat of my jeans from the frost, and then I tuck my knees up to my chest just like I would as a kid.

I watch the light.

I wait for an answer.

I know I can't watch this place get blown to bits. I can't watch some stranger swing a wrecking ball through the windows and leave nothing but a cracked slab of concrete to prove this marvel was ever even here.

"But what else can I do?"

I speak so softly there's no echo of my words, just puffs of hot breath dissipating in the chill.

"What would I even do with this place?"

I know what the old Natalie would have done.

She would have turned the barn into a studio.

She would have put in a supply cupboard, a few sinks, a couple long tables. She would have insulated the walls and put in wooden floors, and she wouldn't care if everyone thought that was a crazy choice for a studio because she would have welcomed the stains, the splatters, the marks of creation left like an autobiography in a secret language scrawled underfoot.

She would have hung plants from the rafters. She would have found a vintage kettle and set up a little trolley for making tea.

Hell, she probably would have said yes to the inn idea the second Jacinthe brought it up. She would organize art classes for the guests. She would plan week-long retreats for people to escape to La Cloche and soak up all the inspiration gushing through town, letting it fuel their desire to create whatever the hell they want.

She would have been up for the challenge. She wouldn't have cared about not knowing how to build an inn. She would have believed she could figure it out.

"But I'm not her."

My voice hitches. I lift a hand to my cheek and realize it's damp with tears.

"Not anymore."

Chapter 8

Brooke

"Not today, asshole."

I glare at the pendulous bulge in my bathroom ceiling like I can will it to shrivel up into nothing. My landlord is now trying to gaslight me into thinking the lump is a paint bubble.

"A paint bubble," I mutter as I finish rinsing my cleanser off. "Ha."

There is no way in hell there aren't several litres of leaking water suspended in that thing, just waiting for the perfect moment to burst and bring the whole ceiling down.

I've started keeping the bathroom door shut and barricaded when I go out, so I at least know the flood will not rain down on Bailey.

Right on cue, my greying corgi comes trotting into the bathroom, wagging her stumpy tail.

"I know you're hungry, baby," I tell her. "Your breakfast is almost ready."

I pat my face dry and then make a beeline for the kitchen when the microwave chimes. Bailey does her best to keep up, her claws click-clacking on the vinyl floorboards.

When I adopted her, the shelter told me we'd only have a few years together, but I didn't care. Nothing was going to stop me from taking her home, not with those adorable brown eyes beaming at me and her white-tipped chin whiskers just begging for a scratch.

I may use her senior doggie status as an excuse to spoil her beyond measure, but she deserves it, even if the frozen organic dog meal subscription box I get for her is criminally overpriced.

I grab her breakfast from the microwave and stir the contents around before dumping them into her bowl. Her whole body wiggles as she waits for me to set the bowl on her food mat, where she begins devouring before I've even removed my hand.

"Enjoy, cutie patootie," I say, giving her a quick pat before I head for my bedroom.

I check the time on my phone and then hurry through picking an outfit. It's still too cold for anything but pants to be practical, but I go with a maroon, long-sleeved dress with buttons up the front, putting my faith in fleece-lined tights and knee-high boots to keep from freezing on the way to work.

Today feels worth dressing up for.

I got back to Montreal early enough yesterday that I was able to email Natalie a proper estimate and some follow-up information before I called it a day. I treated myself to some wine and a romcom last night, and when my brain tried to convince me the consultation was clearly an utter failure and I'd blown my shot at making project manager, I drowned those thoughts out with plenty of Bailey snuggles.

"I am not missing this opportunity," I tell myself as I hop around on one foot while pulling up the leg of my tights.

I survived going back to La Cloche. Not only that, but I survived coming face to face with my ex's sister, and I did not run out of that cafe screaming.

I could have left. I could have made some excuse and slipped out before we even went to the house. I could have turned down the project entirely and never driven to La Cloche at all—but I didn't, and that counts for something.

Maybe it means I'm finally starting to stand on my own without waiting for someone else to come along and hold me up. Maybe it means the life I've built for myself in the years since the wedding fell through is actually working out.

My life. Not a magical happily ever after wrapped up in somebody else, but a real, practical, dependable life of my own. A life I can count on.

Montreal traffic makes my drive to work as gruelling as ever, but I just turn up my music and savor the coffee in my travel mug. I don't even curse when someone cuts me off. I pull into my spot at the office at ten to nine and decide I have time to grab muffins for me and Layla at the cafe across the road. I dig my phone out of my purse to ask what flavor she wants and notice I've got a new work email notification.

I shouldn't open the message. It's literally ten minutes to nine. Whatever it is can wait ten minutes, but when I flick my inbox open just to get a peek at the sender's name, I can't help reading the whole message.

It's from Natalie.

Hi Brooke,

Thanks again for driving out to La Cloche and meeting with me and Maddie. We both really appreciated you coming so far.

I know we weren't the most organized or prepared, and I apologize for taking up so much of your time. I wasn't at my most professional, and I'm sorry if I came across as rude or uninterested.

Your work is incredible, and we were both really impressed by the consultation. However, I've decided that I won't be moving forward with the inn project, so we unfortunately won't be needing the services of Leung Designs.

Again, I'm sorry for taking up your time on this. I wish you all the best, and I hope you're doing well in Montreal.

Sincerely,
Natalie

"Oh no."

A cold sweat breaks out on my back, trickling down to the waistband of my dress.

She can't do this.

I only got this project because no one else wanted it. Eric never would have considered a job this small and remote if by some fluke of scheduling we didn't end up with a gap to fill this quarter. That's not going to happen again, not with the demand for Leung Designs here in Montreal growing stronger every year.

We'll keep taking bigger and flashier projects, and Eric will keep assigning them to the same managers he always does. I'll be stuck waiting to 'circle back' to a promotion that never comes because it's either that or bail on the six years I've put in at this firm and start over at the bottom of the food chain somewhere else.

"No."

I meet my gaze in the rearview mirror.

"No," I repeat. "That's not happening."

Adrenaline surges in my veins. I can barely feel my car keys in my hand as I fish them out of my purse and flick the engine back on.

By the time I come back to my senses, I'm already on the highway. I check the dashboard clock.

Twenty past nine.

I'm late for work.

My stomach knots, and dread creeps in, chilling the sweat-slicked skin of my back and making my knees jitter.

I hit a patch of traffic and use one of my hands to dig out my phone. I punch in Layla's number and put her on speaker.

"Hey, babe." Her bright and airy tone fills the car. "I was just about to text you. Is traffic bad today? I can let Francois know. He's looking for you."

Francois is the manager of the other project I'm currently assigned to. I'm supposed to hand in some drafts to him this morning.

I take a shaky breath and count to three as I let it out.

"Um, actually, I need you to let Francois know I won't be in the office today. I, um, need to go back to La Cloche."

There's a moment of silence before Layla crows, "Whaaaaat?"

The traffic thins out, leaving me with a long stretch of open road ahead. Outlet shops and car dealerships line the highway. I'm already at the edge of the city.

My pulse kicks up another notch, and I focus on keeping the car straight.

"Yeah, there's a few things I want to sort out with the client in person before she signs on."

I still haven't told Layla who the client is. I figured we could have a long chat over lunch today, but that's yet another plan for this day that's now gone out the window.

"Okay. Wow. That's a lot of driving."

"Uh-huh," I say, "but I just have a hunch this is the best way to talk to her."

Paint the Moon

I press my lips together to hold back a manic laugh.

I don't have a hunch. I didn't even know where I was driving to until I announced my destination to Layla.

"Can you tell Francois I'll get his stuff to him by the end of the day? He'll be annoyed, but you can just tell him Eric said I'm supposed to do this."

That's a lie.

I have no idea how Eric would feel about this. He wants this project for the firm, but I doubt he wants it bad enough for me to compromise a bigger, more important job.

I watch the next exit ramp get closer and closer, and my fingers twitch on the steering wheel as I consider turning around. My gaze darts from the ramp to the road and back again, over and over, until suddenly, the exit is behind me and I'm hitting the gas. I scoot over to the inner lane, where the cars are moving faster, zooming farther and farther out of Montreal.

"Are you okay?" Layla asks.

"Oh, um, yeah," I mutter. "The signal is patchy here. I should probably let you go. Thanks for dealing with Francois."

"Okay," she says, her tone wary. "Text me when you get there, all right?"

I agree, and she hangs up.

The rest of the drive to La Cloche is a blur. I'm on autopilot. I switch the radio on, but I can barely hear the songs over the sound of my thumping heart.

Every time I think about what I'm actually going to do in La Cloche, a wave of panicked nausea threatens to crest over me, so I force myself to think of nothing but the road. I coast through the twists and turns as the highway shifts into a simple two-lane country road. I glide along the foothills of the Laurentians, passing looming woods and icy lakes streaked with the first few cracks of springtime.

My fugue state almost makes me miss the turn-off to La Cloche, but I spot the sign at the last moment and manage to round the bend. I drive all the way to the middle of town and park just off Rue Principale.

It's only once I've lost the distraction of the rumbling engine that I actually realize what I've done.

"Shit," I say, giving my reflection in the mirror an accusing glare. "This is crazy. *Shit.*"

I don't know where Natalie is. I don't even have her phone number.

I drum my fingertips against the steering wheel and consider my options.

I could drive back to Montreal. I could try sending Natalie an email, like a normal person, and see if there's anything I can do to change her mind.

If the real reason she isn't hiring me is because our former connection is just too weird, showing up in her town unannounced to track her down on the street isn't going to convince her this can be a perfectly normal business relationship.

I fiddle with my car keys, picturing myself slinking back into the office this afternoon. Eric will want an update, and if I can't get Natalie to sign on with Leung Designs, I'll have to tell him I've wasted two whole days of company time driving out here.

He'll never let me live that down. He'll use it as justification to push off any further discussions of my promotion indefinitely.

I'm still caught up in a mental pros and cons list when the rap of someone's knuckles against the passenger side window makes me shriek.

I whip my head around and find Maddie hunched over to peer at me through the window, a skittish grin on her face as she lifts her gloved hand to give me a wave.

I blink at her and squeeze the car keys so tight my palm stings. I climb out of the car and smooth down my coat before walking around to join her on the sidewalk. She's clutching a takeout tray of coffee cups from Café Cloche, her dark hair pinned back in a tight bun.

For a moment, I'm convinced her arrival has to be a sign, but the time I spent in La Cloche all those years ago taught me you can't go more than five meters in this town without bumping into someone you know.

Still, she's seen me, and that means she'll tell Natalie I was here, and that means I can't *not* find Natalie today.

"Brooke!" Maddie says, still grinning as I approach. "What are you doing back here so soon? Did Natalie want to meet with you again?"

Her voice is edged with excitement, and she sways a little, like she's trying to keep herself from jumping up and down.

"I... Yes. Yes, she did." The lie leaves my mouth before I've even processed what I'm saying, and more of them just keep coming. "But I just realized we've only been communicating via email so far, and I completely forgot to ask for her number until now. Do you think I could just get it from you?"

Nerves are zinging up and down my spine, but my voice must sound at least somewhat normal; Maddie beams at me and bobs her head.

"Of course! I'm so happy she wants to talk about the inn."

She rattles off a phone number as I punch it into my cell.

"Oh, but you might have a hard time reaching her just now," she says, her forehead wrinkling. "I'm pretty sure she's out walking Belle. She doesn't usually bring her phone with her. She's very into the whole sanctity of communing with nature thing. Oh wait! Oh no. Do you think she forgot she's supposed to meet you?"

Her eyes widen, and I shake my head, fumbling for an excuse.

"Oh, no, I'm just early. I wasn't sure how bad traffic would be."

Maddie lets out a relieved sigh. "Oh, good. Well, I've got to run. I have to drive back to Saint-Jovite. Can you believe my boss has me drive all the way home to La Cloche every time she wants me to do a coffee run? I brought her a latte from Café Cloche once, and now she won't accept anything else."

I chuckle and give her a sympathetic shake of my head. "Bosses, huh?"

She takes off to where her car is parked just a couple places down from mine. I wave goodbye, and as soon as she's out of sight, I look down at the new number in my contacts, my finger hovering over the button to give Natalie a call.

I stand there, as frozen as a block of ice, before I crack myself out of my stupor. I shove my phone into my coat pocket and hitch my purse strap higher up my shoulder.

I don't have to call her now. Maddie said she's probably not even reachable. I can go grab a coffee and spend a little more time planning my next move.

As I trudge up to the main street, I wonder if I should get a drink instead. It's not even lunchtime, but if there were ever a day to rely on liquid courage, this would be it.

I turn the corner onto Rue Principale and end up right

outside a restaurant with a painted wooden sign etched with block capitals that spell out MACK'S BISTRO.

The windows are a little foggy, but I can see a few brown vinyl booths and lacquered tables inside. The yellowed menu taped to a glass panel in the door advertises an array of fried foods and beers.

I can't remember if I've been in before, but something has me pulling the door open instead of walking farther up to the café. A blast of warm air hits me, along with the scent of fryer oil. String lights criss-cross along the ceiling, giving the place an evening-time glow even in the middle of the day.

The only other person in here is a middle-aged woman in a caftan sitting at the bar. She's got a huge clip shaped like a butterfly holding up her grey-streaked hair.

I can't help grinning. If there's one thing you're guaranteed to find in La Cloche, it's a middle-aged woman in a caftan.

The bell above the door tinkles, and the woman glances over her shoulder to give me a smile, but no one else appears.

I start to edge back towards the door as I wonder if the place is even open yet, but just before I grab the handle, a bald guy in a Van Halen t-shirt comes out from behind the bar.

"*Salut, mademoiselle!*" he calls.

"Uh, *ouais, salut,*" I stutter.

He tells me to sit wherever I like. I scan the completely empty room and then slip into the nearest booth, the one with a view out the front window. He drops a menu off and asks if I'd like anything to drink.

"Um…"

My gaze flits over the beer and spirits section on the

back of the menu, but I flip it over, slapping my hand down on the cover just a little too hard as I order a tea instead.

The man's eyebrows raise just enough for me to notice, but he nods and says he'll have a tea coming right up.

I get another eyebrow raise when he comes back a couple minutes later to deliver the steaming mug and I tell him that's all I'd like to order today.

"Let me know if you change your mind, miss," he says in French. "I'm making pizzas today. The tourists love my pizzas. I even make vegan ones now. Nothing like good Québécois cheese, if you ask me, but you've got to give the people what they want."

I fake a smile and tell him I'll consider it.

I blow on my tea and stare out the fog-coated glass, watching people wander up and down the sidewalk in their boots and coats. There's a pottery shop across the street, the window display filled with vases and candlesticks in bright pastel hues that contrast with the late winter gloom. A woman about my age and a little girl in a puffy snowsuit come out, the mother clutching a brown paper bag with a few tissue paper-wrapped pieces poking out over the top. The shopkeeper waves them off, holding the door open and bending down to give the little girl a high-five.

I wonder if they're locals on a shopping spree or just out of season tourists passing through.

I wonder if they live in one of the little brick houses just off the main street, with a melting snowman in the yard and a cat sleeping on the windowsill.

That could have been me.

If I'd stayed here, I might have had a daughter that age by now.

The thought nearly makes me drop my tea. I set the mug down, the saucer rattling as my hands shake.

Paint the Moon

I can't think about that. I can't go back to *what if* and *if only*. I need to focus on the present, not some sob story vision of the past.

In the present, I am an independent woman committed to my career. I have a stable and fulfilling life in Montreal I've worked hard to build for myself.

I don't need someone to come along and offer me an escape. I'm not trying to escape anymore.

My phone is pressed to my ear a second later, the steady ringing cutting through my thoughts as I hold my breath and wait to see if Natalie will pick up.

"Hello?"

Her voice comes through after the third ring. I open my mouth to answer, but a zing of panic shoots through me when I can't make any sound come out.

"Hello? Is anyone there?"

I hear her breathe into the receiver for a couple seconds, and then there's a shuffling sound like she's about to hang up.

"Wait!"

My shout is loud enough to make the woman at the bar look over at me again. My cheeks heat up, and I turn my face to the window.

"Um, hi," I add at a normal volume. "It's, uh, Brooke. Brooke Carmichael."

"Brooke," Natalie says, sounding startled. "Oh. Wow. Hi."

"I'm sorry to bother you. Maddie gave me your number."

"No worries," she says. She sounds a little out of breath, and I can hear the crunching of her footsteps, like she's walking somewhere snowy. "What's up?"

"Well, I, um, wanted to talk to you."

I wince. Obviously I wanted to talk to her. That's the whole point of calling someone.

"I'm in La Cloche," I blurt.

I fight the urge to dive under the table and hide forever. I sound like a stalker. I *am* a stalker.

"You are?" Her footsteps stop. "Why?"

I open my mouth to answer, but once again, I can't find any words. Natalie saves me by rushing to speak again.

"Sorry. That came out wrong. I mean, uh, what brings you into town?"

She starts walking again. I hear a dog bark, and I wince. She's out trying to enjoy her life, and I'm harassing her with this unhinged phone call.

"I, uh..." I glance out the window, raking my gaze along the street until I spot the pottery shop's window display again. "Pottery! I saw some, uh, pottery I'd like to buy yesterday, so today I came back to, um, buy it."

"Oh. Cool."

I can hear the unspoken question in her voice, namely: *What the hell are you calling me for?*

I should just hang up. I should abandon this whole plan. I should go back to the office with my tail between my legs and announce I lost the project.

"Have a drink with me."

Natalie makes a surprised sound that's almost a squawk, and I have to clamp my jaw shut so I don't do something similar.

I just asked her that. I really just asked her that.

The silence that follows feels like it drags on for an hour. Finally, Natalie lets out a strained chuckle.

"Is it even noon yet?"

I pull my phone away from my ear to check the screen. "Twelve-oh-five."

She laughs for real this time. "Well, as they say, it's five o'clock somewhere."

"It doesn't have to be a *drink* drink," I say in a rush. "I'm having tea. You can have tea too. Or we can have an actual drink. Whatever you want. I just thought it would be good to, um, talk. You were right. Yesterday was very...unexpected, and I know I got a bit weird, so I wanted to see if we could meet up so I could apologize."

"You don't have anything to apologize for."

The sincerity in her voice hits me straight in the chest. I fall silent again.

"But since you made the trip again, it's the least I can do. Where are you right now?"

I let her know, and she says she's only a five minute walk away. We hang up, and I notice I've been tearing up a napkin with my free hand. The pieces lay in a pile like a miniature snowdrift on the glossy surface of the table.

I force myself to take a few steadying sips of tea while I wait for Natalie to arrive. She pops out onto the main street a few blocks down, her cloud of thick, wavy hair unmistakable even from that far away.

A huge bloodhound trots along beside her, snout glued to the ground and dangling ears flapping.

My breath lodges in my throat.

Belle.

The name stuck out to me when Maddie mentioned it, and now I know why. Belle is the Sinclair family dog. I'd spend half the evening petting her whenever I went to dinner at my ex's parents' place.

I watch the two of them get closer and closer to the bistro. Natalie is wearing the same bomber jacket she had on the other day, hands stuffed into her pockets. She's got loose-fitting jeans on over some Kodiak boots.

She doesn't spot me until she's only a couple steps away. As soon as her eyes lock with mine through the glass, her severe features soften into a smile.

Despite the fact that my hands are shaking so hard I can barely keep hold of my tea, I smile back.

"The city girl returns," she says as soon as she pulls the door open.

Belle comes barrelling in ahead of her, huge paws click-clacking against the floor.

"Belle!" I call out. "Come here, girl!"

She whips her head around, nearly smacking herself in the face with one of her paddle-sized ears, and then lopes over to my table with her tail wagging.

"Hi, Belle!" I coo as I slide over to start scratching her head. "Do you remember me?"

"Oh, right. I forgot you two have met."

Natalie approaches the table, stopping a couple feet away to watch me and Belle with her arms crossed over her chest.

The air in the restaurant seems to get heavier all of a sudden, like the fog clinging to the windows has drifted over to stifle us with the weight of the past.

I look back down at Belle. If she notices the change in the atmosphere, she doesn't show it. Her eyes are scrunched closed, her tongue lolling. I shift my knees over to avoid getting hit with a bloodhound drool bomb.

"She likes you," Natalie says. "She's not like that with everyone."

Before I can think of what to say, the same bald guy from earlier comes storming out of the back room while brandishing a flour-dusted rolling pin at us.

"Get that animal out of here!" he shouts, speaking English now.

Paint the Moon

Natalie just laughs. "Come on, Mack. It's just Belle. Plus, there's like nobody in here."

He gives a pointed look at me. "Are you bothering my customer with your hellhound?"

"I'm *meeting* your customer with my hellhound. She's here to see me."

Mack squints and glances between the two of us like he's checking for signs Natalie is lying.

"Fine. The dog can stay, but you have to order a pizza."

Natalie shrugs and slides into the other side of the booth.

"I'm fine with that." She tilts her head at me. "You down to split a pizza?"

I nod. "Oh, sure. Yeah, pizza would be great."

I don't know if she'll want to stick around for a meal once she finds out why I'm really here, but it doesn't seem like I've got much of a choice.

"Should we have that *drink* drink?" she asks me. "Somehow, I can't see tea pairing very well with pizza."

Chapter 9

Natalie

We've almost finished our beers, and I still have no idea why Brooke called me. I have a hunch she's not really in town for some pottery, which is as much to do with her shaking hands and restless babbling as it is with the fact that no one drives for two hours on a weekday morning just to buy a vase.

She also doesn't have any shopping bags.

"So," I say, "do you want your half of the pizza to go, or should we get another round of beer?"

She's barely picked at her first slice while we've discussed everything from the weather to the housing market, but she's had no trouble with her beer. She's been downing it like water since Mack dropped the pint glasses off at our table.

"I, um...well, I guess we could get another round. I really should eat more of this pizza too."

She stuffs a few bites in her mouth, chomping like a beaver going to town on a log before forcing down a thick swallow.

I'd be tempted to laugh if I weren't so worried. She's

starting to make me think she's about to do something catastrophic, like announce she's been raising my brother's secret love child in Montreal for the past six years.

The thought makes my stomach churn so much I have to put down my pizza.

I don't know why it feels so weird to think about her dating my brother. Jonas has plenty of exes in La Cloche. His class clown charm was practically a lethal weapon back in high school. I don't even think twice about saying hi to his former girlfriends when I bump into them now. Sometimes we'll even trade a few jokes at his expense.

I probably just feel awkward about the way things ended between them. I'm the sister of the guy responsible for what was probably the worst day of Brooke's life.

"Look, Brooke…"

Her shoulders stiffen under the thin fabric of her maroon-coloured dress.

The colour looks pretty on her, the deep berry shade contrasting with her pale skin and the blonde sheen of her hair.

Her eyes flare wide, gawking at me like I've got her at gunpoint, but I force myself to keep going.

"I'm getting the feeling there's something you want to say to me, and I just want you to know, whatever it is, you can tell me."

Her chest strains against the buttons of her dress as her breathing quickens.

I focus extra hard on keeping my gaze glued to her face as heat creeps up my neck.

"I need you to hire me."

I straighten up so fast my back thumps against the booth and knocks the breath out of me. Belle raises her head where she's curled up under a nearby table.

Whatever I was expecting Brooke to say, it wasn't that.

"I know that sounds desperate, but the thing is, I am desperate."

Brooke folds her hands together on the table in front of her, staring down at her interlaced knuckles.

"Your inn would be the most important project of my entire career. I've been with Leung Designs for six years now. I took the job right after...well, after everything that happened here. I've stuck it out despite my shitty boss and all the extra stuff that gets dumped on my plate because I thought it would all pay off someday, but I'm realizing...it's not going to. Not if I keep doing things the same way I always have. This project is my leverage. If I make you the best damn inn to ever grace the Laurentians, I'll either move up in this company, or I'll have what I need to move up somewhere else. I'm not going to get a chance like this again."

She's looking at me instead of the table now. There's a burning sincerity in her eyes that I can only handle staring at for a couple seconds before I have to blink and glance away.

"I shouldn't be telling you any of this, of course. It's extremely unprofessional. I'd probably be fired if my boss knew I said all that. This isn't at all how I'd normally approach a client, but...well, this isn't exactly a normal situation, is it?"

She reaches for her beer and tips her head back to swallow the last sip.

I watch her neck arch, baring her delicate skin as her throat bobs.

She's right.

Nothing about this is normal.

"I don't mind the honesty," I say. "It's refreshing. I just wish I could help you."

She sets her glass down and tilts her head, waiting.

"I've decided I'm selling the house," I blurt, her sea green eyes wearing me down in a matter of seconds. "This whole inn idea...it was just an idea. Like I said in my email, I'm sorry we wasted your time, but the truth is, I have no idea what it takes to open an inn."

"But I do."

I squint at her. She leans a little closer over the table.

"I've worked on enough hotels to have a gist of what it takes to get one running. I can help you. All that stuff I was asking you about during the consultation yesterday, all that stuff you haven't figured out yet—I can figure it out for you."

She jerks backwards, breaking our eye contact to glance down at the table.

"Sorry." Her voice is tinged with embarrassment. "I know I sound a little unhinged. The truth is that even if this project didn't have the potential to change my whole career, that house..."

Her gaze drifts to the window, her eyes unfocused as her face tightens into an expression I can't quite read.

I'd almost call it longing, if it made any sense for her to be *longing* for my dead great-aunt's house she only saw for the first time yesterday.

"That house is perfect," she says, turning back to me. "This is exactly the kind of project that makes me love my job. I can *see* that place as an inn. I can feel it. I had a hard time falling asleep last night because my head was already filled with a million ideas. I *want* to work on this."

There's no affectation in her tone. She's almost vibrating with the passion in her words, and for a moment, I want to tell her what *I* see, what I feel when I look at the house.

I want to tell her about the barn, the light, the vision I have for a studio—but that's all it is. A vision. A shimmering mirage in the middle of a wasteland.

"It is a great house," I say, "but it's just...too much. I can't keep it."

"Why not?"

The directness of the question throws me off, like she's whipped out a magnifying glass to study me.

"I don't...I don't really know what I'm doing with my life anymore."

The words tumble out before I can think twice about being so honest. Brooke tilts her head, as patient as a scientist out observing a creature in the wild.

"I don't know if you remember this," I say, "but I, um, I paint, and—"

"Of course I remember that," she cuts in. "I remember your paintings."

It's a perfectly normal thing to say. It doesn't *mean* anything, but there's a softness to her voice that makes both of us pause. The rock music Mack has playing in the kitchen seems to get quieter.

The whole world seems to get quieter. I can't even hear the muffled rumble of car engines on the street anymore.

I clear my throat and take a long gulp of my beer.

"Well, the thing is," I say after setting the glass down, "I've always thought I'd actually *do* something with painting. I only managed one year of university in Montreal before I dropped out to travel. All I've ever worked are shitty part-time jobs to save up here or on the road. I've taken some art courses here and there over the years, and I've had some success getting into a few exhibitions—real exhibitions, not just, you know, selling watercolours to tourists here in La Cloche."

I shrug, fidgeting with my napkin so I don't have to look at her.

I don't know why I'm saying so much. It's not like she asked for my life story.

"You don't think that's real?"

The shock in her voice makes me glance back up at her.

"Selling art in La Cloche?" she adds. "Isn't that, like, the whole point of La Cloche? That people sell art here?"

I shake my head. "Yeah, but having your own studio and actual collectors who come out to look at your work is a whole different level than me selling prints in a corner of my mom's health food store and running a stall at the Christmas market every year. I thought I could get to the next level, once I actually settled down and put my whole focus on my career, but then…"

Shame ties a knot in my stomach. I focus back on the napkin again, folding it into smaller and smaller squares.

"What happened?"

The softness is back in her voice. The sound of it reminds me of winter nights when the snow drifts down in thick clumps, when the sky is streaked with moonlight and it's so quiet you can almost hear the gentle brush of each snowflake hitting the ground.

"I got selected to be the artist in residence at this really famous institution for the arts in Thunder Bay."

The story slips out of me, like I'm emptying myself into the silence of a snowy night.

"It was six months, fully funded, where I could focus on nothing but painting, and at the end, I was guaranteed an exhibition of my work. It's really hard to get selected, and it puts a lot of eyes on your career. The whole Canadian art world knows about this program. There were some really influential people at my show. It could have changed everything for me."

I huff a quiet laugh as I realize the irony.

"I guess it did change everything for me. I bombed it. Hard. I tried to prove I could paint more than just what people have come to expect from me. I wanted to prove I could be bigger, better, but it... it was an absolute failure. I didn't sell a thing, and the reviews..."

I can't keep from wincing.

"Well, let's just say the *best* feedback I got was being called inoffensive but ultimately forgettable. The rest was...a lot worse. It's not the kind of thing an art career can bounce back from, especially when I didn't even *have* a career to begin with. I know that seems overdramatic, but it's the truth, and I have to be realistic with myself now."

I hate how defeated I sound, how pathetic. Even Belle seems to notice; she scrambles to her feet and lumbers over to lay her giant head on the end of the booth's bench.

"It's barely been three months since the show," I say while hunching over to give Belle a few scratches. "I was only home for a couple weeks before *Tante* Manon passed away, and then this whole inheritance thing took over my life, and now..."

Now I don't know what the hell to do with my existence.

"I'm sorry. That sounds awful."

I shrug. "You don't have anything to be sorry about. You're not the one who put a bunch of shitty paintings on display for the whole country to see."

She winces, and I wish I could stuff the words back in my mouth.

"I'm sorry. I sound so petty. It's just..."

I stare out the window as I gather my thoughts. The

Paint the Moon

banners hanging from the lampposts are fluttering in the breeze, their colours as bright as the vibrant shades of the storefronts all painted in different rainbow hues. Even in the gloom of these weeks between winter and spring, the center of town is always bursting with colour.

We're too far up the street for me to see the banner featuring my painting, but I know it's out there, rippling in the wind.

"Painting has always been my *thing*," I say, still staring out the window. "Ever since I was a kid, it's the thing everyone has known me for. This whole town thinks of me as Natalie the painter. I really let myself believe that meant something."

"You don't think it does?"

I turn back to face her, our eyes locking.

"I don't think it means what I thought it did."

I know I should break the eye contact. I should stop telling her things I can't even say out loud to my best friends, but when she's staring at me like that, all I can think about is moonlight shimmering on snowflakes and the deep, deep quiet of a frozen forest at night.

All I can think about is speaking my secrets into the silence.

Belle lets out a low woof. Brooke and I jerk upright in our seats, and I realize just how far we'd both started leaning over the table.

My heart leaps into my throat, panic squeezing my chest.

This is a *really* weird way to behave around someone who was going to marry my brother.

I focus on Belle to distract myself. I'm clearly not finishing my pizza, so I check Mack isn't watching from over at the bar and then rip off a hunk of crust. Belle gobbles it down in a nanosecond, her tail thumping against the floorboards.

When I sit back up, I manage a straight face while I steer us back to the whole reason Brooke is here.

"So that's why I don't think jumping into building an inn is a good idea."

She peers at me for a few seconds, a couple creases forming between her eyes.

She looks cute with her face all scrunched up like that.

No. Not cute.

I can't afford to think she's cute. Even if we didn't have a weirdly entangled past, today might be the last day I ever see her.

My breath catches at the thought.

"I don't mean to sound rude," she says, "but...how are those things connected?"

"I thought trying something new with my painting was a good idea, and I was wrong. How am I supposed to trust this will be any different?"

"I guess you can't know that," she says. "Not until you try."

She says it with a straight face, but the sentiment is so trite even she starts chuckling along with me when I can't hold back a scoff.

"Okay, yeah," she says, grinning. "I sound like a motivational poster. That was cheesy."

I shrug to let her know it happens to the best of us. She reaches for her drink before realizing the glass is already empty.

I forgot we were going to order a second round.

"Maybe if I understood why Manon left me the house, I'd feel different," I explain. "I just can't figure it out. I've started to believe it was totally random, like she drew a name out of a hat and thought, 'Hmm, yes, it will piss off a lot of my relatives if I give this house to the childless vagabond artist with an Anglophone mother. Might as well do it.'"

Brooke laughs. "You think she gave you an entire house just to piss off some of your French cousins?"

I chuckle and spread my hands out like I've thrown down all my cards. "I've got no other theories."

Brooke nods, that pensive expression of hers returning. I try to look away, but something about those little creases between her eyebrows is mesmerizing. I picture myself leaning across the table and reaching my thumb out to smooth them away.

No. No, no, no, no.

I bark at myself in my mind, using the same voice I'd order Belle to heel.

"What is it?" I ask, partially because I want to know what she's thinking, but mostly because I really need her to stop looking at me like that.

She clasps her hands together and rests them on the table.

"Promise you'll hear me out on this."

I nod my head just a little too hard. "Okay. I promise."

"I think you'd regret selling the house now, and I'm not just saying that for my own sake."

My spine stiffens.

That's what Maddie and Jacinthe have been trying to tell me too.

"You've been through a lot," Brooke continues. "You said it's only been a couple months since your aunt passed away, and with all the stress of the exhibition and moving home and getting surprised by her will, you probably haven't even processed her death. Not really, at least."

I open my mouth to protest but end up clamping my jaw shut instead.

No one's ever put it that way before.

I didn't think I felt anything much about Manon's death, but maybe I'm wrong. Maybe I just got so bogged down with the inheritance I forgot to consider I might actually have some grieving to do.

She was my great-aunt, after all. She wasn't a particularly pleasant part of my life here in La Cloche, but she was a constant one.

Maybe the least I can do for her memory is actually spend some time thinking about her life before I sell everything she ever owned.

"Go on," I say.

"You're not losing anything by giving yourself a little more time before you make a choice you can't take back."

She has a point. There's no undoing the sale of the house. Even if I just gave it to one of the distant relatives who were so interested in sniffing around the inheritance, there's no guarantee I'd ever step foot in the house again.

"So," Brooke adds after taking a deep breath, like she's steeling herself, "here's the part I am saying for my own sake. You also aren't losing anything by hiring me and converting the house into an inn."

She's plastered on her 'doing business' face, that calm and efficient expression I recognize from our surprise meeting in the café, but I can see she's fidgeting, her shoulders shifting as she wrings her hands under the table.

I have to remind myself I definitely don't think she's cute.

"Not to be crass," I say, arching an eyebrow, "but you do realize how much money it costs to hire you, right?"

I lift the corner of my mouth to let her know I'm

teasing her—which is a mistake, because it makes her give me a wry smile of her own and bend her head closer towards me.

"Yes," she says, her professional tone edged with amusement, "but you do realize you can still sell the house after you renovate it, right?"

Despite her joking tone, she still manages to floor me.

I gawk at her, my eyes wide, and her grin gets even wider, like she knows she's played a trump card.

"Considering you got the property through an inheritance, you could make a huge profit if you sold it as a brand new, fully functional inn all ready for business instead of a rundown old house in need of repair. If you complete the renovations and still aren't convinced you actually want to run an inn, there's no harm done. All you'll have done is make selling the place even easier."

She's making all of this sound way too easy.

I narrow my eyes. "Are you swindling me, Brooke Carmichael?"

She tucks a lock of hair behind her ear and pretends to glare at me. "I've never swindled in my life."

The haughty, almost bratty voice she puts on has me diving down to feed Belle another chunk of pizza just so I can get my face under control.

No one as pretty as her should be allowed to use a voice like that.

"You'd still want the job even if we're starting from absolute scratch?" I ask, taking another stab at professionalism after I've sat back up. "It sounds like your clients usually have a lot more prepared than I do."

Brooke shakes her head. "Like I said, I can help you. I've already laid it all on the line, so you know how much you'd be helping me too."

I spend another few moments turning things over in my mind.

"I guess the house would need some work before I sold it anyway..." I mutter.

She nods, barely concealing another grin. "Mhmm."

I chuckle and shake my head. "You really are swindling me."

She shrugs and tucks the other side of her hair behind her ear. "I prefer to think of it as convincing."

I really should argue more. I already decided to sell. When I sent her that email yesterday, I told myself it was the end of this.

Instead, I find myself settling a little deeper into the booth.

"So, say I do want to go through with this, what's our first step?"

Chapter 10

Natalie

"Was she always this hot?"

I whirl around and shoot daggers at my best friend.

"Jacinthe."

She shrugs and stuffs her hands in the pockets of her baggy jeans. "*Quoi?* I'm just saying."

"You're saying it too loud."

I grab her by the sleeve of her flannel and tug her farther into the kitchen, where we're supposed to be cleaning up the snack trays we set out for our meeting with Brooke.

It's Brooke's third time back in La Cloche today, and her first time meeting with all three of us.

The two weeks since she showed up at Mack's Bistro to plead her case have been filled with more phone calls, emails, and business meetings than I can remember. I've consulted with bankers, municipal authorities, tax lawyers, and contractors.

Maddie and Jacinthe have come along to as many meetings as they can fit into their schedules. Maddie has also taken it upon herself to create a plethora of spreadsheets and shared documents to record everything we've learned so far.

The consensus is that we can, in fact, open an inn here in La Cloche.

We have the zoning. We can get the permits. We'd be eligible for a few loans and even a Québec tourism grant. Maddie is confident she could handle the bookkeeping and supply management, and Jacinthe has already put on her tour guide cap to draft a list of local sights and activities she could offer to guests.

All that's left to decide is if we *will* open an inn.

What we have agreed on is hiring Brooke. She was right that renovating makes sense even if I end up selling. Everything I've learned these past couple weeks has assured me *someone* will pounce on the chance to run the business, even if it's not me.

My inheritance from *Tante* Manon is enough to cover the fees from Leung Designs as well as the most essential parts of the construction, so there was nothing stopping us from moving ahead with Brooke.

Then again, if she overhears Jacinthe talking about how hot she is, Brooke might decide to rip up our contract herself.

"They can't hear us," Jacinthe says, waving my concerns away as she dumps some fruit peels off the snack tray into the trash. "They're talking about math. They're on a whole other planet right now."

We left Brooke in the living room with Maddie so the two of them could nerd out in peace.

The more I've talked to Brooke, the more I've realized just how much her job consists of. She's like an architect, decorator, artist, and sociologist all sharing the same brain.

I grab the tray out of Jacinthe's hands so I can wash it.

"Just try not to say anything inappropriate before this meeting is done," I say.

She sidles over to me and leans against the counter. I can feel her eyes on me, but I don't give her the satisfaction of looking up as I scrub the tray.

"Ohhhhh," she drawls after another few seconds of staring. "You *do* think she's hot. Well, well, well..."

I jerk my head up. "I do *not* think she's hot."

I don't know why my face feels so warm. The fact that my own skin is betraying me makes me glare even harder at Jacinthe.

She scoffs and crosses her arms. "I know you have eyes, dumbass. Don't lie to me."

I can tell she won't let this go, and the more we talk about it, the more likely it is Brooke will overhear, so I lower my voice to a sharp whisper.

"Okay, okay, so she's pretty. *Obviously* she's really pretty, but lots of women are really pretty."

Jacinthe scoffs again. "Duh. We're gay. Of course we think lots of women are pretty. You're being really weird about *this* pretty woman, though, *ma belle*."

I fling my sponge into the sink and whirl around to face her, planting my soapy hands on my hips before I can think better of soaking my jeans.

"*I'm* not being weird. *You're* the one who mentioned how hot she is while she's literally in the next room."

I drop my voice again and cast a nervous glance at the hallway, but I can still hear the faint echoes of Maddie and Brooke caught up in their conversation.

Jacinthe squints at me and taps her chin.

"Hmmm."

"What are you hmming at?" I demand. "There's nothing to hmm at. She's my brother's ex, and now she's our interior designer. It doesn't even matter if she's hot or not."

Jacinthe sticks her neck out and leans towards me.

"Hmmmmmm," she repeats, making the sound even longer and louder.

"Oh my god, stop!"

I take a step back, and she counters it with a step forward.

"HMMMMMM!" she all but shrieks, flapping her hands like a deranged bird.

I squeal and flick my wet hands at her, which makes her gasp and then curse at the droplets splattering her face.

Then she lunges for the sink to grab some soap suds of her own.

We've progressed to laughing and chasing each other in circles around the kitchen when the sound of someone clearing their throat stops me in my tracks.

"Uh, guys?"

Maddie is standing in the kitchen's entryway, shaking her head at us.

Jacinthe steps up beside me and flicks a final shot of cold water at the back of my neck. I'm flaming so hot with embarrassment I'm surprised the water doesn't sizzle. There's no way Brooke didn't hear us screeching like little kids.

"I have to go now," Maddie says. "Jacinthe, do you still need a ride home?"

"*Ouais, merci, ma petite cousine.*"

Maddie rolls her eyes and insists she is not Jacinthe's *little* cousin. They're still bickering as I shepherd us out of the kitchen. Brooke is in the living room packing up her laptop. She does us all the solid of pretending she hasn't realized she's been hired by idiots.

"Oh, Natalie," Maddie says, tapping my arm, "Brooke was wondering if you could show her the barn."

I freeze, glancing between her and Brooke as I fumble for words.

"Oh. I, um, I—"

"You don't have to," Brooke interrupts. "I just thought since I'm already done at the office for the day, I could hang around a little longer to see more of the property. I haven't even properly seen the backyard. It's totally fine if you don't have time, though."

I shake my head, which feels heavy with the weight of everyone's eyes on me.

"No, that's fine. I can show you around."

"Great!" Maddie chirps, stepping past me to head for the foyer. "Have fun, you two! Jacinthe, *viens.*"

Jacinthe clomps out after her, but not without shooting me a pointed look.

I'd growl at her if I didn't think that would have Brooke worried to be alone in a house with me.

Once my friends are gone, Brooke and I get our coats and boots on. We're only a few days away from April now, and it's gotten warm enough that anyone new to Québec might be foolish enough to believe winter has finally lost its hold on the province.

I've lived through too many freak snowstorms in the middle of April to believe we're safe until May.

Still, the sound of water dripping off the eaves fills the air out on the porch. A few chickadees twitter and take off from where they were perched on the railing.

Brooke walks over to grip the railing herself and takes a deep gulp of air in through her nose.

"God, that smells good," she says, with what can only be described as gusto.

She proceeds to huff down more of the country air like it's in limited supply.

I press my lips together to keep from laughing as I watch her shoulders rise and fall, her blonde hair cascading over her shoulders where she stands with her back to me.

"Better than downtown Montreal?" I ask.

She chuckles. "Most places smell better than downtown, but wow, you guys have really got it good out here. Like, this is what your guests are going to wake up and see every day. It's incredible."

She sweeps her hand out like the front yard, with its patchy, melting snow heaps and muddy walkway is a stunning vista worth millions.

I don't have it in me to tease her. Her enthusiasm is exactly the reason there's a part of me that's considering running this inn.

So many people live their whole lives without the moments I take for granted: wandering a quiet country road at dusk, listening to the birds serenade the sun's arrival, sipping tea on a cozy porch on a sunny springtime afternoon. I forget just how lucky I am to have a home town that soothes me, that offers me quiet when I need it and community when I crave it, that can serve as an inspiration or a refuge whenever I need somewhere to pull myself back up to my feet and keep going.

I'm not so sure about that last part these days, but at least there's still a place for me here. At least I still feel at home, and maybe it wouldn't be so bad to spend my days running a place that gives visitors the chance to feel that way too.

"We do have it pretty good," I say, stepping down off the porch. "Shall we?"

We walk around the edge of the house, splashing and

crunching our way through puddles and drifts of crystallized snow. Brooke pauses as we pass by one of the two evergreens that flank the house. Dark green needles coat the ground, their sharp, fresh scent like a natural air freshener that tingles in my nose.

"Do you know what kind of trees these are?" she asks, craning her neck to stare up at the conical branches tapering to a point high above our heads.

"They're balsam firs," I answer. "I'm pretty sure these are as old as the house."

She takes another one of her enthusiastic sniffs.

"So good," I hear her mutter under her breath.

"Here." I lunge forward, bending to grab a twig that's dropped from the tree. "Let me show you something."

I need a distraction. If we keep standing here while she says things in a breathy voice like that, I'm going to lose my mind.

"Did you ever do this as a kid?" I ask.

I point at the bubbles in the tree's bark, scattered like boils among the patches of lichen clinging to the trunk. Then I poke the end of the stick into one of them.

A glob of sap shoots out, exploding in a pressurized spray of thick, clear liquid.

Brooke shrieks and jumps away.

"Shit. Sorry," I say with a chuckle. "That was a good one. They don't always shoot out like that."

She presses a hand to her chest. "That scared the shit out of me! Is this supposed to be a game? Poke the tree?"

She's laughing now too, but she still keeps a wary distance as I pierce another sap bubble. This one just trickles down the tree trunk instead of exploding.

"Kind of," I say. "Mostly it's just fun. Sometimes you

can hit your friends with them. I guess it sounds pretty crazy to someone who grew up in the city."

"I didn't grow up in the city."

I drop my arm to my side and nearly stab myself with the sap-covered twig.

"You didn't? Why did I think you grew up in Montreal?"

She shrugs. "I guess we've never talked much before now."

A moment of silence falls, filled with the dripping sound of melting snow.

I clear my throat. "So, um, where did you grow up?"

She takes a step away from me, peering at the tree trunk as she lifts a finger to stroke a flaky patch of pale green lichen.

"I guess I partially grew up in Montreal. I moved there with my mom when I was ten. We used to live in New Brunswick, before my parents split up."

My eyes widen. I never would have guessed she was from so far away.

"Wow. East coast, huh?"

She nods. "Yeah, we lived in a small town, less than an hour's drive from the ocean. My dad has a huge family, so I was related to half the people in town."

I chuckle. "Damn. Guess it's kind of nice you didn't spend your teenage years there. That would have made dating hard."

The corners of her mouth lift, but the faint smile drops off her face a second later.

"I guess," she says with another shrug.

Before I can ask anything else, she takes a step back from the tree and jerks her chin towards the house.

"My grandma had a house out there just like this. Well, not just like this, but same...feeling."

Her gaze sweeps over the white walls and grey shutters.

Earlier, I told her about my idea to paint all the shutters emerald green, and she said that's exactly the colour she would have suggested.

Watching her now, I'm starting to understand the wistful, almost pained expression that crosses her face when she's looking at the house sometimes.

"Why did your mom move you all the way to Montreal?"

The question slips out before I can stop it. I wince.

"Sorry," I add. "That was really personal."

She shakes her head, shifting her focus from the house back to me.

"It's no big deal. My mom is from Montreal originally, and we still have some family out here." She glances down at her boots. "After the move, we bounced around with relatives for...a while. Or with guys she was dating. It just took us a while to get settled."

Her shoulders curl inward, just enough for me to notice, like she's trying to make herself smaller.

My heart swells, and for a second, all I want to do is throw my arms around her.

"That sounds tough," I say instead, "especially if you were only ten."

My parents are the kind of people who seem like they burst into existence as a fully-formed, nauseatingly lovesick middle-aged couple who've been together since the dawn of time. My dad still buys my mom flowers every Friday, and they've been married for over thirty years.

As a child, I couldn't even fathom the concept of divorce.

"It wasn't the best, I'll admit," Brooke says, stuffing her hands into the pockets of her pea coat. "Anyway, I don't know if that makes me a city kid or not, by your standards. I definitely never poked sap bubbles for fun, even in New Brunswick."

She gestures at the stick I'm still clutching and laughs.

It's a real laugh, and the sight of her smiling again feels like watching the first few blades of grass pop up from the ground in spring.

I hold out the stick.

"It's never too late to try."

She accepts the offer, and I stare at the way her mouth purses with concentration while she selects her target on the tree trunk.

She chooses well; a glob of sap shoots out when she pierces the bubble. I only just manage to side-step out of the range of fire.

"Ew!" she shrieks. "That's so gross!"

"How can it be gross?" I demand, laughing at the way her expression sours with disgust. "It's a tree!"

She holds the twig up, pointing at the clump of congealed sap clinging to the end. "It's so goopy!"

I shrug. "Maybe you are a city girl after all."

"Hey!" She flings the stick away so she can wag her finger at me. "Ten years in a small town has to count for something."

I heave a dramatic sigh. "Sure, sure. Whatever you say."

We both break down laughing. I step away from the tree and motion for her to follow me.

"Come on. I'll give you a tour of the rest of the yard."

The barn is looming at the back of the property, but I can't bring myself to take her inside just yet.

I've never taken anyone to the barn before.

Paint the Moon

I guide her over to observe the frozen pond instead. The shrubs lining the water are all shaggy and overgrown. Swaths of dead bulrushes jut up through the ice like skeletal fingers.

"So, since I missed out on it, tell me, what *was* dating in a small town like?" Brooke asks as we amble along the rim of the pond. "Or, is. I assume you still date here."

"Not lately."

She turns her head to glance at me. "Oh?"

"You've taken up most of my time."

My mouth drops open as I realize how totally wrong that came out. Brooke's eyes widen.

"I mean, not you, specifically," I stutter. "You as in, the whole project. You know, with the house."

I point over at the building in question, jabbing my finger in the air several times like an idiot. My face is burning, and I wish I could shove my head in the nearest snow bank to cool off. I settle for yanking my hair over my shoulder to air out the back of my neck.

"The house. Right." Brooke says, resuming our route around the pound. "I know you've been really busy."

I nod, not trusting myself to speak again. "Mhmm."

"But before that?" she says after we've walked a little farther. "You didn't accidentally date a third cousin once removed or anything?"

I laugh a little too hard, latching onto the change in subject.

"My mom is from Ontario, so only half my family even lives in the province," I explain. "I think that spared me from most of the risk of cousin dating. Plus, being a lesbian limited my options to basically nothing."

She stays silent, and a fresh wave of embarrassment hits me.

"You, uh, did know I'm a lesbian, right?"

I assumed she knew. My whole family knows, but like we've already acknowledged, Brooke and I have never really talked before.

"Oh, yes, I knew."

I can't read her tone, so I can't tell if I should be sagging with relief or getting even tenser.

Not that it matters. She's my interior designer. It's not like I even needed to come out to her at all.

"So you didn't have a lot of chances to date?" she asks. "In La Cloche? Really?"

We've started a second lap around the pond, but she doesn't seem to notice, and I'm too focused on surviving this conversation to think of what else to show her around the yard.

I concentrate on answering her question, and I end up fighting back a grin when I realize what she's getting at.

I suppose it is hard to believe a town full of hippie artisans and holistic healing practitioners isn't also home to a thriving lesbian commune.

"La Cloche doesn't have a lot of people in general," I explain. "Plus, I went to high school at a big feeder school for all the small towns around here, and while La Cloche is very queer-friendly, most of the other ones are not. It wasn't exactly cool to be gay at my school."

She raises a hand to her mouth and looks at me with genuine pain in her eyes.

"I'm so sorry," she murmurs.

The depth of her sympathy catches me off guard.

"It's okay," I say with what I hope is a reassuring laugh. "It wasn't like I was getting attacked in the hallways. It really wasn't that bad. Most people just thought I was kind of weird. Thank god I had Jacinthe. My parents thought about sending me to an English high school, but I insisted I stay with her."

She nods and stays quiet for a moment, staring down at the tracks we're re-tracing through the muddy snow.

"So did you two...?"

I bark a laugh. "Oh, god, no. I'm sure it's surprising we never even tried dating each other, but...just no. It'd be like dating a sister. Same with Maddie."

"Is Maddie queer too?"

Her question makes me feel like a fist has unclenched from squeezing my chest.

Any straight person who can comfortably say the word 'queer' without making things weird is usually pretty cool.

"Yep," I tell her. "We're a little lesbian trio. Coming out to each other was hilarious. I said I had something to tell them, and then Jacinthe said she also had something to tell us, and then Maddie did too. Turned out we all had the same thing to tell each other."

"That's so cute," she says, flashing me a smile.

"It was pretty adorable. So, yeah, to answer your question properly, I had a grand total of one girlfriend in high school, and another while I was at CEGEP, and I still have no idea how I even managed that."

She nods. "And since then?"

I make a show out of narrowing my eyes at her. "Do you normally know so much about your clients' love lives?"

All the colour drains from her face.

"I'm so sorry. I—"

I lift a hand to cut her off. "Brooke, I'm teasing you. It's fine. You're not the first person to be curious about what small town lesbian life is like."

We're about to start our third lap around the pond, but neither of us makes a move to change course.

"So what about you?" I ask.

"What about me?"

"You going to share any of your dating lore?"

She shrugs. "There's not much to tell."

I scoff and cross my arms. "Come on. You have to give me something."

"I really don't have much," she insists. "I dated the same guy from when I was fifteen to when I was nineteen. Then I had some, um, years of the single life in Montreal."

I wag my eyebrows at her. "Any salacious stories?"

She lets out a half-hearted chuckle and shoves her hands even deeper into her pockets.

"I was just...a bit lost."

All the amusement has left her tone. Her voice is barely louder than the rustling of the dead reeds.

"Oh," I say.

It's a stupid reply, but I'm so stunned I can't come up with anything else.

"Yeah, it's not a fun answer," she says, "but it's the truth. Yves was my rock for so long, you know? Our life in Montreal was so unstable for so long, and I got pretty dependent on him. Too dependent on him. I went a little crazy when I didn't have him anymore, and, you know, there's always a party to distract yourself with in Montreal."

She looks lost just talking about it, like she's miles away from La Cloche, caught up in a mess of jumbled city streets and late nights.

I want to pull her back from there. I want to keep her grounded, right here with me.

"I can't believe his name was Yves," I say. "That's like, an old French dude name."

I wasn't sure if a joke was the way to go, but it works.

Brooke tips her head back and laughs loud enough to echo through the empty yard.

"It is," she says, still chuckling. "Oh my god, you're right. It really is. How have I never thought of that before?"

I laugh along with her, a rush of satisfaction shooting through me as I see the distant look evaporate from her eyes.

"So, old man Yves left the picture," I say, "you had some single life years in Montreal, and then...?"

"I smartened up right after my undergrad, when I met..."

My steps grind to a halt, reality slamming into me like I've been flattened by a truck speeding up the highway.

"My brother."

My voice rings in my ears. Brooke pauses a step ahead of me.

"Yes."

For the past few minutes, I truly forgot who she was.

I forgot where this story was headed.

I force myself to start walking again. My boots feel like they're made of lead, every step a conscious effort to keep moving.

"Have you...?"

I try to ask how things have been since Jonas, like my own brother leaving her at the altar is just another chapter we can skip over, but the words stick in my throat.

I swallow and try again

"Since him, have you...?"

"I haven't dated much, no." Brooke's voice is stilted, and out of the corner of my eye, I can see her movements are just as stiff. "Some dates here and there, but no serious relationships. I'm very focused on my career."

I nod, turning the information over in my mind.

She hasn't had a relationship since him.

She freezes up whenever he's mentioned.

I don't think I've even heard her say his name at all during any of her visits to La Cloche.

We're still walking at the edge of the pond, but I feel like I've cracked through the icy surface and dropped down into the frigid water.

Maybe she still has feelings for him.

I cross my arms over my stomach, squeezing tight as an acrid taste fills my mouth.

The sudden nausea only gets worse when Brooke drops her voice to barely more than a whisper and asks, "Does...does he know? About the project? About...me?"

She sounds nervous, anxious even, and I can't tell if she's hoping for a yes or a no.

I can't tell what she's thinking at all.

I take a quick breath to steady myself before I say, "I haven't had a chance to tell him yet."

She lets out a relieved sigh so quiet I almost miss it.

Or maybe she's not relieved. Maybe she wants to hear about him. Maybe she wants *him* to hear about *her*.

Maybe that's the whole reason she took this job.

"Are we going to go look at the barn?"

Brooke points towards the barn at the back of the yard. I feel sicker than ever as I think about showing it to her now.

It doesn't make any sense, but I don't have time to question myself. I just need this conversation to be over. I need this whole day to be over right now.

"Oh, um, you know what?" I act out patting down my pockets like I'm looking for something. "It's locked, and I don't have the key with me. It must be at my apartment."

"That's too bad. I guess I should head out anyway. I've still got the drive ahead of me."

"Mhmm," I mumble,

I stride past her, leading the way back across the yard. We don't say anything else until we're a couple meters from her car.

"I can take it from here," she says. "I'll text you to set up our next meeting?"

I nod. "Sounds good."

She hovers for a moment. I nudge a stray pinecone with the tip of my boot to give me an excuse not to look at her.

I'm scared of what she might see if I look at her now.

I hear her car keys jangle.

"Bye, Natalie," she says after another long moment.

I school my face into the most impassive expression I can manage and lift my head.

"Bye, Brooke."

Chapter 11

Brooke

"You smell good." Layla takes a step closer to me, shoving her nose into my hair. "Why do you smell so good?"

I shove her away and go back to arranging the board room table.

"I'm wearing perfume."

Layla clucks her tongue. "Why are you wearing perfume?"

"I often wear perfume," I say, my voice sharpening as I lay a stack of napkins out in a fan shape.

"This is different."

Sighing, I plant a hand on my fist and turn to face her. "It's my usual plain old vanilla perfume, Layla. The same one I've been wearing for years. Maybe you're just smelling my hairspray."

"Aha!" She lifts a finger in the air, her eyes brightening. "That's it! So, why are you wearing hairspray?"

"Because I curled my hair, Layla. And don't ask why I curled my hair. I just wanted to, okay? Same reason I put on mascara and a skirt. I just wanted to look nice today. You should know what I'm talking about. I know for a fact it takes you at least an hour to get ready for work every morning because you enjoy putting effort in, so why can't I?"

I cross my arms and cock my head, waiting for Layla to look properly chagrined, but all she does is smirk.

"You like someone, don't you?"

I throw my hands in the air and consider tossing the napkins at her.

"Did you hear any of that? I said you dress nice all the time, so why can't I—"

"You dress nice too," she cuts in, "but I've only seen you curl your hair, like, twice, and you have way more than mascara on today."

"And that means I must like someone?" I fume. "Maybe I just like myself!"

She tilts her head and observes me like I'm a science experiment.

"There's also this uncharacteristic defensiveness to contend with."

I let out a sound somewhere between a growl and a screech. "I am not being defensive!"

My voice echoes in the empty conference room. I gasp and clap a hand over my mouth.

I glance at the glass wall that puts us on display for the whole rest of the office. Sure enough, a few of my co-workers have popped their heads up from their computers to stare.

I force my mouth into a grin and give them what I hope is a reassuring little wave.

They lose interest a few seconds later, and I whirl around to face Layla.

"I am *not* being defensive," I say in a measured voice, at

a volume the whole office won't be able to hear. "I'm just trying to prove a point."

"Yeah, okay, you've stuck up for feminism," she says while inspecting her nails. "Women can dress nice for themselves. I agree, but I am also your best friend, and I can tell when you're trying to impress someone."

I'm going to impress her with my throwing aim if she doesn't let this go.

"The only person I'm seeing today is a client, hence *this*," I hiss, pointing at the glass plate full of biscuits and the varied selection of tea bags I still need to organize on the table, "which you are totally distracting me from."

That perks her up way too much. She props her hip against one of the board room chairs and raises an eyebrow.

"Who's the client?"

"Natalie," I answer, unable to keep the satisfaction out of my voice.

That will at least put an end to her insinuations.

"Oh." She blinks a couple times, clearly thrown off her game. "She's coming here?"

"Yes," I say, shuffling the colourful packages of the teabags around as I wonder if I should arrange them by hue or by flavour. "She said she felt bad about me commuting so much and that she had to come to the city for the day anyway. I tried to tell her it's no trouble, but she insisted."

"So now you're building her an ornate napkin display? Is this some sort of courtship ritual?"

My spine stiffens.

"*Layla.*"

I glance between her and the board room door before dashing over to make sure it's shut as tight as possible.

"What the hell are you talking about?" I hiss.

Paint the Moon

"Is it her you're dressed up for?" she asks, dipping her eyes down to give my skirt and blouse a once-over.

I feel like my own eyes are about to pop out of my skull.

"Layla, are you crazy?"

She shifts her weight off the chair and straightens up, ignoring my question.

"You know I really don't care if you like girls, right?"

I spin around, scanning the office for signs anyone is listening, but they're all still at their desks, well out of earshot.

"I don't," I say, focusing back on Layla. "I've only hooked up with, like, four girls. In *college*."

I emphasize the last part to remind her that all happened during the era of my life I refer to as the Dark Ages, AKA the post-Yves era in which I was partying my face off and ending up in random clubs and even randomer basements and living rooms every weekend.

I ended up in some pretty random bedrooms too.

Layla isn't fazed.

"And I've always said that to me, that sounds like liking girls."

"I like guys!"

She frowns at me like a teacher disappointed by my answer.

"You can like both, you know. There's this really cool thing called bisexuality."

"It's not about that," I insist, after another glance at the office. "It's like I've told you before. If I *actually* liked girls, I would have dated at least one by now, right? I'm thirty. It's a bit late to do the whole figuring out my sexuality thing."

She squints at me. "I might not be an expert, but I wasn't aware there's a deadline."

I roll my eyes. She's missing the point on purpose.

"There's not, but I mean, if I hooked up with girls, and then I didn't ever actually date a girl, and then I almost got married to a man, don't you think I would have had some big crisis of sexuality at some point? Don't you think I would have at least *thought* about coming out as bi?"

I did think about it, briefly, somewhere between all the binge drinking and Redbull-fuelled study sessions as I barely scraped through my Bachelor's degree, but I always pushed the idea aside.

I doubt you can push it aside if you're actually queer. It seems like the sort of thing you can't just ignore for the rest of your life.

Layla is quiet for a few seconds. Her expression shifts from amused to a guarded pensiveness, and when she speaks, her voice is much softer than before.

"I don't know," she says. "I think it's different for everyone."

For some reason, her tone makes a lump form in my throat. My heart is beating way too fast, and I have to step away from her and pretend I'm still busy with the teabags before I can talk again.

"Well, I'm not bi, and I don't have a crush on my ex-fiancé's little sister."

I wait for her to argue, but she doesn't say anything at all.

I turn back around.

"I do, however, have a meeting with her in less than five minutes."

Layla peers at me with that same guarded look. I can feel sweat gathering under the neck of my blouse. I have to stop myself from sighing with relief when she chuckles and raises her hands in surrender.

"Okay, okay. I know when I'm not wanted."

She heads for the door but stops just before she grabs the handle.

"Hey," she says, looking over her shoulder at me. "You know there's nothing you could ever do that would make me love you less, right?"

I huff a laugh.

"Okay, *Mom*," I joke, but I'm smiling in spite of myself.

She blows me a kiss before letting herself out of the board room. I watch her traipse back over to her desk, her plaid skater dress swishing around her knees, before I turn back to the table. I'm still fidgeting with my little spread when there's a knock on the conference room door. I turn around, expecting to find Layla standing behind the glass to let me know Natalie is on her way up to the office.

My heart jumps into my throat when I find Natalie herself standing there.

She's wearing black jeans and a blue button-up under her usual bomber jacket. Her hair is doing its best to escape from the low ponytail she's pulled it into, a few frizzy curls slipping out to frame her face. Her cheeks are flushed like she's been walking around in the cold, and when she steps inside the room, I realize she's out of breath.

"Sorry I'm a few minutes late," she wheezes as the glass door swings shut behind her. "I forgot how bad Montreal traffic is. Some guy let me in downstairs, but the elevator was taking forever, so I just ran up the stairs. That was a mistake."

She flashes me an apologetic grin and takes a deep gasp of air.

I notice she's wearing black leather boots with a low heel instead of her usual Kodiaks. The extra inch of height means she's still taller than me even in the short pumps I picked for our meeting.

She clears her throat, and I realize I've been staring at her for just a few seconds too long.

My cheeks burn as I step back over to the table.

"Would you like anything?" I ask, gesturing at the assortment of snacks. "That thermos has hot water for tea. I figured it's a little late in the day for coffee, but if you'd like that instead, we actually have a pretty good machine in the break room. I can make you something."

"No worries," she says, still hovering by the door. "Tea would be great."

I give her the rundown of flavours. She chooses honey and ginger. I pour it for her and fix a mug of chamomile for myself before we sit down across from each other.

My face still feels like it's on fire. The whole reason I made this little snack display was to avoid the awkwardness we ended our last meeting with, not prolong it. I thought cookies and tea would be a perfect way to start things off on the right foot.

It's been almost a week since our stroll through the house's backyard, and I've spent more hours than I can count replaying everything I said and wondering where it all went wrong.

I must have crossed a line.

In fact, I know I crossed a line. Talking about our love lives at all was crossing a line. I might ask a client a polite question about their spouse here and there, or chat about what they did on the weekend, but anything more would be unprofessional.

Natalie and I might have a faint former connection, but that doesn't mean she isn't, first and foremost, a client.

She's the client for the most important job of my career. Eric has even taken me off all my other projects so I can focus solely on managing the inn design.

I'll have absolutely no excuse if I screw this up.

"Sorry you had to deal with the traffic," I say, breaking the silence. "It was particularly brutal this morning. It was actually faster for me to take the metro and two buses than my car today, but I was hoping you'd miss the worst of it."

"It's okay," she says. "Like I said, I had to come to the city anyway."

"What for?"

The question slips out before I can stop it. I take a gulp of my tea to hide my wince and end up scalding my tongue.

I'm supposed to stop asking her personal questions.

"There's this one stockist for my mom's shop that won't deliver outside of Montreal, so I came to pick her order up."

I bob my head a little too enthusiastically. "Oh, cool. I remember your mom's shop. It's so cute in there."

I can practically feel Natalie tense up, even from across the table. Her shoulders clench, her arms stiffening in the middle of reaching for her tea.

My heart pounds loud and fast in my ears.

"Is…is the tea okay?" I ask.

She opens and closes her mouth a few times like she's working out what to say.

"Look, I really want to be normal about this," she says after a long moment. "I told myself I wasn't going to bring it up. It doesn't matter either way. You're amazing at your job, and you're really going above and beyond for us. I just…"

Panic makes the few sips of tea I've managed to take slosh around in my stomach.

She can't be firing me.

She shoves some of the flyaway hairs out of her face and takes a deep breath.

"I have to ask you something. I realize it's an insane question."

All I can do is bob my head.

"Did you..." She trails off for a moment, and I see her fingers clench tight around her mug. "Did you take this job because you still have feelings for Jonas?"

For a second, I consider rubbing my ears with my knuckles and then asking her to repeat herself, like a cartoon character miming disbelief.

There's no way *that's* what she wanted to ask me.

I realize my jaw has dropped open. I snap it shut, but I have no idea what to say.

The board room is now so quiet I can hear the ticking of the clock on the wall, even with the rattle of the heating system blasting.

"I shouldn't have said that." She shakes her head, her face pinched. "That was so stupid. I'm sorry. It's just, it's so awkward when we talk about him, and I'm sure that's my fault, and I just want to make sure I'm doing the right thing and not making you uncomfortable, and—"

A cackle fills the room, and it takes me half a second to realize I'm the one laughing.

Natalie's eyes flare, her mouth hanging half-open as she blinks at me.

I can't stop laughing. I wrap my arms around my stomach and squeeze my lips together to keep the sound in, but that just makes it burst out as an embarrassing guffaw.

It's too absurd: the idea that I'd take on a whole project with a two hour commute to the job site just for the chance to maybe run into the man who left me at the altar.

Natalie's expression is shifting from shocked to horrified. She glances past me out at the office, like she's considering calling for help.

I cough a couple times, urging myself to snap out of it before she tells the whole company I'm having a nervous breakdown. I smooth my skirt out and then take a sobering sip of tea.

"Natalie," I say, shaking my head from side to side, "I do not still have feelings for...for him."

Her eyes narrow.

"You don't say his name."

My breath catches at the accusation, and Natalie's face floods with regret.

"Sorry," she blurts. "I'm a mess today. I was nervous about this meeting. I need to shut up. Maybe I should—"

"You're right."

My head spins as I sift through my memories of the last few weeks, digging for proof that she's wrong, but I've got nothing.

I haven't said his name at all since I went back to La Cloche.

"I didn't even notice," I say. "I...I guess I've been trying to protect myself. The only reason I could convince myself to even take this job at all is by reminding myself just how far I've come since...Jonas."

I stare into space, the room around me a blur. Somewhere in the back of my head, I know I should be embarrassed about rambling like this. It's the exact opposite of the professionalism I was so intent on maintaining today, but I forgot what talking to Natalie is like.

It's *easy* to talk to her—almost too easy, like slipping into the tug of a river's current without knowing just how fast the water flows.

"I guess I was scared saying his name would make the past feel...closer," I admit.

I pause for a moment, waiting to see if that might be true.

I force myself to picture Jonas: his curly overgrown hair,

the goofy smile that stopped me in my tracks the night I first saw him in the crowd at a bar.

The details are hazy. I remember liking his smile, but I can't quite see it in my mind. I remember the way his laugh made everyone around him laugh too, but I can't quite hear the sound of it.

Saying his name doesn't sharpen the memories. If anything, it just emphasizes how thick the wall between me and my past is, like an opaque chunk of glass that only reveals hints of figures and shadows on the other side.

"But it doesn't feel closer."

I'm somebody else now.

I'm not so desperate for a stupid fairytale ending that I'd get engaged to a man I'd known for less than two years.

There are no fairytales. There's no one coming in to sweep all your problems away and whisk you off to a new life where nothing bad happens.

That doesn't happen in cities, and it doesn't happen in small towns either.

I know that now.

I should be blushing and apologizing, but the rush of clarity feels like an endorphin high pumping me up with confidence. I straighten my posture and speak in the same calm, affirming voice I'd use for a board room presentation.

"It was over six years ago, Natalie. I'm a completely different person. I'm not looking for the same things I was back then."

"Oh," she says, the sound edged with relief.

"Did you really think I was still in love with your brother?" I demand. I can't keep myself from snorting as soon as I finish my sentence.

Natalie chuckles, some of the tension draining from the room as we laugh together.

"I don't know what I thought," she says, shaking her head.

"I was twenty-two when I met Jonas," I remind her. "Our whole relationship only lasted a little more than two years. I...well, let's just say I learned my lesson."

She squints at me, and my curiosity surges enough for me to ask, "Did Jonas ever tell you why he called the wedding off?"

She drops her gaze to the table, her jaw tightening with an expression that almost looks like shame.

"He said he rushed into things, that he wasn't ready for that kind of commitment."

For a moment, I hear his voice in my head, telling me the exact same thing in the churchyard after he finally showed up to face me.

I just can't give you what you want, Brooke. I can't be the guy you need.

"That's just not who he was," I tell Natalie, "and I should have seen it coming. I was looking for something that wasn't there. I'm not looking for that anymore, not with anyone else, and definitely not with *him*."

I shrug and take a gulp of my tea.

"I don't want this to be awkward anymore," I say once I've swallowed. "If we want to design the best inn Québec has ever seen, we probably need to figure this out first."

Natalie nods. "I agree."

"Maybe we just need to accept it," I say, floating the idea as it arrives in my head. "The weirdness. I mean, it *is* weird that I almost married your brother. It's weird that I've been to your mom's store already. It's weird that I used to play with your family's dog. I've had dinner in your parents' house a bunch of times. It's all very, very weird."

Natalie flashes me a grin. "It is. It is super fucking weird, isn't it?"

"So fucking weird."

We've both lowered our volume a little, sharing a covert smile like we're kids cursing in the back of a classroom instead of adults having a professional meeting in an office.

"So how about we just...call it as we see it?" I suggest. "If a weird moment happens, we just acknowledge it and move on instead of pretending it isn't happening."

Natalie props her elbow on the table and grips her chin, her eyes narrowing as she thinks for a few moments.

Then she nods.

"I like that," she says. She glances around the board room and then fixes her attention on my laptop, which is still lying closed on the table beside me. "So, should we talk about some interior design now?"

The rest of the meeting flies by. We're making much faster progress than I expected, given Natalie didn't even know she wanted to build an inn a few weeks ago. I've been guiding her and her friends through much more than an interior designer would normally help with, but they've all been more than willing to cooperate and have come up with some great ideas themselves.

Natalie has been especially impressive. Her artistic instincts have helped her notice a few details even I've missed, and when the two of us get on a roll, it's easy to forget I'm not talking to someone trained in the field. It's like she can visualize my ideas and run with them before I've even finished explaining what they are.

That's what today is like. By the time the meeting comes to an end, we've blasted through every item on today's to-do list and made a start on some tasks I didn't even have on the agenda yet.

Paint the Moon

"I'm so glad you want to keep the arched entryways," I say as I close down my laptop. "They already add so much character, and it's really going to continue the flow of the first floor if we stick to that with the new additions."

"I wouldn't have it any other way," she says, beaming at me while she pulls her coat on.

I grab my phone off the table and swipe to unlock the screen. "Let me just write myself a quick memo to get in touch with that flooring guy I told you about, and then I'll walk you out."

I blink down at the screen and wonder if there's something wrong with my phone.

I've been so caught up in the meeting I haven't checked my phone since Natalie arrived, but there's no way I've gotten seven voicemails in the last hour.

There's also a string of texts.

Dread sweeps through me like an ice storm numbing my body when I see they're all from the same person.

My landlord.

"Oh no," I moan.

I don't have to bother with the voicemails. The texts are a jumble of typos and exclamation points, but I can make out the French well enough to get the general idea.

"Oh *no!*" I yelp. Panic surges in my bloodstream, the sickening waves of adrenaline threatening to pull me under.

"What?" Natalie urges, her face pale.

"Bailey!" I shout, glancing between her and the phone and then back again. "My dog! My apartment!"

She zooms around the table so fast I don't have a chance to realize what's happening before she's crouched down in front of me, spinning my swivel chair so I'm facing her.

She places a gentle hand on my knee.

"Slow down," she says, staring straight into my eyes, her voice low but clear. "Breathe."

She takes an exaggerated inhale, scrunching her shoulders up before slowly relaxing them as she breathes out.

I find myself copying her on instinct, our eyes locked as we breathe in sync with each other.

Her irises are like flecks of clear winter sky.

Suddenly, all I can think about is the weight of her hand on my knee.

"What happened?" she asks.

"My apartment is flooding," I say, shocked at how much calmer I sound. "My landlord is there now. He's got my dog. She must be terrified. All my stuff is getting ruined too. I have to go home."

Natalie nods and pushes up to her feet. I feel like there's a burning ember where her hand used to be, singing its way through my tights.

My skin must be extra sensitive from all the panic.

"Right," Natalie says, already heading for the door. "Let's get you out of here. Are you okay to drive yourself home?"

"I think so. I—"

I gasp and clap a hand over my mouth.

"Oh shit," I mutter from behind my fingers. "I don't have my car today. I took the bus because of the traffic, but it takes forever. It would be way faster with a car at this time of day. Shit. I better order a ride."

I fumble for my phone on the table.

"I'll drive you."

I look up in time to see Natalie yank the door open.

"Huh?"

"I said I'll drive you. It will be faster than waiting for a ride. Come on. Let's go."

Chapter 12
Natalie

Two hours after leaving the Leung Designs office, I'm sitting on the couch in Brooke's apartment with a cowering corgi trying to bury herself in my shirt.

"Well, where am I supposed to go?" I hear Brooke saying in French from behind the wall that separates the living room from the entryway. "This wouldn't have happened if you'd dealt with it weeks ago!"

Before her landlord gets a chance to reply, the emergency plumber who showed up twenty minutes ago turns on the machine he's been using to suck up all the water from the floor. The whirring and slurping blocks out the rest of the conversation and makes Bailey burrow even deeper into my lap.

"It's okay," I soothe, stroking her back. "It's just a big vacuum."

I doubt that's much of a comfort. Even Belle, my family's giant bloodhound, is terrified of regular-sized vacuums.

I keep patting Bailey as I look around the room, wincing

at the noise. I can tell Brooke must have a beautifully decorated apartment—when it's not torn to shreds.

The living room's colour scheme is pink and pale green, with lots of light wood accents and a huge plant collection on display in front of the floor-to-ceiling windows with a view of the concrete balcony.

It's also stuffed with chaotic piles of furniture and random items that have been rescued from the bathroom and the bedroom, where the worst of the flooding hit. Apparently, a leak in the bathroom exploded and took the whole ceiling down with it.

The plumber said it must have happened right after Brooke left for work, given the amount of water damage. Brooke's landlord came to investigate when the downstairs neighbors complained about their ceiling dripping. In addition to the demolished bathroom, he found the water had already pooled all through Brooke's hallway and was trickling into her bedroom.

Brooke and I spent the first hour here hauling things out of the danger zone while we waited for the landlord to find a plumber willing to come over immediately.

Bailey risks lifting her head when the water sucking machine shuts off but tucks it back under my elbow when the apartment door slams shut.

"I can't believe him!" Brooke shouts.

She comes storming into the living room. She's still wearing her tights, which are soaked all the way up to her ankles. Her hair is a mess, and there's murder in her eyes.

"He won't do anything!" she says, raking her hands through her hair and leaving it even more rumpled. "He says he can't get his usual plumber in until Friday, and that's just to assess how long this will take to fix. The toilet and shower aren't even functional anymore, and who knows how bad the flooring is damaged? It could be weeks before the repairs are done!"

I shake my head. "What the hell? And you said he already knew the leak was a problem?"

"Yes!" She throws her hands in the air and then starts pacing the room, which is quite a feat of agility given the piles of stuff. "I sent pictures! I sent videos! Multiple times! I did everything short of threatening him with legal action, but I guess I should have gone that far."

She freezes mid-step when she notices Bailey wriggling under my arm.

"Oh, Bailey!" she cries before clapping a hand over her mouth, her eyes widening. "I'm scaring her even more."

She sidesteps around her nightstand, which is currently lying on its side in the middle of the living room rug, and gingerly takes a seat next to me on the couch.

"It's okay, baby," she croons. "I won't yell anymore."

Bailey shimmies out from her hiding spot. She snuffles and gives a tentative wag of her nubby tail before sniffing Brooke's outstretched palm.

"I'm sorry for freaking out like this," Brooke says, shifting her attention to me as she strokes Bailey's head.

"Don't be," I urge. "Your home has literally been destroyed due to your landlord's negligence. I think you deserve to freak out even more."

She slumps against the pale green couch cushions and sighs.

"He said he doesn't owe me any compensation for alternative accommodation, even though he ignored all my warnings. He said all he's obligated to do is not charge me rent for the days the apartment is unusable."

I frown. "That can't be right, not if you let him know something was wrong and he did nothing."

She rubs her temples, and all of the fight seems to seep out of her, leaving her looking so exhausted I'm scared she's going to slide off the couch and drop to the floor.

"I can't even think about it right now. I guess I have to find a hotel for tonight. Oh god, finding a dog-friendly hotel at the last minute will be a nightmare. It's going to be so expensive..."

Her eyes drift closed, and she sighs again.

"There's no one you can stay with here in Montreal?" I ask.

She shakes her head, her eyes still closed.

"My best friend's boyfriend is allergic. As in, his face swells up like a balloon if he gets even a whiff of dog. I'm sure she'd still say yes if I asked, but I can't do that to them."

She's quiet for a moment, her forehead creasing like she's running through a mental list of options.

"I do not want to deal with my mom's reaction to this. Not today. She could be an option for later if I really need it, but she's just so...unpredictable."

Her mouth screws up like she's tasted something sour. I wait for her to list some more options, but she seems to have run dry.

I hesitate, petting Bailey a few more times and stealing glances at Brooke's haggard face while I wonder if I should keep my idea to myself.

Today actually felt normal between us, once we hashed out the whole Jonas thing.

What I'm about to suggest is not normal, not for an interior designer and a client.

The plumber bangs around in the bathroom, the clanking and crashing making Bailey tuck in closer to Brooke, but he doesn't turn the vacuum thing back on.

I was kind of hoping he'd give me an interlude to think

about this more, but I guess I'm just putting off the inevitable.

"Why don't you come stay in La Cloche?"

Brooke's eyes fly open. She blinks a couple times but doesn't say anything.

I wonder if there's a chance she didn't hear me, if maybe I could pretend I never spoke at all, but then she sits up straight and asks, "What? In La Cloche?"

I steel myself with a sharp inhale and then nod.

"Uh-huh. I know it's a long drive, but I've got an entire six-bedroom house with no one in it. I'm sure Bailey would be way more comfortable there than stuffed into a hotel room. Plus, we could move our meeting for next week up to tomorrow, so you'd be killing two drives with one stone. You could come back to the city and sort things out after that."

She starts tracing shapes into the velvet cushion, her gaze fixed to the tip of her finger as she swirls it along the fabric while she thinks.

"That's very generous," she says, still staring down at the cushion, "but I couldn't impose on you like that. It feels—"

"Weird?"

She looks up, and when our eyes lock, we both chuckle at the reference to our meeting.

"Honestly, yeah," she says. "It does feel kind of weird."

"Well..." I drop my gaze to start tracing a few shapes of my own into my side of the couch. "You know what we said about weird."

"That we should acknowledge it and then move right on past it."

I nod. "That is what we said. Specifically, it's what *you* said."

She lets out a soft laugh.

"Look, there's no pressure," I tell her. "It's whatever is best for you. It's just an option I wanted to put out there in case it would be helpful, no matter how weird it is. I'm not using the house. You could stay as long as you want."

She cups Bailey's face with both her hands. "*You* would like to go to La Cloche, wouldn't you?"

Bailey's stump of a tail wags, her whole butt jiggling.

We both laugh.

"It would be really helpful not to stress about finding a place, just for tonight," Brooke says, speaking to me now. "It must be almost five already. If I don't have to hunt down a hotel, I'll have time to make sure everything is all set here before I leave."

"I can help," I offer. "If it's almost five, it's traffic hour anyway. We can wait it out. I can go get us a pizza for dinner or something."

"You'd do that?"

Brooke's eyes get all shiny, and I realize she must be even more upset than I thought. She's literally staring at me like I'm the Messiah because I offered to buy her a pizza.

"Of course," I say with a chuckle. "As long as we acknowledge how weird it is for your client to be eating pizza in your apartment with you, I think we'll be fine."

~

It's past eight in the evening by the time I turn onto the road into La Cloche. I see Brooke's turn signal flashing in my rear-view mirror, her silver Honda following along behind my trusty old Toyota.

The end credits of the art history podcast I'm listening to begin to play through my speakers. I shut the volume off and wonder what Brooke is listening to.

I have no idea what music she likes, or if she has any favourite podcasts. Maybe she listens to the radio.

I shake my head before I can wonder anything else.

I'm not supposed to *wonder* about her. I'm only thinking about her so much because of all the time we've spent together today. I've seen into her world: her city, her workplace, her home. I know what colour her couch is, where she keeps the tea in her kitchen, what kind of bowl she uses for Bailey's food.

It's a glazed ceramic dish with Bailey's name painted on the side in shaky brushstrokes and dotted all over with little white polka dots. When I asked about it, Brooke laughed and said she decorated it herself at a paint and sip bridal shower for one of her friends. Then she snatched it away so I wouldn't judge her painting skills.

I realize I'm grinning like an idiot, alone in my car, and I wipe the expression off my face.

I focus on the road instead, leading Brooke to the house. I roll to a stop in front of the gate before hopping out of my car to unlock it so Brooke won't have to park on the street all night.

She pulls into the driveway, and I laugh when I see Bailey's head pop up in the passenger side window. Brooke throws her door open and then hauls Bailey into her lap before lifting her down to the ground.

"Her hips are getting so bad she can't even get in and out of the car anymore," Brooke explains.

I squat down and pat my thigh to call Bailey over. She takes a few hesitant sniffs of the night air before waddling over and bumping my hand with her greying snout.

"It's really nice that you adopted her," I say while I scratch Bailey's head. "Not a lot of people would take on a senior dog."

"I literally couldn't leave the shelter without her," Brooke calls over her shoulder as she lifts a small suitcase out of her car's trunk. "She stole my heart."

I lead the way into the house, flipping a few light switches on to cut through the gloom. Bailey sniffs around the entryway while Brooke takes off her scarf and pea coat.

"I'm going to turn the heat up for you," I say. "I've been keeping it pretty cold in here to save on power bills, but it should warm up by the time you're going to sleep. Then I've got to pop over to my parents' place to get you some bedding and stuff, but it'll only take a few minutes."

I called my mom on the ride home to ask her to get a few things ready. All the bedding the house came with is currently sitting in a giant pile of laundry I have yet to finish.

"You can use whatever bedroom you want," I say. "Feel free to pick it out while I go deal with the heating."

I head for the thermostat in the living room while Brooke carries her suitcase upstairs, Bailey clattering along behind her. They're both still up there when the glare of headlights streaks across the dim living room. I dart over to the window and see a car pulling into the driveway.

I squint, the lights too bright for me to even make out what kind of car it is. It's not until the headlights shut off and the driver climbs out that I recognize her.

My mom.

"Shit," I mutter before racing over to the front door.

My mom doesn't know Brooke is working for me yet. I still haven't addressed that with my parents. There hasn't really been an opportune moment to say, 'Remember that girl you thought was going to be your daughter-in-law before your son ruined her life? Now she's designing the inn

I may or may not end up running as a replacement for my failed art career! Aren't you proud of your children?'

All I told her tonight is that a friend of mine is dealing with a flooded apartment and needs a place to stay. She was supposed to wait for me to pick up the supplies myself. I already insisted there was no need for her to come here.

"Mom!" I bark when I yank the door open and find her already climbing up to the porch with a giant plastic storage bin in her arms. "What are you doing here?"

She wobbles a little. I rush forward to take the bin from her, then gasp when the weight of it nearly snaps my back in half.

"And what the hell is in this bin?"

She gives me her usual cheery, ethereal, 'I just meditated for an hour in a woodland meadow' smile.

"Well, hello to you too, Natalie." She lets out a tinkling laugh as she steps past me.

"Mom, wait!"

I'm still staggering under the weight of the bin, and there's nothing I can do to stop her from letting herself into the foyer.

"I can't believe you're making your friend sleep in this empty old house instead of at our place," she says, clucking her tongue as she peers around the room. "You know we have a lovely spare bedroom always ready for guests. You could have even slept in your old room for the night if you were too embarrassed to leave your friend alone with me and your father. She could have had Jonas's room. I just put in the funkiest new headboard! You really need to come over and see it someday."

I wince at how loud her voice sounds. I keep glancing at the stairs, my heart racing. My stomach is a twisted knot.

I need to get her out of here before Brooke comes down.

"I'm sure it's super funky, Mom," I say, grunting as I squat down to release the bin.

It lands with a heavy *thunk* on the floor.

"Well, thanks." I straighten up and shake out the strain in my arm muscles while casting another glance at the staircase. "I appreciate you bringing all this over. You really didn't need to leave the house, though. Anyway, it's late. You probably want to get going."

She is not going, though.

She is already slipping her fleece-lined Crocs off and wandering into the living room.

I stare at the back of her grey-streaked head, her hair that's almost as thick as mine gathered into a low ponytail that fans out over her purple puffer jacket.

The jacket clashes violently with the mustard yellow velvet lounge pants she's got on, but my mother has never been one to let the laws of the colour wheel determine her outfits.

"I don't think I've been in here since that day you first got the keys," she says, her voice echoing back to me as she strolls even farther into the living room. "Wow. You've cleared out a lot of stuff."

I fight the urge to growl as I traipse after her.

"Mom, Dad is going to worry about you if you don't get back soon."

She waves off my protests, her back still to me as she makes her way over to the fireplace, where she runs her hands over the stones.

"This is *such* a lovely fireplace," she says. "Your guests are going to love it, honey."

My jaw clenches.

I've told her I *might* be interested in running the inn and that all I've actually committed to is the renovations,

Paint the Moon

but she keeps talking like I'll be hosting the grand opening any day now.

Everyone does. Even Maddie and Jacinthe seem to have forgotten I'm not ready to make up my mind yet.

The creaking of the staircase makes me freeze. I whip my head around, nearly jumping out of my skin when a rapid *click-clack, click-clack* sound approaches.

Bailey comes lumbering into the living room.

"Oh, who is this angel?" Mom coos, swooping over to kneel down and shower Bailey with affection.

I can't speak.

I can barely even breathe.

My whole body has gone rigid with horror as I listen to the sound of human footsteps following Bailey's path down the stairs.

"Sorry!" Brooke calls out. "I was trying to keep her upstairs with me since I heard someone come in, but she wanted to say hi."

I have about point two seconds before she'll be in the living room.

I scan the exits, panic making my vision swim as I wonder if I could football tackle my mom out the window in time to stop this interaction from happening.

It's too late, though.

Brooke steps into the living room, mere feet away from the woman who almost became her mother-in-law.

"I hope she isn't bothering you," she says, an apologetic smile on her face as she looks from me to Bailey, and then, finally, at my mom.

Her smile drops.

Shock takes over her features, her mouth gaping as she takes a fumbling step backwards.

My mom is still hunched down in front of Bailey. She

blinks at Brooke a couple times, and all I can do is watch while her confusion slowly shifts into recognition.

"Brooke."

Her voice is hoarse, her eyes bulging even more than Brooke's as her hand goes still on Bailey's back.

Bailey does her best to elicit more scratches, jostling my mom's hand and letting out a low whine, but my mom is completely frozen.

We all stand there like a melodramatic tableau in some low-budget community theater project.

Then Mom turns her chin to look at me.

"What...what is Brooke doing here?" she croaks.

This is the moment I should step in and start making apologies while offering up a smooth and concise explanation that will hasten us out of this mess, but all I can manage to say is, "Um..."

She straightens up, shaking her head like she's casting off her stupor. Her raspy tone is replaced by a jittery, almost excited buzz.

"What's going on? Is Jonas here?" She glances around the room like she's expecting him to jump out of a corner and then fixes her attention back on Brooke. "Have you reunited with Jonas?"

I don't know what makes me cringe more: her asking if Brooke is dating my brother again, or her describing it as *reuniting*.

Brooke still looks so shocked I half-expect her to press the back of her hand to forehead and faint away like a frail Victorian lady.

Either that or have a heart attack.

"Mom, no," I say. "Brooke is just staying here tonight. She... Well, she's the interior designer I've been working with."

Paint the Moon

Mom squints at me.

"She is?" She looks around the living room again. "So where is your friend with the flooded apartment?"

I try not to scream.

"That *is* Brooke. I just...I didn't know what else to say on the phone." I pause to take a deep breath and wrack my brain for the quickest way to say this. "Maddie set up our first meeting without realizing who Brooke was, and she turned out to be the perfect fit for the project, and...well, I've been so busy with the house I just hadn't had a chance to tell you yet. I didn't know you were going to come over tonight."

She crosses her arms, bobbing her head like she's replaying my explanation in her mind. The moment seems to stretch on for at least a decade. Bailey has retreated over to Brooke, where she's sitting at her feet and pawing at Brooke's sock while she whines.

Brooke doesn't even seem to notice her. She's backed up far enough to lean against the edge of an armchair, but she doesn't take a seat.

All she does is stare.

Finally, my mom gives a last nod of her head, like she's accepted my story.

"I see," she says.

Then it's like her personality reboots itself, recovering from the shock and firing back up to maximum levels of Cynthia Sinclair friendliness and effusive displays of emotion.

"Oh, Brooke, sweetie, it is *so* good to see you again!" She bounds over to Brooke's side and beams at her. "You look lovely! May I hug you?"

A fresh wave of horror descends over me as she holds out her arms.

Brooke blinks at her. "Oh, um, sure."

Mom pulls her into a tight hug. All I can do is watch, wondering how many seconds I'm supposed to let Brooke suffer for before I intervene, but the longer I look, the more I realize Brooke doesn't seem like she's suffering at all.

She stays rigid for the first couple seconds, but then it's like something in her releases, like a valve is thrown open and all the tension whooshes out of her body. She wraps her arms around my mom, her eyes closing and her shoulders drooping.

When they let go of each other, Brooke gives my mom a soft smile.

"Oh, Brooke, honey," Mom says, her eyes shining. "I didn't know if we'd ever see you again."

I realize Brooke's eyes are all shiny too, and my panic swoops back in at full blast.

My mom is going to make her cry.

I made Brooke drive all the way out here, and now she's being forced to listen to my mother dump a whole dramatic monologue about the broken engagement on her with zero warning.

"You just disappeared," Mom continues, her voice watery. "I mean, of course you did. I don't blame you. I just wish I'd had the chance to tell you how much you meant to us, no matter what, and—"

"Mom."

Both of them jerk with surprise, like they forgot I was still in the room.

"Brooke has had a really long day," I say, balling my fists behind my back as I fight to keep from snapping at her. "I think she just wants to go to bed."

Mom turns back to Brooke and pats her on the arm.

"Of course, of course. I'm sorry. I just got a bit

emotional, seeing Brooke here after all these years. It's surreal!"

I stride over towards the exit, hoping that will encourage her to do the same, but she just gives Brooke another pat.

"Honey, are you sure you want to stay in this musty old place? We have the spare bedroom all ready to go."

I raise my gaze to the ceiling, begging for divine intervention.

There is no way she still thinks it's appropriate to offer up Jonas's childhood bedroom.

"Oh, that's fine," Brooke answers. "I'm more than happy here. Plus, I've got Bailey, so I wouldn't want to be a bother."

She reaches down to scratch Bailey's ears. Mom grins at both of them.

"Oh, you could never be a bother!" she urges. "Belle would love a little buddy for the night. You know what a gentle giant she is."

This woman truly knows no bounds.

Brooke lets out a polite chuckle. "Really, I'm fine here. Spending the night will really help with my design work. I'm getting the full immersive experience, you know?"

Mom squints at her for a few seconds before she admits defeat. "Well, if you're sure, then I'll let you rest, but you've got an open invitation to pop by my shop whenever you like. We can have a cup of tea and catch up. I would love to hear all about you and your work!"

"Thank you," Brooke says. "That's very kind."

The misty look is back in her eyes. I give up on all sense of restraint and literally grab my mom by the coat sleeve to tug her over to her shoes.

"Okay, off I go," she calls back to Brooke. "Sleep well, sweetie!"

Once she's zipped her coat up, she pries the lid off the bin still sitting in the middle of the foyer.

"Now, Natalie, pay attention. There are sheets and blankets in here, and I've packed you up some healthy snacks for tonight. There's muesli and oat milk for breakfast, so please put that in the fridge."

She holds up each item as she describes them to me, shifting the collection of packages, bags, and bottles around inside.

"There's also a lavender room spray and a lovely patchouli candle. Oh, and towels! I didn't know if there were any good ones in the house. There are some shower products too. I put in that new organic bubble bath I'm stocking in the shop, and I also grabbed one of our spare yoga mats in case Brooke needs one."

I don't know what the hell Brooke could need a yoga mat or organic bubble bath for, considering she's insisting on only staying one night, but the flames of my frustration die down slightly as I look at all the effort she put in.

"Thank you, Mom," I say. "Really. You've been so thoughtful."

"*You* are so thoughtful," she replies, grinning at me as she presses the lid back into place. "It was very kind of you to offer Brooke a place to stay. You make me proud."

She motions for me to come closer, and I bend my head so she can press her lips to my forehead.

"*Bisous!*" she says, smacking me with a kiss. "I love you."

"Love you too, Mom."

I open the door for her, and I stand leaning against the frame to wave goodbye when she pulls out of the driveway. I spend an extra few moments breathing in the cold night air, letting it fuel me up with resolve to go back in and face Brooke.

When I return to the living room, she's sitting in the same armchair she was leaning against before, Bailey curled up on her lap. She's got a thousand-yard stare on her face, and it takes her a couple seconds to realize I've walked in the room.

"So..." I say. "Weird, right?"

She nods. "Weird."

I cross my arms and lean against the wall, wishing I had a bottle of whiskey to pull out for a shot.

Or three.

Then I remember the fridge is still stocked with the remnants of a twelve pack I bought as a reward for one of the marathon cleaning sessions Maddie, Jacinthe, and I endured when I first got the house.

It won't quite hit the spot like a shot, but a cheap IPA is better than nothing.

"Do you want a drink?" I ask.

Brooke's face lights up like I've just offered her the elixir of eternal life.

"God, yes," she groans.

Chapter 13

Brooke

"What are you going to name it?" I ask.

I'm halfway through my second beer, watching Natalie stoke the fire she's built in the living room.

The furnace is taking longer than expected to warm up, so we've got the coffee table pulled up in front of the fireplace, its surface spread with a selection of the snacks Natalie's mom dropped off: stuffed olives, pita chips, and multiple flavors of hummus.

We're sitting on throw pillows on the floor to be closer to the heat. I have an old Hudson's Bay blanket draped around my shoulders. Bailey is curled up under the heavy wool, her nose twitching as she dreams.

Natalie pokes at the logs she hauled in from a stack in the backyard. They've started to burn down to embers, but with a few strategic nudges, she gets the flames back up and roaring again.

"Woo!" I say. "Look at you go, fire master."

She chuckles. "You're easily impressed, city girl."

I grimace. "Not a city girl, remember? Also, you didn't answer my question."

She drops back onto her stack of pillows, arranging them so she can stretch her legs out in front of her while she tucks her hands behind her head. The firelight dances in her eyes and makes her skin glow.

"What was your question?"

She shifts her gaze from the flames to my face.

I blink and look away, busying myself with loading up my plate with a fresh round of snacks.

"I asked what you're going to name it. The inn."

I hear the sloshing of her beer bottle as she takes a couple swigs.

"I mean, if you don't sell the house," I add, scooping up a few olives and dropping them onto my plate.

"I guess we *would* need a name. I hadn't even thought about that."

"Any ideas coming to mind?"

I set my refilled plate down on the end of the coffee table and take a few sips of beer myself.

I wouldn't say I'm tipsy, but the alcohol has definitely helped mellow out the end of what has been the most stressful day of my whole month. Combined with the soft glow of the fire warming my cheeks, I'm pretty sure I'm only a few sips away from my eyelids drooping.

"Hmmm." Natalie taps her chin with the lip of her beer bottle. "Nothing that I'm sure Jacinthe and Maddie would agree to as well. We'd all need to get on board. If we did end up running the business ourselves, we'd all have equal shares."

"I think it's so cool that you might do something like this with your best friends," I tell her.

She nods, the corner of her mouth quirking up into a smile that doesn't quite reach her eyes.

"Yeah," she says, "it would be pretty cool, you know, if we actually did it."

She shrugs like she's shaking off a chill.

"So," she says in a brighter voice, "what do *you* think we should name it?"

I scoff. "*I* can't name it."

"Why not?"

"It's *your* inn!"

She tips her beer at me. "Well, you're designing it. You really haven't thought about a name at all?"

I'm about to lie and say I haven't considered it, but instead, I find my gaze drifting over to the window, where the shadowy outline of one the towering evergreens flanking the house is just visible through the glass.

"What are those trees called again?" I ask.

Natalie's eyes follow the direction of my gaze. "Balsam firs."

"Right. Balsam firs."

I nod a few times, wondering if I should keep my thoughts to myself, but they come rushing out anyways.

"When we were out there playing with the sap bubbles, I felt like a kid again, you know? But it was more than that. I felt like I could remember a time when life was so...limitless, when it felt like I could do anything, *be* anything, without worrying about it."

I keep staring at the shadows of the trees, like traces of my childhood are clinging to the branches.

"After we moved to Montreal, I had to worry about my mom so much, and where we'd live, and just, you know, *everything*. Sometimes I think maybe my whole life has been shaped around trying to escape all that worry, instead of...well, I don't know what else, but maybe that's what people come out to a place like this to try and find."

My cheeks warm with more than the heat of the flames, and I take a sip of my beer while I avoid Natalie's eyes.

"So, I don't know," I say, doing my best to sound matter of fact, "maybe you could name it for the trees. They're a very distinct landmark, the way there's one on either side of the house. They'd look great in a logo design."

"Balsam Inn," Natalie murmurs.

I steal a glance at her and see she's staring straight into the fire.

"Yeah," I say. I'm murmuring too. "Something like that."

"Balsam Inn."

She repeats the words like she's testing their flavor on her tongue, like she can't tell if she wants to go in for a bite.

We're quiet for what feels like a few minutes. She keeps peering into the twisting flames and pulsing coals like she's caught in a trance, and I wish I could see whatever she's envisioning.

"It's just an idea," I say. "I can put coming up with a name on the agenda for our meeting tomorrow."

"Right." She snaps her attention back to me, the hazy look clearing from her eyes. "I forgot we have a meeting."

She swoops her hand out towards the fireplace.

"Is it still weird to be having a fireside beer with your client?" she asks.

I reach for an olive off my plate and pop it in my mouth, chewing while I think the question over.

"Actually...no," I answer.

Her eyebrows jump up. "Oh?"

"I..."

I focus on the simmering red coals at the heart of the fire, like they'll somehow spell out the words I need.

"I'm actually really glad your mom stopped by," I admit.

Natalie drops her head into her hands.

"Oh my god," she groans. "I'm still so sorry about that."

"I know. You've told me like twenty times," I say, laughing at her dramatic pose. "But I mean it. Of course I would have preferred a little warning, but having her be so kind to me, just like she always was...it reminded me that I don't want to forget *everything* about those two years of my life."

Natalie lifts her head, giving me a perfect view of her regal profile silhouetted by the firelight: her harsh brow, strong nose, sharp jawline, and the pillowy, generous lips that add just the right amount of softness.

She's entrancing. Somehow, when I'm around her, all my thoughts just tumble out of my mouth.

"I thought that was the only way to get over it," I say. "I thought I just had to pretend like it all happened to somebody else, but it didn't. It happened to me, and maybe I can trust I'm not going to fall apart if I accept that. Admitting that there was a lot I liked about my time here doesn't mean I'm going to make the same mistakes all over again."

She's turned her whole face towards me now, the angles of her features softening as her lips curve into a gentle smile.

I reach for my beer bottle. I've only got a couple sips left, and I wonder just how hard the drinks are going to hit when I stand up to go to bed.

I have no idea how late it is.

I draw my knees up to my chest, making Bailey let out a snuffle of protest, and drain what's left of my drink.

"And," I say, setting the empty bottle down on the table, "it also means that maybe us hanging out isn't that weird after all. You're not just my client."

Paint the Moon

I meant to add something about how it's okay for us to be friends too, but the words get lodged in my throat when I see the way she's looking at me.

She looks *hungry*.

Her gaze rakes over my face like I'm the sweetest, most delicate pastry, and she hasn't had sugar in years.

I shiver like she's traced the shape of me with her fingertips instead of her eyes.

Sparks pop and crackle somewhere low in my stomach, and all of a sudden, it's like I'm hollowed out with need, with a craving to fill myself up with more, more, more, until I'm full.

My breath catches, my skin searing hot.

I'm hungry too.

"So what am I?"

Her voice is like dark velvet, like the smooth expanse of an inky black sky just waiting to swallow me whole. Everything has flipped. I'm falling through the ceiling and into the night, scrambling to keep my grip on gravity.

She watches me without blinking. The blue of her eyes looks icier than ever as they reflect the firelight, like the elements themselves are waging war in her stare.

I don't know what she is.

I don't know what I am.

I don't know what's happening to us.

"I don't know."

The confession is barely more than a mumble, but it's still enough to shock me out of my trance, like the wail of a siren in the dead of night.

I whip my head around, shifting my body away from her as I pretend to be looking for my phone on the couch behind me.

I'm not supposed to talk to her like this. I'm not supposed to look at her like that.

I grab my phone off the cushion and twist back around, faking a yawn even though my heart is beating so fast I'm not sure I'll ever be sleepy again.

"Oh, wow," I say, feigning nonchalance as best I can. "It's past eleven. I should get this cleaned up."

I lean over the coffee table and start piling a few plates up, but Natalie shakes her head and jumps to her feet.

"I'll take care of it," she says, taking over my task. "You're my house guest, after all."

She sounds like her usual self: polite and to the point.

She doesn't sound like she's battling an inferno of inner turmoil.

My face burns as I'm given all the proof I need to believe the last few minutes were nothing but me making a fool of myself.

Chapter 14

Natalie

I show up at the house the next morning with two steaming takeout coffees and a paper bag filled with a chocolate croissant, a mini quiche, an apple turnover, and a sausage roll tucked under my arm.

All I meant to buy was the chocolate croissant. I figured Brooke might want something more substantial than muesli for breakfast, but by the time I got up to the counter at Café Cloche, I'd convinced myself I needed to get her a savory option in case she's not a sweets in the morning type of person.

Then I thought I better get her a second sweet option just in case she does like pastries but isn't a fan of the flaky kind. Then I decided quiche is pretty flaky too so I should probably get her a back-up savory option as well.

As I shuffle the coffees around so I can pull out my keys when I reach the front door, I realize I'm going to look like an absolute idiot presenting her with more baked goods than anyone could hope to consume in a single morning.

It takes me three tries to get the key in the lock, and I

can't blame my precarious grip on the coffees. My hands are shaking. My breath shakes too as I prepare to step inside.

It's only nine in the morning, but the coffee I'm holding will already be my second of the day. Caffeine is the only thing keeping me standing after getting barely more than five hours of sleep last night.

All I could think about were those last few minutes we spent sitting in front of the fireplace: the way her skin glowed like a sunset, the way the whole room seemed to get soft and hazy when she looked at me, the way her voice dropped to a whisper when she answered the question I still can't believe I was stupid enough to ask.

'So what am I?'

'I don't know.'

I tossed and turned for hours last night replaying those two sentences over and over in my head, scratching at them like lottery cards that might be hiding my claim to millions under their surface.

Or my claim to nothing at all.

In the light of day, I've realized just how lucky I am the conversation ended there.

Brooke was not flirting with me, no matter how much the beer in my system tried to convince me otherwise. Two drinks have never been enough to completely knock the sense out of me before, but I guess last night marks a first for that.

We were just chatting. She'd had an upsetting day, and she needed a chance to relax and settle down before bed. That's all that conversation was, and that's all any conversation we have today will be too.

"Be cool," I order myself, swinging the door open.

The hinges creak like a scene from a horror movie, and I remind myself to get some oil for them.

"Good morning!" I call out once I'm standing in the foyer.

I listen for an answering shout or the approaching clatter of Bailey's paws, but there's nothing.

"Hello?"

I've just started to wonder if Brooke might still be sleeping when I hear the groan of the floorboards outside. I pull the door back open just as Brooke comes around the far corner of the wraparound porch, with Bailey waddling along at her heels.

She's wearing her pea coat over a pair of pale pink pajama pants stuffed into the tops of her boots. She's got a dopey-looking pink pompom hat pulled down over her ears. It's the least fashionable thing I've ever seen her wear, and something about it has me smiling so wide my face hurts before I've even said hello.

"Natalie! Hi! Good morning!" she calls, beaming at me as she walks over. "Isn't it a gorgeous day?"

Up close, I see the crisp morning air has stained her cheeks a rosy pink to match her hat. Her eyes are glittering in the soft light, like the crystalline frost coating the front lawn. The sunbeams are streaking under the porch's roof at just the right angle to make the locks of blonde hair framing her face glow like polished gold.

"Yeah," I say as I continue to stare at her. "Gorgeous."

I feel a scratching sensation against my foot, and I quit gawking at Brooke to look down and see Bailey pawing at my boot.

I welcome the distraction and squat down to pet her. She wiggles in appreciation for a few seconds and then, without warning, takes off tearing up and down the length of the porch with more speed than I would ever suspect from an elderly corgi with bad hips.

"Wow," I say, straightening back up. "Someone has the zoomies."

Brooke chuckles, shaking her head as she watches Bailey's antics.

"She's been zooming around like she's a puppy all morning. I don't think I've ever seen her this energetic."

"I guess the country air is doing her good."

Brooke nods. "It's doing me good too."

She steps up to the porch rail, wrapping her hands around the peeling white paint clinging to the wood, and takes a deep, indulgent breath.

Her eyes close, an expression of pure bliss taking over her face.

My throat goes dry, and for a moment, I can see it: the exact shades of paint I'd grab to capture the pink in her cheeks and the golden filaments of her hair.

"God," she says, with so much fervor it's almost obscene. "I can't get enough of that."

I squeeze the coffee cups so hard I'm scared I'm going to crush the cardboard and end up with a face full of scalding hot water.

I could paint her.

I don't paint people I know very often, but if I ever find my way back to a canvas again, I could paint her.

There is art in every breath she takes.

"Did you, um, sleep okay?" I ask through a clenched jaw.

"Like a baby!" She whirls around to flash me another one of those radiant smiles. "I never sleep like that in the city."

A rush of satisfaction fills me, like I really am the proud owner of an inn receiving a compliment from a guest.

"So it wasn't too creepy being here on your own?"

Paint the Moon

"Not at all!" she says before pursing her lips to think for a moment. "Well, maybe a little when I first turned out the light, but then I slept so well, and I woke up to the most beautiful morning. I didn't even stop to make myself a coffee before I rushed out to enjoy it with Bailey."

I hold out one of the cups, still struggling to keep from crushing the pastries under my other arm.

"Coffee, you say?"

"Oh, is that for me? You are so sweet!" she gushes, taking the drink from me and inspecting the logo stamped on the side. "It's from Café Cloche?"

"The one and only. I got pastries too."

I grab the bag with my now free hand and give the pastries a little shake.

"You're my hero! They looked so good last time I was in there, but I was a little too preoccupied to eat anything."

We both chuckle at the memory of coming face to face for the first time with a guilty-looking Maddie cowering beside us.

"I'm making you freeze out here," she says. "We should go inside."

I follow after her into the foyer. She sets her coffee down on a small table and points at the stairs.

"I'll go change real quick, and then I have something to show you."

"Show me?"

She pulls off her pompom hat and toys with it, a grin somewhere between embarrassed and mischievous taking over her face.

"I was doing a bit of snooping around my room this morning, and I, um, found something."

I prop my hand on my hip, making the bag of pastries

crinkle. Bailey is sitting just below them, drooling and making pleading eyes at me.

"You have me intrigued," I say.

"I'll bring it down with me," Brooke calls back as she jogs up the stairs.

The scent of the pastries is strong enough to keep Bailey glued to my side while I head for the kitchen. She stalks my every move as I pull out a plate big enough for everything I ordered and arrange the pastries on top.

"I'd give you some, but I don't know if you're allowed," I tell her.

She's still making eyes at me when Brooke comes into the kitchen, dressed in some light wash jeans and a cozy-looking cream sweater.

She looks gorgeous in all her professional office girl clothes, but there's something about this casual ensemble that makes her look absolutely radiant, like she's soaked up all the sunlight from out on the porch.

Even her body language is different in this outfit. She's lost any trace of her reserved poise. Instead, she's practically bouncing as she comes over to join me, her hair swishing and an even more mischievous grin than earlier lighting up her face.

I notice she's got one hand tucked behind her back.

"What's that?" I ask.

"I'm about to show you," she says, "but first, I have a proposition for you."

I tilt my head. "Oh?"

"Mhmm. I'll show you what I found, but I have something I want to see in return."

I feign aloofness even though my heart is pounding for no good reason.

Paint the Moon

"And what would that be?"

"While I was walking Bailey around the backyard, I noticed the barn isn't locked anymore. I'd like to finally see it."

My spine stiffens. I have to bite my tongue to keep from telling her the barn is never locked as I remember the lie I told her last time she was here.

I scramble for another excuse, but I can't come up with anything.

There's no reason for me not to show her. It's just a barn I used to play in as a kid. Sure, I have some special memories there, but it's not like it's a sacred temple or anything. I shouldn't feel like I'm baring my soul showing it to Brooke.

"Um, okay."

"Good," she says with a satisfied nod. "Here's what I found."

She swings her arm out from behind her back to reveal a white envelope pinched between her fingers.

My name is spelt on the front in swooping, old-fashioned cursive letters.

"There's one of those antique covered desks in the room I slept in," she explains. "You know the kind that you can lock up? I just tried it out of curiosity, and it wasn't locked, and there were all these papers inside. I didn't go through them or anything. I just saw your name. I think maybe your great-aunt wrote you a letter or something. It had a sticky note on it reminding her to give it to Monsieur something or other, but maybe she forgot."

My heart is beating so fast I can feel it thumping against my ribcage. I can't take my eyes off the envelope.

"Maybe it was supposed to come with the will," I murmur.

Brooke nods. "That's what I was thinking too."

"I don't know how we missed that desk," I say. "I thought everything important would be in the study."

I let out a squawk of surprise when, instead of handing the letter to me, Brooke takes off out of the kitchen with it still clutched in her hand.

"Guess we better get out to that barn if you want to read this," she calls.

I stand there frozen for a few seconds before sprinting to catch up with her in the foyer, where she's tugging her boots back on.

"I'm kidding, you know," she says, nodding at where she's set the letter down on the table. "You can read it now if you want."

I stare at the crisp white paper, my mind whirring with a thousand possibilities.

I've been asking for a reason. I've been begging to know why Manon chose me.

At times, it's felt like that could be the answer to everything—not just the mystery of the house, but the whole mess of doubt and uncertainty my life has become these past few months.

I haven't been able to trust anything, not myself, not my talent, not even the encouragement of my friends. Their support hasn't helped the way it used to. Nothing has.

Through it all, there's been this house, looming like a hulking reminder that I've been given yet another opportunity to mess up the chance of a lifetime.

Maybe this letter could change all that, or maybe it could simply confirm what I'm afraid of: I won't be able to measure up.

I hover in place, fighting the conflicting urges to tear the letter open and get as far away from it as I can.

"A deal is a deal," I say, ripping my gaze away from the envelope and lunging for my boots instead. "You hold onto that until I've shown you the barn."

Chapter 15

Brooke

Natalie hauls the barn door open, the walls groaning in protest like she's woken the building up from a long nap.

Bailey darts behind my legs, giving the dark space beyond the doorframe a wary look.

"Well, here it is," Natalie says, shoving her hands into her pockets. "The famous barn."

I step past her, blinking as my eyes adjust. My footsteps echo against the bumpy concrete floor.

As soon as I can see properly, I gasp.

The wide, cavernous space is mostly empty, just a couple stalls remaining where I imagine there may have been rows of them housing a collection of animals before. Some bits of yard work equipment are scattered around the room, and there's a dusty old workbench housing a collection of tools along one of the walls, but that's not what has my mouth gaping and my eyes widening with disbelief.

It's the light.

Two rows of windows face each other high up in the

Paint the Moon

rafters, letting criss-crossing beams of morning sunlight filter inside.

The soft, buttery light is straight out of a Renaissance painting. It catches on the dust particles dancing in the air, turning them to shimmering specks of gold. The spider webs in the rafters sparkle like intricate tapestries woven with ancient patterns.

Even though we're standing in a crooked old barn, I'm hit with the same full-bodied reverence I feel when I'm staring up at the vaulted ceilings of a lofty cathedral, like even my very bones recognize the magnitude of what I'm seeing.

I hear Natalie step up beside me.

"It's beautiful," I whisper.

My voice sounds so small.

"It is," she whispers back.

I don't know how long we stand there. Even Bailey seems to pick up on the solemn moment. She plops down just a few inches from my feet and waits while I watch the dust continue to dance in the sunbeams.

"I don't...I don't even have words," I say. "I mean, I know it's just a barn, but...but..."

I trail off and turn to look at Natalie, spreading one of my hands to gesture up at the windows.

She gives me a soft smile. "I know."

I stay fixed in place while she takes a few steps over to the work bench, running her finger along the edge and leaving a long streak through the dust.

"I used to sneak out here during holiday dinners and stuff." She stops with her back to me, shifting her weight from foot to foot before she speaks again. "This is... This is where I first realized I wanted to paint."

I picture her out here as a child, a wild tangle of poofy

hair framing her face as she sat on the dusty concrete getting a party dress she probably didn't want to wear all covered in dirt.

I burn with the urge to ask her a dozen questions: what the first painting she made was, who bought her first set of brushes, how it felt to turn a blank page into art.

Something tells me to stay quiet, though. Something tells me she's not ready for that yet.

Instead, I pull the envelope out of my pocket.

"Here," I say, holding the paper out as she turns back around. "You've earned it."

She walks over to me, but instead of grabbing the envelope, she stares at it like it's about to jump out of my hand and bite her.

"I'm scared to read it," she says, her voice low.

"It's okay to be scared."

She hesitates for a few more seconds before she grips the corner of the paper. I let go, watching as she traces her fingertip over the letters of her name.

"I should probably just get it over with, right?"

She looks up at me with an almost childlike longing for guidance in her eyes. My chest tightens.

"Only if you want to," I say.

"Okay." She nods and then takes a deep breath. "I'm going to at least check what it is."

She wanders back over to the work bench, and I stroll over to the stalls to give her some space. I listen to the sound of the envelope ripping as I peer into the empty stalls. Natalie stays silent, but I hear the rustling of a few pages. I glance over and see she's standing with her back to me, completely still. I wonder if I should offer to leave the barn altogether, but I don't want to interrupt her reading.

The next stall is unlatched, so I let myself inside, Bailey

sniffing around behind me. I wonder if there were ever horses in here. The musky scents of the barn reminds me of the horses I used to visit down the street back in New Brunswick.

I get so caught up in the memories of home that I don't process the sound Natalie is making until it's been going on for a few minutes.

Then I freeze.

She's crying.

I speed out of the stall and find her trembling, her shoulders shaking as she leans against the workbench like it's the only thing keeping her standing. The letter is still clutched in her quaking grip.

"Natalie!" I rush over and then freeze again when I'm right beside her, not sure if I should touch her. "What's wrong?"

She fights the tears dripping down her cheeks, grimacing like she's embarrassed by her reaction, but they keep coming.

"I never knew," she chokes out, shaking her head. "I never even guessed. I…I…"

"Hey." I loop my arm under hers when her knees begin to shake. "Hey, it's okay."

She hesitates and then leans her weight against me. She sniffs a few times and swipes at her eyes.

"She was here for…for so long," she croaks.

The pain in her voice pierces straight through my heart, despite the fact that I have no idea what's going on.

"What happened?" I ask, keeping my voice as gentle as possible.

She tries to speak, but the tears won't let her. I pat her arm, letting her lean on me as she fights for control.

I want to tell her she doesn't have to do that, that she

can let it all out with me, but she tries to speak again before I get the chance.

"I...I..." She trails off and shakes her head before thrusting the letter at me. "Here. Just read it."

I look between her and the sheets of paper.

"Are you sure?"

Whatever is in that letter, it's got to be extremely personal. I don't know if Natalie will regret showing it to me once she's thinking straight, but when she practically shoves the letter in my hand, I take it.

With my other arm still supporting her, I lift the bundle of papers up and realize there's a glossy page torn out of a magazine tucked in among the plain sheets of notepaper.

I shift it to the front of the pile, and a quick scan reveals it's an old article about an exhibition Natalie's work was featured in a few years ago. It seems to have come from some sort of local publication in La Cloche, praising Natalie for being part of a big art festival in Montreal.

I read through the first few sentences.

A favourite local artist and lifelong resident of La Cloche, Natalie Sinclair, has made it all the way to Montreal for her artistic studies. Two of her paintings have been selected for display in Festival Q, a burgeoning celebration of LGBTQ artists in Canada being hosted for the second time this year in Montreal.

The text is interspersed with two large photographs of Natalie's paintings. Even though they're only a couple inches large, I still have to stifle a gasp when I see them.

They're stunning.

In the first one, a nude woman stands with her back to the viewer in the middle of a forest clearing. Thick, dark hair hangs down her back. Towering evergreen trees stretch up around her, sunlight dappling through their branches to gleam on the woman's skin.

Flecks of paint in a rainbow of hues give the light an almost fantastical quality, like it's shimmering with bioluminescent filaments.

The second painting features the same surreal, prismatic lighting, but this time, it's twined around two joined hands, almost like a DNA spiral. The hands stretch out towards each other from either side of the canvas, adorned with stacks of mismatched bracelets and a few rings. One of them has dark green nail polish that's flaked off in a few spots. Even printed in a magazine, the details are so realistic I can hardly believe the hands are actually done with paint.

My eyes land on a quote from Natalie included in the article.

"I draw a lot of inspiration from thinking about the relationship between queerness and nature. Being from a small town, I'm used to the idea of cities being a place of refuge for queer people to escape to, but I think sometimes we forget how much healing and belonging we can also find just by escaping to the woods. Nothing in there will ever judge us for being who we are."

An ache pierces my chest, so sharp I almost cry out, and it takes me a second to place it as longing.

Longing for a place with no judgement. No expectation. No right and no wrong.

I look at the painting of the hands again, fingers intertwined, palms pressed together.

Two women's hands.

I want to finish the article, but I know Natalie is waiting for me to read the letter. She's still sniffling, her shoulder pressed against mine.

I shuffle the magazine page to the back of the pile and

find the beginning of the letter. The text is written in French, in the same looping cursive from the envelope, and it takes me a couple seconds to adjust to the handwriting. Then I begin to read.

My niece Natalie,

When you read this, I will be gone, and you will know I have left my house, my possessions, and all the money I have left to you.

You will be wondering why.

The truth is that I hadn't considered leaving you anything until almost seven years ago, when I saw the article I'm enclosing here.

That was the first time I saw any of your art.

Many people have wondered why I never remarried, why I have stayed alone in this house for so many decades. I know what they think of me, a woman tragically widowed just a few short years after her marriage began, left to wander old and childless through the empty house she cannot bear to leave.

They think I am a ghost. They think I haunt this place, or that it haunts me with all the memories of the things I never got to have.

But I will tell you, Natalie, because you will understand something no one else in this family ever has: I never wanted any of it.

I never wanted this house. I never wanted my husband. I never wanted a marriage or children or any of the things a good Catholic girl is supposed to have.

I was born with something wrong with me. Something bad. Something I was never supposed to talk about. Something I needed to swallow up inside me and hide forever.

I think you know what it is.

I used to pray things would change, but they didn't. I

used to pray I'd be fixed, but I never was, so instead, I prayed I could go far, far away. I prayed for the strength to leave my family behind, but it never came.

In my day, us girls did what we were told. We had to. Out here, things were done a certain way, and you'd lose all respectability if you tried to do anything else. If you lost respectability, you lost your community, and community was all we had.

You stayed with your family until you found a husband, and then you stayed with him. There were no opportunities for women who did anything different. Not here. Here, we were all like little dolls. We were all supposed to be the same: pretty and neat and obedient.

I look back now, and I know I could have left. It would have been hard, but I could have done it, if I'd had the strength. I was weak. I was scared. When they found a nice man for me to marry, I said yes.

And slowly, I began to hate them for it. My own family. My own husband. I hated them all, even though it was me with the horrible secret.

When my husband died, I was relieved. Relieved to be a widow. Can you think of anything more evil than being relieved when your husband is killed? A nice man who wanted nothing more than a wife and a family, and I was glad he died.

At first, I stayed in this house to punish myself. If I was evil, I didn't deserve to leave. After a while, my family began to ask questions. My mother wanted me to remarry. My sister wanted to move into the house with her family. Everyone said I didn't need this place anymore.

But didn't they put me here? Didn't they want me to live this life? Didn't they look past all the lies and the hiding and let themselves believe I was a good girl, a good little doll who'd make a good little wife?

After that, I stayed out of spite. Even after my parents died, and then all my siblings, I stayed.

Even when all those English people came to town and filled La Cloche with idiotic tourists who offered me more money than I'd ever dreamed of to buy it, I stayed.

This was the life they built me for. I swore to myself I'd never leave it.

When I saw your art, my niece, I saw something I never knew was possible. I know it never would have been possible for me, but the world is different for you. You don't have to hide.

I wanted to hate you for it. At first, I really did, but I've hated so many people for so long. I'm old. I'm tired. I'm ready to leave this world. It's not mine anymore. It's your world. It's a world for people like you, and so this house should be for you too.

Maybe you can be happy here. Maybe you will fill the house with dreams. Or art. Or even children. I don't know you well enough to know what you want, but whatever it is, I hope this place will lead you to it.

Maybe you'll sell it and go far, far away just like I dreamed of, but there is a selfish part of me that hopes you will stay. I hope you will stay and show all the girls here things are different now.

I still think you are impertinent and don't speak very good French, but you deserve everything I am leaving you. Don't let anyone tell you otherwise. Do whatever you want with it, but make sure it is what you want.

Do what I couldn't, Natalie. That's all I ask in return.
Your aunt,
Manon

Paint the Moon

It takes me three tries to read the last paragraph, and I realize it's because my hand is shaking.

"Did you know?" My voice is trembling too. "About...her?"

Natalie shakes her head. She's not sniffling anymore, and she's shifted her weight off my arm. She hasn't moved away from me, though.

When she speaks, her voice is low and hoarse. "I had no idea. I don't think anyone did."

She stares at the papers in my hand, wincing like she's watching something precious get smashed to bits

"She thought she was *evil*," she says with a shudder. "For decades. I can't even imagine..."

She trails off, and for a moment, it's like the horror of all those long years fills the barn with a silent scream.

All the air is pushed out, leaving nothing but a suffocating grief.

I look at Manon's signature—no last name, not her own or her husband's—and the letters begin to blur. My eyes burn, and the next time I blink, I feel the searing trail of a tear slide down my cheek.

"Brooke?"

Out of the corner of my eye, I see Natalie peering at me, her forehead wrinkled with concern, but all I can do is shake my head while a wave of guilt crests over me and threatens to pull me under.

All this time, I've been making excuses.

I've been pushing things aside.

I've been denying something I've known for years—maybe even my whole life—because I didn't want to deal with the complications.

I just wanted a stable and predictable future, something to ground myself with, something to hold onto no matter how much my life seemed to slip out of my control.

Liking girls would have been just one more thing I didn't see coming, one more thing I had to feel confused and scared about.

What a cowardly reason to pretend it wasn't true.

"I'm sorry," I say around the lump that's formed in my throat. "It's not about me. She was *your* aunt. I just..."

I squeeze my eyes shut, but more tears still seep out, dripping down my cheeks to splash onto my coat.

"What is it?" Natalie murmurs.

The gentleness in her voice just makes my guilt rise even higher, like a tidal wave towering high above my head, higher than the barn itself.

"I'm so mad at myself," I whisper, my eyes still shut.

I try to slide my arm out from around her, but she grips my elbow and holds me in place.

"Why?" she asks.

My face burns with shame, hot enough to make the salty tears sting my skin.

"I..." I open my eyes as I fumble for the right words, but I still have to stare down at the tips of my shoes instead of at her. "In the past, I've...I've hooked up with...a few...women."

A moment of silence passes. I feel Natalie shift against the workbench, leaning slightly away from me.

"And you're mad at yourself...for that?"

There's an ache in her voice I can't bear the sound of.

"No!" I say, loud enough to make Natalie jump. Bailey perks her ears up and lets out a low whine.

"No," I repeat, quieter now. "I'm mad because I had every chance in the world to accept something about myself, and I chose not to."

Natalie stiffens. I glance at her face and see the hurt in her expression has morphed into shock.

"It was just...so much, you know? So much to figure out. So much to change. So much to be afraid of. But this letter..." I hold up the pages still clutched in my hand. "I had it so much easier than her. It's like she said. Our world is so different from hers. I feel selfish for convincing myself I could just blow it all off when there are countless people who would give anything to take my place."

I drop my gaze to the floor again, bracing for Natalie to agree with me, but instead, she gives my elbow another squeeze.

"You're not selfish for being afraid."

She stays quiet for a moment, like she's giving her words a chance to sink in.

I wish they would, but I can't believe her, not with the evidence clutched in my hand.

"It doesn't matter where you live or what your family is like or how supportive your friends are," she adds. "It's always scary."

Part of me knows that's true, but the rest of me is convinced I didn't deserve to be scared.

"I didn't think it counted, you know? A few drunken hookups. I didn't think it was enough." I let out a scoff that grates my throat. "But maybe I was just choosing the easy way out."

Natalie slides away from me, and for a moment, I'm convinced she's going to walk out of the barn, so disgusted she can't even bear to be in the same room as me.

She's out here changing lives with her amazing queer artwork, and I haven't even been able to admit the truth by the age of thirty.

Instead of leaving, she steps over to stand in front of me, our boots tip to tip as she lays her hands on my shoulders.

Her grip on me is strong. Solid. As stable as the foundation of this barn that has kept on standing despite years of neglect.

"It's enough, Brooke. If you want it to be. Whatever you feel is enough."

I tilt my chin up and meet the cobalt blue of her eyes.

I shiver.

Her fingers flex around my shoulder blades.

"And you didn't do anything wrong," she adds. "Even now, we don't live in a world that makes it easy."

She's so close I can almost feel the warmth of her breath on my skin.

"That's true," I say, "but we still live in a different world than Manon."

We live in a world of possibilities. I can feel them sparkling in the air around us, like the flecks of rainbow light in Natalie's painting.

"And I don't want to waste it," I murmur.

Natalie shakes her head, slowly, her gaze still locked on mine.

"I don't either."

She's even closer now.

I have never seen eyes like hers.

Or lips like hers.

Somehow, I'm looking at her mouth, and then my eyes are closing, but I can still see the speckled light swirling around us like a thousand tiny prisms.

Her fingers disappear from my shoulders. My eyes fly open to find she's taken a step back. She shoves her hands in the pockets of her jacket.

"I'm, uh, keeping the house," she says, her voice a little

breathy before she clears her throat and straightens her posture. "I'm running the inn."

I blink a couple times, my heart pounding.

Was I about to kiss her?

Was she about to kiss me?

"You are?" I say, fighting through the daze of the last few minutes.

She nods and chuckles, dropping her gaze to the floor as she kicks at a pebble with the tip of her boot.

"Tell me Manon's gay grand-niece and her two gay best friends running a super gay inn at the house she was supposed to live out her heteronormative nightmare in isn't the best flip of the script you've ever heard."

She looks back up, grinning at me, and even though my head is still spinning, it's impossible not to grin back at her.

"It's pretty damn great."

She nods, and she seems to grow taller, fuelled with a stronger sense of certainty than I've ever seen in her before.

"I know I can do this. There was this part of me that kept thinking I didn't deserve it, that I'd just mess it up, but this really is what she wanted, and...it's what I want too."

She looks around the barn, raising her eyes to the windows above our heads.

"I love this town," she says. "There is so much beauty in La Cloche. So much inspiration. I want to make sure everyone gets to experience that, and this is how I'm going to do it."

I watch her with the same hushed awe I felt when I first stepped into the barn.

"You're going to be amazing at it," I murmur.

She flashes me another grin, and then her attention lands on the bundle of papers still sitting on the workbench beside me.

"I wish I'd known," she says, the ache back in her voice. "I wish she'd told me while she was still here. Maybe I could have made things better for her."

"You did."

She gives me a confused look, her eyebrows wrinkling.

"Your art," I remind her. "It changed everything for Manon. Maybe she didn't get to live the kind of life she wanted, but she died knowing someone in her family would. She said you showed her things she didn't even know were possible, just through your paintings. You gave her hope in the world, even after everything she'd been through."

She blinks at me, her thoughts hidden behind a blank face, and then goes back to kicking at the pebble.

"I don't know..." she mutters.

There's no way I'm letting her get away with that.

I push off the bench and grab her hands.

"Well, I do. Your work matters, Natalie."

Her head snaps up, her eyes flaring wide.

I don't back down. I squeeze her hands in mine and refuse to look away.

"It matters to *me*."

She glances between me and our entwined fingers, her chest heaving.

I don't know how long we stand there, only that I couldn't let her go if I tried.

"Your hands are cold," she murmurs, her thumb sweeping over my knuckles. "Come on. Let's get you inside."

Chapter 16

Brooke

I don't know how I make it through the meeting. For the sake of my job, I hope I at least managed to take some notes, because by the time I'm packing up my laptop at the kitchen table, I realize I have absolutely no memory of what Natalie and I discussed over the past hour since we came in from the barn.

I've used up every spare brain cell and then some just trying not to stare at her mouth.

"So what's your plan for tonight?" Natalie asks while piling our breakfast dishes into the sink.

My heart leaps into my throat, but then she keeps talking.

"Are you going back to the city? Did you find somewhere to stay?"

Heat creeps up my neck, and I pretend to be busy rooting around in my purse.

Of course she wasn't asking to make plans *with* me.

Sharing an emotional moment together and letting her know I'm attracted to women doesn't mean there's anything going on between *us*.

I got carried away in the barn. We both did. The letter touched us both, far more than we expected.

I don't know what's happening to me, or where I'm supposed to go from here. All I can be sure of is that I'm definitely not supposed to ruin the most important business relationship of my career by making a move on a client who is also my ex-fiancé's little sister.

"I'm not sure," I say, fidgeting with a couple lipsticks and a pack of gum I didn't even know were lurking at the bottom of my bag. "I'm going to call my landlord before I drive back and see if there are any updates. Then I'll probably go to my mom's place. I think it's my only long-term option in the city."

My jaw is clenching just thinking about calling my mother, never mind sharing a house with her again for the first time since I moved out at eighteen.

Natalie throws another look at me over her shoulder.

"You don't sound thrilled about that," she says with a sympathetic grin.

I shrug. "She's just a little...chaotic sometimes, but it will be fine."

I sound about as convinced as I feel, which is not at all, but Natalie does me the courtesy of nodding and saying she's sure things will be okay.

I offer to help with the dishes, but she says she's fine and that I should go make my phone calls. I head into the living room and flop down on the couch. Bailey is still hovering in the kitchen, hoping for food scraps, so I tug a throw pillow onto my lap to use for emotional support instead.

I get sent straight to voicemail the first time I dial my landlord, so I try again a couple minutes later, in case he's busy, or maybe screening my calls and hoping I'll give up so he can ignore me.

Paint the Moon

The phone rings this time, but it still takes him a while to pick up. Our short conversation confirms he's at least got an estimate on how long I'll be out of an apartment.

Apparently, it will be a two week job, but in over half a decade of interior design, I've yet to see a contractor ever finish on time. Still, it's much less time than I expected.

We hang up, and I'm left to face the moment I'm truly dreading.

She picks up after the third ring.

"Hi, Mom!" I say, forcing a cheery note into my voice.

But not too cheery. She always knows when I take it too far on the faking.

"Brooke! I haven't heard from you in so long!"

A pang of guilt stabs me.

"Yeah, I'm sorry. Work has been kind of crazy."

"Did they promote you yet?"

The guilt is wiped away by a surge of irritation.

Of course that's the first thing she asks about. All she ever wants to know about work is if they're paying me more yet.

"Sort of. I have this trial project to give managing a go."

The fewer details I give her, the better. We've already gotten sidetracked from the reason I called.

"Just a trial?"

I squeeze the pillow so hard I'm grateful I don't have Bailey to cuddle. I'd probably be crushing her lungs without even realizing it.

"Yes. They want to see how I do with it first."

She lets out a heavy sigh. "You've been there forever. You deserve to be making more money, you know."

I keep pulverizing the pillow with one hand and use the other to rub my temple. "You're preaching to the choir, Mom."

She grunts. "So are you calling me on your lunch break or something?"

I grimace as I prepare to drop the bomb.

"Uh, yeah. Sort of. I have something to ask you."

"Oh? What is it?"

I can hear the alarm in her voice, and I know I've already messed this up. She's on guard now, which means an explosion is imminent.

"Well, don't worry, but—"

"Why are you always telling me not to worry?" she snaps. "You and Stan. I do *not* worry too much, okay?"

At least she's still with Stan. She went back and forth between so many boyfriends when I was a kid I couldn't even keep their names straight.

That would have been fine. I wouldn't have cared how many guys she dated if we hadn't also moved in with several of them, sometimes for just a few months at a time.

I can't even say for sure how many rooms I had to pack up and leave between the ages of eight and eighteen. Some of them just blur together now.

"Okay," I say. "I'm sorry. It's just, my apartment flooded, and—"

"*WHAT?*"

I clench my jaw so hard my teeth squeak.

"It's fine," I cut in. "It wasn't that bad. I—"

There's no stopping her, though. I know that all too well.

"*Not that bad?*" she shouts. "You're telling me a *flood* was *not that bad?* When did it happen? Where are you? What's going on?"

"I'm trying to tell you," I snap, which was not the right thing to do.

She switches straight into guilt tripping.

"Well, forgive me for being concerned about my daughter! Do not raise your voice at me just because I care about you!"

I squeeze my eyes shut, pressing the pillow between my palms like it's a talisman grounding me in the present.

I'm not a teenager anymore. I'm a thirty year-old adult. I have a job. I have my own money and my own home.

Her moods do not control my life anymore.

I can be stable. I can be strong.

"Okay," I say, stroking the surface of the pillow as I take a deep breath.

"Are you going to tell me or not?"

"It happened yesterday. I wasn't home. I'm fine. Bailey is fine. The landlord is getting it sorted out."

"Do you have to move out?" she demands, questions pouring out of her like a geyser. "You're staying here, right? Oh god, I'll need to clean the spare room. It's a mess. Are they still charging you rent? You know you can't accept that, right? How long will it take to fix? What's the damage? Is your stuff okay? Do you need to move things over here? I'll tell Stan to bring the truck. STAN!"

I hear the sound of footsteps and doors banging as she charges through the house.

"Mom, hold on."

"STAN!" she shouts, like she hasn't even heard me. "Brooke had a flood! A *flood*, Stan! STAN!"

I can hear the distant sound of his muffled replies, and it takes everything in me not to do more than roll my eyes.

They're going to end up having a twenty minute interlude before she even remembers she's still on the phone.

That's when it hits me.

I can't do this.

I can't stay with her for two weeks. I can't even stay with her for a night.

This can't be my life again.

"Mom," I say, as loud as I dare.

"What is it?"

"I don't need to stay with you. I'm staying with a friend."

The silence that falls is so loaded I can feel the weight of it crushing my chest.

"What do you mean?" she says, her panicked shouts replaced by a bone-chilling calm. "Of course you're staying with us."

All the instincts I developed as a child are begging me to back down, to make myself small and obedient, but the cost of giving in on this is too high.

"I'm already at her place," I explain. "She's got a spare bedroom and a yard for Bailey and everything. I just wanted to let you know."

I hear her suck in a breath.

"Do you not *want* to stay with us?"

I wriggle even deeper into the couch, like I can slip between the cushions and disappear from this conversation.

"Mom, it's not about that," I try to soothe.

"Who even is this friend? Is it that Layla girl?"

"No, it's not Layla."

I know she won't be content with just that, so I wrack my brain for the quickest explanation possible. "It's a new friend. Her name is Natalie."

She huffs. "You're staying at the house of someone you don't even know?"

I tug at a lock of my hair, holding my breath to swallow a scream.

"She's a new friend, Mom, not a stranger." I chuckle like

this is all just a silly little joke we can share. Sometimes that works to diffuse the tension. "I've known her for a bit. Everything is okay."

I bite my lip, bracing for her response.

"I'm just worried about you."

My shoulders loosen when I hear how much her tone has softened.

"I know," I tell her. "I know you are, but like I said, everything is okay."

"You're sure?"

"I'm sure."

She sighs again, all the fight seeping out of her. "All right, well, you let me know what that landlord is up to. You should *not* be kept out of your apartment for too long."

"I will."

"Okay. I guess you have to go. I love you."

My eyes begin to sting. I squeeze them shut.

"I love you too, Mom."

As soon as we've hung up, I hurl my phone at the closest armchair. It hits the cushions so hard it bounces onto the carpet, landing with a *thunk* that makes me extra grateful I splurged on a quality phone case.

"UGH!" I shriek.

Then I remember where I am.

I'm sure I'm beet red by the time Bailey and Natalie come flying into the living room to see if I'm all right.

"Sorry," I say while Bailey licks my hand. "I'm fine. How much of that did you hear?"

Natalie shrugs. "I was doing my best not to eavesdrop."

"It's fine." I lift Bailey onto my lap and slump against the back of the couch. "I know I wasn't quiet. My mom is just...exhausting."

Natalie grins. "As is the way of mothers."

I try to smile back, but I can only hold it for a second.

"I guess so. She's just...so hard to predict. You never know what's going to set her off."

Natalie leans against the arched entrance into the living room and nods. "That must be hard to deal with."

Stroking the white ruff of fur around Bailey's neck has already started calming me down. I don't know what I ever did without this dog.

"I've learned to just do my best to tiptoe around her," I say. "It's a lot better now that I'm an adult and we don't live together."

"I bet."

I keep petting Bailey as I scramble for what to say next.

I hadn't thought this far ahead on the call with my mom.

"Speaking of..." I begin. "I, uh, don't think it's going to work out for me to stay with her."

Natalie frowns. "Oh no. Is everything okay?"

"Yeah, it's just...not a good time, but I've been thinking, and..."

I'm literally thinking of it now, working through the plan in my head as I explain it to her.

"The landlord says it's only going to be two weeks of repairs, which means it will probably be at least three, but that's still less than I expected. Since this house is my only official project at the moment, I'm thinking maybe I could ask my boss for permission to work from home for the next couple weeks, and maybe pop into the office for the day from time to time."

She nods. "That sounds reasonable."

"I hope so. So, um...is it really okay if I stay here for a while?"

I can't keep my voice from raising half an octave with nerves.

Natalie chuckles and comes over to sit in the armchair beside the couch. "Of course! That's what I told you."

I sag with relief, my spine liquefying. "I just wanted to check you weren't saying that to be polite without really meaning it."

She leans over the edge of the chair and forces me to meet her gaze. "I mean it."

"You're sure?"

"Yes, Brooke." She tilts her head, one of the curls that has slipped out of her ponytail falling into her face. "You don't ever have to tiptoe around me, okay?"

My eyes start to sting all over again, but I can't look away.

I don't *want* to look away. For a moment, it's like we're back out in the barn again, just us, alone in a pool of golden light.

"Okay," I murmur.

Chapter 17

Brooke

By the time my third day in La Cloche rolls around, I've gotten myself into a routine. I wake up at eight, make breakfast, feed Bailey, and log in for work by nine. I've set up my work station in the study, where the huge oak desk and leather-backed office chair make me feel like I'm a mystery novelist writing my next bestseller at the turn of the century, rather than an underpaid interior designer scrambling for a promotion.

Lunchtime is the best part of the day. That's when Natalie shows up with Belle, and we spend an hour taking the dogs out on one of the local trails. Today, we're going far enough that we'll need to drive out to the trailhead in Natalie's car.

When she pulls into the driveway, I laugh out loud at the sight of Belle squished into the back seat of Natalie's little Toyota. Her hulking head looms over Natalie's shoulder, tongue lolling, as Natalie waves at me through the windshield.

"You ready for walkies?" I ask Bailey, heading over to pull on my boots.

Paint the Moon

Bailey yips her agreement, doing her usual excited Corgi wiggle and bounding out the door as soon as I've opened it.

She still has more energy than I've ever seen before, and even though the vet said the best we can hope for is slowing the progression of her hip issues, I swear she's gotten more agile in just the few days we've spent out in the mountains.

I still lift her into the car just to be safe. Despite their size difference, Bailey has taken to Belle like they were litter mates in a former life. She begins attacking the bloodhound's wrinkly jowls with kisses the second I've deposited her onto the backseat.

"Well, someone's excited," Natalie says with a laugh as I climb into the passenger seat. "I can't even remember the last time anyone slobbered all over my face just to say hello."

"Oh really?" I joke. "You haven't even gotten a *little* slobber lately?"

She shakes her head and shifts the car into gear. "I've been too busy hanging out with you."

My heart does a weird fluttering thing in my chest.

"Right," I say.

I watch the houses of La Cloche go by outside the window, with their yellowed lawns and bare trees in the yard. The snow has almost completely gone now, with nothing but a few mud-streaked clumps remaining here and there. The air is warm enough that I didn't even need to bring a scarf today.

"Oh, did you hear about the storm?" Natalie asks, guiding us out to a bumpy back road dotted with potholes. She slows the car down to swerve around the worst of them.

"What storm?" I ask. I jumped straight into work this morning without even checking my phone.

"There's an ice storm rolling in tonight. The worst of it is supposed to pass us by, but apparently it's still going to be pretty nasty."

I peer at the blue sky streaked with only a few wisps of white clouds, but I don't doubt her. Winter always seems to have one final trick up its sleeves.

"I knew we'd get one last storm," Natalie says. "There's always at least one in April. Anyway, my mom keeps bugging me to get you to stay at their house tonight because of the weather, so I figured I should at least offer, even though staying with them would definitely fall under the category of weird."

I chuckle. "I'll be fine. It's not my first ice storm, you know. Plus, you said we're not even supposed to get the worst of it. I'm sure I'll just sleep through the whole thing."

We pull up to an abandoned field that seems to come out of nowhere, tucked in amongst the thick forest of maple, birch, and evergreens. The dead remains of last year's tall grass cover the ground, flattened by the weight of the snow that blanketed them all winter. The field is surrounded by a rotting wooden fence that's missing half its rails, with a rusting gate closing it in.

A set of tire tracks have been worn into the ground in front of the gate. Natalie uses them to drive straight up to the gate before she cuts the engine.

"I know it doesn't look like much," she says, "but there's a really nice stream just past the field."

The dogs take off the second we open the back door, Bailey flying out after Belle before I can stop her. I wince as she leaps down to the ground, but she seems fine despite her wobbly landing. She shuffles along behind Belle as the bigger dog begins sniffing everything within reach, tail wagging.

The gate is unlocked. Natalie swings it open, the groan of the hinges cutting through the calm of the woods around us. A few birds are twittering, and I can hear small animals scuttling around in the grass, fleeing from Belle's nose as she interrupts their afternoon adventures. The air is teeming with the pungent odor of mud and wet, decaying leaves.

It's a good thing the trees are still bare. Everything out here will be sprayed with a thick layer of ice by morning, if the storm really does come through.

Natalie and I walk side by side through the field. The mud sticks to the bottoms of my boots in thick clumps, but there's a narrow trail that keeps us out of the worst of it.

"So, I told Jacinthe and Maddie I'm all in on the inn," she says.

"That's great! Were they excited?"

"Very," she answers, grinning. "We've already got a few more business meetings set up with the bank. Jacinthe is a tough negotiator, as you can probably imagine, which has really helped with securing funding, and Maddie already has a spreadsheet for everything. We're registering as an LLC, and we're working on a tourism grant application."

"That's such good news! Let me know if there's anything I can do to help."

We break apart to step around a huge puddle in the middle of the trail and then fall into step beside each other again.

"Thanks," she says. "That's really nice of you. You're already going above and beyond. Seriously. You even came up with the name. Balsam Inn wouldn't exist without you."

I shrug and then tug at the neck of my jacket. "Oh, it was just an idea. I'm sure Jacinthe and Maddie can help you think of something better."

She shakes her head. "I already ran it past them, and

they love it. The trees are almost as iconic as the house itself, so it's a perfect fit."

Up ahead, Belle lifts her head to check that we're still behind her. Bailey is waddling along a few steps in front of us.

"I did think about naming it after Manon," Natalie says after we've walked a little farther.

Her tone has a somber note now. I nod, waiting for her to go on.

"But it didn't feel right. She didn't ever want that house. It was basically a prison to her. I didn't want to chain her name to it now."

I nod. "That makes sense."

"But I do want to honor her somehow," she continues. "I, um...well, I have this idea for the barn."

She stuffs her hands in her pockets and stares straight ahead, pressing her lips together like she's nervous to share.

"I bet it's great," I encourage. "You have great instincts for using spaces. I think if you'd studied interior design, you'd be giving me a run for my money."

She chuckles. "Nah, you'd be the expert no matter what. That's actually why I want to run this past you. I, um...I've been thinking about turning the barn into a studio. I could name that after her. Studio Manon."

I can't hold back a gasp.

As soon as she says it, I can see the whole thing take shape in my mind. Walls are sliding into place. Furniture is assembling. The floor is getting redone. Calculations swirl through my head as I imagine the final result: all that gorgeous light flooding into a lofty, open-concept studio with custom storage and some cozy corners for lounging. There'd even be room for a little kitchenette.

"That's perfect!" I say, loud enough to make both the

dogs turn their heads. "Oh my god, Natalie, that's an amazing idea."

"You think so?" she asks, glancing at me with a sheepish smile on her face.

"I love it!" I gush. "With all that light. Wow. You have to do it."

"I was thinking we could hire some local artists to teach classes for our guests out there," she explains. "I'd love to create some art retreat programs for people who want to escape into nature and get inspired. We could even rent it out as an artists' space during the off season. I'd like to set up a program for people who can't afford to pay for it too, so they could have a free place to work. We could support people from communities that get overlooked in the art world."

She's practically vibrating, and her energy is infectious. There's a bounce in my step as we near the edge of the field.

"That all sounds incredible. You could teach some classes yourself too! I'm sure people would love to learn from you."

Her grin tightens into a grimace.

"Maybe," she says.

I'm hit with the urge to grab her arm, to stop her in her tracks and make her understand how powerful she is. I thought learning about the effect her work had on Manon would help.

Before I get the chance to say anything, we reach the decaying fence, and Natalie ducks under one of the lichen-covered beams.

"Anyway," she says, "I also wanted to tell you Jacinthe and Maddie think we should have a celebratory dinner at the house once our LLC is registered."

"Oh, of course." I bob my head as I duck under the

fence too. "Just let me know whenever it is, and I'll make myself scarce for you."

Natalie scoffs. She plants her hands on her hips and shakes her head at me.

"Brooke," she says, like she's talking to a kindergartner, "I'm not asking you to get lost. I'm inviting you to the dinner."

"Oh." I blink a couple times as I re-process the last few seconds. "Really?"

She shakes her head again, letting out an incredulous chuckle.

"Of course. Like I said, Balsam Inn wouldn't exist without you. Of course I want you at our celebration."

I want you.

I know there was more to that sentence, but for some reason, those are the only words I hear.

My heart stutters, my breath catching in my throat.

We're standing face to face, just a few feet apart, squared off like we're about to have a fistfight.

Or make out.

I guess we also sort of look like we might be about to do that.

My heart beats even faster.

Natalie breaks eye contact first.

"I mean, everyone wants you there," she adds, turning around and continuing our progress up the trail.

My head is spinning, but I force myself to keep walking too.

"I get if it's too weird for you," Natalie is saying while I jog through the mud to catch up with her. "It's probably not a normal thing to do with your clients."

"I want to be there."

I sound way too intense, and I avoid Natalie's eyes when she turns her head to look at me.

We're headed into the forest now, the muddy trail covered with twigs and desiccated leaves. There are lots of balsam firs out here. I recognize the bubbles on their trunks, the fresh scent of their needles filling my nose.

"That's great," Natalie tells me, before she lets out a soft laugh. "I guess you're already living there, so it would be a little weird if you didn't show up for dinner."

I laugh too. "The weird just keeps coming for us, huh?"

"Yeah, but I think we're doing a good job taking it in stride."

I meet her gaze when she looks at me this time. Her hair is loose and wild today, framing her face like a dark halo.

"Yeah," I say. "Me too."

We keep the conversation light for the rest of the walk. Bailey and Belle get absolutely filthy splashing around in the small stream at the end of the trail, but they look so cute chasing each other through the water that it will be worth wrangling them with towels before we let them back in the car.

Natalie and I race twigs through the current while we let the dogs play, cheering the sticks on while they shoot around the stones and logs that rise up to block their paths.

I feel like I've stepped back into my childhood in New Brunswick, where nature was always close by and even the simple things like racing sticks or jumping in puddles could keep me occupied for hours on end.

Life got so much more complicated once we moved to Montreal.

Natalie and I are still giggling like kids when she drops me back off at the house. After we've said goodbye, I make myself a quick sandwich with the load of groceries I picked up a couple days ago and settle into the study for an afternoon of work.

Not even a series of very annoying emails from Eric can throw off my good mood. I trudge through them one by one, nibbling on my sandwich and taking sips of chamomile tea.

Out here on my own, I'm remembering why I fell in love with interior design in the first place. I can get lost in plans for the inn for hours on end, ideas blooming in my mind like a sprouting garden bed spilling out across the yard. I haven't felt this creative in years.

If I could just get Layla out here to be my personal secretary, there'd be nothing about the office I'd miss.

As my graze drifts out the window while I blow on my tea, my usual jazz music filling the room, I let myself imagine what it could be like: working on my own.

My own office.

My own clients.

My own business.

I wouldn't even have to be based in the city. I could specialize in projects just like this: restoring old buildings in historic towns, preserving their roots while allowing them to grow into something new.

I could even live somewhere like La Cloche.

I nearly drop the mug as the thought enters my head.

I gave up on that idea a long time ago.

I committed to Leung Designs because it was the smart thing to do and I was done looking for fairytales.

A few weeks in the countryside isn't going to change that.

I double down on work for the rest of the day, barely lifting my head from my laptop until dinnertime. I eat some cheap noodles and pre-made pasta sauce while Bailey gobbles down her kibble. I take her for a quick walk around the yard before curling up with some reality TV for the evening.

The mind-numbing effect of the show works a little too well. I end up falling asleep on the couch, wrapped in an old quilt, and I wake up in the pitch dark to an ear-splitting whistling punctuated with sharp raps against the windows.

I jump to my feet, a dizzying rush of adrenaline shooting through me as I search for the shadow of an intruder trying to get inside. It takes me a couple seconds to realize what I'm hearing are actually ice pellets smacking the glass while a vicious wind howls through the night.

I collapse back onto the couch, patting around for my phone to check the time. I can't see anything. I let out a yelp of surprise when my hand brushes over Bailey's fur.

She's cowering under the quilt, the eerie sound of the wind making her whimper.

"It's okay, baby," I croon, petting her with one hand while I keep hunting for my phone with the other.

The glare of the screen blinds me for a moment once I've finally clicked it on. I blink and focus on the clock.

It's past one in the morning.

"Shit," I mutter.

I have a few missed calls and texts. I lean over to switch the closest table lamp on before I read them.

Nothing happens.

I try the switch a couple more times. Then I get up to try the overhead light.

Still nothing.

The wind moans like a phantom, whipping the ice pellets against the windows. I shiver without the warmth of the quilt and realize how cold the house has gotten.

If the power is out, that means there's no heat.

I pad back over to the couch, the hair on the back of my neck rising as I realize I'm completely alone in an old house in a storm with no way to turn on the lights.

This is the perfect start of a horror movie.

I check who's been calling me and find all the messages are from Natalie. Her latest text came in just twenty minutes ago, asking me if I'm awake and to let her know if I've still got power.

I press the button to call her, and she picks up on the second ring.

"I'm so glad you called," she says, her voice shaky with relief. "I hope I didn't wake you. I just wanted to check on you. It's awful out there. Half the town has lost power, but my apartment is still okay. Please tell me the house is okay too."

"I fell asleep in front of the TV," I admit. "Sorry I wasn't answering. The wind just woke me up. There's no power here."

She curses.

"But it's okay," I add. "All I'm going to do is go to bed."

"You'll freeze!" she shouts, sounding so much like an overly concerned mother I almost want to laugh. "Seriously. A house that big without heat all night will not be good for you. Or Bailey."

I'm about to protest when the most massive gust of wind yet shakes the house, making the windows and even some of the furniture rattle.

Bailey whimpers and burrows into my lap.

"It is a little creepy here without the lights," I admit.

"I'm coming to get you."

I gawk at my phone.

"Natalie, no! You can't drive in this. I'll be fine."

I can already hear the sound of her car keys jingling.

"It's just a couple minutes away. I'll go slow. I know the roads. I don't want you driving yourself. Just hang tight, and I'll be there."

I try to sputter out a protest, but she says she'll see me soon and hangs up.

Chapter 18

Natalie

"You are so lucky we didn't die!"

Brooke is fuming by the time we're scrambling up the staircase around the back of my mom's shop. I can barely hear her over the sound of ice pellets pinging against the rickety old roof that hangs over the stairway.

She does have a point. By the time I was crawling up the road to get her, with zero visibility and my wiper blades in danger of flying off at any moment, I realized I'd put my life on the line, but it was too late to turn back.

I had to get to her.

As soon as she said the power was out, there was no way I was leaving her alone in that house all night. I didn't think. I just moved.

I fling the apartment door open once I reach the top of the stairs. Brooke storms past me and then crouches down in a squat. I yank the door shut behind us and turn to watch as she unbuttons her coat to reveal Bailey tucked against her chest like a baby. She lowers her to the ground and then straightens up, whirling around to face me.

Paint the Moon

"Seriously, what the hell?" she demands, eyes blazing. "You could have crashed! I was fine. You did not have to do that."

"I was worried about you."

The admission slips out before I can stop it.

A strained moment of silence passes before Brooke's shoulders slump and she slides her coat all the way off.

"Well, thank you," she says. "That's sweet of you. Stupid, but sweet."

"Here." I reach for her coat. "Let me hang that up for you."

All I've got is an overstuffed wooden coat rack by the door. This place is seriously lacking in storage. I rearrange a few things to make room for Brooke's coat while she takes her boots off and then wanders into my living room.

Technically, the living room is also the kitchen and the dining room and the office, but she's peering around like she's in a fascinating museum and not a cramped and cluttered apartment.

My face heats up as I take a look around the room myself, imagining what she might think of it. It's nothing like her airy, plant-filled oasis in the city, with its crisp white walls and coordinated throw pillows.

My own plants are arranged in a mismatched collection of dusty thrifted containers. The fake leather of my ancient sofa has a pitiful sag in the middle. My bookcase is stuffed with a mishmash of hefty art textbooks, spindly collections of poetry, and random paperbacks. The walls are a buttery off-white that looks sunny and cheerful in the daylight, but in the glow from the table lamp and the string of fairy lights strung around the bookcase, I worry they just look like an ugly, faded beige.

A framed piece I painted years ago hangs above the

couch as the focal point of the room, the large canvas and minimalist white wood frame adding what I hope is a touch of maturity to the space. Brooke hones in on the painting, stepping closer to get a better look.

I watch her hair swish against her back. She's wearing her pink pajama pants again, under a pale blue long-sleeve shirt that clings to her waist and hips like a glove. The ribbed fabric is thin enough that I can see the darker colour of her bra straps underneath.

My throat goes dry, and I realize this rescue mission was an even stupider idea than I thought.

I brought her here—to my one-bedroom apartment—in the middle of the night.

I don't even know where she's going to sleep.

"What's this painting called?"

She looks at me over her shoulder, her hair rippling like sheets of silver in the dim room.

I don't know how her hair can do that: shift through so many different shades of silver and gold.

She's like the light in the barn, always unveiling something new, always making me itch to pick up a paintbrush.

Even when I'm not sure I can paint again.

"Oh, that one?" I say, like an idiot.

She chuckles. "Yes. This one."

Even though I've already seen countless people scrutinize my work, I still shiver as I watch Brooke take in the painting. Her head swivels, her gaze sweeping over the full expanse of the piece, and for a moment, I feel like it's me she's looking at.

My body, laid as bare as the canvas on display.

"It's called *Moon Girl*."

Not my most mysterious title, but it does a good job

describing the painting: a glowing full moon hangs in a deep indigo sky, filling two thirds of the canvas, its surface rippled with craters.

Silvery moonbeams emanate down towards the shadowy outlines of a forest below, and in the moonbeams, the vague shape of a nude woman slips in and out of view, just hints of curves and muscles shimmering in wisps of gossamer light.

Jacinthe is always calling me a douchebag for having a naked lady painting in my living room, and the longer Brooke goes without saying anything, the more I start to worry she's thinking the same thing.

"Moon girl," she whispers.

"I painted it after my first big trip to Australia," I say, hoping some back-story will rule out any douchebag accusations. "I made a lot of queer friends on that trip, from all over the world, and it got me thinking about how similar our experiences were. A lot of us could look back and see we knew we were queer at a very early age, but in the moment, it was like glimpsing something out of the corner of your eye. We didn't have a name to pin it down with. We didn't have the language to understand ourselves, to truly see our queerness for what it was, but it was always there, waiting, shimmering like a vision in the moonlight every night."

"That's what it feels like for me."

My breath lodges in my throat. I feel like I've stumbled upon a deer in a clearing and any sudden movements might send her sprinting away from me.

"Like it's...*there*," she says, "but I can't quite see it, you know?"

There's a note of yearning in her voice, so plaintive it's almost mourning, and my chest aches at the sound.

I risk taking a step closer, and then another, padding along the floor in my socks until we're standing side by side.

"You must think I'm ridiculous," she says with a bitter chuckle, shaking her head. "You came out in high school, and I'm thirty and haven't even figured this out yet."

I hate how embarrassed she sounds.

I hate anyone and anything that ever made her feel shameful.

"I don't think you're ridiculous."

She shrugs and smooths down the front of her shirt.

That's not good enough for me. I need her to understand this.

I lean in a little closer, waiting until she lifts her head to meet my gaze.

"I don't think you're ridiculous at all, Brooke."

She peers at me for a moment, taking me in with wide eyes, before she fixes her gaze on the painting again.

"I just never really had time to figure it out. I was with Yves for so long, and then when he left, my life got so messy, I just thought...I thought sleeping with a few women was part of the messiness."

She cringes.

"That sounds horrible. I know," she adds. "I don't mean—"

"It's okay. I understand." I sweep my hand out towards the canvas. "That's what this painting is about. We don't get to grow up thinking this is even an option."

She nods. "Yeah. That's it. I couldn't even picture what life with a woman would look like, so I figured I must not really be bi, but I think maybe it's just because I never got to see anyone living a different sort of life. No one outright told me being gay was wrong, per se, but no one told me it was right, either."

Paint the Moon

"That's really common. My parents taught us a lot about acceptance and embracing people who are different from us, but still, no one really thinks to say to kids, 'Also, *you* could be gay, and that's okay too.'"

She nods and crosses her arms, still staring at the speckled beams of moonlight.

"I wonder how different things could have been," she murmurs.

I wonder too. My eyes wander over the brushstrokes I traced across the canvas years ago, and I wonder how different we all might have turned out if we didn't have to taste love in the same breath as confusion and fear.

"I know it's stupid," Brooke says, squeezing her arms even tighter around herself, "but I sort of feel like…it's too late for me now, you know?"

"What do you mean?"

"I mean, even if I do the whole coming out thing, who wants to date a thirty year-old whose only experiences are a handful of drunken hook-ups during college?"

She grimaces, her forehead creasing, and I want to smooth the lines in her skin away. I want to take her hands in mine and unfurl her arms as I guide her to stand tall.

"I don't even know what dating means to me anymore," she continues. "For so long, it was about stability, about having something I could count on, even if it was just the idea of a less chaotic life, but I don't want to rely on someone else for that ever again."

I see the flicker of pain cross her face, and I know she's thinking of her ruined wedding day, of the life she thought she was starting here in this very town.

"I don't know where that leaves me. Maybe I've just missed my chance."

She seems to curl up even tighter, growing smaller with defeat, and I can't take it anymore.

"That's not how it works."

I lay my hands on her shoulders, spinning her to face me.

"You don't run out of chances, and there's no such thing as too late. If somebody tries to tell you otherwise, they're wrong."

I'm practically glaring at her, like if I focus hard enough, I'll be able to transfer my certainty over to her.

The storm is still howling outside, battering the roof with icy shards like shrapnel pinging off the shingles. I realize I haven't let go of Brooke's shoulders. I let my hands drop to my sides, heat creeping up my neck.

She hasn't said anything. I take a few shuffling steps backwards and then walk over to my tiny kitchen, opening and closing a few random cupboards to fill the awkward silence.

"Are you, um, tired?" I ask. "Hungry? Can I get you anything?"

When I look back at her, she's moved away from the painting and crouched down to pet Bailey in front of the old bamboo papasan chair tucked into the corner beside my bookshelf.

"Actually, do you have any herbal tea?" she asks. "If you've got anything without caffeine, I think that would help get me sleepy again."

I chuckle. "Do I have herbal tea?"

I dig through the vast collection of tea that occupies one of my drawers before I set a selection of boxes and tins down on the counter for her.

"Your options are chamomile, lemon and ginger, rose

and apple, mint, dandelion leaf, or decaf green tea with jasmine."

She comes over to observe my offerings and gives an approving nod that makes me way too proud considering it's just tea.

"An impressive collection. I'll take chamomile, thank you."

I tell her to have a seat while I get the water ready. A few minutes later, I bring two steaming mugs of chamomile over to the couch and set them on the coffee table.

"Is that where you paint?" she asks once I've taken a seat next to her.

She points over at the wide desk under the window. It's spread with a protective vinyl cloth, the entire surface cluttered with paint pots, stacks of brushes, and a few splattered palettes.

I wince at how messy the desk looks, like a classroom art station for kindergartners who don't know how to clean up after themselves.

"Sometimes," I answer. "I should clean it up. It's not like I've been working on anything lately."

"Do you want to be working on anything?"

The directness of her question startles me into silence. She grabs her mug, blowing onto the steaming liquid while she waits for my answer.

I try not to look at the way her lips are pursed, the way her fingers look so dainty wrapped around the handle.

"I...I do, yeah," I say, the truth slipping out before I can stop it. "Since that letter from *Tante* Manon, I've felt like...like I want to keep going. I mean, it's stupid to quit painting over one failed show, but I can't get what they said about me out of my head. I tried so hard to be something new, something better than I've ever been before, and it didn't work. They didn't want it. I don't know how to come back from that."

I slump against the couch cushions, the fake leather cold and slippery against my back.

"Sometimes I feel it, that urge I used to get, like I couldn't do anything *but* paint, but then it just...dies." I stare down at the coffee table like I'm watching all my ideas crumble into dust. "It's like just the thought of a blank page turns into this vast, empty wasteland where nothing can survive. I can barely even look at a canvas."

I reach for my tea. I should change the subject. We should talk about something easy, something normal, something to distract me from the fact that there's an exceptionally beautiful woman sitting in her pajamas in my apartment and I still have no idea where she's going to sleep.

"What if you didn't paint on a canvas?"

Brooke shifts to sit cross-legged on the couch, a glimmer in her eye like she's got the answer to a riddle.

"Huh?"

"Maybe you just need to do something totally out of the box to trick your brain into painting again. When I'm really stuck on a project, I ignore my laptop and just start drawing on random napkins or a cardboard box or something. Maybe it would work for you too."

I'm not sure how a napkin is going to reinvigorate my art career, but I nod anyway.

"An interesting theory."

She rolls her eyes like she knows I'm bullshitting her.

"I'm serious!" she insists, twisting around so she can point over at my desk. "Go grab a paintbrush right now."

She looks so cute when she gets bossy—cute enough that I can't say no. I gather up a couple thin brushes and a tray of some cracked old watercolours, and then I fill a glass up in the kitchen sink.

"Okay," I say once I've deposited my supplies and a few scraps of paper towel on the coffee table. "What am I painting on?"

"Hmm." Brooke taps her chin and scans my apartment. "How about...?"

Her eyes light up, and she flexes her hand out in front of her.

"How about you paint something on my hand?"

"Your hand?"

"Yes. Look." She plops her hand palm-down on the coffee table. "That's not so intimidating, is it?"

I grin and bend my head over her hand. "You're right. You have very tiny hands."

She pouts at me. "They're not *very* tiny. They're normal size."

My pulse speeds up, reverberating in my ears as I watch her push her bottom lip out.

Brooke Carmichael's pouting face could end up being the death of me.

"Okay," I say, forcing a chuckle. "You have normal size hands."

She sweeps her hair over her shoulder and then snaps her fingers at me.

"Come on," she says, gesturing at her waiting hand. "Get painting."

"So bossy," I say, laughing for real this time. "What should I paint?"

She shrugs. "You're the artist. You tell me."

I don't get to see her all playful and teasing like this very often. Tonight reminds me of that first morning I brought her coffee at the house, when I caught her walking Bailey in her pajamas. Then, she glowed like a soft sunrise, but tonight, she shines like a star, like the first pinprick of silver light in a dark winter sky.

"You're the one running this show," I tease back. "I thought maybe you had an idea."

"Well, since I have to do everything..." She feigns a scoff before perusing the room again. "You should paint..."

Her head swivels, searching for a worthy subject among all my clutter. She scans every corner, only stopping once she's glanced behind us.

Then she looks back at me.

"Paint the moon."

In that moment, I can see it: a gleaming, silvery orb against her pale skin, the faint blue of her veins streaked beneath the paint. I already know exactly what shades of pearly white and smoky grey to choose. Maybe a faint halo of purple.

My fingers twitch, desperate for a brush.

Without a word, I slide off the couch and take a seat on the floor, settling onto the carpet and shifting the coffee table back to give us more space. Brooke climbs down to sit beside me, both of us cross-legged, and spreads her hand out on the table again.

"Can I bring your hand a little closer?" I ask, shifting around to find the best angle to work from.

She nods, and I lift her hand up with one of mine, cradling her like a delicate bird as I lay her palm down exactly where I want it.

She's so close I can smell the faint shampoo scent lingering in her hair, something floral like lilies or peonies. I examine her skin, the dainty ridges of her bones and the creases of her knuckles.

She was right. This is nothing like painting on canvas,

and somehow, there's nothing holding me back anymore. The doubts have all melted away.

In this moment, painting feels just like it used to: as easy and as vital as breathing.

I select one of the brushes and dip it in the water glass before loading the tip up with a silvery grey.

I hover over Brooke's hand for a second before I sweep the first stroke over her skin.

She shivers.

"Is it too cold?"

I'm whispering, and I don't know why.

"No," she says. She's whispering too. "It's...it's good."

I can hear her breathing, hard enough to tear my gaze away from my work and make me look at her face.

She's staring at the swirl of colour on her hand, her lips parted. I can see the rise and fall of her chest under her shirt

My own breathing has gotten faster now too. The room feels like it's charged with a low, humming current, like the snapping power lines outside have loaded the atmosphere with electricity.

I keep painting.

My throat is dry, and I can feel sweat beading on the back of my neck, but the longer I work, the more I get lost in the process, until I'm not even thinking about Brooke at all.

All that exists is the brush and the paints and the vision of the moon in my mind, like I'm calling it down from the sky to capture it here with these colours.

I'm not sure how long I work. One of my feet starts to go numb, but the tingling sensation is only a dim discomfort at the edge of my awareness.

I swirl the grey with pearly white, creating the dappled outlines of craters, before reaching for the palest shade of purple in my set.

Somewhere in the back of my mind, I remember one of the critics saying I had an 'unsuccessful use of poorly selected colours.'

The brush hovers above Brooke's hand, my muscles clenching. Unusual colours have always been a theme in my work, splashes of vibrant hues dotting otherwise muted scenes, but for my exhibition, I tried to stick to more realistic palettes. I wanted to prove my style could mature, that I'd evolved into an artist worth displaying in huge galleries filled with important people.

Maybe that's where I went wrong.

"Natalie?"

"Sorry," I say, blinking my eyes back into focus. "I just spaced out."

I take a deep breath, and as I let it out, I lower the tip of the brush to Brooke's skin. I'm only painting on her hand. This isn't a canvas. This won't go in an exhibition. This painting won't even last until tomorrow.

There is only now, just me and just her, and this moon that wants to be purple.

So I let it be purple. I give in to the process, surrendering myself, letting the moon take over, like it's capturing *me* now, using my fingers to tell the story of its watch over the night.

Both my feet are asleep by the time I'm finished. My back is aching, but there's a huge smile on my face as I drop the brush into the water glass and sit up straight.

"It's done."

A thrill shoots through me, like the crackling electricity in the air has entered my bloodstream.

Brooke lifts her hand, turning it back and forth in the twinkling glow of the fairy lights.

I hold my breath, waiting for her to say something.

"It's beautiful." She stares at the moon like it's a precious diamond strapped to her palm. "I wish I had something more profound to say, but it's just... so beautiful. It's just like the one in your painting."

She looks between the moon on her hand and the one on the wall. I do the same, my eyes catching on the wispy outlines of the woman's body dancing in the moonbeams.

I wonder if I could paint Brooke like that, if I could capture the silvery blonde of her hair, the curve of her jaw, the way every detail of her has been shifting in and out of view in my dreams for weeks.

There's no point trying to deny it to myself anymore.

I want her.

I can't have her, but that doesn't mean I don't want her so bad I'd walk barefoot through the howling storm outside if it meant I got to touch her.

There are so many ways I want to touch her.

"Oh, shoot! I smudged it!"

The sleeve of her shirt has slipped down, smearing a bit of the paint. She looks absolutely horrified with herself, her eyes gone cartoonishly wide, and I can't keep myself from laughing.

"It's fine. Come here. Let me fix it."

I grab one of the sheets of paper towel and dip the edge into the murky water for my brush. I scoot in close enough to lay Brooke's hand over my knee and then dab at the smudge. It's a minor fix, cleared up in just a few seconds, but when I set the crumpled paper towel back on the coffee table, Brooke keeps her hand on my leg.

My heart jumps into my throat, and suddenly, it's like I can feel her touch burning straight through my sweatpants to sear the skin underneath.

I don't know why I didn't wear something sexier than

sweatpants. I don't know why I didn't think this through at all.

She's here, and she's touching me, and I'm going to make a fool of myself. I'm going to do something I can't take back.

"Thank you," she murmurs. "For trusting me with this. I know it wasn't easy."

I nod, pressing my lips tight together. My knee is still on fire, my body begging for her to light the rest of me up too.

"And thank you for coming to get me."

Her voice gets quieter. Shakier too.

Or maybe I'm just imagining that.

All I can look at is the moon on her hand.

My art on her skin.

It strikes me, then: the intimacy of what we've just done.

I've created something with her body.

I've done something I wasn't sure I'd ever be able to do again, and I did it because of her.

"Brooke..."

I don't know what else to say. If I keep talking, she's going to know how I feel, but I can't let us sit here in silence. She'll figure it out if I don't talk, and she'll figure it out if I do.

I'm trapped. I trapped myself by bringing her here, and now she's going to realize I forget how to breathe every damn time I look at her mouth.

"Natalie."

My name is like the sweetest song on her lips. I could drink the sound of it up like summer wine.

She starts to say something else, but the words turn into a shriek when the lights cut out.

I gasp as we're plunged into darkness.

The lights flicker before blinking back on. Brooke is

gripping my knee so tight her fingertips are digging into my shin.

Bailey lifts her head over on the footstool and whines.

"It's okay," I soothe. "We're okay."

I should get up and start gathering candles. I should figure out our sleeping arrangements. I should do *something* besides just sit here, but she's still clinging to me, and I couldn't move if I tried.

The lights flicker again. The wind howls, rattling the walls.

Brooke shudders.

I slide closer on the rug, bumping her leg with mine.

"Sorry," I murmur.

She shakes her head.

"I keep thinking," she says, staring at me with that same hazy-eyed look she was giving my painting, like she's caught in a waking dream, "about how I wish we'd gotten to know each other better before."

She pauses, her gaze dropping to her hand on my leg. I watch her throat bob as she swallows.

"But then I realize I don't wish that." She sounds hoarse now, her chest heaving. "Because if I'd known you better then, I...I..."

The lights cut out again, but this time, neither of us says a word. Her face is hidden by shadows, and the dark makes my voice sound extra loud when I ask, "What, Brooke?"

Her fingers twitch on my knee, sending an electric shock zinging up my leg.

"I might have ended up feeling like this about you."

The howls of the storm make it feel like the rest of the world has been wiped away, like there's nothing beyond these walls and maybe soon we'll lose this room too. We'll lose ourselves. We'll lose everything.

Maybe that's what makes me tell her the truth.

"I can't stop thinking about you."

The lights flick back on, the sudden glow of the table lamp blinding me, but it's too late to stop now. I've said it in the dark, and now she'll hear it in the light.

"I've tried to stop, but I...I can't."

Her hand slides from my knee to my thigh.

"I can't stop thinking about you either."

Chapter 19

Brooke

I'm going to kiss her.

I know it as surely as I know the sun will rise tomorrow, as I know this storm will end, as I know I'll have to face what it means to have her art seeping into my skin.

My hand slides up the top of her thigh. I watch the pearly, purple-tinged moon move along her body like it's arching across the night sky.

My fingertips brush the waistband of her sweatpants.

"Brooke."

She's leaning closer now, or maybe I am. The whole room is shifting, and I can't tell up from down.

I hook a finger around her waistband. She gasps.

We're so close now, close enough that I have to close my eyes just to find the nerve to keep leaning in.

The first thing I feel is one of her curls brushing my cheek. Then there's the fluttering warmth of her breath on my lips.

Our noses bump together. She rubs the tip of hers along

the side of mine. A whimper catches in the back of my throat.

I can almost taste her already. Every part of me is straining to close the last few millimetres between our mouths. I'm shaking, my whole body trembling so hard I'm sure she must be able to feel it.

I don't think I've ever felt this weak for someone before.

Somewhere in the back of my head, I know that should terrify me, but right now, it just makes me want her even more.

The lights flicker, splashing the backs of my eyelids with flashes of gold.

I press my lips to hers.

It's like throwing myself into the heart of the storm.

My need for her tears through me like a gale force wind, and there's no room to be embarrassed or hesitant or even smart about any of this.

This might be the stupidest thing I've ever done, but nothing can stop me. I'd freeze for this. I'd burn for this. I'd walk out into the bitter ice and hail just to feel the fire that crackles through me when her tongue brushes against mine.

Her hands are in my hair. Both of mine are clutching her sweatpants now. She's pushed herself onto her knees to lean over me, tugging my head back with a gentle but insistent pressure that makes me moan into her mouth.

Her thick hair falls around us like a curtain, brushing my cheeks and neck. I slide one of my hands around to press against her lower back. Her hips jerk, and a hot rush of satisfaction burns through me.

I made her do that.

She wants me too.

Her teeth scrape my bottom lip, and I moan again,

louder this time. Her grip on my hair tightens before she slides her thumbs down to caress my neck.

I arch my head back, breaking the kiss. Her lips brush over my chin and then slide down to my throat.

I gasp and tug at her sweatpants. The lights aren't flickering anymore, but I can still see the streaks of gold when I shut my eyes, pulsing in time with my thundering heart.

She's practically straddling me now, and I'm desperate for the pressure, desperate to feel her hips flex against mine.

I've been desperate for so long.

I think part of me wanted her since she walked into that coffee shop, as shocked to see me as I was to see her.

My back hits the carpet, and she tumbles down on top of me, our legs tangling as her arms cradle my head. Her lips are still locked to my neck, her kisses punctuated with gentle scrapes of her teeth that have me writhing underneath her.

I'm dimly aware that we're sandwiched between the couch and the coffee table, but I don't care. I wrap my arms around her and thrust my hips up.

She swears, burying her face in the crook of my shoulder. I dig one of my hands into her hair.

So much gorgeous, gorgeous hair.

"How do you do this to me?" she pants, her words muffled against my skin. "Do you have any idea how bad I want you?"

I'm breathing too hard to answer, but I thrust my hips up again to let her know I want her just as much.

"Fuck," she hisses. "What do I have to do to get you off my floor and into my bed, Brooke Carmichael?"

"You'll probably have to get off me first."

She chuckles, the throaty sound enough to make my thighs squeeze tighter around her.

"We're not going to get anywhere if you keep doing that," she says, her lips brushing the soft skin behind my ear.

I mutter an incoherent reply, my eyelids fluttering.

The truth is, I don't care if we make it anywhere else. The floor. The couch. The bed. It's all the same to me if it means I get to keep touching her.

She doesn't seem to share my opinion. With a groan, she pushes away and then does an awkward backwards crawl to get to her feet. She shoves her hair out of her face and grins down at me.

"Need a hand?"

I push up to a seat, my head spinning. She tugs me up until I'm standing. I take a wobbly step forwards, momentum propelling me straight into her chest. She wraps her arms around me, and I watch, mesmerized, as the blinking fairy lights behind me reflect in her eyes.

"You're so pretty," I murmur.

Maybe it's not the smoothest line, but it's the truth. In the daylight, she's striking, all bold features and a commanding stare, but here in this half-darkness, with her hair wilder than ever and her cheeks flushed, her blue eyes like a sky full of stars, she is *so* pretty.

She slides her grip down my arms and then takes my hands in hers.

"Come with me."

She starts walking backwards, guiding us to her bedroom. When we reach the threshold, she lets go of me and steps inside to switch on another string of fairy lights, this one twined along the bars of her black metal headboard.

The pulsing glow is just enough for me to make out the shape of the room. A double bed takes up most of the floor, a shag rug laid underneath it. There's a closet with a couple shirts slung over the doorknobs, and another painting hangs over the bed, but it's too dark for me to make out the subject.

"Do you want to come in?" she asks.

The question feels loaded, like she's lit the fuse of a firework and is waiting to see if I'll snuff it out or let the explosion go off.

A shiver runs up my spine. I cross my arms, huddling in my pajamas. The whistle of the wind outside fills the silence.

I think about running, but there's nowhere to run. We're the only thing in the eye of this storm.

I step into the bedroom.

Natalie closes the door behind me, turning the room even more dim. My heart is thumping so hard I'm sure she must be able to hear it, even from a couple feet away.

"Brooke..."

She starts to ask me something, but I don't give her the chance. I don't want questions or answers. I just want her. Everything else can wait. It *has* to wait, or I might not let myself have her at all.

"Kiss me again."

Her mouth finds mine, her arms snaking around my waist to pull us chest to chest. Without breaking the kiss, she begins backing me towards her bed. My calves bump against the edge of the mattress, and then for the second time tonight, I'm tumbling down with her on top of me.

She slides her hands under my waist to help me shimmy up the bed until I land with my head on the pillows. I feel dizzy, but instead of fighting the sensation, I throw myself into it, like I'm riding a swirling current. I tug at the neck of her sweater, and she sweeps her tongue along my bottom lip before sitting up enough to pull the whole thing over her head.

She's wearing a sports bra underneath. I stare up at the smooth expanse of her stomach while she tosses the sweater aside, watching the fairy lights dapple her skin. The ache that's been building between my legs gets even sharper.

"You doing okay?" she asks, arching an eyebrow.

I realize my jaw has gone slack, hanging wide open while I gawk at her.

I snap it shut and nod, my cheeks blazing. It's like she's got the keys to all my defences. I have no choice but to show her exactly how I feel.

I reach for her, running my hands up her back as she lowers herself over me. I sigh as I trace the curve of her spine. She nuzzles into my neck, her lips brushing the soft skin behind my ear.

My toes curl. I wrap my fists around the straps of her bra.

"Come here."

She shifts us around until we're both sitting up. She peels the hem of my shirt up a few inches and then locks eyes with me, tilting her head.

All I can do is nod my permission. She lifts the shirt off me. I shiver and reach for the clasp of my bra. Her eyes are locked on my chest, and she curses when I get the bra unhooked and tug it down my arms.

She reaches for me, skating her fingertips up my stomach, and then higher, until she brushes my nipples. I gasp, arching my neck and squeezing my eyes shut as she flicks her thumbs across my nipples a few times. My thighs twitch, my hips jerking.

I should be ashamed of how out of control my body is, but there's no room for shame now, not when her fingers are making sparks pop and sizzle in the darkness behind my closed eyelids. I push my chest into her hands, and she starts caressing me, her hair brushing my shoulders as she leans forward to capture my mouth again. She rocks against me, our bodies curving in a rhythmic serpentine.

Just when I think I can't take it anymore, she pulls back and tugs off her sports bra before tossing it to the floor.

My jaw drops again, but this time, I can't make myself close it, not even when she smirks at my reaction.

She's perfect. With the shadows of the bedroom accenting the sharp angles of her face and the indulgent curves of her hips and chest, she looks like a goddess rising to rule the underworld.

She cups my face in her hands and traces one of her fingers along my lips, which are still parted in awe. I tremble as she slips her finger in my mouth.

I close my lips around it on instinct. Her eyes flash when my teeth scrape the pad of her finger. Slowly, I slide my lips up to her knuckle, my gaze locked on hers.

She strokes my hair out of my face, tucking it behind my ear as I keep sucking her finger. Something about the tenderness of the gesture combined with the obscenity of the moment makes the need building inside me a thousand times more intense.

I know I'm wet for her, and I want her to see it. I want her to feel it.

I need her to know what she does to me.

I release her finger and roll onto my back before shimmying out of my pajama bottoms. Once I'm lying there in just my underwear, I look up and see Natalie is staring straight between my legs. I'm only wearing some plain old beige bikini briefs, but she's looking at them like they're a jewel-encrusted silver platter serving up her last meal on earth.

"Fuck," she groans.

She plants her hands on the mattress to crawl over and position herself between my legs. She grips my thighs, spreading them wider while she keeps her eyes locked on the thin strip of fabric. Her fingers dig into my thighs with just enough force to ache in the best way possible. I'm sure she can see me soaking through the fabric.

I've never done something so intimate with a woman before.

Hell, I don't know if I've ever done anything so intimate with *anyone*.

All my other times with women were rushed and clumsy, fueled by a few too many drinks a little too late at night. With Natalie, there are no excuses to hide behind, no alcohol dulling our senses, no anonymity to cloak the moment.

I'm exposed, vulnerable, spread open to show Natalie how much I want this.

Me. Her.

Us.

She slides her hands up my thighs, tracing my hip bones before she hooks her thumbs around my underwear and tugs to make the fabric taut between my legs.

"Fuck," she says, her voice low and raspy. "Look how wet you are."

Her tone is commanding, and I find myself shifting up onto my elbows, lifting my head so I can obey.

I'm even wetter than I thought, and with the soaked fabric stretched tight like that, I can see the outline of every fold between my legs put on display for her.

She lets go with one hand and uses it to trail a finger down the edge of my underwear, her touch feather-light on my inner thigh. My muscles strain with anticipation as I wait for her to touch me where I need it most.

She takes her time, teasing around the edges before she goes in for one long, drawn-out stroke.

I moan, fisting the blankets as my head drops back.

She repeats the action again, and then again, each stroke as torturously slow as the last.

I need more. I need to feel her without anything between us.

"I need you inside me."

The words come out on a whimper. Her hand goes still, and I crack my eyes open, wondering if I went too far, but then she whips the underwear down my legs so fast I hear a few threads snap.

She rolls over me to dig through her nightstand for a second before letting out a satisfied grunt when she finds a hair elastic. She's still piling her curls into a haphazard bun as she settles into position with her face between my legs.

Her face.

Between my legs.

I collapse against the pillows, my thighs quivering as she guides them even farther apart. Her nose glides up the crease of my inner thigh before she trails a row of kisses across the bottom of my stomach.

"You still want me inside you?" she murmurs against my skin.

"Yes," I gasp in between gulps for air.

She begins to tease me with her fingers, sliding the wetness up to stroke my clit. The whole room feels like it's rumbling, like the world is about to cleave in two. My hands dig for something solid to cling to, and I end up gripping the rails of her headboard, the metal cold and solid in my fists.

"That's it," Natalie croons. "Take it for me."

She gives up on the teasing and thrusts her finger inside

me, millimetre by millimetre, while I moan and clutch the headboard.

It's not enough. It's not nearly enough, and she seems to agree. After only a couple thrusts, she slips a second finger in, curling them at just the right angle to rip a guttural groan out of me.

"That's good," she coaxes. "Like that. Squeeze my fingers."

I clench around her, whimpering at how good it feels to do something so filthy just because she asked.

No one has ever told me to do something like that before. No one has ever ordered me around like that, in such a sweet voice laced with so much undeniable power, like concrete wrapped in silk.

She could get me to do anything.

"So good," she murmurs. "You take it so good. I want to make you come, okay?"

The words alone push me even closer to the edge. I bob my head, not caring how pitiful I look as I keep thrusting down on her.

She lowers her mouth, her lips ghosting over my stomach before she strokes my clit with her tongue.

I let out a strangled cry as white hot light streaks my vision.

She keeps going, lavishing me with strokes and swirls while her fingers continue to thrust. Somehow, she keeps her rhythm steady, like a maestro conducting a symphony that builds and builds until everything blurs together.

Her hands. My skin. Her tongue. My breath.

The smell of her. The taste of me.

It's all mixed up. We're mixed together, and I don't know how I'll ever tear us apart.

"Come for me, Brooke." Her voice is muted, murky, like we've plunged deep underwater. "Come for me."

I can't deny her.

I can't *not* do what she says.

In this moment, I'm hers, and there's nothing else I want to be.

I come so hard the headboard groans, the metal straining in my grip. I'm sure I must be making sound, but I can't hear it over the roaring wind in my head as I'm sucked up into the storm she's made of me.

I rage for her, my body howling with desire. My back arches, my legs shaking as she guides me back down to earth.

My vision is hazy as I stare at her. She lifts her head, her mouth glistening in the blinking light, wet with the taste of me.

I shiver, and she crawls up to lay her body over mine, pulling a blanket over us both.

I close my eyes, nuzzling her neck, but even as the warmth of her soaks into me with all the peace and reassurance of an afternoon sun, I can't help wondering what the hell we've just done.

Chapter 20

Natalie

I wake up to the pale light of early morning streaming through the window and the sound of someone rustling around beside me in bed. I roll over and see a head of tangled blonde hair, followed by an absolutely stunning back and a particularly gorgeous ass as the woman climbs out of bed, completely naked.

I blink, trying to figure out what angel from on high has deemed fit to visit me in my sleep.

Then it all comes rushing back to me.

"Brooke?" I croak.

She whirls around, her eyes flaring wide when she sees I'm awake.

Then she claps her hands over her tits to cover them, like I didn't just have them in my mouth mere hours ago.

"Oh no," she moans. "Oh no. Oh no. Oh no."

She keeps her chant going as she snatches the blanket off the bed and wraps it around herself like a toga, leaving me with nothing but a thin sheet.

I shiver, the fog of sleep still clearing from my brain. I rub my eyes and fumble for my phone on the nightstand.

"What time is it?" I ask, yawning as I swipe at the screen to answer my own question.

Just past seven.

Last time I checked the clock, it was four in the morning, and we'd just wrapped up round three of sex, following a quick interlude of sleep between rounds one and two.

"I can't believe we did this."

Brooke is still clutching the blanket like a scandalized old woman. She glances around my room like she's expecting the boogeyman to jump out of a corner.

"Brooke," I say, the alarm in her voice snapping me out of the last of my brain fog, "you're freaking out."

She gawks at me. "Of course I'm freaking out! We had *sex*!"

She drops her voice on the last word, gesturing between the two of us with a frantic hand motion. I have to bite back a grin. Despite the gravity of the situation, I can't help noticing how damn cute she is.

"We sure did," I say with a nod.

She glares at me like I'm a teenage boy making inappropriate comments during high school health class.

"You're my *client*," she says. "This is...this is beyond unethical! This is the most unprofessional thing I've ever done."

She starts pacing along the carpet, which is quite the feat, considering the room is so small the bed almost fills the whole floor.

Her forehead wrinkles, her lips pursed in a grimace as she keeps her blanket-toga secured with one hand and uses the other to rub her temple.

Then she freezes mid-step and turns to look at me in absolute horror.

"Oh my god," she whispers. "I'm so sorry."

Clearly, her brain is still working way faster than mine this morning. I have no idea why she's apologizing.

"For...what?" I ask when she doesn't go on.

"You're my client. You deserved better from me."

She shakes her head and presses her fingertips to her lips, her shoulders hunching.

I figured waking up today might be a little awkward, but I had no idea she'd think it was *this* bad.

"I mean..." I begin, grasping for a way to lighten the mood. "I really can't think of how last night could have been any better."

I give her a small smile before sitting up in bed.

The sheet pools around my waist, and I remember I'm just as naked as her. The cool air of the room makes goose bumps rise on my skin, and I can feel my nipples get hard.

Brooke's eyes drop to my chest.

For a moment, all I can think of is the way she looked at me last night: like she wanted to worship me, like she'd get down on her knees right there in my bedroom and pray for my touch.

I wanted her just as bad. I could have spent all night tasting her, listening to the sounds she made and feeling her legs tremble.

I think I could make Brooke Carmichael come a thousand times and still be desperate to shove my face between her legs and do it all over again.

When she finally looks up from my chest, I risk giving her another smile.

Her eyes flare, and for a second, I think she's going to crawl back into bed and forget all about professionalism.

Then she jerks back, taking a few fumbling steps away from me while shaking her head.

"Don't look at me like that!" she orders. "You're making me....think things! Things I shouldn't be thinking!"

"Brooke, seriously," I say, in what I hope is a soothing tone, "it's fine."

She does her frantic gesture between the two of us again.

"*This* is fine?"

I shift the sheet up to cover my chest.

"We're adults," I say. "We slept together. Yeah, it wasn't...professional, but I really don't think it's worth a moral crisis."

She squints at me like I'm speaking a foreign language.

"You don't?"

I shake my head. "No, I don't."

She wrinkles her nose like she's caught the scent of something rotten. "Not even considering I've, like, slept with your brother?"

I cringe. "Okay, ew."

I hadn't even thought about *that* part, and I don't want to start now.

"See!" Brooke crows, like my momentary grimace was all the evidence she needed. "It *is* a moral crisis. There are so many layers here, so many reasons we should *not* have done this."

The bite in her tone makes me swallow whatever argument I was going to make about my brother not being a big deal.

I look at her—really look at her: the way she's hiding her body from me and practically cowering at the end of the bed.

My stomach twists.

"You regret it?"

"I..."

She glances away, her voice fading into silence.

"Oh," I say. "I see."

There's a weird ringing in my ears. I bundle the sheet up even tighter around me.

"It's not that I regret it," she says, staring down at the carpet. "It's just...this is way more complicated than I gave myself a chance to consider."

I should drop it.

It's clear how she feels. She won't even look at me. It's like the daylight has seared away everything we found in the darkness, like we've burned down to nothing but cold, flaking ash.

Still, I can't let it go.

Not like this.

"Does it have to be complicated?"

I sound plaintive, desperate. I might as well be begging her, and maybe part of me is.

Maybe it's me who would get down and pray for her.

"I think it does."

She says it softly, almost tenderly, and her gentleness stings far more than if she'd cursed me out.

"So that's it?" I ask. "This was just...a mistake?"

I brace for her answer like I'm preparing for a slap across the face.

"No."

My head jerks up, and when my eyes lock with hers, I see it again, just for a moment: that fire from last night, roaring back to life.

It's only a moment, though. All the heat is extinguished when she glances away.

"It wasn't *just* a mistake. If we were different people, then maybe..."

She trails off, and her silence is like a gaping hole opening up in the floor between us.

I finish her sentence for her.

"But we're not."

She shakes her head, and she looks more pained than ever, her face twisted with something that looks a lot like panic.

The longer I sit here watching her struggle in silence, the more reality dawns on me.

She has so much more at stake than I do.

"Brooke," I say, loud enough to make her look at me again, "I don't want you to think I'm going to fire you because you won't sleep with me again."

She opens her mouth but closes it again without speaking.

"You're right," I add. "This is complicated. I see that, and if you...if you want to forget all about last night, that's okay."

She's quiet for what feels like an eternity.

Then she nods.

"I think that would be best."

I take a deep breath, willing myself to become hard as stone.

I can't crack. Not now. Not in front of her.

"Okay," I say. "Then that's what we'll do."

I swing my legs off the bed, keeping my chest covered as I bend over and hunt for my sweatpants. Luckily, they're on this side of the floor, along with my sweater. I pull them both on while Brooke gets dressed with her back to me.

I jump to my feet, plastering on a smile that feels like trying to lift a thousand pounds with my cheeks.

"I'm still making you breakfast though, okay?" I say as I

sidle past her. "I'm not kicking you out without a nice meal first."

Bailey trots over from where she's been laying on the living room floor to come sniff at my feet.

"Nice-ish, at least," I call back to Brooke while bending down to pet Bailey and ponder our limited breakfast options. "Don't get your hopes too high."

She lets out a laugh that's too strained to sound real.

I get to work on some toast in the kitchen while Brooke heads for the bathroom. The second she closes the door, my eyes begin to sting.

I brace my hands against the counter, my throat thick as I swallow a silent sob.

Chapter 21

Natalie

"*Qu'est-ce qui se passe avec toi et Brooke?*"

I glance over both my shoulders and then shoot Jacinthe a glare, like someone might be listening in on her asking what's up with me and Brooke.

Considering we're at a grocery store half an hour outside La Cloche, it's unlikely, but I still lower my voice and lean closer in the middle of the baking aisle.

"Nothing," I say. "Why do you ask?"

She raises an eyebrow. "Bullshit, *ma belle*."

I make a show out of rolling my eyes and grab a bottle of vanilla extract.

"We've been over this. I've agreed she's pretty and admitted I like spending time with her, but that doesn't mean there's anything happening. Those are just facts."

"Is it a fact that you are boning?"

I make a choking sound and try to pass it off as a scoff.

"Oh my god, how old are you, Jass?"

She plants her hands on her hips. "You did not answer my question."

It's been five days since the ice storm. Five days of trying to forget the way Brooke tasted, the sounds she made, the warmth of her curled up beside me in bed all night long.

We've still taken the dogs out together. I've still shown up to our meetings about the inn. For all intents and purposes, we've acted like that night never happened, like it was nothing but an April snowstorm: just a minor inconvenience of nature that melted away the very next day.

The accusatory arch of Jacinthe's eyebrow proves how naive I was to think *all* the evidence had disappeared, but still, I'm not about to disregard Brooke's privacy, especially not when we're all having our celebratory dinner as official business associates tonight.

"We are *not* boning," I assert before pulling out the shopping list Maddie gave us. I turn my back to Jacinthe and walk farther down the aisle to indicate this conversation is done.

She just stomps along behind me, hands still splayed on her hips.

"Did you have a fight or something, then? You seemed weird together today."

Despite my best efforts, I flinch.

I kept telling myself our stilted conversations and sparse text messages weren't a big deal, that the awkwardness between me and Brooke would smooth itself out after a few days. I convinced myself I was the only one who even noticed things were a little weird, but hearing it from someone else makes the reality so much harder to ignore.

Things have been *really* weird with Brooke. Our lunchtime walks have been filled with nothing but small talk about the dogs and what we had for breakfast before one of us makes an excuse to head home. During our design meetings, she talks more to Jacinthe and Maddie than to me, and I can't even blame her; ever since that night, it's like a huge lump swells up in my throat every time I do so much as look at her.

I keep thinking about what she said about us being different people, that maybe if the situation were different, maybe...

The *maybe* is so vague and pointless it feels like I'm back to staring at blank canvases again.

There's no point imagining a different life, a different future, a different Natalie.

I'm finally getting a grip on the Natalie I am now, on *this* life and the future I'm building. I have direction. I have a plan. I have goals and timelines and friends who are counting on me.

The tinny sounds of a pop song are pumping through the grocery store's speakers, filling the silence between me and Jacinthe. A couple old ladies push their carts past us, giving us weird looks as we stand frozen in front of the shelves stacked with flour and sugar.

"We..." I start to say once we've got the aisle to ourselves again.

I only manage the one word before I give up on finding an excuse.

If Jacinthe knows something is up, that means Maddie knows too, and just the thought of navigating weighted silences with the two of them *and* with Brooke for an entire evening makes me feel like I'm trying to heft the whole shelf of flour sacks over my head.

Maybe I could put *some* of the weight down while still protecting Brooke's privacy.

"We had, like, a...moment...a few days ago," I say after shoving a few packages into our cart and crossing them off Maddie's list.

Jacinthe grabs the cart's handle and pushes it along behind me as I begin a hunt for cherry pie filling.

"A moment, *hein*?"

Her tone has shifted from teasing to cautious, like I'm a wild animal she wasn't expecting to get this close to.

"Yeah, just one of those little moments, you know? When you become, like...*aware* of each other. I think we both realized that maybe if she wasn't working for me, and maybe if she'd never met Jonas..."

I spot the jars of pre-made pie filling and make a beeline over to grab the cherry flavour.

"Then maybe," Jacinthe says as I drop it in among the rest of the ingredients, "something might...happen?"

I press my lips together and nod, doing my best not to think about how much already *has* happened with Brooke.

We've covered the dessert items for Maddie, so I lead us over to our final stop in the beer aisle before we can head back to La Cloche.

"Is it really such a big deal?" Jacinthe asks while perusing the brightly-coloured labels of the craft brew section. "All that stuff? You're adults, right? You're not breaking any laws by having a crush on each other."

I turn away to hide another wince.

It sounds so simple when she says it like that, and there's a part of me—a part of me I've been trying my hardest to bury over the past five days—that wants to believe it could be simple.

It felt simple in the moment: the way our bodies fit together, the way she said my name, the way she dug her hands into my hair and pulled me closer.

It felt as simple as picking up a brush, like that whole night was a painting I'd had in my head for weeks before finally getting it down on paper, every stroke blending into the next with effortless harmony.

"I felt that way too, at first," I say, wandering along the row of frosty refrigerator doors, "but the more I thought about it, the more I realized it *is* a big deal. This job means a lot to her. It's really important for her career. If anything happened between us...it just puts her in a much more vulnerable position than me, and that's not fair."

Jacinthe nods, stacking some cans with cartoon logos on them into the cart.

"Hmm. Okay, I see. It's more of a risk for her."

"And the whole Jonas thing..." I add, traipsing back over to the cart. "Well, to be honest, it's just awkward. It was so long ago, and they're both different people now, but I don't know if it would ever not be weird, and there's only so much weird a relationship can handle, right?"

Jacinthe's head jerks up.

"A relationship, huh?"

All the blood drains from my face.

"I mean, I don't *actually* want a relationship with her," I blurt. "I'm just talking through all the reasons why we shouldn't have more than...a moment."

She squints at me, staring me down for so long I drop my gaze to the cart and pretend to be busy rearranging the groceries.

"You know you're my best friend, right?"

I flick my gaze back up to meet hers, squinting in confusion at the earnest look on her face.

"Um, yeah?"

"So, you can talk to me." She takes a step closer before shrugging and tugging at her sleeves. "I know Maddie is the more, ah, gentle one, but I care about you, and I want you to be happy. Always. So if there's anything you want to tell me, you can."

For a second, all I can do is blink at the uncharacteristic sight of Jacinthe looking downright bashful, but then a rush of tenderness fills my chest. I pull her into a hug, right there in the middle of the aisle.

"Merci, Jass," I say, squeezing her tight.

I hold onto her for another moment, wishing I could tell her everything, but there's nothing else to say.

Not to her, and not to Brooke.

There's nothing to do but move on.

Chapter 22

Natalie

After we've loaded the back seat of her mud-splattered pick-up truck with the groceries, Jacinthe drives us back to La Cloche.

"How's your mom doing this week?" I ask, watching the shadows of the forest whip by as we weave along the bends of the road we've been driving our whole lives.

"*La même,*" Jacinthe answers. "Good days and bad days, like always. This week has been okay, though. She's excited about the inn."

She grins, and relief makes me sag against the seat.

Her mom's MS took a turn for the worse a few years ago, and the stress of trying to manage a whole barn of horses just the two of them only complicates things more.

"Oh yeah?" I say.

She nods, still grinning. "*Ouais,* she wants to know everything about it. It's getting annoying, but it's also cute. I think it's just nice for her to have something else to think about, besides the farm."

"You know, if you guys need more help out there, Maddie and I can—"

"*Non.*" She cuts me off with the same stubborn insistence as usual. "*Merci.* We're okay. This time of year is always tough. We're used to it. Just need all this *maudit* mud to dry up so tourists want to go out on trail rides again. Summer will fix everything. It always does."

I bite back the urge to argue, to remind her that summer didn't fix everything last year and that the off-seasons are only getting harder for them.

I know it will only turn into more denial and refuted offers of help that will eventually result in a fight neither of us wants to have.

"Right," I say instead.

Jacinthe rolls her shoulders back, bobbing her head along to the French pop song on the radio.

"Once we get this inn going, *mon amie*, we're gonna have more customers than we know what to do with. I'm gonna set up a really fucking romantic sunrise ride for all our honeymoon suite guests."

I cackle. "I wasn't aware we were building a honeymoon suite."

"*Câlice, là!*" She lifts one of her hands from the wheel and gestures at me like I'm crazy. "We can't have an inn without a honeymoon suite! Where are the horny people gonna have all their freaky hotel room sex?"

"Right," I say, still chuckling. "We definitely need a place for that."

The rest of the ride home stays light and breezy, filled with jokes about the inn that help to balance out all the serious financial discussions and endless business calls our week has been filled with.

By the time we pull up in front of the house, the sky has faded from pink to dusky purple. A plume of smoke from the chimney curls up into the twilight, and I can see the glow of a roaring fire through the living room window. I know Brooke is waiting inside, already working on dinner with Maddie in the kitchen.

I pause halfway to the porch with a load of groceries in my arms and inhale the scent of damp earth tinged with a hint of wood smoke in the air. My chest wells up with a bittersweet rush of emotion as I wonder how many times *Tante* Manon had to come home to a house that was empty and cold, waiting to swallow her back up into endless hallways filled with guilt and grief.

Grief for all the things she never got to be.

I wonder what she'd say if she could see the place now, already so much brighter and warmer than it ever was during her lifetime. I wonder how she'd react if I could tell her about Balsam Inn.

I wonder if she'd think I'm making the right choice. I wonder if she'd be proud of me.

Jacinthe glances back at me from the front door, raising an eyebrow to ask what the hell I'm doing standing in the middle of the yard. I hurry after her, and we set the groceries down in the foyer so we can peel off our boots and coats.

"*Salut*, bitches!" Jacinthe calls out over the sound of jazz music tinkling in the living room and the clanging of dishes echoing out from the kitchen. "We have the food."

Maddie comes rushing around the corner, Bailey at her heels. Her hair is tied up in a haphazard bun, and she's wearing an old-fashioned frilly apron over a simple sweater dress. She must have dug it up from one of the drawers in the kitchen.

"Finally," she says. "You guys took forever."

"Show some gratitude, *fantôme*," Jacinthe shoots back, "or no beer for you."

She heaves the bag holding the beer cans back up onto her shoulder and crosses her arms.

"Praise be to you, Jacinthe." Maddie rolls her eyes while she mimes out bowing to her cousin. "Our most noble and gracious provider."

Jacinthe nods her approval. "That's more like it."

She fishes out a can for Maddie, and the three of us load up with the rest of the groceries before heading to the kitchen.

"Brooke, do you want a beer?" Maddie asks as we step inside.

Brooke is kneeling in front of the oven, peering at the shepherd's pie inside with her back to us while clutching a glass of white wine.

"I think I'll stick with this for now," she says before turning around.

Her eyes widen when she spots me. My face burns like I'm the one with my nose pressed against the oven door.

"Oh. Hi," she adds, blinking a couple times before straightening up.

"Hi," I answer.

There's an awkward silence that only breaks when I force myself to walk over to the table and dump my grocery bags on it.

"Anything we can help with?" I ask.

"I think we're just about done," Maddie says, shaking her head. "Brooke has been amazing. I just need some time to whip up dessert and get it in the oven, so why don't you all clear out and chill for a bit?"

Maddie has taken charge of this dinner with her usual gusto for organizing, and she succeeds in shooing us all out of her way.

"*Venez*," Jacinthe says, once the three of us have been

herded into the hallway like clueless cattle. "Let's go outside. It's actually warm tonight."

She sneaks back into the kitchen to grab a couple beers while Brooke and I get our shoes on. Outside, the three of us sit down on the porch steps with drinks in hand, watching Bailey sniff around the shoots of new grass just beginning to push up through the yellowed remains of last year's lawn.

"Wow. Look at that sky," Brooke says, her voice pitched low with awe. "You've got to get a sunset like this on your brochure."

The edge of the purple sky is still streaked with bold ribbons of rosy pink, like a vibrant tie-dye sheet stretched over our heads.

I wonder if there'll ever be a night I sit out here with an easel and capture the sky.

"It's really happening, isn't it?" I say. "We're really doing this."

Jacinthe thrusts her beer up in the air. "We sure fucking are! Bring it in, girlies!"

Brooke and I laugh as we clink our drinks to hers. Bailey pauses her sniffing to look over at all the fuss, and I notice she's got a stick that's a little too big for her clutched in her mouth. She comes waddling over, half-dragging it along the ground, and then plops it down at Jacinthe's feet.

"Aww, look!" I say. "Bailey wants to play with you."

Jacinthe gives Brooke a questioning look. "Does she fetch?"

"She does, but she gets tired out easily. She should be good for a few rounds, though."

Bailey wags her stumpy tail as Jacinthe gets to her feet. Still clutching her beer, she mutters to Bailey in French while carrying the stick out to the middle of the yard.

"She's going to be so sad to leave this place," Brooke says

while we watch Bailey trot after the stick. "I swear she's like a whole other dog out here."

She lets out a soft laugh, but there's a hollow note to the sound.

"I was just thinking," she adds, "I'm like a whole other person out here too. I just feel so...light. I didn't realize how heavy life had started to feel in the city. I think I'll always be a small town girl at heart."

She's quiet for a moment, quiet enough that I can hear the thump of my heartbeat ringing in my ears. Then she shakes her head and chuckles.

"Wow, who am I? I sound like a cheesy country song."

I grin, staring at her profile as she continues to watch Bailey. "I like it."

I hear her breath catch, and I wish I could take the words back.

I don't know how to be around her anymore.

I don't know how to let that night go. I just know I have to.

The silence turns strained, cloying, and I have to swallow past a lump in my throat to take another sip of my beer.

"I'm sorry," she murmurs. "I know I've been awkward since...you know."

The can nearly slips out of my grip.

That's the first time she's mentioned our night together so directly.

"It's okay," I say, fighting to keep my voice even. "I've been awkward too."

She shifts to face me. "It's really nice of you to still want me at your dinner tonight."

"Of course I still want you here," I urge. "Just because

we...you know...doesn't mean I don't still like hanging out with you."

She drops her gaze to my lap and then flicks her eyes back up to meet mine.

"I like hanging out with you too."

I have to look away and gulp down a huge sip of beer to steady myself. Before I can think of what to say next, Jacinthe starts walking back over. The three of us spend the next few minutes taking turns being the fetch master and making small talk until Maddie calls us back inside.

We manage to hassle her into letting us help set up the dining room table. Soon, the whole thing is spread with bowls and dishes holding a feast of shepherd's pie, balsamic salad, the best bread rolls La Cloche's bakery has to offer, and a piping hot cherry crumble.

We're about to tuck in when Jacinthe pushes her chair back, the feet scraping against the floor with a screech that most certainly has *Tante* Manon rolling in her grave.

"I propose a toast!" she says, swinging her beer—which has been deposited in a glass to make it seem fancier—out in front of her.

Maddie sighs, but I can see her suppressing a grin.

"Here we go," she drawls.

"To Balsam Inn!"

Maddie and I exchange a look, bracing for Jacinthe to launch into a soliloquy.

"And to us! The sexiest innkeepers Québec has ever seen!" She does a little shoulder shimmy and wags her eyebrows. "You two are my best friends, and we're going to run the best business together. We first dreamed of this when we were teenagers, and now it's finally coming true. We've been through a lot, but that's what got us here, and I have a feeling things are turning around for us all. I know I'm a lot to handle sometimes, but you put up with me, and I promise to pay it back by showing up for you and for Balsam Inn for the rest of my goddamn life."

Jacinthe's voice cracks, her hand shaking just enough for me to notice the tremor. My chest gets tight at the sight of her looking even more vulnerable than she did back in the grocery store. I share another look with Maddie, this one filled with a mix of shock and tenderness.

Jass is rarely the one to get sappy on us, at least not until she's had a couple more beers. With all her swearing and stomping around, sometimes I forget she's not always a pint-sized pinnacle of crude determination.

Sometimes she's soft too.

Brooke is the first to lean over and clink her glass to Jacinthe's. In silence, Maddie and I follow suit.

"Now hurry up and make toasts too," Jacinthe demands after clearing her throat, "so we can get drunk already."

She settles into her chair and stares the rest of us down with a steely glare until Maddie grumbles and gets to her feet.

"Okay, fine. I'll go." She picks up her wine glass. "Jacinthe is right. We've been through a lot. We've all had some struggles lately. I've realized my internship is burning me out, and I don't feel respected there. It's not what I hoped it would be, and that's been...a lot harder than I've let on."

She stares down at the table, and for a moment, she seems to get so small.

Then she jerks her head up, lifting her chin high.

"But this house, this project...it's been a light for me. It just feels right, and maybe we've got a long road ahead of us, but when has that stopped us before? I don't know exactly how things will work out, and that's scary, but I don't care. I have my friends, and we have a dream, and maybe I can trust that's enough."

She chuckles at herself, and maybe it is a cheesy line, but it still has my eyes stinging.

"To you, my friends. That includes you, Brooke," she says, grinning at her. "You're part of this whether you like it or not."

Jacinthe bobs her head. *"Ben ouais*, we couldn't do it without you."

I know I should voice my agreement too, but my throat feels too thick to speak. Instead, I clink my glass to Brooke's. The other two join in, and then I feel the weight of Jacinthe's expectant glare zero in on me.

"Natalie, *c'est ton tour.*"

I make a show out of sighing and getting to my feet, but my heart is racing, and my mind is nothing but a blank sheet.

I have no idea what to say, no clue how to put everything I'm feeling tonight into words.

"Okay, okay," I say with a shrug. "I guess there's no way out of this."

I resist the urge to tug at the collar of the button-down I put on for tonight—an actual dress shirt, rather than my usual plaid. Jacinthe has gone for a similar get-up, but Brooke is in a dress like Maddie.

It's one I've seen her wear before, a maroon number with a floaty skirt and long sleeves. A row of buttons runs up the front, and I have to squeeze my eyes shut as my blank mind decides to fill itself with images of all the smooth, soft skin I know is hiding under the fabric.

I take a deep breath and let it out.

I have to talk. I have to do something other than stand here thinking about a woman I can't have.

"When I first found out I was getting this house, I didn't believe I deserved it."

The words come flying out of me. I'm speaking a little too loud, my voice echoing through the room, but it's too late to turn back.

"I didn't think I was worth it. I mean, why me, right? The college dropout. The broke artist. The critical flop who crawled back home with her tail between her legs thinking she might never paint again."

I shake my head, shame still smoking inside me like acrid remains clinging to the bottom of a burnt pot.

"Jacinthe is right, though," I add. "All of that...it's what led me here. If my exhibition had been a huge success, I wouldn't have thought twice about selling this house and moving away. I would have used the money to try and chase more of that success, to try and make something of myself, but I know now I would have ended up even more miserable than the last time I tried to live in the city."

I take another steadying breath, and I begin to fill myself up with something new, something that isn't bitter and charred.

Something that feels a lot like a fresh start.

"I don't have to book huge galleries and sell to famous clients and get amazing reviews from everyone who sees my work. I thought I needed all that to make a difference, but I don't. I can make a difference here, and...here is where I want to be. With all of you. Doing what we love, in a place we love too."

I look around the dining room, already so different than the austere setting for the grim holiday meals of my childhood.

We have candles burning and a cheery gingham cloth on the table. We have music filling the air. We have more food and drinks than the four of us could possibly get through alone.

We have each other, too.

"*Tante* Manon didn't get a chance to love this house because she couldn't be herself here. I don't want anyone who walks through the doors to ever feel that way again. I don't want anyone to feel like they have to hide themselves, or change themselves, or fit somebody else's idea of what enough looks like."

I smack my glass down for emphasis, and Jacinthe copies the gesture.

"Hear, hear!" she shouts along with nods from Maddie and Brooke.

"I've always felt like enough in La Cloche, and I'm tired of acting like I need anything more than that. *This* is enough."

I sweep my arm out to include them. All of them. Even Brooke.

"This is more than enough. I get to run an inn with my best friends, an inn where people can create and explore and find themselves, whatever that looks like. How fucking cool is that?"

The three of them whoop with agreement, stamping their feet like we're at a football game.

"This is what I want, and I'm so grateful to have it. I'm so grateful to have all of you." I beam at them as I thrust my glass high above my head. "So here's to us, and to Balsam Inn, and…to Manon. She said all she wanted in return was for me to do exactly what I want with this place, so that's what I'm going to do."

"To Manon," my friends echo, raising their glasses up like mine.

My eyes are still stinging, but I can't stop smiling, and before I sit down, I add one more thing.

"And I'm going to paint. I don't know what, and I don't know when, but I'm going to paint again."

My chest heaves, a thrill of nerves shooting up my spine, but my friends don't even blink. They break out into cheers and more foot stamping. Jacinthe jumps up and pulls me into a bone-crushing hug that nearly sends my beer spilling over us both.

It takes a few minutes for us to quiet down and give Brooke a chance to ask, "Can I say something too?"

She's looking at me, and for a second, it feels like she can see *through* me, straight into every thought of her I can't get rid of no matter how hard I try.

"Of course," I say.

A hush falls over the room as Brooke pushes her chair back. She stands up and clears her throat.

"Thank you for having me here tonight. I know we haven't known each other for very long, but being here, being part of this...it means more than I can say."

She glances at Jacinthe and Maddie, but her eyes keep coming back to me.

"Coming back to this town was tough. I had no idea what to expect. I didn't think there was anything left for me here, but you've proved me wrong. There's friendship. There's beauty. There's...love."

My heart leaps into my throat when she murmurs the last word. She presses her lips together, glancing away from me as she goes on.

"I look at the love you all have between you, and I just feel so lucky to be here seeing it. The three of you are a force to be reckoned with, and I truly think this will be the best inn the province of Québec has ever seen. I mean, it has to be, right? I'm designing it."

Maddie and Jacinthe burst out laughing.

"But seriously," she adds, "thank you. Thank you for this opportunity. Thank you for trusting me with something so important, and thank you all for being so kind. I needed it more than I knew."

She pinches the stem of her wine glass between her fingers and holds it up to the light.

"To your future. May all your dreams keep coming true."

As we all join in one last toast together, I can't help wondering if she'd still say the same thing if she knew she's what I've been dreaming of every night.

Chapter 23

Brooke

Natalie and I stand in the doorway waving goodbye to Jacinthe and Maddie as the two of them stagger up the street towards town. I can't help laughing as I watch them clutch each other and shriek while side-stepping around puddles, even though I doubt I'd fare much better if I had to walk anywhere tonight.

We're all a little tipsy after keeping the drinks flowing well past dinner. We topped up the fire with a couple new logs and spent a few hours swapping stories in the living room, all of us bundled up in blankets and sprawled on the furniture or the floor.

My cheeks are warm from the wine, and the glow of the fireplace seems to have seeped into my body, making everything feel soft and hazy.

It's almost like the house has turned into a cocoon, a safe and secret place for things to grow until they're ready to bloom with possibility and transform into something new.

Like Natalie said, it's really happening. We're doing this. I might not be around for the whole metamorphosis,

Paint the Moon

but I'm part of this too. My ideas, my choices, my dreams—they're all wrapped up in this chrysalis waiting to burst.

I'll be a piece of this house forever.

I lean against the sturdy wood of the doorframe, and I realize the connection goes both ways.

This house will be a piece of me forever too.

"God, they are so drunk," Natalie says, shaking her head as she takes a fumbling step back inside the foyer.

The fumbling makes it clear she's well into tipsy territory herself, but I suppress a grin instead of calling her out on it.

"I'll go finish those dishes," she tells me as I close the door.

"Let me help," I insist, following her down the hall to the kitchen.

She and Jacinthe made a stab at the dishes as a thank-you to Maddie for doing most of the cooking, but Natalie decided it would be wiser to send the two cousins home together rather than letting Maddie stumble into town alone.

That leaves just the two of us in the house.

It's the first time we've been alone inside together since the ice storm. Our business meetings have all been accompanied by either Maddie or Jacinthe, and we've kept our walks close to town these days, where it's normal to bump into other dog owners and have someone else break the silence between us.

There's no one coming to interrupt us now.

I stare at the back of Natalie's head as she hunches over the sink, her hair tied back in a low ponytail that's inches from escaping its bonds and springing free.

My breath catches as I think about what it felt like to

have my hands buried in those thick locks, tugging her closer.

My skin prickles with heat, like I've sat too close to the fireplace. Despite Natalie's protests, I step up to the counter and start drying dishes with a vengeance.

I need the distraction. I need to give my hands something else to do besides itch with the urge to slide the elastic out of her hair myself and pull her to me all over again.

It was only one time.

The mantra I've been repeating for the past five days echoes through my head, and I dry the pot I'm holding in time with the words.

Just one time.

That has to be enough. I can't let myself want more.

"Have you heard anything from your landlord?"

I pause with the dish towel clutched in my hands.

"Oh, um, yes, actually." I force myself to continue drying. "Apparently things are pretty on schedule. It won't be completely done by the end of next week, but I'll be able to move back in."

Out of the corner of my eye, I notice her expression harden into a frown for a second before she smoothes her features back out.

"Next week," she says, her voice eerily monotone. "Wow. That went fast."

I nod. "Uh-huh."

The atmosphere in the kitchen has turned suffocating, like the chimney is backed up and the room is filling with smoke too thick to breathe. Coughing up small talk feels like choking on the fumes.

We finish the dishes in silence. I've memorized where everything goes now, and I help get the pots, pans, and trays settled back into their places.

"I think you know this kitchen better than me now," Natalie says after she has to ask me where the rolling pin lives.

I force a chuckle. "Well, the whole thing is getting renovated in a few weeks. You can put stuff wherever you want after that."

She rests her back against the counter and crosses her arms over her chest. I mimic her pose, leaning up against the wall on the other side of the room.

"It's gonna be weird," she says. "You not living here anymore."

I nod. "Yes. It is."

It hasn't even been two weeks, but my routine in the city already feels like it belongs to somebody else, like the woman who battled traffic every morning and had to walk a whole block just to find some grass for her dog to play on is someone I read about or saw in a TV show.

That woman is everything I wanted to be, everything I spent years shaping my life into, but somehow, right now, she doesn't feel like me.

"Bailey will miss it here."

I can't talk about myself. I can't think about what leaving this house will mean for me.

It shouldn't mean anything at all. It was a temporary solution, a simple getaway, a one-time thing.

It was only one time.

Just one time.

"I'm sure she will."

Natalie's eyes feel like they're piercing straight through me, pinning me to the wall. My gaze darts down to her mouth.

Those full lips of hers. I can still feel them teasing mine apart, opening me up, her tongue sweeping out to taste me.

I shiver, and I know she sees it.

There's no way she doesn't see how much I want her.

She stands there like a statue, like her regal features are carved from stone. My hands begin to tremble. I clench them into fists at my sides.

I feel it again: the same aching urge to obey her.

I want her to command me. Order me. Tell me to drop to my knees and admit I will miss this. I will miss her. I will play the one night we had over and over in my head for the rest of my life, like a record caught in a loop, the sound of her—the sound of *us*—spinning around and around years after I've forgotten exactly what colour her eyes were.

I don't want to forget.

A pang of longing hits me like a blow to the chest, making me sag a couple inches down the wall.

I don't want that stormy blue to fade. I want to memorize the streaks of grey and cobalt, the way her irises always look like a shifting storm howling across a lake. She is a dance between calm and chaos, and I want to hurl myself straight at the point where her edges crash together.

I want to get swept up in the eye of her storm.

Again.

Once was not enough, and as I look at her now, all poise and defiance while we both brace for the end of this, I don't know how I ever thought it could be.

I don't know how I ever thought I could stop this.

"Natalie…"

My voice breaks, and the trembling travels from my clenched fists all the way up my arms.

"Yes?"

"I…"

My knees are shaking too.

"Brooke, what is it?"

The few feet of space between us feels like an endless chasm in the middle of the kitchen floor.

I don't know how to cross it. I *shouldn't* cross it, but every inch of my body is begging me to try.

"I can't...I can't stop thinking about you."

I stifle a gasp as the truth slips out. Natalie flinches, and then all the concern in her face morphs into a stony glare.

"Don't. Don't do that."

The bottom of my stomach drops.

"You can't say that to me." She stares at a spot on the wall just above my shoulder. "We said one night. We agreed on one night, and I've been...I've been trying my damn hardest to respect that. I've been trying to let this go. I understand your reasons. I'm not mad, but, Brooke, you can't say things like that to me, okay? Not if you really want this to stop."

I can see her chest heaving, straining the buttons of her shirt. Her voice is raw, her words ground out through a clenched jaw. A blistering heat races along my skin as I realize the bite in her tone isn't just for me.

She's angry with herself too, angry at how much she wants this.

I can see it in her face, hiding behind all the bitterness. There's a naked desire that wants to spring free.

"What if I don't want this to stop?"

Her brow furrows even more, her glare somehow ice cold and scalding all at once.

She thinks I'm playing with her, but I've never been more serious in my life.

"I know what I said," I tell her. "I know there are so many reasons not to do this, and none of them have changed. I shouldn't want more, but I...I do. I want you.

Again. It makes no sense and I wish I could stop it, but I can't."

I have nothing else to give her. I have nothing to offer except the truth.

She stares at me for so long it feels like the moon outside must have crossed the whole sky by the time she answers.

"I can't either. It's still there. Every time I look at you."

She's whispering, a coarse longing edging her words. I feel the sound trail over my skin, tracing the shape of me.

"So what do we do?"

"What do you want to do?" she murmurs. "You have to call this one, Brooke."

I want her to give me the answers. I want her to take the lead. I want nothing more than to follow wherever she'll take me, but she's right.

It's my terms we're breaking. It's my choice we're undoing tonight.

"I'm still...I'm still leaving."

I have to squeeze my eyes shut before I can continue.

I can't think when I'm looking at her.

"I have a whole life to go back to, and I still work for you. There's still...so much in the past too."

I pause again, panting as I call up the courage to throw everything I've just said straight out the window.

"But I can't go the whole rest of my life without tasting you again."

My eyes fly open when I hear her suck in a breath.

She looks ready to pounce. I can see the muscles of her neck straining. My pulse surges, the sound of rushing blood filling my ears.

"It's driving me crazy, Natalie," I rasp. "Wanting you this bad."

A muffled sound lodges in her throat. Her eyelids flutter for a moment before her gaze turns steely again.

"Tell me what you want."

My body jerks like it's coming to life, like I've been sleep-walking for decades and her command is the only thing that can wake me up.

"I want..."

I trail off and press my lips together, wondering if I should lie, if I *could* lie.

What I want is obscene.

It's far too much.

But she asked.

She asked, and I need to tell her. I *want* to tell her. I want her to see the quaking, vulnerable parts of me and make them feel safe and strong.

"God, I want to be on my knees for you right fucking now."

The counter groans, the wood creaking under Natalie's grip.

"Damn it, Brooke," she hisses.

My thighs twitch, squeezing together. I can already feel the pressure building between them.

"I can't change the future," I say, still panting. "I can't change the past either. I've only got right now, Natalie. Do you understand?"

I sound frantic. I feel frantic, like the walls are closing in and all the air is being sucked out of the room.

"I do."

She nods, and I focus on her.

Only her.

"And right now...I want you again." My tongue darts out to lick my bottom lip, like I can already taste her there.

"I want you as many times as I can possibly have you before I need to leave."

She stares me down, and I wonder what she sees. I'm a shaking, breathless mess, so weak for her I can't even stand without the weight of the wall behind me.

Still, I know I'd tear through every wall of this house just to have her again. I'd fight anything for her, including myself.

"You mean that?" she asks.

"I do." My thighs twitch again, and her gaze darts down to the hem of my dress. "You have no idea how much I mean that."

"Show me."

My spine jerks again, snapping to attention at the sound of her command. Goose bumps break out along my arms. The hairs on the back of my neck stand up, and I shiver like she's thrown open the window behind her to let the night air in.

I glance at the dark yard through the glass and see it's dappled with silver streaks of moonlight.

Like her painting.

Like the strokes of her brush on my body.

It was always there, waiting, shimmering like a vision in the moonlight.

That's what she said about the moon girl on her wall.

Maybe there's always been a moon girl in me too, waiting to come down from the sky.

I sink to my knees.

Natalie sighs, a sharp burst of air that spurs me on despite the burning in my cheeks.

I crawl.

With my head bowed and the knees of my tights skimming the floor tiles, I crawl to her.

My dress brushes the backs of my thighs, hitching up higher with every shift of my hips. My hair hangs in curtains around my flaming face, and it's the best burn I've ever felt, this mix of shame and desire. I can't tell where one ends and the other begins. They flow into each other, feeding on one another.

By the time I raise myself to my knees at Natalie's feet, I can't tell if I'm about to cry or come or dissolve into some tumultuous mix of both the second she touches me.

I wait, and when her thumb brushes my chin, I tremble.

She tips my chin up, and slowly, I raise my eyes to meet hers.

"Good girl."

Everything blurs.

The whole world melts, liquefies, dissolves into sweet, sticky syrup like she's bathed me in the honey dripping from her tongue.

Any part of me that still had a hope of warring against this gives in and lays down its arms.

I don't want to fight this. Not ever. I want to drown in her sweet and sting myself on her sharp.

"This is what you want?" she asks, her thumb still hooked under my chin.

"Yes," I rasp.

She nods, pulling her hand back, and it's all the invitation I need.

I shove the edge of her shirt up so I can trail my lips along the bottom of her stomach. I kiss along the ridges of her hip bone, and she curses, giving up her grip on the counter so she can hold my hair back for me instead.

It takes me a couple tries to get the button of her jeans unhooked. I tug the zipper down and then inch the jeans lower down her thighs, following along with my mouth.

She's wearing a plain pair of burgundy underwear, and somewhere in the back of my mind, I notice they almost perfectly match my dress.

The rest of my mind is busy revelling in how smooth her skin feels under my lips. I kiss along the top of her thigh, darting my tongue out and then moaning when that makes her grip my hair a little harder.

I grab her hips and press my mouth between her legs, kissing and licking her over the damp fabric. My eyes roll back, another moan bursting out of me as the taste of her hits my tongue.

I pull back just long enough to yank her underwear to the side and then dive in with my tongue again, her skin slick and warm against my lips. The hard kitchen floor is starting to make my knees ache, but I don't care. I pull myself in deeper, burying my head between her legs as her fingertips dig into my scalp.

I can hear her gasping. Her hips flex into my hands. She's grinding on my face, and it's the hottest thing I've ever felt in my life.

I could stay like this all night, her hands buried in my hair and her pussy rocking against my tongue, but the clothes still tangled around her legs are keeping me from getting as deep as I want.

With a growl I've never heard myself make before, I pull back and help her scramble out of the jeans and underwear. Then, still on my knees, I push her up against the cupboards and hitch one of her legs over my shoulder.

She gasps in surprise as the new angle lets me lick up the length of her. I dip my tongue inside her, moaning at the taste, and then trail the tip of my tongue up to circle her clit.

She cries out, and I glance up to see her with her head

thrown back, one of her hands scrambling to find purchase on a cupboard door handle.

I wrap my arm around the thigh slung over my shoulder, giving myself leverage to slide in closer and truly fuck her with my tongue.

It's the first time I've done that with anyone, and I moan as loud as she does while I thrust my tongue in and out of her.

I want her everywhere. I want it messy. I want the taste of her all over my face, dripping down my chin and seeping into my dress.

The desire comes out of nowhere, the need for it overpowering.

I want to devour her. I want to consume her like a feast.

I want to kneel here like her good girl and let her feed me.

She starts rocking her hips again, riding my tongue. I tip my head back farther and let her have her way with me.

She really is dripping down my chin by the time I slide my tongue up and curl the tip so she can grind her clit against it while I slip two fingers inside her. She's so soaked I gasp, the fingers of my other hand digging into her thigh. Her hips are bucking uncontrollably now, the cupboard door banging as she yanks on the handle.

"Brooke," she gasps. "Brooke."

My name.

My name on her lips.

I find just the right pace with my fingers and the perfect strokes with my tongue to have her gasps turning into screams. I put every ounce of concentration I have left into keeping my movements steady, clutching her leg tight, pressing into her until there's hardly any room left for me to breathe.

She comes with a spasm that makes her spine arch, her head knocking against the cupboards with enough force I'm almost worried about her.

She doesn't seem to care. She bucks against me again and again, her shouts fading to a keening moan and then a shuddering sigh. I don't stop licking her until she tugs my head up, her chest heaving.

Her eyes are hazy, just glittering slits under drooping lids. Her cheeks and neck are flushed.

I'm breathing almost as hard as she is. I try to ask if she's all right, but I can't get enough air in my lungs.

She slides her leg off my shoulder and then sinks down off the counter to sit beside me on the floor. Her hair is a mess, and she's still got her shirt and socks on. The corner of her mouth lifts in a lopsided grin, and my heart swells at the sight.

"Come here," she slurs, holding her arms out.

I fold myself into her embrace, straddling her lap so she can hold me. I wrap my arms tight around her neck, and she tucks her head under my chin.

"Brooke," she murmurs into my chest.

"Yes?"

She tips her head back to meet my gaze, her expression still a little loopy. I grin back at her.

"I just want to tell you," she drawls, "that you are a very, very, *very* good girl."

A fresh thrill of desire shoots through me. My hips flex into hers.

She starts kissing up the side of my neck, and I wonder if we'll ever make it to bed or if we'll spend the rest of the night right here on the kitchen floor.

Chapter 24

Brooke

"I have a proposition for you."

Natalie's fingers trace along my spine under the covers. I wiggle in closer to her, until my butt bumps against her hips and she lets out a satisfying groan.

"And what might that be?" I ask.

She catches a lock of my hair between her fingers and gives it a gentle tug.

"God, you're mischievous in the morning," she mutters, her voice laced with just enough of a threat to make me shiver.

This is our third morning together in a row. We passed out in bed around 2AM the night of the dinner with Maddie and Jacinthe. At that point, it was just a necessity, but the way we lingered under the sheets the next morning certainly wasn't, and the two nights she's ended up sleeping here since then haven't been last-minute arrangements either.

She could have gone back to her apartment. I could have asked her to leave. We could have limited ourselves to sex with no cuddles or sleepovers, but there's something about lying in a bed with our bodies tangled together and the morning sun peeking through the blinds that feels almost as irresistible as the sex itself.

The thought has alarm bells going off in my head, but I do my best to turn their volume down.

We both know what this is. I'm still leaving. I'm going back to my life in the city, and she's staying here in La Cloche. The lines we've blurred will solidify back into stark dividers.

We both understand that.

"You mentioned a proposition?" I remind her as her fingertips brush the nape of my neck.

"Right," she says. "You distracted me."

Instead of continuing her path along my body, she rolls away from me and onto her back. She reaches behind her head to fluff the pillows and then sits up straighter.

I do the same, a few pinpricks of worry needling my stomach.

"My parents want to know if you want to come over for dinner tonight," she says once I'm settled.

My mouth drops open.

Whatever I was bracing for, it wasn't that.

"They don't know about...this," she rushes to add, gesturing between us. "Obviously. It's just that yesterday, my mom asked how much longer you'll be in La Cloche for and then said they really want to have you over for dinner while you're still here. I think they're worried you might feel like they're not happy you're working on the inn."

A pang of guilt hits me. I never got around to having that cup of tea with Natalie's mom.

The guilt is quickly followed by a jolt of surprise.

I don't know when I started thinking of her as Natalie's

mom instead of Jonas's mom, like she's always been in my head.

"Oh, I don't think that at all," I stammer. "I'm sorry if I made them feel that way."

"No, no." Natalie shakes her head. "It's nothing you did. They're just, you know, very into peace and harmony and stuff. I think they feel like they need to make a gesture of repair towards you, or whatever my mom would call it."

I chuckle along with Natalie, but I still feel a surge of gratitude for her mother, just like I did that night she showed up at the house and gave me a hug I didn't know I needed.

She might be a bit cheesy sometimes, but a little more peace and harmony would have gone a long way when I was growing up with my own mom.

"Anyway," Natalie says, "I haven't given her an answer yet. I told her you're pretty busy with work and getting ready to go back to the city in a few days, so she won't be offended if you say no. I get that it's a little weird."

"It's not weird at all."

I pause, and the weight of history seems to press down on us, like a heavy blanket thumping down on the bed.

The bed in which I am naked with my ex's sister.

"Okay, so maybe it's a little weird," I amend, "but I actually think it's really nice of them."

"So you'd like to go?"

I press my lips together, pulling the sheets up higher over my chest as I force myself to really think about this.

I haven't stepped foot in that house in over six years. It's the house where I've had at least a dozen dinners with the people I thought would be my in-laws someday.

That was a different time, though. A different me. I've

spent six years building a wall between who I was then and who I am now.

A simple dinner isn't going to bring it all crashing down.

"Yes," I say. "I would."

Natalie gives me a doubtful look. "There's no pressure, just so you know. I don't want you to feel like you have to do anything."

The concern in her voice makes a twinge of tenderness tug at my chest. Over the past few days, she's been extra careful to remind me she doesn't ever want my job to be the reason I say yes or no to anything with her.

I roll onto my side, clutching the edge of the pillow as I smile at her. "I know. I appreciate that. I really do want to go."

She turns onto her side as well, our faces just inches apart. "Okay, great. I'm glad."

I lift my head enough to glance over at the alarm clock and check just how much time we've got left to lie here.

Among other things.

She follows the direction of my gaze and groans when she spots the clock.

"Shit. I have a phone meeting with some suppliers for the inn in like twenty minutes," she says, rubbing her eyes. "I'm covering a shift at the shop this afternoon, but how about I pick you up after that and drive you over for dinner?"

I shimmy in closer and only hesitate for a second before pressing the tip of my nose to hers.

"That sounds nice."

We both end up giggling when she rubs her nose against mine, but as soon as she nudges my head back and locks her lips to mine, all the laughter whooshes out of me with a gasp.

I decide there's a lot we can do in twenty minutes.

∽

"Come on in, *les filles*!"

Natalie's dad pulls open the front door of the small, two-storey house before we've even had a chance to knock. Belle comes galloping down the hallway behind him and nearly knocks his legs out from under him in her rush to say hello.

Bailey yips in greeting behind me, and the two of them take off running circles around the small front yard.

"Sorry I'm not *that* excited to see you," Natalie's dad jokes.

We all chuckle. He takes a couple steps back into the house to give us room to come into the entryway.

"It would be hard to match that enthusiasm, Marcel," I say.

I hold out the bottle of organic wine I hunted down in the only *dépanneur* in La Cloche during my lunch break. I was only mildly surprised La Cloche's corner store carries organic. It also has a section for low-budget art supplies and some cheap essential oils.

"Here," I say. "This is for dinner."

"Why, thank you, Brooke!"

Marcel takes the bottle, and the two of us get a good look at each other for the first time. He looks almost exactly the same, save for a bit more grey hair around his temples and a few extra lines creasing his forehead. He looks far more like Jonas than Natalie does. Same square jaw and long nose. Same bright, charismatic smile that verges on goofy.

For a moment, all I can do is blink at him while a

hundred memories flash through my mind like the frames of a film strip.

Jonas's smile is what got me. It was a smile that said everything was going to be all right. All my life, I'd been looking for someone to tell me that, someone who could make it true.

In the end, it wasn't him.

In the end, I had to do it myself.

"So good to see you, Brooke. What's it been? Six years? Almost seven?"

Marcel's voice pulls me back to the present. I bob my head and plaster on a grin. The dogs come charging inside and zoom past us to take off towards the smell of something spicy wafting out of the kitchen.

"I think it's close to seven now, yes," I say, using my coat and shoes as an excuse to turn away and get my head on straight.

Jonas isn't here. This dinner isn't about him. It's about me and my client and her parents wanting to make a nice gesture.

Everything else is in the past.

Natalie steps up beside me and holds her arm out. It takes me a moment to realize she's offering to put away my coat.

"Oh, right," I mutter, after Marcel says he's going to go put away the wine.

I hand my pea coat to Natalie, and she slings it onto a hanger before tucking it away in the closet beside the front door.

Then she comes close enough to murmur, "Are you okay?"

My breath catches at the sudden proximity and the way her eyes glimmer in the dim light of the entryway. My heart

Paint the Moon

clangs against my ribcage like a warning bell, but I squeeze my hands together behind my back and remind myself I'm fine.

This is all fine.

I can handle it.

"Just a little...weird," I whisper back.

"Not too weird?"

I shake my head. "It's fine. Just strange to be back in this house."

She opens her mouth like she wants to say more, but we're interrupted by the arrival of her mother, who swans into the room in a billowing blue tunic dress with the bottle of wine I brought clutched in her hands.

"Brooke, did you go out and find me an organic syrah?" she asks. "How did you know this would go perfectly with dinner?"

I practically leap away from Natalie with a jerky hop that's anything but subtle. Thankfully, Cynthia seems too caught up admiring my wine selection to notice I was just nose to nose with her daughter.

"Lucky guess?" I say.

She gives the swirling pattern on the bottle's label an appreciative tap. "You are such an angel."

She turns to Natalie and opens her arms for a hug. Once they've let go of each other, she lifts her arms out towards me and tilts her head.

"Up for another hug, sweetie? No pressure."

No pressure.

That's always how I felt in the Sinclair house—like I could actually breathe without choking on all the goddamn pressure to do the right thing, say the right thing, be in exactly the right place at the right time.

Growing up, a calm and uneventful night seemed to

hinge on me being six steps ahead of my mother's reactions at all times, but in this house, calm seemed to be the status quo. Sure, I'd see the family squabble or snap from time to time, but there was a baseline harmony they always returned to, a true north that never moved.

I step into Cynthia's waiting arms, and just like when she hugged me that first night at the house, I find myself sagging into her touch.

She squeezes me tighter.

"Thank you so much for coming over, honey. It's lovely to have you back." She pulls away and beams at me, giving my arm a pat before tugging me down the hall. "Let's go chat in the living room. Marcel is finishing up the skewers on the grill."

The living room hasn't changed much. The old-fashioned woodstove has a cheery fire blazing inside. The saggy corduroy couch is piled with paisley cushions, and the walls are covered with mismatched frames displaying a selection of artwork and photos.

By now, I've seen enough of Natalie's paintings to recognize a few of the pieces as her work, but there's something charmingly juvenile about these ones, like a teenager's awkward attempts to find their personal style.

The paintings are still gorgeous, of course, with her signature use of vibrant, almost psychedelic colours. I wander over to look at one that shows a landscape of gold and crimson mountains. I can almost smell the crisp scent of falling leaves,.

"Did you know Natalie was only twelve when she painted that?" Cynthia asks from where she's pouring three glasses of wine on top of a credenza.

"Twelve?" I echo, wheeling around to look at Natalie for confirmation.

She nods and tries to play things off with a casual shrug, but I can see the bashful smile tugging at her lips.

"I'm pretty sure I couldn't draw more than a stick man at twelve," I say.

Cynthia chuckles as she brings me my wine glass. "Me neither. I still can't draw more than a stick man, come to think of it, but Natalie was an artist from the start."

"She's very talented," I say, clinking my glass to Cynthia's before taking a sip.

The syrah is earthy with a slight spicy kick, and I mimic Cynthia's hum of appreciation.

"It's nice to have someone around who appreciates a good wine," she says, casting a fake glare at Natalie. "My children are too hipster to enjoy anything except their precious craft beers."

Natalie rolls her eyes. "No one even says hipster anymore, Mom, and I do drink wine sometimes."

She lifts her own glass off the credenza and takes a pointed sip.

Cynthia guides me over to the couch and takes the armchair for herself. Natalie claims the other couch cushion. Belle and Bailey decide to make an appearance, settling onto the yellow rug in front of the woodstove now that they've realized there are no scraps waiting for them in the kitchen.

I grin at the sight of squat little Bailey tucked up against the giant bloodhound before getting sucked up into a conversation about Balsam Inn. Natalie and I take turns answering Cynthia's dozens of questions, and despite the inquisition, it's impossible not to catch some of her enthusiasm.

"This is just what the town needs," she says, clapping her hands and almost sending some of her wine sloshing over the rim of her glass. "So, Brooke, how much do you take care of on-site once the renovations begin?"

"Oh, well, I don't really need to be on-site much at all," I explain. "Once the design is all approved and in the hands of the contractors, I only need to come in if something is really wrong. There are usually some tweaks that come up along the way, but I can do all that remotely. To be honest, I'm pretty close to finishing everything Natalie needs me for."

"Oh."

I look over at Natalie and see she's gone rigid, staring at the bulb of her wine glass like she's just spotted a vision of doom swirling in the sediment. She jerks her head up and clears her throat when she realizes I'm staring at her.

"I, um, didn't realize you were that close to done," she says. "That's good news."

Her voice sounds oddly monotone.

"I mean, of course I'd love to see the finished product," I add, "and I'm here for whatever you need through the whole process."

She nods. "Right. Yeah. Of course. It's just, um, kind of crazy to think it's all really happening. Like, it's not just plans anymore, you know?"

Cynthia claps her hands again, letting out a little squeal.

"It's happening!" she sing-songs. "Gosh, I am so proud of you. Both of you. So much talent right here in my living room."

She climbs out of the armchair and gives us each an approving pat on the shoulder before announcing she's going to check on Marcel.

As soon as she's disappeared with a flourish of blue fabric, I shift to face Natalie.

"You okay?"

"I'm fine," she says, avoiding my eyes.

She sets her wine down on the clunky wooden coffee table and adjusts the clip holding her hair out of her face before she looks at me.

"I guess I just didn't realize that when you leave this week, you're, like, *really* leaving."

I open my mouth to protest, but then snap it shut when I can't think of an argument.

There is no argument.

I've run out of excuses to spend time in La Cloche.

The only reason left to be here is her, and that's not going to work.

This is never going to work.

Still, I find myself leaning in towards her, lifting a hand to cup her cheek and smooth my thumb along her jaw, like I can wipe all the tension away.

"I'm not gone yet," I murmur.

Her eyelids flutter closed, but she doesn't pull away. She leans into my touch, her lips parting.

"Cynthia says I just *have* to try this wine."

Natalie gasps, her eyes flying open as Marcel comes bumbling into the living room. I snatch my hand back and slam my back against the arm of the couch in my attempt to scramble away from her.

Meanwhile, Natalie leaps to her feet like the couch is on fire and charges for the credenza, where Marcel is giving us a confused look that seems blessedly oblivious to what he almost walked in on.

"Uh, yeah, here, let me pour you one," Natalie stammers.

She fixes him a drink just in time for Cynthia to announce that dinner is served. We file into the kitchen, Natalie and I silent and avoiding eye contact. I get seated across from her, and when our hands brush as she passes me the salad bowl, we both jerk like we've been shocked.

"What is it?" Cynthia demands. "Don't tell me there's a bug in the salad. I picked one out when I was making it, but I thought that was the only one."

Natalie gags as she settles back into her seat. "Ew, Mom, you gave us a bug salad?"

"It's *organic* salad," Cynthia says with a wave of her fork. "From a small farm, so yes, sometimes it might have a little bug or a bit of dirt. It's *nature*."

The two of them launch into an argument about their differing standards for salad. Marcel takes a hearty bite of lettuce like he couldn't care less either way, but when I look down at the leaves on my plate, my stomach rolls in a way that has nothing to do with bugs.

I almost kissed Natalie.

Right there in the living room.

The living room where at least five photos of my ex-fiancé are hanging on the walls.

I'm sitting at the table where I planned a wedding that never happened, in the town where I swore I'd never make the same mistake again.

I'm sitting across from a woman I quite literally can't resist, who makes me weak at just the thought of her.

I told myself this was different. I told myself I wasn't the same, but I'm still making stupid decisions just to try and cling to something that feels good even though, deep down, I know it can't possibly be right.

"Is that a car?"

Marcel squints past the table and into the living room, where the front window gives a view of the dark driveway outside.

Sure enough, a pair of headlights is beaming straight through the glass.

"Who could that be?" Cynthia asks, with the casual curiosity of a small town resident who's used to neighbors stopping by.

We all strain our ears to listen as the faint rumble of the car's engine shuts off. The thud of a door closing comes next.

"Might be Jean-Claude returning my tool kit," Marcel says, pushing his chair back. "I'll get it."

Before he's even had a chance to leave the kitchen, the sound of the front door swinging open echoes down the hall.

"What up, family?" a man's voice calls out.

I freeze, my blood turning to ice.

Natalie's face is ashen, her eyes growing wide with horror.

Even Marcel and Cynthia look stricken, their gazes darting back and forth between me and the hallway.

"Hello?" the man shouts.

The sound of paws clacking on hardwood fills the silence.

"Hey, Belle. Oh, hey. Who are you?"

A quick glance at the spot Bailey just occupied tells me she's gone to greet him too.

"Mom!" he yells. "Dad! Hello? Who is this corgi?"

None of us move. The creaking footsteps coming down the hall might as well be the soundtrack of a horror movie.

There's nowhere to run. There's nowhere to hide. There's nothing to do except sit here and wait as the man I thought I was going to marry, once upon a fucking time, comes striding into the room.

"Was anyone going to answer m—"

He cuts himself off, stumbling to a halt when he finds everyone staring, and I get a split-second to look at him before he notices me.

He seems a little older, his face a bit leaner with a few creases around his eyes, but mostly, he just looks like Jonas: floppy, golden-brown hair, thick eyelashes, wide shoulders and a towering build under his usual construction guy get-up of faded blue jeans and a flannel.

He looks like the kind of guy who'd swing you over his shoulder and carry you up the street when your heels are killing you after a long night. He looks like the kind of guy who's always got a dirty joke to make you smile when all you want to do is cry.

He looks solid.

He looks like he'll always be there.

But he wasn't.

I wish I could blame him for it. This would all be so much simpler if I could blame him, but looking at him now, it's clearer than ever that when I fell for Jonas, I was just falling for what felt like a solution to a problem.

The problem was me.

It's still me.

"Brooke?"

I watch the emotions flit across his face when his eyes lock with mine: confusion, shock, panic, and—for just a flash so quick I almost miss it—shame.

"Brooke," he says again, as solemn as a eulogy.

Natalie jumps to her feet, pushing her chair back so hard it tips over and crashes to the ground. Belle and Bailey both whine.

"Jonas, what the hell are you doing here?"

She's got her back to me now, but I can see her shoulders are set in a tight line, and I imagine her expression is just as stern.

Jonas's eyebrows draw together. "Uh...laundry?"

Someone snorts, and it takes me a second to realize it's me.

Everyone's attention snaps back to me, and I cover my mouth with my hand as a bellow of laughter threatens to force its way out of me.

This is surreal. I almost expect a reality TV crew to burst out of the cupboards and tell me I'm being pranked.

My thirty year-old ex-fiancé still drives a half hour to do laundry at his parents' house, and I can't even judge him for being an immature mess because I'm literally screwing his sister.

All of a sudden, it's like the house is crashing down around me, like the whole town is caving in and dragging me down, down, down into a deep, dark chasm where there's nothing to do except face the reality of my choices.

I said I'd never do this again, and I did.

I came crawling back to the town where I thought I'd get my fairytale. I let myself get swept away all over again, only this time, it's worse.

This time, I'm not running from a nightmare. I'm running from the perfectly stable, reliable, independent life I built so I'd never need to rely on anybody else the way I let myself rely on Jonas.

Or Yves.

Or any other man.

Or woman.

I wasn't supposed to need anyone.

It wasn't supposed to be like this.

"Brooke?"

I'm not sure when Natalie came over, but I look down

and find her kneeling beside my chair, staring up at me with frantic concern.

"Brooke. Talk to me."

I can't speak. I can't move. My whole body is numb, like I've plunged into the icy depths of a frigid lake, so deep the light can't find me and there's no way to tell up from down.

Or past from future.

It's all tangled together, bound in endless knots I can't undo.

"I need some air."

It feels like I'm breaking out of a coffin, but I manage to get to my feet. I keep my gaze fixed to the floor as I rush past Jonas and down the hall.

"Brooke, wait!"

Natalie is right on my heels, but I don't turn around. I head straight for my boots, fumbling to get them on and then digging blindly through the closet until my fingers brush the familiar wool of my pea coat.

I shove my arm through one of the sleeves and don't even bother with the other as I reach for the door.

"Brooke, please."

The ragged plea in Natalie's voice makes me pause. Bailey waddles up to me in the meantime, her ears twitching with agitation.

"I need some air," I repeat, tugging on the door handle. I step outside without a glance back. "Come on, Bailey."

I brace for Natalie to grab the door, or shout, or do something else to stop me, but she lets me go.

I wait, hovering on the front step, but there's no sound of movement on the other side of the door.

Bailey whines.

"Come on," I say, patting my leg while my voice hitches on a sob. "Let's go for a walk."

Chapter 25

Natalie

I find her at the church.

Brooke is huddled under the small shingled roof above the doorway, backlit by the single light left on to illuminate the concrete steps. The rest of the churchyard is dark, nothing but a meager glow emanating from the solar-powered string lights lining the white picket fence.

She's got Bailey on her lap. She stares down at her hand as she strokes her fingers along Bailey's fur, and she doesn't seem to notice me approach.

I stop on the sidewalk, just before I reach the path up to the church. In the shadows, I let myself drink in the sight of her. The light above her head turns the edges of her blonde hair into a halo.

I remember the first thought I had, the first time I ever saw her: that she looked like a Christmas angel, like some ethereal visitor from the heavens splashed in watercolours across the pages of a children's book.

My hands are stuffed into my pockets, but they still twitch with the urge to paint her, to capture the planes of her cheeks, the swell of her lips, the swoop of every golden eyelash.

I keep walking, making my footsteps heavier on purpose so I don't startle her. She jerks her head up, squinting into the street before she spots me.

It's been almost half an hour since she left my parents' house. She only had a few minutes' head start before I took off after her, but there was no trail to follow, no sign of her for several blocks. I thought I'd have to go back and start searching for her with my car.

"Hi," I say once I'm only a couple feet away from the stairs.

"Hi."

I nod my head towards the steps, asking permission, and she shifts over so I can join her.

"I think everybody in this town must think I'm crazy."

I can't read her tone. She looks as dazed as she did when she seemed to go into a trance at my parents' table, but at least she's talking now.

"Why's that?" I ask.

"Because I had a bit of a panic attack and really needed to run, but Bailey can't go that fast, so I picked her up and started sprinting. I was running through town with a dog in my arms and my coat falling off. I'll go down in history as the crazy corgi lady."

She lets out a strangled laugh.

"There are worse things to go down in history for," I say, forcing myself to chuckle along with her.

We lapse into silence. My gaze drifts over to the picture-perfect view of Rue Principale. The sidewalks are dotted with chatting pedestrians piling into restaurants and bars. The streetlights cast a warm amber glow over the scene, a few blinking neon signs adding pops of colour.

"Are you okay?" I ask. "The panic attack? It's...good now?"

I sound like a Neanderthal, but her silence is so unnerving I can't keep my thoughts straight.

"I'm okay," she says, in that same hollow, almost alien tone.

A second later, she shakes her head.

"Actually, no, I'm not okay, but I'm not having a panic attack anymore."

The thought of her all alone out here, gasping for breath and reduced to huddling in a churchyard, makes guilt slice through me like a vicious knife.

"I'm so sorry," I say. "I had no idea he would be there. My parents didn't either. I grilled them on it as soon as you left. Trust me. I promise they weren't setting you up."

I'm sure that doesn't make it any better, but I at least want her to know nobody planned this.

"I know they wouldn't do that," she says.

She winces, and I resist the urge to slip my arm around her shoulders.

All I want is to make everything okay for her, but I don't know how.

"I'm sorry I ran out."

"Brooke, you don't have to be sorry," I urge. "You needed some space. That's perfectly understandable."

She shakes her head. "It's not."

I squint at her face while she continues to stare into the street, but it's no use. I can't read her.

"It's not perfectly understandable," she says, her voice taking on a jagged edge. "It's pathetic."

"What?" I bark. "What do you mean?"

"I..."

She tips her head back, staring up at the beam of light emanating down from above the door.

"I thought I was going to get married here. Right here. Right in this church. Or non-denominational community center. Whatever it's called."

She huffs a bitter laugh and straightens her neck out.

"That was so long ago," she says. "I thought I'd become a completely different person since then, but I haven't, have I?"

I really need to stop squinting at her, but none of this makes any sense. She's told me herself what a different person she is, how much she's changed, how she doesn't want the same things she used to.

Maybe she just needs someone to remind her.

"I think you have."

She shakes her head again. "You don't know me."

I can't stop myself from gasping. My body goes rigid, hardening itself against the pain.

I don't know what we are, but we sure as hell aren't strangers.

At least, I didn't think we were.

"I mean, you haven't known me that long," she adds, her voice softer.

She looks so pale, almost translucent, like she's fading away right here on the steps.

I'm not gone yet.

That's what she told me. She held my face and said that to me not even an hour ago, but here she is, already miles away.

But I won't let her leave.

Not like this.

Not so soon.

"That doesn't mean I don't know you well."

Her head jerks up at the force in my tone.

"I know you're strong, Brooke," I continue. "You're incredibly strong. You're tough. You're independent. You're—"

"I'm not."

She looks anguished, her face creased with pain, and I have no idea why.

She should be angry or frustrated or even sad about seeing Jonas, but she shouldn't be *shrinking* like this.

It doesn't make sense.

"Why do you say that?"

"Because I...I'm just doing it again, aren't I?"

She spreads her hands, jostling Bailey in her lap, and gives me a pleading look, begging me to get it, but I don't.

"Doing what?"

She squeezes her hands together, hunching over like she's got a stomach ache.

"Falling for...this town." Her voice cracks. "Falling for a fairytale. Falling for something that doesn't exist."

My pulse flares, thumping so hard and fast I can feel it in my throat.

"I don't know about a fairytale," I say, "but I know this town exists. I...I exist."

Our eyes lock. Her bottom lip quivers, and before I can think better of it, I start leaning in, closing the gap, pushing aside everything and everyone between us.

I don't want anything between us ever again.

Just as my eyes start to close, she pulls back.

"I let this go too far." She's panting, scrambling to pull her coat tighter around her like it's a shield. "I shouldn't have let it start at all."

The words slam into me like a blow to the chest, shattering my ribcage, jagged fragments splintering straight into my heart.

She nudges Bailey off her lap and gets to her feet.

"I'm sorry," she says without looking at me. "You didn't deserve to get caught up in my mess."

She gets all the way to the bottom of the staircase before she glances back and realizes Bailey isn't following.

The corgi is standing at my side, ears pinned back as she whines and looks back and forth between the two of us.

Brooke pats her thigh, the tapping getting more and more frantic the longer Bailey refuses to move.

The ache in my chest is getting sharper, hotter, morphing from pain to a searing anger.

She doesn't get to end it like this.

Maybe it was always going to end, but she doesn't get to write us off as nothing but a mistake.

"You are *not* a mess, Brooke." My voice echoes through the yard. "You're acting like your life is falling apart, but it's not."

Her eyes narrow at the harshness in my tone, but I can't bring myself to be gentle anymore.

I have to get through to her.

"How would you know that?" she asks.

"Because I just spent months doing exactly the same thing."

I take a step down, and then another, until I'm towering just a couple feet above her.

"Everyone kept trying to tell me one failed art show didn't have to define my life. *You* kept telling me that, and you know what? You were right. So take a leaf out of your own book and remember that just because things went wrong once before, doesn't mean they're just going to keep going wrong again."

I cross my arms, watching her struggle to come up with a response.

I wish I felt satisfied, but her stunned silence just makes another sharp ache radiate through my ribcage, and it only intensifies when all the fight seems to seep out of her like a candle snuffed by the wind.

She pulls her coat tighter around her, a shiver wracking her body.

"But they are going wrong," she says, so quietly I have to take another step closer. "This is wrong."

She nods between the two of us, like everything we are can be encompassed by a dismissive jerk of her chin.

A chill sweeps up my spine, and part of me wants to collapse right here on the cold concrete steps and accept defeat.

Maybe it would hurt less. Maybe the icy despair would be better than this white-hot pain, but I've spent months giving into the stagnation of despair already.

I'm not doing that with her.

"Why does it have to be wrong?"

Her jaw drops, and she blinks a few times, like that's the last thing she expected me to say.

"You're my-my client," she stammers, "and—"

"But I won't always be. You just said yourself you're practically done designing the inn."

I cross my arms tighter over my chest and tilt my chin up, daring her to contradict me.

"You're still his—I mean, you're still Jonas's sister."

Her eyes are wide, and she glances around the churchyard like there might be more arguments hiding behind the bushes or strung along the fence, ones I can't refute.

"So what?" I say with a shrug. "You hadn't seen me for six years. We barely even knew each other before that.

We're not committing some incestuous crime. Why is it wrong?"

Bailey has clambered down the steps to butt her head against Brooke's legs, but Brooke doesn't even seem to notice.

She swallows and shakes her head. She almost looks like she's trying not to puke, and I'm about to ask if she's okay when the words she's holding back shoot out of her as a hoarse shout.

"Because I'm just repeating the same mistake!"

Mistake.

The word echoes through the yard, through the street, through the whole fucking town.

I take a step back, shaking my head.

"Is that really what you think of me?" I ask, my voice as hollow as I feel.

She lifts her foot like she's about to rush towards me, but then she plants it back down on the ground. Her hands are balled into fists at her sides.

"No, that's not...that's not what I mean." She squeezes her eyes shut for a second, breathing hard through her nose. "I mean I'm latching onto this town, this life... I'm too *happy* here, Natalie. Don't you get that?"

She slashes one of her arms out, swiping at the air in desperation, but all I can do is shake my head again.

"No, I don't. I don't get that at all."

She digs her hands into her hair, spinning on her heels to stare out into the street. A few tourists shriek with laughter, clutching each other as they stumble into Mack's Bistro. A pick-up truck rumbles past us, the bed loaded up with firewood. I recognize the driver as one of my dad's buddies.

"I used to think small towns like this were this magical place where nothing bad happens," Brooke says once the truck has disappeared down a side street. She's still standing with her back to me. "All the bad in my life happened *after* we left our small town, and I just kept looking for something or some*one* who could make life feel that safe again, that simple."

Her shoulders slump as she turns back to face me, that same distant, haunted look from before returning to her eyes.

"But it's not simple. Nothing is ever that simple, and I promised myself I would never rely on another person for my happiness again. *I* need to take care of me. *I* need to make me happy."

She sounds so far from happy I almost want to laugh at the irony, but mostly, I just want to hold her.

I want to hold every version of her who had to live through the pain and loneliness that made her believe this about herself.

"Brooke..."

I climb down the stairs until we're standing face to face. The light from the church silhouettes the side of her cheek and glints on her hair.

"There's a difference between completely relying on someone else for all your happiness and just...*being* happy with someone."

I pause, hoping she hears me, hoping that somewhere deep inside her, she can accept the truth.

Then I tell her the rest.

"I'm happy with you."

She winces, squeezing her eyes shut again. She doesn't open them back up this time.

"Natalie," she whispers, "don't."

I shake my head even though she can't see me.

"No, I'm going to. I have to. I need you to know."

Maybe it will change everything. Maybe it will change nothing, but I'm done acting like I don't get a say in the course of my own life.

People can tell me I'm wrong. *She* can tell me I'm wrong, but I know how I feel. I know it as sure as I know what colours I would use to paint every strand of her hair and each of those delicate eyelashes.

"Nobody in my life was able to pull me out of the hole I was in. I was stuck. I couldn't see a way forward, and you...you made me *want* to move forward."

I rake my gaze over her face, committing every curve and angle to memory.

"You made me want to be somebody again. You made me want to create and...and thrive. You made me get up in the morning and feel excited again, just by being yourself."

She doesn't open her eyes, but she makes a soft sound in the back of her throat.

"I'm not going to tell you this town is magic, but you..." I lean in as close as I dare, dropping my voice lower. "*You* are magic, Brooke. What happens when we're together—*that's* magic. Being with you...it's like painting with colours I've never even seen before."

Her eyes flutter open, and she's Brooke again, not some distant ghost of the past.

My Brooke.

Here. Now. With me.

"Natalie..." she murmurs.

My heart lurches. My arms ache to reach for her, but I don't want to go too far, not until she knows everything.

"I don't want it to end, okay? Not when you leave this week. Not when the inn is done. I want to try this. I want to *trust* this."

I'm shaking now too, but I keep my gaze locked on hers and force myself to keep going.

"I want more nights with you. I want more days with you. More walks with the dogs. More dinners with my friends. I want to meet your friends. I want to stay up all night in front of a fireplace, telling each other the stories of our lives. I want to get lost in the woods together. I want you there when the inn opens. I want to cheer you on at your job. I want...I just *want* you, Brooke. I know I wasn't supposed to, but I do. I'm not going to pretend like that's wrong."

I'm panting by the time I finish, my breath clouding in the air between us.

"I...I don't know what to say."

Brooke is standing stock-still, not even blinking.

"Say you want me too."

She makes that choked sound again.

"I want you, Natalie. Of course I want you."

My breath catches. My arms start to reach for her, but before I get the chance, she turns away.

"But I don't think I can let myself have you," she whispers. "Maybe you can trust this, but...I don't think I can."

It feels like all the streetlights burn out one by one, plunging the night into total darkness.

Everything goes dim and cold.

"I'm sorry," she says without looking at me.

Then she starts to walk away.

She gets as far as the sidewalk before Bailey lets out a whine. The dog is still standing right where Brooke's feet used to be. She makes a few anxious snuffling noises while tossing her head.

"Bailey. Come," Brooke orders, in a harsher voice than I've ever heard her use before. "*Now*, Bailey."

Bailey yips and hesitates for another moment before taking off down the path.

I don't feel anything as I watch her waddle away from me.

I'm numb, like I've been standing out here for hours, the damp of the night seeping into my bones.

"Where are you going?" I rasp.

Brooke shudders. "I just...I need to be alone. I'm going back to the house."

"Let me drive you," I say, my voice flat.

I have to focus on the practicalities. I can't think about what any of this means.

"I'll walk."

I start trudging up the path towards her. "It's far. It's cold out. I—"

She shakes her head. "I'll be fine."

"You—"

"I'll be fine, Natalie."

She takes a step back.

Away from me.

"Just...just let me go."

I stumble to a halt. All I can do is watch as she crosses the road, heading up the sidewalk into town.

Bailey is the only one who looks back at me.

Chapter 26

Natalie

"So yeah, that's the end of it. She left. Just like that."

Maddie and Jacinthe watch me with the exact same expression: mouths hanging wide open like fish in an aquarium, eyes bulging. Jacinthe is holding her beer bottle halfway to her mouth, and Maddie is slowly tilting her head to the side, like she does on the rare occasions when she's faced with an equation she can't solve in three seconds flat.

We're sitting at our favourite booth in Mack's Bistro. The place is bumping tonight, loaded up with locals buzzed on beer and the rush of spring fever. The room is stifling from all the body heat.

I'm still wearing my jacket, despite the sweat beading on the back of my neck. I know my skin is heating up, but I don't feel it.

I've been numb since that night at the church with Brooke.

"*Câlice,*" Jacinthe swears, just loud enough to be heard over the music and chattering voices.

That's how I know she's truly shocked. Normally, Jacinthe's swearing occurs at the top of her lungs.

"I mean, we had a hunch something was going on with you two," Maddie says, sharing a glance with her cousin, "but this is..."

"Bananas," Jacinthe summarizes. "Fucking bananas *de criss.*"

She gives the table a slap for emphasis and takes a swig of her beer.

I have to laugh at how ridiculous the phrase 'bananas of Christ' is. That's a new one for her.

My amusement only lasts for a couple seconds before the numbness sets in all over again, just like it has every time I've gotten a momentary distraction from thinking about Brooke.

She left La Cloche the day after Jonas showed up at dinner. She called me, but I was working a shift in my mom's shop and missed it. By the time I listened to her message about needing to leave in time to check into a hotel in Montreal, she was already gone.

In the message, she told me it'd be better for everyone if we kept things strictly professional from now on. That was almost a week ago, and all I've heard from her since are a couple design related updates sent via email, with Maddie and Jacinthe included as recipients too.

I know they're my business partners, but it still felt like a slap in the face, like even the intimacy of a direct email is too much for us now.

I do have plenty of direct messages from my whole family sitting unanswered on my phone. They all want to make things right with Brooke and apologize for the shock of Jonas showing up out of nowhere. I can't tell them what's wrong with Brooke is actually *me*. I wasn't even sure how to

Paint the Moon

tell Maddie and Jacinthe. I'd retreated into my apartment for three whole days, like a hermit in a cave, before the two of them showed up on my doorstep and dragged me out to the bar tonight.

I can't even blame the alcohol for telling them the whole story. I'd only had a couple sips of beer before it all started pouring out of me like a burst pipe, the pressure to handle this all by myself finally too much to contain.

"So how are you...feeling?" Maddie asks, blinking at me from behind her glasses like a therapist poised to jot down some notes.

"Honestly?" I say with a shrug. "I have no idea. I haven't felt much of anything since she left."

Maddie nods. "It sounds like you're still in shock. That makes sense. A lot happened to you in just a few weeks."

"God." I prop my elbows on the table so I can bury my face in my hands. "Has it only been a few weeks?"

I could have sworn I walked into Café Cloche and found Maddie sitting there with Brooke months ago.

Jacinthe claps me on the back, hard enough to make me cough.

"There, there, *là*," she says, rubbing an awkward circle along the back of my flannel.

I lift my head and grimace at her.

"Has anyone ever told you you're, like, really bad at being comforting?"

There's a split-second of silence before the three of us burst out laughing.

"What?" Jacinthe barks. "This is how I comfort the horses! It's good enough for them."

"They don't even speak English," I shoot back.

She gasps and places a hand on her chest. "Of course

they do not. They are good Québécois horses. They only speak French."

I give her shoulder a shove. "You are so ridiculous."

I can't keep myself from chuckling, and she flashes me a devious grin.

"Aha! I made you laugh. Not so bad at comforting after all, *hein*?"

I concede with a resigned shake of my head. "No, not so bad at all."

I take another sip of my beer and then look between the two of them.

"Thank you, guys. Really. I needed this. Saying it all out loud...well, it fucking sucks, to be honest. It makes it all real, but maybe I need it to be real. I just...I don't know how to process it. I wasn't even sure who I *was* when Brooke showed up in town, and now..."

Their expressions turn serious again.

"And now?" Maddie prompts.

I slouch against the back of the booth and spare a glance around the room, at the crowds of people revelling in the irresistible vigor of the earth coming back to life.

The whole town is thawing, stretching its limbs like a bear coming out of hibernation to sniff the springtime air. The trees are budding. The birds are flying back from down south. The days are getting longer, stretching into the kind of lingering twilight that always makes you want to stay out just a little later than you planned.

I've seen La Cloche come back to life like this every year, felt the whole community breathe a sigh of relief when the tourists begin to trickle back in. All the local business owners are hard at work making plans, dreaming of the busy summer days to come and flinging themselves into action to prepare.

I thought I'd be one of them. I thought that rush of energy springing up from the blooming earth would be coursing through me too, but I can't feel it.

I can't feel anything.

"I'm still not sure who I am," I say, picking at the edge of the peeling label on my beer bottle, which is dripping with condensation in the steamy room. "I know what I *want*. I want to run the inn. I want to give it my all, but...how do I know I've got enough to give?"

I gave Brooke everything. I laid it all on the line for her, right there on the sidewalk. I gave her the truth, and it wasn't enough.

"You are enough, Natalie."

Maddie's voice pulls me out of my thoughts. She reaches over to grip my shoulder, squeezing hard.

"You are more than enough."

Jacinthe grabs my other arm.

"*Ben ouais, c'est vrai*. Remember when you made that speech at our dinner? You spoke from your heart, man. You were so brave. Yeah, Maddie and I have had our shit to deal with too, but you didn't even think you *wanted* to do the inn, and now look at you!" She gives me a little shake. "Being a badass business lady and everything. You've got this. It feels right, so you're doing it, even when it's tough. *That* is enough. Don't forget that just because some hottie from the city can't do the same."

I chuckle at her description of Brooke, the sound thick and watery. My eyes sting, and I tilt my head so I can rub my cheek along Jacinthe's knuckles where she's still clutching my shoulder.

"Thank you," I say. "That genuinely was very comforting, Jass."

She scoffs. "That wasn't just comforting. That was some damn poetry!"

I tip my head back enough for her to see me roll my eyes. "Okay, let's not get ahead of ourselves. It was nice."

She tuts but doesn't pull her hand away. On the other side of me, Maddie sighs.

"As much as it pains me to inflate my cousin's ego, Jass is right." She pauses to give Jacinthe time to let out an obligatory whoop. "You've come so far, Natalie, and nothing should make you doubt that."

With the two of them by my side, as steady and solid as the two fir trees standing sentinel on either side of Balsam Inn, I give myself a chance to believe what they're saying.

Brooke might be gone, but everything else I've found over the past few weeks is still here. My life is still blooming with potential, and I have two of the best friends in the world to help it grow.

I just have to let them.

"I don't want to be stuck again." The burning in my eyes has gotten worse, and I blink to clear my blurring vision. "But I'm scared moving forward means that first, things are going to really, really hurt."

Maddie gives me another squeeze. "They probably are."

I'm about to give her a look to demand if she's bent on stealing the Worst Reassurance crown from Jacinthe, but then she slides out of the booth so she can come close enough to wrap me in a proper hug.

"But you've got us to help you," she says, nuzzling into my hair. "Always."

Jacinthe joins the pile, and I don't even care that we're getting a bunch of weird looks or that a rowdy group of guys is shouting 'Awww!' at us from over at the bar.

Paint the Moon

I let them hold me, sniffling as a couple tears finally manage to escape and run down my cheeks.

Somewhere deep inside me, the numbness begins to crack and flake away, like an old coat of paint. Underneath, I'm raw and weak, in need of some serious repair, but I can handle it.

I've already taken on one fixer-upper project. I can do it again.

"God," I say, wriggling my arm through our tangle of limbs so I can swipe at my face. "Running an inn is already making me such a fucking sap. Since when do I cry this much?"

Maddie strokes my back. "It's okay to let it out sometimes. It's okay to lean on people."

On cue, I slump against her, making her wobble on her feet before she catches her balance. We all laugh.

"You're right," I say. "It is. I just wish…I wish Brooke saw that too."

She could have leaned on me. We could have figured it out together.

I picture her walking away into the night, and all I can think about is how alone she looked, like a tree without a forest to call home.

"*Je sais, ma belle,*" Maddie murmurs.

We stay twined in our group hug for a few moments longer while I get myself under control. It might be okay to let things out with my friends, but becoming fodder for town gossip about 'that girl who was sobbing in Mack's last night' is taking things a little too far.

Once we're all settled in our seats again, I lunge for my beer, draining what's left in just a few gulps. Jacinthe gives me an approving slap on the back and says the next round is on her.

She shuffles over to the bar, and by the time she comes back balancing three fresh bottles in her arms, the speakers are pumping out an old pop song that stirs some vague memories of miscreant teenage behaviour.

They get clearer when the chorus hits and I recognize the song as one of the biggest hits of the summer Jacinthe and I graduated high school. It became the backing track for some extremely cringe-worthy but somehow wildly entertaining life choices.

"*Mon dieu*," Maddie says as Jass sets the beer bottles down. "I don't think I've heard this since I was a teenager."

Jacinthe is already jamming out, bobbing her head and mouthing the lyrics.

"Fuck yeah!" she shouts. "This was our jam! Mack kicked me out of the bar for trying to dance on a table to this."

I somehow convinced her to wear a crop top that night. She claimed to hate every second of it and said it was cramping her style, but as soon as she brings up the story, I'm hit with an image of her swaying her hips and proudly gyrating her bared midriff for half the town to see.

She hikes a knee up onto the booth's bench like she's about to grant us a follow-up performance, but Maddie tugs her back down.

"You do not need to repeat that event," she hisses.

I'm cackling at the sight of them, and I can't stop swaying in my seat. The music feels like it's seeping into my bloodstream even quicker than alcohol.

"Maybe we do," I say.

"Huh?" Jacinthe squawks as I slide out of the booth and snatch my beer off the table.

"Let's dance!" I call over my shoulder, already leading

Paint the Moon

the way to the only somewhat empty space on the floor. "There hasn't been a dance party at Mack's since last summer."

I have to shimmy my way past some middle-aged women in polar fleeces having what sounds like a very intense discussion about tulip bulbs, but I manage to secure a spot big enough to begin swaying in time to the beat.

"Mack does not like dance parties in here," Maddie says, casting an apprehensive look at the bar once she and Jacinthe have squeezed in beside me.

Sure enough, Mack is glaring straight at us while pouring a soda.

Jacinthe shrugs. "Since when have we ever listened to Mack?"

Even Maddie can't argue with that, and soon the three of us are all shoulder shimmying and whipping our hair around. I fling my jacket off in time with a crescendo in the music, laughing as it lands on Jacinthe's head.

She starts dragging it along her body like a burlesque dancer with a feather boa, which makes the crowd of people gathering laugh along with me. Within a couple songs, there's at least a dozen of us all rocking out.

We dance for so long my face gets flushed and my back turns slick with sweat. I take turns spinning around with friends and acquaintances and even a few random tourists. Everything gets brought to an end when Jacinthe decides to give her table dancing routine another shot and ends up getting chased out the front door by Mack, armed with a broomstick.

Maddie and I decide we'd better not leave her unsupervised and dash out after her. We all end up leaning against the building and gasping for breath, making each other laugh with our imitations of Mack's frantic broomstick waving.

"How about a nightcap at Maddie's place?" Jacinthe says once we've calmed down.

Maddie squints at her. "You know, you could *ask* to come to my house."

She shrugs. "My place is too far."

I cross my arms and watch them squabble with each other, grinning at the familiar sight.

No matter how old we get, these two can always find something to argue about.

"I think I'm gonna turn in, actually," I say once I've decided it's time to break things up.

Jacinthe pouts. "It's so early."

I chuckle. "Yes, but it's also a weeknight, and as you put it, we are badass business ladies now."

We say our goodnights, and I thank them for getting me out of my apartment and listening to my life update.

"Of course," Maddie says, stepping out of our hug goodbye. "Who knows? Maybe Jass and I will finally find people to date and you'll get to return the favor."

Jacinthe barks a laugh that carries all the weight of a jaded small town lesbian. The two of them take off, headed for Maddie's car parked on the other side of the road.

I shove my hands in my pockets and make the trek over to my place. The wooden stairs up to my apartment creak and groan, and I can't help thinking about the night Brooke and I climbed them together in the middle of the ice storm, the wind howling in our ears.

Inside, I switch my fairy lights on and make myself a cup of mint tea before sprawling out on my couch. I was planning on binging some mindless sitcom before bed, but I end up staring over at my desk instead.

Paint the Moon

I never did get it cleaned up. The surface is still scattered with paint sets, brushes, stray pencils, and a few sketchpads with mug ring stains on their covers.

I blow on my tea, staring at the mess for another few minutes before I get up and grab one of the sketchpads and a pencil to bring back over to the couch.

I swipe at my phone screen, pulling up my favourite Maggie Rogers album, and turn the volume up until the soft guitar notes fill the room. There's an errant scrunchie on my coffee table, and I use it to pile my hair into a haphazard bun.

I cross my legs before pulling the sketchbook onto my lap and flipping to a blank page.

I close my eyes, toying with the pencil, and take a deep breath before forcing myself to picture her.

Every detail.

Every soft inch of skin.

The bow of her lips.

The hollow at the base of her throat.

The little pink birthmark just behind her ear, so tiny you'd never find it unless you kissed her there.

I wince, all my instincts telling me to pull back from the memory, to shut it down, to go numb.

I make myself feel instead, and it hurts. It hurts far worse than it should. We only had weeks together, just the first few chapters of a story she decided not to tell, but I ache like the empty shelves of a library watching tome after tome get set alight.

Still, I feel it.

I feel it because in every beautiful thing I've made, there has been some measure of hurt, some pain I healed with a paper, a pencil, and a riot of dazzling colour.

That's what my art does. It heals. It heals me, and even

if it's not hanging in huge galleries far away from this little town, I know it heals other people too.

I keep the image of Brooke shimmering in my mind, and I press the tip of the pencil to the blank page.

Chapter 27
Brooke

I look up from my computer screen to see Eric dipping out of his office, jacket already on and a pretentious leather briefcase clutched in one of his hands.

Who even uses a briefcase anymore?

I click over to my inbox, giving it a refresh just in case Eric managed to answer my email within his last couple minutes of work.

There's nothing.

I sent him a message yesterday morning to ask if we could schedule a review of my work on Balsam Inn and talk about future opportunities. I've been back in Montreal for four days, and he hasn't even remarked upon my return to full-time hours at the office. On my first morning, he made a passing joke about catching me looking for a jazz playlist on company time again and then kept walking straight into his office, like he didn't even notice I'd been gone.

My skin crawls at the memory, and before I can give myself time to have second thoughts, I pop up from my chair and make a beeline over to him just as he's walking past the reception desk.

"Hey, Eric."

He glances over his shoulder but keeps moving towards the door. "Oh, hey, Brooke. Have a nice night!"

I plant my feet in a wide stance. "Wait a minute."

Out of the corner of my eye, I notice Layla shooting us curious glances while pretending to be engrossed by her laptop at the reception desk.

Eric finally grinds to a halt once he's got a grip on the door handle.

"Gotta go, Brooke! It's past five. Can you shoot me an email instead?"

I swallow down the urge to remind him of all the times this firm has sent me frantic pleas for help well past five in the evening.

"I did," I say instead. "Yesterday morning. I wanted to check that you got it."

He screws up his face to show this isn't ringing any bells. "What was it about?"

The urge to back down and tell him not to worry about any of this rises up from some ancient part of me, threatening to swallow my courage like some monster from the deep, but I widen my stance on the floor and brace for a fight.

I *have* to fight. I've got too much hanging on this job. This is the job I shaped my whole life around after Jonas walked out on the wedding. This is the cornerstone of my existence here in Montreal. I've spent years building this career, ignoring all the parts of me crying out for something different. I committed to practicality instead, to stability, to cold hard reality instead of a dream that might not come true.

I told myself it would be worth it.

I told myself the same thing when I walked away from Natalie.

So I'll *make* it worth it—even if that means having a showdown with my boss when he's already halfway out the door.

"Me," I answer Eric, "and my future at this company. I've almost finished my first job as a project manager, and I'd like to review my performance with you and talk about what comes next."

My tone is still professional, quiet enough that the few remaining staff members at their desks won't be able to overhear, but I keep my delivery firm and enunciate my words despite how fast my heart is beating.

Eric lets go of the door handle.

"Right. Yes." He turns to face me, his mouth turned up in a tight grin that does nothing to reassure me. "The thing is, this quarter is not such a great time for that. Now that your schedule is clear, Pierre's been asking to have you back on his team. I think that's a great place for you for now. We can talk more once we do the company-wide performance reviews in August."

My jaw drops.

"Are you serious?"

Eric's eyes dart around the room as he lets out a strained chuckle.

"Dang, Brooke. Did you skip your cup of coffee this morning?"

My hands are starting to tremble, but not with nerves. I clench them into fists behind my back as betrayal and rage race along my skin like searing flames.

"No, I didn't," I say, somehow managing to keep myself from shouting. "I'm confused. We planned on discussing future management opportunities for me if everything went well with this project."

Eric nods, turning up the dial on his fake smile. "And we will! Just not right now."

I can feel my eyes bulging. My whole body feels like it's swelling up with the effort to keep myself in check.

Eric lifts a hand like I'm a growling stray dog he can tame.

"Look, you're a great employee, Brooke," he says, in the world's most condescending attempt at a comforting voice. "You're one of the rocks of Leung Designs. You've been with us since the start, and we need you where you are. For now."

This is exactly what he said *before* I took the job in La Cloche—the job that was supposed to change everything.

I shake my head like I haven't heard him correctly.

"I'm sorry," I say, my voice rising half an octave, "but how long is *for now*?"

Eric sighs and then makes a show out of pulling his phone out of his pocket.

"Look, I've really got to go," he says, flipping the screen around to face me and jabbing a finger at the time. "Let's circle back to this another time, okay?"

He's serious.

He's actually serious.

This project hasn't changed anything at all.

I watch him turn back to the door handle and slip outside into the hall. The floor seems to drop out from under me, dragging me down to another dimension, another reality, where Natalie is still standing in front of the church, the steeple rising behind her like a looming white specter against the night sky.

I left her.

Paint the Moon

I left her standing right there, ready to give me everything.

"Break room. Now," Layla's voice says from behind me.

Her hands clamp down on my shoulders. She spins me around, steering me across the office. I know I must be walking, but I can't feel my feet.

Layla yanks the frosted glass door open and ushers me inside. I stand like a zombie in the middle of the room, where the usual sticky coffee mug rings are coating the top of the glass table and the smell of someone's egg sandwich from lunch is still lingering in the air.

This is what I left La Cloche for. This is all I've got going for me.

"Okay, babe," Layla says once she's pulled the door shut to cut us off from the rest of the office. "Let it out."

Just minutes ago, I was fighting back a shriek, but now, I can barely manage a whisper.

"What just happened?"

Layla comes to stand in front of me, wagging her chin from side to side and peering into my face like she's a paramedic scanning for injuries.

"He's an asshole," she says. "I can't believe him."

"He promised we'd talk about me moving up to manager after this project." There's no way I made that up, but he brushed it aside like it was a figment of my imagination. "It's the whole reason I agreed to do it."

Layla rubs her hands up and down my forearms. "I know. He's being ridiculous."

I stare at a stain on the tiles behind the break room sink. The congealed, reddish-brown glob looks like it might have been ketchup at some point.

My stomach churns.

"I don't know what to do," I rasp. "I don't know where to go from here."

Layla rolls her shoulders back like she's gearing up to ride into battle with me.

"I can make sure you get in to speak with him tomorrow. I'm not above *accidentally* cancelling one of his other meetings."

I shake my head. "I don't think it would make a difference."

"He'll listen," she says, crossing her arms. "He has to."

"He actually doesn't have to. He doesn't have to do anything at all. It's his company."

I chose to work for a firm because it was supposed to be stable, reliable, a guaranteed path to career growth and achievement if I just put in the time, stayed patient, and proved my worth.

It was supposed to outweigh all the benefits of my long shot, fairytale dream of going freelance.

"I need this to work out," I say, squeezing my fists so tight my nails dig into my palms. "I need this to be worth it."

Layla purses her lips and stares at me for a moment.

"This job?" she asks.

"This...this life," I admit. "I need my life to work out, Layla. I'm supposed to be able to make the right choices. I'm supposed to be able to make things work. I need to know I can do it."

I start pacing the room, struck by the sudden urge to move as my thoughts go from sluggish to racing out of control.

"I've built my life here around making the practical choice again and again. It's practical to live in the city. It's practical to work for someone else's firm instead of trying to build my own. I won't let myself chase some stupid fairytale of what life could be, but what life actually *is*...well, it's...it's..."

A lump gets lodged in my throat, forcing me into silence.

"It's not working out?" Layla murmurs.

I shake my head, stumbling to a halt and squeezing my eyes shut like I can block out the truth.

"It *has* to. I need it to. I've...I've given up so much."

I crack my eyes open and find Layla watching me with her head tilted to the side.

"No one who knows you would ever doubt your ability to take care of yourself and make good choices, Brooke," she says. "You're extremely self-sufficient."

She presses her lips together, and I can tell there's more she wants to say. I brace for whatever is coming next.

"Have you ever thought maybe...maybe you don't need to be quite so extreme? Like maybe you've, I don't know, overcorrected?"

I narrow my eyes. "I'm not overcorrecting by making sure I don't keep making the same mistakes."

"I think you've made a lot fewer mistakes than you think," she tells me. "Some people you loved let you down, in some pretty big ways, and I get that it sucks. Your mom, Yves, Jonas... It really fucking sucks, but it doesn't have to say anything about *you*."

It does, though. There had to have been *something* I could have changed if I was smart enough, or strong enough, or less desperate to have somebody else fix things for me.

"I shouldn't have let myself get in those situations in the first place."

Layla huffs and uncrosses her arms before a taking a step closer.

"Brooke," she says, locking her eyes on mine. "Listen to

me. You weren't wrong. You weren't bad. We all have to be at least a little vulnerable if we want a chance to be happy. That's the trade-off. Sometimes it's a shit deal, but it's the truth."

I grunt in agreement. If that's true, then it really is a shit deal.

Layla hesitates for a second before she asks in a soft voice, "Is any of this about...Natalie?"

I can't keep myself from flinching. She's gotten the whole story out of me over the past few days, piece by tattered piece, but she hasn't given me much input of her own. I'm still not sure where she stands on the whole me hooking up with my ex-fiancé's sister angle.

"Maybe," I blurt. "Yes. I don't know."

I shake my head and then press my fingertips to my temples as the whole room seems to spin.

"I know you feel like you had to leave her," Layla says, "but—"

"I don't know what I think," I cut in. "Not anymore."

Nothing makes sense. This job. Natalie. My life in Montreal. All of it is a tangled mess.

"Okay." Layla takes a deep breath. "Well, just so you know...if *she* is your chance to be happy, I don't think it's too late to give it a shot."

I flinch again. I can only meet her stare for a few seconds before my shoulders slump, sagging under what feels like a hundred pound weight dropping straight on my back.

I want to believe her. I want it to be that easy. This is all so fucking heavy I can barely stand.

Like she can read my mind, she pulls me into a tight hug, letting me lean all my weight on her for a long moment before she helps me straighten up.

"Thank you," I murmur. "God, I'm so tired."

My eyelids are drooping. I feel like I've run a marathon in the past ten minutes.

"You should go home," Layla says. "Get some takeout and watch a movie. Have a bath. Pet Bailey."

I bob my head and raise my hand to stifle a yawn. "Takeout does sound nice."

Layla slips into maternal mode, ushering me out to my desk so I can pack up my things and then making sure I'm okay to drive home.

"Thank you again," I say while she waits outside the elevator with me.

"Of course. You're stubborn as hell sometimes, but I know you'll figure this out."

I wish I shared her confidence, but currently, just getting out of the office feels like it's depleting the last of my strength.

I blast the radio in my car to keep myself alert, but as soon as I'm back in my apartment, I collapse onto my couch and consider skipping dinner all together. Even scrolling through delivery apps sounds exhausting.

Bailey hops up and tucks herself against me while I huddle under a blanket. There's still a pile of renovation supplies sitting outside the bathroom, and the workers have at least a week of finishing touches left, but the place is at least functional enough for me to live in.

"At least I've got you," I say to Bailey while scratching her ears. "Why can't everything be as straightforward as us, huh?"

She sighs, her eyelids fluttering.

"Cutie," I coo before letting out a sigh of my own and working up the willpower to order some food.

I switch the TV on while I wait for the takeout, but I

don't pick out a show. Instead, I let the screensaver bounce around, staring at the brand's logo pinging from side to side.

Within the darkness of the black background, I see Natalie standing outside the church again.

I see myself walking away.

She wasn't supposed to mean anything. She wasn't supposed to change my life in a matter of weeks.

She wasn't supposed to make it so damn hard to say goodbye.

I sniff and realize there are already tears running down my face, leaving salty trails on my cheeks.

"I don't know what to do."

I can't tell if I'm talking to Bailey or myself or the phantoms in my TV screen. I just know I desperately want someone to give me an answer.

For a wild second, I wish I could call my mom.

I play that conversation out in my head for a grand total of two seconds before realizing it's not an option. It's not even *her* I want to call. It's the idea of a mom, some wise, all-knowing figure who will soothe me and untangle this whole mess with the same gentleness she'd brush out a knot in my hair.

My throat gets thick, and I curl myself up into a tight ball around Bailey. There's a sharp pain just under my sternum, and it only gets worse as the minutes tick by. Soon, I feel like I can't breathe at all, like I'm choking on the need to simply *talk* to someone and have them tell me it will be all right.

Someone who understands. Someone who could find a way through this.

I'm not sure where the idea comes from. The thought arrives so fast I barely have time to register what I'm doing before I'm looking up the number on my phone.

I think about hanging up as soon as the first ring sounds in my ear.

This is pointless. She's probably not even at the store this late, and even if she was, I have no idea what I'd say.

Just as I'm about to disconnect the call, someone picks up.

"Hello?"

It's her.

"H-hi," I say, my voice weak and watery. I pause to clear my throat. "It's, um, Brooke. I'm sorry to call like this, but I-I don't really know who else to talk to, and I was...I was wondering...could I still come by for a cup of tea sometime?"

Chapter 28

Brooke

Cynthia brings two steaming mugs of tea over to the table by the window in the back room of her health food shop. Afternoon sunlight is streaming through the glass, warming my cheek and painting a golden sheen along the varnished top of the wooden table.

There's a sun catcher splashing tiny rainbows all over the shelves stuffed with products and packaging. The room smells like sandalwood incense and the rich, earthy aroma of dried herbs. From out in the main room, the faint strains of an Enya album echo back to us.

I grin at the sound. If there's one thing you can count on Cynthia for, it's an Enya playlist.

"There you are, honey," she says, setting my mug down in front of me and pulling out the chair opposite mine. "Do you want anything to sweeten it? I just got this new stevia syrup in stock. They've completely gotten rid of that bitter taste stevia usually has. It's like magic!"

"I'm actually great just like this," I tell her, taking a whiff of the tea. "I love lemon ginger on its own."

She nods in agreement and takes a seat. We spend a few

moments blowing on our tea and staring out at the sunshine before she breaks the silence.

"Is there something in particular you wanted to talk about today, Brooke?"

There's no judgement in her voice, just an open-hearted invitation, but I still feel my cheeks heating up.

I can't believe I really drove out here. After my altercation with Eric at the office last night, I called in sick this morning and went back and forth on driving into La Cloche for the entire morning before deciding I should just hop in the car and figure things out on the road.

It's like there's a part of me that's come loose and hopped into the driver's seat of my brain—a wild part of me that doesn't have any trace of my usual obsession with consequences and deliberation.

I can't tell if I'm terrified or thrilled to be stuck in the passenger seat.

I tuck my hair behind my ears before clasping my mug. The ceramic is a little too hot to be comfortable, but I let the slight burn fuel me into action.

"Did you ever suspect things wouldn't work out with me and Jonas?"

Cynthia blinks, her eyes widening. She wipes the surprise off her face a second later and settles a little deeper into her chair. I find myself hanging on her every movement, so desperate for a response I'm practically vibrating.

I still have that craving for answers, for a way forward, or even just a hint of where to go next.

Somehow, that craving has called me back to La Cloche, and as I watch Cynthia ponder her next words, I wonder if my future has always been tied to this part of my past.

It makes no sense. I moved on. I moved on from this

place so long ago, but lately, time seems to be unravelling, looping itself into riddles I can't figure out.

"Well..."

She drums her fingers against the side of her mug. The mugs are both a pearlescent blue that shimmers in the light.

They remind me of the painting in Natalie's living room.

Moon Girl.

"It *was* a quick engagement," Cynthia says, "for sure, but Jonas has been known to dilly-dally, so I knew things must be quite serious if he was ready to move that fast."

My stomach twists with the echo of an old wound.

"But he wasn't ready."

Cynthia winces at the sharpness in my tone, and I remind myself it's her son we're talking about here.

"Sorry. I—"

She shakes her head. "It's okay, honey. You're right. He wasn't ready, and while I always had my fingers crossed for you, I can't say I was totally shocked."

My heart sinks. My whole body gets heavier, like I'm turning to stone.

"So I *was* an idiot. I should have seen it coming."

This confirms it. Everyone else saw it coming. Everyone but me.

Cynthia reaches for my hand, pausing to see if I'll pull back before she gives me a squeeze.

"Brooke." There's a sternness in her voice, a steely edge I've never heard before. "You were *never* an idiot."

She makes sure I look at her before she lets my hand go, her usual serene demeanor returning.

"Jonas wanted it to work," she tells me. "Very, very much. I had a talk with him to make sure he was serious as soon as you two got engaged."

"You did?"

She nods, the corners of her mouth lifting in a bittersweet smile.

"He said you were the best thing that ever happened to him."

My breath catches.

"That's how I felt about him," I murmur, "when we met."

I can't imagine myself with him now, not even in my wildest dreams, but knowing that at the time, I meant so much to him he'd tell his mother something that sweet—it counts for something. It's like a balm soothing an old burn I forgot all about.

"We adored you too, Marcel and I," Cynthia continues. "We still do. You're a wonderful person, and you fit in here so well. You were not stupid to believe everything would work out. It's what everyone wanted. You and Jonas just weren't...quite right."

She makes it sound simple, like we were just two people who almost fit together before we fell apart.

Just a simple mistake made by two well-meaning people. No villain. No fool.

Just two people looking for love in the wrong place.

I take a deep, shuddering breath as the possibility pushes up through the soil in my mind, like a seedling that desperately wants to bloom.

"I thought I was past all this," I mumble. "It was years ago. I thought I'd left it all behind."

Cynthia lets out a chuckle filled with more understanding than I expected.

"Time works a little different in a place like La Cloche."

"It really does," I say, reaching for my mug and taking a steadying sip of the zesty lemon and ginger.

Cynthia does the same. She looks out the window, at the small parking lot where Natalie usually keeps her car.

When she invited me to the shop last night, Cynthia mentioned Natalie would be over in Saint-Jovite all day taking some meetings about the inn. I couldn't tell if I was being paranoid or if there was a loaded intention behind her mentioning that.

I have no idea what Natalie has said since I left. I wonder if it's even possible for me to ask Cynthia how Natalie is doing without making a fool of myself.

"I'm going to suggest something," she says before I get the chance, "and you can tell me if I'm wrong, but...I'm getting the feeling I'm not really the person you need to be talking to about this."

"Oh. Oh, I'm so sorry," I stammer, my face burning. "We don't have to talk. I didn't mean to, um, offend you, or anything. I can, um, go."

She leans over the table, reaching for my hand again.

"I'm not offended, Brooke. I'm honored. It meant so much to have you call. What I mean to say is that Jonas is coming by the shop to help me put up some shelves in about an hour."

I almost choke on my tea.

"You think I should talk to...*him*?"

I thought she was either kicking me out of the shop or about to make some dramatic declaration about Natalie. Jonas didn't even cross my mind.

"You never really did, did you?" she asks. "After he called the wedding off?"

My mind jumps back to the days after it happened. They're all a blur. We dealt with most of the practical matters over text. I told him I didn't want to see him, didn't want to talk.

I just wanted to get over it and put as much distance between me and the girl I was to make sure I'd never become her again.

"No," I say. "Not really. I didn't think there was anything to say."

Cynthia nods like she was expecting as much.

"I can tell him you're here and want to speak with him, if that is what you want. It's completely your choice."

There's no pressure in her tone. I can tell she'd let me walk away right now without a single protest.

Which leaves *me* to figure out what I want.

I think about it for a few minutes before the wild part of me that's in the driver's seat stomps on the gas pedal.

"Okay. Yes. I'll talk to him."

After I finish my tea, Cynthia offers to let me hang around the shop until Jonas shows up, but I'm too jittery to peruse the latest super foods for an hour.

Instead, I ask her to have Jonas meet me at Café Cloche and take myself out for a walk up Rue Principale in the meantime. All the shop windows are filled with colourful springtime displays, housing everything from hand-spun yarn in pastel ombre shades to ornate origami wall hangings made out of old sheet music.

I'm too anxious to do anything but window shop. I know caffeine is the last thing I need, but I kill some time by waiting in the long line running out the door of Café Cloche and order two coffees when I finally get to the cash register.

Jonas is standing on the sidewalk when I come back outside.

The shock is less intense than when I saw him at his parents' place, but I still feel a jolt when I lay eyes on him, like the mix of familiarity and estrangement is a physical wall I'm bumping into.

He spots me from a few feet away, and we both can't seem to figure out if we should smile or not.

"Hi," I say when I reach him.

"Hi," he echoes.

I thrust one of the takeaway cups at him. "I got you a coffee. I didn't know if you still take it black. I can go back in and get some—"

"I do."

He grips the cup, and for a second, I forget to let go.

His words ring in my ears—the same words he was supposed to say to me so long ago, on such a different day.

I drop my hand to my side.

"I do still take it black," he adds. "Thanks."

We hover on the sidewalk, avoiding each other's eyes. He's wearing heavy work boots and dusty blue jeans, like he came straight from whatever construction site he's working on.

"I hope my mom didn't put you up to this," he says with a nervous chuckle.

"No, not at all," I assure him.

We decide to take a walk and end up strolling along the sidewalk in silence for so long we reach the end of the shops, striding past cozy-looking stone houses with muddy yards instead. We've just walked past a house with a tire swing tied to the tree out front when he stops in the middle of the sidewalk and turns to face me.

"Brooke?"

There's an intensity in his gaze I've ever seen before. Even when we were preparing to get married, Jonas was never a serious guy. He was always grinning like a mischievous class clown and coming up with his next joke.

His solemnity today makes him look older, carving new lines into his forehead.

"Yes?" I say.

My pulse has kicked up, thumping hard against my sternum.

"I'm sorry."

I almost lose my balance and have to take a fumbling step back to stay upright.

"O-oh," I mumble.

The lines in his face deepen.

"I know you didn't want to talk after...after what I did, and I wanted to respect your wishes, but I should have tried harder to find a way to give you a proper apology back then."

The diehard urge to keep the peace crawls out from the corner I've tucked it in for the past couple days, whispering in my ear to tell me *I'm* the one who pushed him away after the wedding day.

"You don't have t—"

"I do," he cuts in. "I'm sorry I embarrassed you. I'm sorry I hurt you. I'm sorry I let you down."

It's him speaking, but when the words hit my ears, it's almost like I can hear a chorus of other voices joining in.

Voices I didn't know I needed.

My mom. My other ex, Yves. Even Eric, my boss.

"I should have figured things out way before the wedding day," he continues. "I should have been more honest with myself, and with you. You were, like, the most amazing girl I'd ever met. I couldn't believe how lucky I was. I kept telling myself I must have tripped into somebody else's life or something crazy like that, because no way was a girl like you supposed to end up with a guy like me."

He shrugs, the corner of his mouth lifting into one of the saddest smiles I've ever seen.

My chest aches.

We weren't right for each other, but he still made me laugh more times than I'd ever be able to count. He still pulled me out of some of the darkest years of my life.

"Jonas—"

"It's true," he says, shaking his head, "and we both know it. You were so ready to build this grown-up life, and I...I wasn't. Truth be told, I still don't think I am, but I told myself I could do it for you."

I can't speak. All I can do is press a hand to my lips as I stare at him.

"That's not enough though, is it?" he asks. "You can't make something work just by telling yourself it has to."

His words hit me like a punch to the gut. I wrap my arms around my stomach as I think back on what I was saying to Layla just last night.

"No," I say. "You can't."

He wrings his hands as the truth settles over us both.

"You were all in, Brooke, and I wasn't. That's on me, not you, and I am so fucking sorry I couldn't step up."

I still want to lie and tell him it wasn't that bad. I still want to smooth over any bumps in the road even if it means I'm flattening myself in the process.

But I don't.

Even if it's just now, just this once, I choose another path.

"Thank you," I say instead.

With those words, I set something down, and the lightness that fills me in return is so overpowering I get dizzy. I take a tottering step, my nose and eyes stinging as a sudden rush of tears fills my eyes.

Jonas lifts his arms, and I step into them, letting him steady me as more tears drip onto the concrete below our feet.

"Aww, Brooke," he says, giving me an awkward pat on the back.

I take a shuddering breath as the dizziness subsides. I get a whiff of him: tangy sweat and the faint, metallic trace of motor oil.

My nose wrinkles.

I can't believe I used to kiss this guy.

Before I can stop myself, I let out a garbled laugh.

"What's so funny, huh?" Jonas asks.

"I really appreciate the apology," I tell him as I step out of the hug, "and yeah, I wish you hadn't left me at the damn altar, but...can you even picture us married now?"

He squints at me, tilting his head.

"No," he says. "No, I really can't."

He barks a laugh, and then I'm laughing again too, both of us howling at the complete lack of chemistry we've got now.

It takes us a couple minutes to calm down and decide to walk back into town.

"I wish you'd found a different way to call things off," I say as we head off, ready to be serious now, "but it *was* the right choice. We'd only been dating for two years, and I...well, a big part of me was just looking for some fairytale to escape into. I ignored a lot of things that weren't right about us. I could have been way more honest with myself. I'm sorry too."

I catch his eye to let him know I mean it. He wags his eyebrows in response.

"Fairytale, huh?" He does what I think is meant to be a

superhero pose, chest all puffed out and arms flexing. "So basically, you're saying I'm Prince Charming?"

I snort and roll my eyes at him.

"Basically," I concede.

He winks. "Then no apology needed."

When we've almost reached the middle of town again, I pause and take a deep breath, closing my eyes and tilting my head back as the exhilarating sensation of being so damn light continues to spread through me.

"Wow," I say. "I didn't know how much I needed this. I wish we'd talked years ago."

He grins. "Me too."

We stroll along, taking sips of our coffees and making a few comments about the shops we pass.

I'm not sure how we're supposed to wrap this up.

"So have you...found anyone?" I ask, just after we've passed a young couple with their arms slung around each other. "Since then?"

"Nah, nothing serious," he answers. "I'm happy living the bachelor life, at least for now. Like we just said, I'm not the world's most serious guy."

He does his signature eyebrow wag again, and I chuckle.

"I'm glad you're happy," I tell him, surprised by just how much I mean it.

"What about you?" he asks.

"Oh, well..."

A rush of blood warms my face, and I pretend to be engrossed by some crocheted sweaters on display at the next shop.

Jonas isn't deterred.

"Aw, come on. Don't be shy, Brooke. Who's the lucky guy?"

"Lucky girl, actually," I blurt.

All the blood drains from my cheeks. I whirl around to face Jonas and find him staring at me with wide eyes.

He rallies after a couple seconds, bobbing his head and shoving his hands in his pockets.

"Oh. Oh, cool. That's great."

I stop holding my breath when he gives me a genuine smile. We start walking again.

"So," he prompts, "who is the lucky girl?"

"I'm not so sure she's lucky," I admit. "I really messed things up with her recently. I think we might be done."

He thumps me on the back like I'm one of the bros.

"You can get her back! Guarantee it. You just need a good plan."

I chuckle and spread my hands out. "I'm open to suggestions."

Then I freeze.

My brain is miles ahead of me, zooming towards one of the craziest ideas I've ever had in my life.

"Wait."

Jonas stops walking when he realizes I'm no longer beside him, glancing back to give me a curious look.

"Actually," I say, "you might be the perfect person to help me come up with a plan."

He jerks a thumb at his chest. "Me?"

"Yeah. She..."

I stop, the words catching in my throat.

There's no going back from here, but I've done enough going back for today.

I want to move forward.

For good.

"I'm going to tell you something, and you have to

promise not to freak out, even though it's kind of weird, okay?"

His eyes narrow. "Okay?"

"This girl..." I glance down at the sidewalk and then force myself to look him in the eyes. "She's your sister."

Chapter 29
Natalie

I pull the sheet off the canvas. Maddie and Jacinthe gasp from where they're standing behind me. I take a step back so they can crowd in closer to get a better look at the painting.

The jittering nerves zinging through my body get more intense the longer the two of them go without saying anything.

"Well?" I demand, just as I'm about to crawl out of my skin.

"*C'est magnifique,*" Jacinthe murmurs as she continues to stare at the canvas, transfixed. "*C'est...c'est...elle.*"

It's her.

I wasn't sure they'd be able to tell, and I don't know if I'm relieved or embarrassed to have the truth displayed so clearly on the canvas.

"Natalie, it's..." Maddie rips her gaze away from the painting, and I'm stunned to see her eyes are shining with unshed tears. "It's stunning. Is this...is this really how you feel about her?"

I take a moment to look at the piece myself.

The canvas is a hulking five feet tall, taking up most of my couch where I've wedged it against the cushions to keep it upright. The piece looks nothing like the art I made for my Thunder Bay exhibition, all filtered through the lens of what I thought other people wanted.

Here, every choice I've made, every colour and brushstroke, is an affirmation of what the past few weeks have taught me: my art is meant to be *mine*.

The background is painted with the inky blue of twilight, tinged with purple at the edges. At the bottom of the canvas, I've painted a small border of stones, tufts of grass, and spotted mushrooms. Their silhouettes are streaked with the silvery rays of the full moon above them.

The glowing orb stretches almost all the way to the edges of the canvas, like those rare nights when a swollen super moon seems to hang so low in the sky it commands a shock of wonder. At first glance, the moon appears to be dappled with its usual craters and crevices, the pockmarked patterns nothing but random markers of the eons passing by. With a closer look, though, the shades of grey, silver, and pearly white coalesce into a distinct shape.

A woman.

She sits with her knees tucked up to her chest, like the moon is a cozy cushion she's curled into. Her long hair fans out around her shoulders. Her chin is lifted, her eyes closed and her lips slightly parted, like she's drinking in the heady scent of the night air.

She's draped in a gossamer gown that clings to the curves of her waist and chest, giving her an elegant sensuality. She looks like the personification of the moon itself, like she holds the power to turn the tides with a flick of her dainty hand. She looks like she could call all the night-blooming flowers of the world up out of the earth, like they

Paint the Moon

would turn their faces to follow her as she floated across the sky, like they'd weep and wither when she sank below the horizon and left them to face the glare of the sun.

"Yes," I murmur, my eyes lingering on the woman's face. "This is how I feel about Brooke."

My breath hitches, and before I can say anything else, Maddie tilts her head onto my shoulder while Jacinthe slings an arm around my waist.

They hold me steady while I take a few deep breaths and prepare to tell them what's happening next.

"I'm going to give it to her."

Maddie jerks her head up. Jacinthe stiffens.

"*Quoi?*" she asks. "You're going to get rid of it?"

"I'm giving it away," I correct, "to Brooke."

Maddie's eyes narrow behind her glasses.

"Are you sure?" she asks. "It must have taken you ages. You don't want to display it anywhere?"

I shake my head. "Not this one."

I extract myself from Jacinthe's grip and reach for the sheet on the floor. I lay it back over the canvas, hiding the piece from view.

It's almost like I've turned off a light. Despite the morning sun streaming through the window, the whole apartment seems to get darker.

"There'll be more," I explain. "I have so much more to paint. I don't think I've ever had so many ideas at once. We're going to need to speed up the timeline on the inn so I can get some cash to afford all these canvases."

They both indulge me with a laugh, but I can see the concern lingering in their eyes.

"This one, though..." I trail off and stare at the sheet for a moment. I can still feel a pull towards the piece, even with the moon out of sight, like the painting has its own field of gravity. "This one I have to let go of. I didn't paint this for me. I painted it for her. She might not be able to see herself the way I see her, but I still want to show her. I want her to know how strong I think she is, how much I believe in her...even if she wasn't ready to believe in us."

I brace for them to ask me again if I'm sure, but all they do is come in for a hug.

"I'm doing it today," I say with their arms around me. "I'm driving to Montreal."

∽

I try to get into my usual art history podcast as I wind along the familiar bends in the road, but the words won't stick in my brain. I give up and drive in silence instead.

The painting, wrapped in its sheet with some bubble wrap to protect the corners, takes up the whole backseat. I keep glancing at it in the rear-view mirror.

I still have Brooke's address in my phone from when I went to grab us a pizza that night her apartment flooded. I have no idea if she'll even be home. I still haven't decided if I should try to talk to her. I've got a notebook and pen stashed on the front seat in case I decide to leave the painting with a note taped to it instead, but I don't have the first clue what my note would say.

I've already put everything into the painting. I've poured myself into every brushstroke, dipped into my heartache like it's the deepest of pigments.

I notice my phone is lighting up where I've tossed it into the cup holder. I set it on my lap and keep steering with one hand while I swipe at the screen, stealing glances to see what the notifications are about. There's a string of text alerts and at least three missed calls.

Paint the Moon

I frown, alarm bells ringing in my ears, and end up taking the next bend in the road way too fast.

"Shit," I mutter as the car swerves out.

I breathe a sigh of relief when I see there's no one coming at me on the other side of the bend, but my heart is still racing, and I scan for a place to pull over.

The winding highway doesn't offer many opportunities, but when I spot the flash of the sun glinting on a distant lake behind the trees, I remember there's an old, abandoned dirt road just a couple kilometers ahead. I ease myself off the highway once I reach it, cutting the engine once I've driven a few meters up the bumpy surface.

My chest constricts when I check my phone again and see all the calls and messages are from Jonas. I don't bother reading past the first couple texts demanding to know where I am before I stab at the button to call him and press the phone to my ear.

"What's the matter?" I ask as soon as he picks up.

"Where are you?" he says instead of answering. "Weren't you supposed to be home today?"

He doesn't sound like anyone has died. If anything, he sounds mildly pissed off at me.

"Um, not that I'm aware of?"

"Mom said you were."

Despite my alarm, I roll my eyes. "Well, I'm twenty-six. Mom does not keep constant tabs on my actions."

He responds with an equally sassy voice. "Well, I'm at your apartment, and you're not here. So where are you?"

I glance out my windshield at the desolate stretch of dirt road covered in mud-filled potholes. A slight breeze shakes the dense trees surrounding my car.

"I'm...driving," I say. "Well, actually I've pulled over on

the side of the road because you scared the shit out of me with all those texts. What the hell is going on?"

His older brother snark evaporates, replaced with a nervousness that has me even more on edge.

"Uh, nothing. I just have to, um, give you something."

"Give me something?"

"Yeah." He pauses, and I think I hear him gulp. "Something important."

"Well, can you leave it at my apartment?"

"No!" he barks before lowering his voice. "No, it has to go, uh, to you."

I catch my own eye in the rear view mirror and squint at myself.

"You're being weird," I tell him.

I expect him to bicker, but instead, he just asks when I'll be home.

"I don't know," I answer. "I'm out for the day. I have, uh, an errand to run in Montreal."

He sucks in a breath. "Montreal? Shit."

My blood pressure ratchets up a few notches.

"Jonas, seriously, what is going on?"

Once again, he ignores me.

"Where are you exactly right now?"

I sigh and decide it's probably easier if I just start answering him. Maybe it will get us to the bottom of this faster.

"I'm on that dirt road just before Labelle."

"That one that goes to the dump?"

"No, the other one. Nasty Road."

I cringe as I say it. In high school, this place had a reputation for being a sure-fire spot to sneak out and hook up in the back of a car without getting caught. Hence the nickname.

My brother in particular had a reputation for taking his fair share of ladies out to Nasty Road.

"Oh, Nasty Road!" he says, his voice brightening. "Why didn't you just say that?"

"Because we're too old to be calling it Nasty Road."

He tuts. "You're never too old for some nasty times on Nasty Road."

I make a gagging sound. "Jonas, come on. Can I continue driving now or what?"

"No!" he shouts, loud enough to make me pull the phone away from my ear. "Uh, actually, just stay there."

"You want me to stay here?" I demand. "I'm just supposed to sit here alone in my car on Nasty Road?"

"Yes. Just for a bit."

I groan. "Jonas, I have things to do."

"Just sit for like...twenty minutes. Half an hour max."

"Half an hour?" I squawk.

He lets out a heavy sigh, like I'm the one being unreasonable.

"Look, Natalie, can you just trust me on this?"

"No! You're not telling me anything."

He pauses for a few seconds, and when he speaks again, there's a strained note of sincerity in his voice, one I don't hear very often.

"Look, just stay there for twenty minutes, okay? Can you do that?"

I smack the steering wheel and then slump in my seat.

"I fucking guess," I concede.

"'Atta girl!" he quips before ending the call without another word.

The sheet-shrouded painting behind me is like a specter in the corner of my vision. Sitting still is not what I need. Doubts begin to creep in, like the wind creaking through the tree branches is whispering questions to me, demanding to know what the hell I think I'm doing showing up on Brooke's doorstep unannounced with a giant painting of her.

I switch the car back on and get my podcast pumping through the speakers. I still can't focus on what the hosts are saying, but at least their voices drown out the sound of the wind.

By the time eighteen minutes have eked by, there's still no sign of Jonas. I've swung the car around to face the highway, and I've only seen the occasional pick-up truck go by, along with the roaring parade of a mid-life crisis biker gang enjoying the country roads.

I haven't gotten any new texts or calls. I'm about to call Jonas again when a silver Honda comes into view, its turn signal blinking.

My relief only lasts a second before I remember Jonas drives a truck and that I only know one person with a silver Honda.

She pulls over in front of me and gets out of the car, her pea coat hanging open over a pair of light jeans and a white shirt.

Despite the absolute shock freezing me in my seat, I still feel a jolt of desire. Her hair is loose, the ends curling around her shoulders just like in my painting.

She shuts the car door and takes a couple steps towards me before stumbling to a halt. There's something clutched in her hands. It looks like a sheet of paper, but I can't be sure from here.

I blink a few times, just to make sure she's not going to disappear. I haven't been sleeping well, but I didn't think I was at the level of experiencing hallucinations yet.

Brooke remains standing outside her car, refusing to evaporate like a mirage in the desert.

She's here.

She's really here.

I need to go to her.

My legs feel like they're filled with sand. I heave myself out of the car, clinging to the door for balance before I find the strength to slam it shut.

The sound echoes through the empty road, louder than I anticipated. We both flinch.

I shove my hands in my pockets and trudge over to her, the wind snatching at my hair.

I can hear the throb of my heartbeat in my ears. There's a hopeful fluttering sensation in my chest, but I squash it down before it can take flight.

She already walked away from me once.

When there are still a few feet of space between us, I stop. Pebbles crunch under my feet as I shift my weight, working up the nerve to keep holding her gaze.

"What are you doing here?" I ask.

My voice is hoarse, and Brooke flinches again at how raw I sound.

"Jonas said you'd be here," she answers. "I was on my way to La Cloche."

A fresh bolt of shock zings through me. "What?"

The breeze ruffles the papers in Brooke's hands, but I'm too stunned to do anything except gawk at her face.

"Jonas was supposed to find you and tell me where to meet you, but then he found out you'd left town."

I squint at her. "You've been talking to Jonas?"

She nods. "Yes. He's, um, been helping me."

My stomach churns, and for one wild second, I feel the

urge to take a leaf out of my mom's book and demand to know if the two of them have 'reunited.'

Brooke seems to sense my line of thinking. Her nose wrinkles.

"Ew, no, it's nothing like that," she urges. "We talked last week. He apologized for how he ended things. I never gave him the chance to do that before, and I...I didn't realize how much I needed someone to just say sorry. It helped me realize a lot of other things too."

She glances down at the papers, and I realize they're actually some kind of magazine, with a glossy cover tilted at an angle I can't see from here.

"Jonas has kind of turned into my wingman on this. He's helped me with putting this together." She thrusts the magazine out towards me. "It's for you. I was coming to give it to you today."

I step closer, reaching out on instinct.

"What is this?" I ask as I flip the magazine around to read the title.

Brooke wraps her arms around her stomach, rocking back and forth while she watches me read.

"I'm no graphic designer," she says, her voice pitched high with nerves, "but I did my best with the layout and things."

The words *Art in Review* are spelt out in a trendy font stretched across the top of the page, with a subtitle that reads *Spotlight On: Natalie Sinclair*.

The cover image is a painting of a full moon hanging in an indigo sky, with the hazy shape of a woman half-hidden in the silvery beams of light spilling across the canvas.

It's my painting.

It's *Moon Girl*.

I tear my gaze away and look back up at Brooke. "Is this...?"

She's chewing on her lip, still rocking with nerves.

"Open it," she urges.

I flip the cover open and find a photo of me inlaid inside what appears to be a short biography of me and my work, covering a brief timeline of my life in La Cloche, my travels, and the art shows I've been featured in.

I skim the text and turn to the next page, then the next, my breathing getting faster and faster as I go.

Every page is filled with a photo of a different piece I've made, accompanied by a review.

Only the reviews aren't from critics.

They're from my family. My friends. The people of La Cloche. Everyone who's seen me grow from a child who spent way too much time with her crayons to the artist I am today.

Each of them have written something about their favourite piece of my work.

There's a photo of a small painting I gave Maddie for her birthday when we were teenagers, showing three girls playing in a tree house together, just like the one my dad built for us when we were kids.

In her review, she talks about keeping the painting in her locker after Jacinthe and I graduated two years ahead of her, and how sometimes, it was the only thing that could comfort her when she was getting bullied.

There's a review from my mom's best friend, who was the first person to buy one of my watercolours when I started selling them in my mom's shop. It was a Christmas scene of La Cloche in the snow. She talks about hanging it up in her living room every December, and how her grandkids always know Santa is coming soon when they come over and see their favourite painting.

The stories range from simple and sweet to achingly soul-baring. Some of them are about pieces I can't even remember making, paintings that have somehow gone on to hold a permanent place of honor in somebody else's life.

On one of the last pages, there are two pictures of the same pieces featured in the clipping *Tante* Manon included with her letter to me.

The text is from her letter too, just a single sentence with her name underneath.

When I saw your art, my niece, I saw something I never knew was possible.

-*Manon*

The page blurs, and it takes me a second to realize it's because I'm crying. I lower the magazine and take a shaky breath before looking back at Brooke.

Tears are streaming down her cheeks too.

"I never want you to have to doubt how powerful your art is, Natalie."

A sob catches in my throat. My heart feels like it's swelling up, ballooning against my ribs.

"Brooke," I choke out.

Her breath hitches at the sound of her name, and she takes a step closer to me.

"I shouldn't have left like that, Natalie. I was just so scared. I was afraid to get hurt. I was afraid to feel stupid again. I was afraid...I was afraid to feel what I feel for you."

Her eyes lock with mine, and for a moment, it's like we're back in bed on that last morning before everything fell apart.

Her hair splayed on the pillow, catching the morning sun.

Her little smile when she blinked her eyes open and caught me marvelling at her.

The warmth of her breath on my lips when she rolled over and leaned in for a kiss.

"What do you feel for me?" I whisper.

She nods at the magazine in my hands. "Read the last page."

I do as she says, and there it is again: *Moon Girl*.

The review is from Brooke.

I could say knowing Natalie Sinclair has changed my life, but that would be a lie.

Knowing Natalie hasn't changed me into something new. Knowing Natalie has stripped away everything I'm not, everything I hid myself with in an attempt to cover up the truth.

Knowing Natalie has shown me the truth was the most beautiful part of me all along. Like she's done for so many others, she's taught me I don't need to hide. Her work reflects pieces of me, buried so deep and dark I didn't think they could ever reach a mirror, but when I saw this painting on her wall, there they were, staring straight back at me without fear or shame.

Natalie has shown me there is no shame in love. There is no weakness. There is no guilt. We may try to paint it with those ugly shades, but love's true colours always find a way to shine through.

In Natalie's work, I see my true colours. I see a life I've denied myself for too long, one shining with truth and integrity. I see a brave life. I see a life governed by me, my desires, my hopes, my dreams. I see a life where pain no longer burns me like the sun.

I see a life where I dance in the moonlight.
-Brooke Carmichael

My tears are falling on the page now, leaving wet splotches on the letters as the magazine trembles in my hands.

"Brooke..." I say, staring down at the words.

Her words.

For me.

"I know it might be too late," she says. "I know I hurt you by not giving this a chance the first time you offered. I know that offer might not still stand, but you were brave enough to tell me what you wanted, and I want to do the same for you."

Her boots crunch against the rocky dirt road as she closes the gap between us.

"I want to give this a chance—a real chance, without any hiding or holding back." Her voice is shaking, but she doesn't stop. "I want to walk around holding hands with you. I want to go on dates. I want to cook you dinner. I want to wake up beside you without anywhere else to be for the whole rest of the day. I want to introduce you to my best friend. I want to be there for the rest of your journey opening Balsam Inn, and not just as your interior designer. I want to be *with* you."

My chest feels like it's cracking open, the feeling building inside me too much to contain. The mix of tenderness and absolute determination on her face steals my breath away.

"But it's more than just wanting," she says. "I'm ready for it. I'm ready to stop letting the past control my future. It won't always be easy for me. In fact, it will probably be really hard, at least at first, but I'm tired of acting like my life is going to fall apart the second I admit I...I need somebody."

Her hands flex at her sides, like it's taking all her self-control not to reach for me.

"I need you, Natalie. I don't need you to give my life meaning or fix every pain I've ever felt. I don't need you for what you can do for me. I need you for what you *are*. I need your laugh, your smile, that look in your eye you get when you're thinking about painting. I need your mind and your heart, and goddamn it, I *really* need your body."

She pauses again, her gaze flicking down the length of me, and a trail of sparks shoots along my skin.

"I can make it on my own," she says, dipping her chin in a determined nod. "I know that. If you say no, I can find a way to be okay. I trust myself. I just…I want to be the kind of person who can trust you too. Will you…will you give me another chance?"

I still can't speak, so instead, I move.

I lunge for her, throwing myself into her arms and wrapping mine tight around her neck.

The scent of her fills my nose: vanilla and floral shampoo. I close my eyes and bury my face in her neck.

When I finally pull back, it's only so I can tilt my head and press my lips to hers.

It's like sinking into a hot spring. My whole body relaxes, nearly going limp against her as I ease into the certainty that somehow, everything is going to be all right.

She kisses me back, her hands sliding into my hair and her soft moan filling my mouth. I let my tongue dart between her lips and earn another moan before I force myself to step away for real this time.

"I have something to show you too."

I take off jogging back to my car, and she follows me, waiting with a confused look on her face while I get the painting unwrapped. I slide it out off the backseat and hold it up for her to see, most of me concealed behind the canvas.

I don't get to watch her reaction, but I hear the moment she realizes what she's looking at.

"Natalie, it's beauti—"

She cuts herself off with a gasp.

"Wait. Is that...?"

"It is," I tell her. "It's you. This is...you. To me."

"This is how you see me?"

She's speaking so softly I can barely hear her above the wind in the trees.

"Every single day," I answer.

I can't stand not looking at her any longer, so I shuffle the canvas back onto the seat. She's still standing there with her hands pressed over her mouth when I turn back around.

"I was on my way to Montreal," I explain. "To give it to you."

"What?" she says from behind her fingers, her eyes bulging.

"It's yours. I made it for you. I thought I'd be giving it to you to say goodbye, but..."

She drops her hands back to her sides and steps closer to the car.

"Yes?"

I reach my hands out to grip both of hers, pulling her to me.

"I want everything you want, Brooke. I want to give us a chance."

She kisses me first this time, with a fierceness that has me stumbling backwards to lean against the side of the car. Her hips bump into mine, pressing hard. She cups my cheeks, stroking her thumbs along my jaw in a way that instantly has heat building between my legs.

She breaks the kiss to trail the side of her nose up mine, and I can't help flinching when I feel how cold her nose is. I realize her fingers are clammy too.

"You're cold," I say, gently prying her hands from my face. "Come on. We can sit in my car."

As I clear my bag off the front seat, she looks around the deserted road, squinting like she's trying to find something.

"Is this place really called Nasty Road?" she asks. "That's what Jonas called it on the phone, but I didn't see a sign."

She gives up on her search when she sees I'm done with the arrangements, but instead of sliding into the seat, she hooks her fingers through the belt loops of my jeans and tugs us flush together again.

"It's just, um, a dumb local nickname," I stammer, my brain already melting.

She gives me a peck on the lips.

"It's not very nasty out here," she says in a teasing voice. "It's actually quite nice."

She plants a kiss on my jaw, and then my neck, before giving my skin a slight scrape with her teeth.

"Brooke," I hiss, "if you keep kissing me like that, you're going to find out exactly what happens on Nasty Road."

She tips her head back, her laughter echoing through the woods, and I decide it might be my favourite sound in the world.

Chapter 30

Brooke

Natalie pauses in front of the door and turns to face me.

"You ready for take two?" she asks.

I take a deep breath and smooth down the front of my dress.

"As ready as I'll ever be."

Instead of opening the door, she takes my hand and rubs her thumb over my knuckles.

"We can leave whenever you want," she says in a soothing tone. "If it's too much, you just tell me, and we'll go. No questions asked."

I give her hand a squeeze and smile despite the gymnastics routine going on in my stomach. Still clutching my hand, she turns back to the door to her parents' house and pulls it open.

Marcel is standing on the other side, striding forward like he was about to let us in himself.

"*Bonsoir, les filles!*" he calls out. "We heard the car pull up. I was just coming to check if you're all right."

"We're great, Dad," Natalie says, tugging me in after her.

Marcel's eyes drop to our joined hands. I brace for things to get awkward, but instead, he beams at us for a moment before plastering on a fake mocking glare.

"Don't tell me you were, ah, what is the word?" He wags his finger at us while he thinks for a moment and then exclaims, "Canoodling on my porch!"

Natalie makes a retching sound. "Dad. Ew. Seriously."

I just laugh, my shoulders sagging with relief.

"We would never, Marcel," I assure him while Natalie takes my coat.

Bailey trots into the house ahead of us. There's music playing in the living room. The warbling sounds of oldies tunes drift out to greet us, along with a shout from Cynthia in the kitchen bidding us hello.

It's the first time I've been back in this house since Natalie and I started officially dating.

Part of me still can't quite believe that afternoon on the side of the highway really happened. As soon as she stepped out of her car, I knew if there was even a hope she'd give me another chance, I'd never let myself lose her again.

That thought would have terrified me just a few weeks ago. In fact, it still does, but whenever a panicked sweat breaks out on the back of my neck and my feet get jittery with the urge to run, I look at Natalie's painting.

The canvas hangs on the wall of my apartment now, front and center above my couch like a mirror image of *Moon Girl* on display in Natalie's living room.

I look at that painting, and something in me goes still. The piece of me that's been restless and anxious my whole life lies down and takes a break.

I wish I could look at it right now.

I roll my shoulders back and clench my jaw as Marcel leads us into the living room. There's a fire burning down to embers in the woodstove despite the warm April evening, which makes the room just a little too sluggishly warm. That probably explains why Belle is sprawled out half-asleep on the rug in front of it, completely unaware she has guests.

Then again, that could also be because Jonas is crouched down beside her, stroking one of her giant ears.

He looks up at the sound of our arrival, and for a moment, I can feel tension crackle through the atmosphere as we all wait to see what will happen next.

I knew he would be here. We all agreed to it. Having a family dinner together is the whole point of the evening, but the memory of what happened the last time Jonas and I came face to face in this house looms like a shadow, threatening to swallow us all up into the past.

Jonas stops petting Belle. She lifts her head in protest and then leaps to her feet when she spots the new people and extra dog in the room. Natalie squats down to give her some scratches, but even Belle's wagging tail whacking against my leg isn't enough to break the expectant trance we've all fallen into.

Another few seconds go by before Jonas gets to his feet.

"Hey, sis," he says, nodding at Natalie when she straightens up to face him.

Then he turns to me.

"Hey, sis's girlfriend."

My spine stiffens. Natalie and I haven't had 'The Girlfriend Talk' yet, and I hear her breath catch from beside me.

Jonas doesn't seem to notice. Instead, he starts stroking his chin, putting on an exaggerated quizzical expression that barely hides the start of his usual goofy grin.

"You know what?" he says, squinting at me. "You look kind of familiar. Have we met before?"

It's a stupid joke, but that's Jonas for you. I feel the corners of my mouth begin to lift too.

"You know what?" I say, mimicking his baffled tone. "I was thinking the same thing about you."

He raises an eyebrow. "Weird."

I nod. "Weird."

He shrugs and then spins on his heels to head for the kitchen.

"Anyway, who wants a beer?" he calls back over his shoulder.

I glance at Natalie, and that's all it takes for the two of us to burst out laughing. The tension in the room drains away, like someone has pulled the plug. Marcel joins in, chuckling and shaking his head like he's not sure what just happened but is happy to come along for the ride.

Things stay smooth for the rest of the night. We talk and laugh our way through the curry Cynthia has prepared for dinner. She calls me a traitor for letting Natalie and Jonas coerce me into trying a craft beer instead of splitting a bottle of wine with her.

I even end up telling everyone about my plan to start working freelance by the end of the year. Natalie already knows, but I explain that I want to keep working on heritage buildings and small business projects instead of the larger, more urban direction Leung Designs is taking.

I have to bite my tongue to keep from launching into a rant about how much time I wasted working for Eric. I'm not financially ready to quit at the drop of a hat, but picturing the look on his face when his trusted 'always keeps her head down and goes along with anything' lackey hands in a two week notice has helped me find the bravery to step out on my own.

We eat dessert in the living room, balancing plates of chocolate lava cake on our knees while enjoying the glow of the fire, which is much more comfortable now that the sun has gone down. Belle and Bailey mope on the rug when they can't charm anyone out of some crumbs, and Marcel tells me the two of them will probably try holding us hostage in the kitchen next time.

Next time.

I look around the room, at the cozy paisley cushions, the frames holding Natalie's art on the walls, the purple sky outside the window. I look at the people surrounding me, Cynthia and Natalie piled onto the couch beside me while the guys perch in the armchairs. The firelight gleams on their faces, turning everything soft and slow.

I could get used to there being a next time.

And another.

And another.

And another after that.

I wait for the panic to hit. I wait for the urge to run to send me fleeing out the door, but it never comes.

By the time Natalie and I pull our shoes and jackets on, the beer has begun to go to my head, and I can't stop grinning at her.

"What?" she says, smiling back at me even though I'm sure I look silly trying to stuff my uncooperative arms into the sleeves of my coat.

"I just...really like you," I say.

She pecks me on the cheek. "I really like you too."

I press my fingertips to the place her lips just were, like people are always doing in sappy movies, and she grins even wider before kissing my other cheek too.

"Come on," she says. "Let's get you to my place."

There's a hunger edging her words that makes me shiver.

We get through our goodbyes and then head outside. I've made it all the way down the driveway with Bailey when I realize Natalie is still hovering on the front step.

"What is it?" I ask when she catches up with me.

She chews on her lip for a moment before she answers with a question of her own.

"Was that still weird? I didn't think it was, but I wanted to check with you. I just...I know we agreed to just let it be weird when it's weird, but I don't want it to be weird forever, and—"

"Natalie."

I take her hands, brushing my thumbs over her knuckles just like she did to me when we first arrived.

I look into her eyes and tell her the truth.

"It wasn't weird at all."

Chapter 31

Natalie

Four Months Later

"We really don't have time for this."

I push Brooke's dress a little farther up her thighs and stifle a groan.

"I beg to differ," I tell her.

Despite her complaint, she still threads her fingers into my hair.

"You beg, do you?" she says, her attempt to sound haughty thwarted by the way her voice hitches.

"If that's what it'll take to get you to let me eat your pussy," I shoot back, trailing my lips along her thigh and pushing the edge of the dress up high enough to expose the periwinkle lace thong she's wearing underneath.

It even has a little bow in the center of the waistband.

"Fucking adorable," I mutter before planting a kiss on top of the bow, letting my lips linger on her stomach.

She gasps, her hands flexing in my hair.

"Someone could come in," she hisses. "This place is crawling with people already."

Paint the Moon

I pause for a moment and listen for the sound of anyone approaching, but as far as I can tell, we've still got the whole barn to ourselves.

We're due to open the doors of Balsam Inn any minute now—literally. A crowd is waiting in the front yard for the start of our open house, which will be followed by our first ever round of guests checking in tomorrow night. There are even a few reporters coming today to feature us in some Québec tourism publications and the local newspaper in Saint-Jovite.

Everything is ready. The rooms are made up. The kitchen is stocked. The booking system, website, and social media accounts are good to go.

The barn is finished.

The whole room gleams, the glorious light that taught me I wanted to be a painter now spilling over a gorgeous studio filled with supply closets, work tables, easels, and a quaint kitchenette stocked with every kind of tea La Cloche has to offer.

Studio Manon is ready for the world.

I'd be nervous if I weren't crouched on my knees with my mouth just inches from slipping between Brooke's legs.

"We have time," I insist. "No one is even looking for us yet."

We were supposed to be doing a final walkthrough of the property, but when I walked into the barn and spotted Brooke bent over to rub out a smudge on one of the shiny new work tables, the hem of that burgundy dress riding up the backs of her thighs, all bets were off.

I had to have her.

"I haven't properly thanked you for being here today," I murmur, my lips continuing to brush along the seam of her thong. "This is how I want to do it."

"You don't have to thank me," she says, the hazy tone leaving her voice. "I'm your girlfriend. Of course I'm here. This is one of the most important days of your life."

I realize this has become a conversation we should probably have face to face. I give the thong one last longing look before pushing myself to my feet.

I cup her cheeks in my hands, careful not to mess up the soft waves she curled into her hair in my apartment this morning.

"I still appreciate it," I say. "I'm never taking you for granted. We have defied far too many odds for me to ever do that."

She huffs a soft laugh. "God, yeah, we've really had our fair share of odds, haven't we?"

I take a step back to drink the sight of her in: this woman who skirted around the edge of my life years before she found her way into my heart.

She looks gorgeous today, the deep shade of the dress a perfect contrast to her pale skin and shimmering hair.

"My moon girl," I murmur.

Truth be told, the long sleeves must be a little too warm for the August day, but I have a sneaking suspicion she wore it just for me.

She knows exactly what this dress does to me. Even now, I'm fighting the compulsion to drop straight back to my knees and taste her for hours, open house be damned.

She closes the gap between us, twining her arms around my neck so she can whisper in my ear.

"I have something to tell you."

Goosebumps rise on my skin.

"Oh?"

She leans back enough to look me in the eyes.

"I'm quitting early. I'm leaving the firm at the end of next month."

I gasp. "What?"

She didn't think she'd be able to leave the firm until Christmas. She's had everything ready to go for at least a month now, from getting a website and portfolio built, to hiring a lawyer to help her draft client contracts, to scoping out some potential leads. I know of at least three businesses in La Cloche alone that would hire her at the drop of a hat, and once the world gets a look at what she's done for Balsam Inn, I'm sure she'll be fielding calls for weeks.

I haven't pushed her on it, though. Just like I've let her take the lead on easing into our relationship, I've trusted that she'll take this step in her career when she's ready. All I want to do is be here to cheer her on.

"It's sooner than planned," she says, her eyes lighting up, "but I just had this thought the other day when I was calling Layla. I realized it doesn't matter how long I wait. There's never going to be any guarantee this works. It will always be a risk, but taking some risks has paid off pretty well for me lately, so why stop now?"

A rush of tenderness sweeps through me. I kiss the tip of her nose and then beam at her.

"I'm so fucking proud of you."

She giggles, and the sound undoes me. We've only just started saying it, but I risk pushing my luck and blurt the words.

"And I love you so much."

Her breath catches, her eyes widening for a moment before her face settles into a smile.

"I love you too."

She tilts her head, and I lean in to kiss her. We start off

soft and slow, but it only takes a few seconds before she's gripping my hair again and I'm panting against her mouth.

"Now," I say, trailing my lips down her neck, "are you going to be a good girl and let me get back on my knees?"

I feel a tremble rock through her body.

"Natalie," she hisses, pretending to be scandalized even though her hips are flexing against mine.

I kiss all the way down to the collar of her dress and dart my tongue out to taste the hollow at the base of her throat. She moans.

"Okay," she whines, "but we have to be fast."

I glance up and give her a wink. "That's never been a problem before."

I sink to my knees and hitch the dress up again. Her skin pebbles with goose bumps.

"Hold this for me," I order.

She clutches the edge of the skirt, already squirming.

"Am I going to have to stand you up against the wall?" I ask. "Or can you stay still for me?"

She squeaks and squeezes her eyes shut. "I can stay still."

That soft little voice has me fighting the urge to rip her thong down her legs and devour her right this second, but I conjure up the strength to prolong this just a bit more.

I press my lips to the tiny bow again and then grab the waistband of the thong with my teeth. Brooke shudders as I use my mouth to slide it down, inch by inch, until it sits halfway down her thighs.

Then I devour her.

By now, I know exactly what strokes and flicks of my tongue drive her crazy. I grab her ass to pull her closer, so close I can't even breathe, but I don't care.

I just need her: the taste of her, the smell of her, the

sound of her stifled moans and whimpers as she bites her fist to keep quiet.

True to my word, the lack of time isn't a problem. We're both spurred on by the urgency, and it's only a few minutes before she's bucking against my face, her muscles tensing.

"Come for me," I urge. "Be a good girl and come."

She throws her head back and explodes with a silent scream. Her legs shake, her hips jerking. I muffle a moan of my own against her skin and don't let up until she pushes me away.

"You're going to destroy my clit if you keep making it feel that good," she gasps, her chest heaving.

I chuckle as I get to my feet. "Destroy your clit, huh?"

I rub my thumb along my lips and then pop it into my mouth, sucking off the taste of her. Her eyes narrow to hazy slits.

"That is so sexy," she mutters

I step closer and smooth down her hair. "You are so sexy."

We're still standing like that when there's a knock at the door.

"Natalie, *tu es là?*"

We both freeze at the sound of Jacinthe's voice and shoot each other a panicked look.

Brooke only just manages to yank her thong back up under her dress as the door swings open and Jacinthe pokes her head in.

A smirk instantly takes over her face.

"Oh ho ho," she drawls. "What do we have here, *hein?*"

Even though my heart is still racing with alarm, I manage to shoot her a death glare.

"*Tais-toi,*" I snap.

She is not deterred.

She strolls in with her hands in the pockets of the blazer she's wearing over some dark blue jeans and a crisp white shirt.

"So when *I* joke about christening all the beds at the inn, you say that's gross and unsanitary, but when *you* do it, it's fine?"

I raise an eyebrow. "We didn't use a bed."

Jacinthe cackles while Brooke splutters behind me.

"Brooke is a lady," Jacinthe chides, giving my shoulder a shove. "You're embarassing her, you horny ass."

Brooke clears her throat and steps up beside me, tossing her hair over her shoulder.

"Who says I'm not a horny ass too?"

Now I'm the one spluttering. Jacinthe gawks at her for a second before raising her hand for a high-five.

"Hell yeah!" she shouts before turning to me and dropping her voice to a conspiratorial whisper. "I like her."

"Me too," I whisper back.

Brooke laughs and smoothes down the front of her dress just as a distant shout echoes across the yard.

"*Voyons*, we gotta go." Jacinthe waves for us to follow her. "Maddie wants to open the doors, but first, I'm gonna tell her I caught you two boning."

"You are not telling her that!" I call out as we make our way across the grassy yard. "Or I'll tell your hot new farrier you think she's cute."

Jacinthe whips her head around to glare at me. "I don't think she's cute!"

I scoff. "You've met her once, and you've already mentioned her like five times."

"Because she overcharged me!"

She whirls around once we reach the back door, and I give her a teasing shove out of the way.

"You didn't need to describe her eyes to tell me she overcharged you."

"I wanted you to get the full picture!"

Before I can think up a comeback, Maddie comes zooming into the renovated kitchen to meet us, all dressed up in a no-nonsense navy shift dress and a delicate silver necklace that makes her look extra grown-up.

"There you are," she scolds, only sparing us a glance before going back to swiping at the screen of the tablet we bought for the inn. "Jass, you need to come help me with the final checks on the food. Natalie, can you make sure the banner in the lounge hasn't fallen down again? Brooke, your friend Layla just pulled up outside, but she said she wants to wait there until we're ready."

She snags Jacinthe's arm and tugs her away before any of us have a chance to reply.

"You can go check on Layla if you want," I say to Brooke once we're alone.

She shakes her head. "I'm sure she's buried in the crowd. I'm so glad she made it, though. She said the traffic was terrible leaving Montreal. Maybe I can convince her to move out here too."

A thrill shoots through me as I realize Brooke's new timeline for quitting her job means she can leave the city sooner. We've only talked about it in the abstract, but at this rate, we'll need to start making plans. Maybe touring rental properties together.

Before I can get too ahead of myself, I catch Brooke smirking at the distant sound of Maddie ordering Jass around in the kitchen.

"Maddie really seems to be thriving here," she says.

"That's one way to put it," I say, only managing a grimace for a moment before I go back to smiling.

Maddie might get a little intense sometimes, but Jacinthe and I would most certainly be floundering without her.

I lead the way into what used to be referred to as the living room but is now known as the lounge. The layout hasn't changed much, aside from some new built-in storage integrated into one of the walls and some updated furniture. The river rock fireplace is still the showstopper of the room, and Brooke's design choices have highlighted its charm.

The grand opening banner we had made for the party is still in place on the wall, which gives me an extra few minutes to pull Brooke into my arms and kiss her some more before Maddie and Jacinthe come speeding into the room.

"It's go time!" Maddie announces. "Everyone is ready. They're just waiting on us."

Despite her haste, she doesn't head for the foyer. Instead, she hovers in place, pressing her lips together as a wave of nerves seems to crash over us all.

I stuff my hands in the pockets of my slacks, rocking on my heels.

"This is it, huh?" I say.

Maddie jerks her head in a sharp nod. "This is it."

"Sure fucking is," Jacinthe adds.

I look at the two of them, and despite their grown-up business clothes and the years that have passed on their faces, I can still see the girls they once were.

These are the girls I climbed trees and got lost in the woods with. These are the girls I'd pull all-nighters with at countless sleepovers. They're the girls I snuck out to parties and tried my first illicit sips of beer with.

They're the girls I came out with.

They're the girls I worked all those shitty summer jobs

with, the three of us dreaming and scheming about the day we'd run a business all our own.

"Whatever happens..." I trail off and shake my head before starting again. "I mean, I'm not saying things won't be amazing, but whatever happens, I'm so glad I'm doing this with you."

Jacinthe piles in for a hug first, followed by Maddie, and then Brooke when I look over my shoulder and motion for her to join. We squeeze each other tight, breathing deep for a moment before we all end up giggling.

As we break apart, Brooke grabs my arm.

"It *will* be amazing," she asserts, staring into my eyes with such confidence and pride I feel like I could take the whole world on and win.

Maddie claps her hands and leads the way to the foyer.

"Okay, here we go!" she calls, reaching for the door handle.

Sunlight spills into the room, bright and bold, followed by a chorus of cheers so loud I stumble to a stop.

I had no idea this many people would show up for us. I can't even see them from here, but it sounds like the entire town must be out on the lawn.

Brooke takes my hand as a fresh surge of nerves threatens to keep me frozen in place. "You ready?" she asks, giving my fingers a squeeze.

I meet her gaze, finding that same look of pride still blazing in her eyes.

My nerves melt away.

For a moment, everything melts away, until it's just me and her in this house.

The house that changed everything.

The house that's about to change everything all over again as soon as we step out that door.

When I answer her, I put everything I have into loading my voice with enough conviction to let her know I'm not just talking about the inn.

I'm talking about us.

Our future.

Me and her and whatever the hell else the world decides to throw at us.

"I've never been more ready in my life."

About the Author

Katia Rose is not much of a Pina Colada person, but she does like getting caught in the rain. She loves to write romances that make her readers laugh, cry, and swoon (preferably in that order). She's rarely found without a cup of tea nearby, and she's more than a little obsessed with tiny plants. Katia is proudly bisexual and has a passion for writing about love in all its forms.

www.katiarose.com

Club Katia

Club Katia is a community that comes together to celebrate the awesomeness of romance novels and the people who read them. Joining also scores you some freebies to read!

Membership includes special updates, sneak peeks, access to Club Katia Exclusives (a collection of content available especially to members) and the opportunity to interact with fellow members in the Club Katia Facebook Group.

Joining is super easy and the club would love to have you! Visit www.katiarose.com/club-katia to get in on the good stuff.

Acknowledgments

Thank YOU, dear reader, for taking a trip to La Cloche with me. I'm beyond grateful to each and every person who gives some of their precious reading time to my stories. It will never cease to fill me with joy and wonder to know my work has a home on bookshelves all around the world, and I wish I could hug every one of you.

To my incredible beta team: Jen, Jaime, Fiona, Shelby, Izzie, Maggie, and Mari. Thank you for the time, effort, and enthusiasm you put into helping me make this story the best it can be. You all brought something special to your observations and feedback, and this book wouldn't be what it is without you.

To all my Club Katia friends: you rock my socks! I am the luckiest author in the world to have such sweet, caring, and hilarious readers helping to create such a fun community for us to enjoy together. Thank you for your endless enthusiasm, whether I'm deep in the writing cave for months or flouncing around on release days.

Thank you to the many loved ones in my 'beyond the book world' life for cheering me on and building me up. Special thanks to Warmonger for being an excellent merch model and lobster sculptor extraordinaire.

Thank you to my Star, for surviving the insanity of living with me while I write a book and only getting a little bit terrified. You have never failed to make me feel seen and celebrated, and I will never stop being grateful for your support.

Also by Katia Rose

Standalone Novels

The Summer List

Girlfriend Material

Just Might Work

The Devil Wears Tartan

This Used to Be Easier

Catch and Cradle

Thigh Highs

Latte Girl

Three Rivers Series

Passing Through

Turning Back

Chasing Stars

The Barflies Series

The Bar Next Door

Glass Half Full

One For the Road

When the Lights Come On

The Sherbrooke Station Quartet

Your Rhythm

Your Echo

Your Sound

Your Chorus

Up Next

Passing Through

Emily Rivers does not have time for love.

Or dating.

Or even a one night stand.

As the eldest of the Rivers sisters, she's too focused on keeping her family's campground running in the wake of a devastating tragedy to even think about romance.

When Kim Jefferies shows up at the local small town bar looking like a lesbian snack on a stick, Emily writes her off as yet another tourist just passing through—no matter how much the butterflies in her stomach try to tell her otherwise.

Only Kim's plans of 'passing through' fade the second she sees Emily Rivers, despite the fact that the whole point of her soul-searching journey was to stop falling for random women in bars who only lead her to heartbreak.

The last thing they're looking for is a love story, but with the help of some conniving sisters, an interfering bartender, and the magic of the great outdoors, that might be exactly what Kim and Emily are going to get.

Read on for a free excerpt from book one in Katia's other bestselling sapphic small town series: Three Rivers!

Chapter 1

Emily

The toilet makes a gurgling sound. I freeze, the wrench going still in my hands as the pipes in front of me start to rattle.

The gurgling gets louder.

I give up on the pipes and rush over to the stall housing the broken toilet I've spent the past two hours trying to fix. The relief that washes over me when I see the bowl is finally refilling swells into panic when the water climbs higher and higher up the sides of the bowl with no sign of slowing down. If anything, the water is speeding up. A few more gurgles ripple the surface of the rising tide before the pipes let out a keening groan.

That's the only warning I get before the whole toilet erupts like Old Faithful—with me standing right in the splash zone.

I shriek as cold—but mercifully clear—toilet water douses the front of my leggings and chambray button-up. A cascade of droplets splatters against the floor tiles. I lunge for the toilet's handle and jam it down a few times, but water continues to gush over the edge of the bowl to form a rapidly expanding puddle on the washroom floor.

The swear words I've been muttering under my breath turn into a full-out bellow of "FUCK!" when the pipes give another rattle just before the toilet in the next stall over erupts too.

The chain reaction continues all the way down the line of stalls like some kind of fancy fountain show at a resort, only instead of being synchronized to classical music, the jets of water shooting out of the toilets are timed to my curses and screams.

I race back over to the pipes and start yanking on every bolt I can reach with the wrench, twisting and turning in the vain hope that I can do something to stop this entire block of the campground's toilets from turning into a waterlogged wasteland we absolutely do not have the money to fix.

We barely had the money to get *one* toilet fixed—hence me going the DIY route armed only with my dad's tool bag and a few YouTube videos.

I'm still flailing the wrench around and screeching in despair when my sister Trish comes careening into the room with her eyes wide and a jagged rock brandished above her head like she's prepared to fight off an attacker.

"What the hell?" she demands, still holding the rock up with one hand as she scans the washroom. Her eyes get even wider as she takes in the chaos.

"They won't shut off!" I wail. "I don't know what to do."

Her head whips back and forth between me and the row of stalls before she takes a few tottering steps back towards the door.

"I'll get Dad."

I shake my head and shift the wrench back over to a bolt

Paint the Moon

I've already tightened. With the washroom just minutes away from turning into a lake, I don't have many options besides trying the same bolts all over again.

"He's out in the boat," I tell Trish while I crank the wrench. "He's been out there all damn day. *Again.* Goddammit."

My wrist twinges in protest of my particularly vicious crank, and I hiss at the pain.

"We've got to shut the water supply off," Trish says.

"That would be great if I actually knew where the thing to do that is."

I know pretty much everything there is to know about running this campground. I can file taxes, balance a budget, and troubleshoot the online booking system. I can also split firewood, jump start a truck, and use a chainsaw.

I might as well be known as a renaissance woman of the woods, but one of the very few things I cannot do is plumbing.

Dad was always the one who handled that—back when he actually handled things.

My groan of frustration is tinged with guilt. It hasn't even been two years. I should be more patient. I know grief works differently for everyone, but in moments like this, I can't help wondering when the grief is going to clear enough for him to see he still has three daughters who need him.

"I think it's coming out of here."

I blink and realize Trish has come to stand beside me in front of the white cinderblock wall lined with exposed pipes that have all been painted white too. She squats down in front of a valve and tries to twist it, but the thing doesn't budge.

I have no idea how or why she thinks that valve is the

problem, and I don't get a chance to ask her before she hoists up her anti-assailant rock and starts smashing it against the side of the valve.

"Trish!" I scream. "What the hell? Stop it! You're going to break something and make it worse!"

"We. Need. To. Shut. It. Off."

She emphasizes each word with a strike of the rock. The clanging sound rings out over the splashing and gurgling still filling the room as the pooling toilet water creeps further and further towards the edges of the floor.

"Trish, stop!"

I hover over her and try to grab her arm. She swats me away with her free hand and keeps bludgeoning the valve. After a couple more strikes, the valve creaks and shifts a fraction of an inch.

"AHA!" Trish crows.

I shout for her to stop again and make another lunge for her arm. Just when I've finally got her incapacitated, the pipes make a weird sucking sound before they go totally silent.

"Oh my god," I say, my fingers still wrapped tight around her wrist. "Did that work?"

We stay frozen in place, blinking at each other as we strain our ears to catch any hint of an incoming toilet explosion.

Nothing happens. I can still hear the drip-drop of the remaining overflow trickling over the edges of the toilets, but the relentless gushing has stopped.

Trish pries my hand off her before straightening up and making a show out of tossing her hair over her shoulder.

"I think a 'thank you' is in order."

I walk over to pace the length of the stalls and ensure the water really has shut off. The metal sides of the stalls are all coated in droplets and the floor looks more like a pond, but there's nothing else pumping through the pipes.

"Thank you for not smashing the pipes up like a maniac," I say as I do one more round of pacing to double-check. "Oh wait, that's exactly what you did."

She lets out a humph. "That's no way to be grateful to your savior."

I'd never give my second-youngest sister the satisfaction of calling her a savior; she'd probably end up recording my voice and then blasting the sound through a megaphone while parading around the whole campground. Still, I give up on my pacing and lean against one of the sinks before I thank her for real.

"I don't know how the hell you figured that out," I say, "but thanks. I probably would have flooded the entire washroom block if you hadn't shown up."

She shrugs. "Probably."

I turn to face the mirror over the sink. The harsh fluorescent lighting makes me look even more sleep-deprived than I already am. My haphazard bun can't hide how greasy the roots of my hair are, and my face somehow looks both puffy and gaunt at the same time.

I lean forward to squint at the space between my eyebrows and then work my features through a few different expressions as I observe the shifts in my skin.

"Ugh," I say after leaning back. "That's definitely a wrinkle."

Trish scoffs. "Right. Yeah. You're an ancient hag at the age of twenty-eight."

"Just because you've got that whole smooth as a baby's bottom thing going on doesn't mean the rest of us aren't suffering," I tell her.

She makes a face as she comes over to stand beside me, leaving her trusty rock on the floor.

"Ew. Don't compare my face to a baby's butt, you weirdo. Also, you spend like seven thousand dollars a year on all those hippie skincare products. Your face probably has the same genetic makeup as, like, tree sap by now. I think you're fine."

That gets me to crack a smile. "I do not spend seven thousand dollars on skincare."

Trish gives me some side-eye.

"It's more like...two thousand," I admit.

I could blame it on wanting to support all the small businesses I get most of my products from, but really, I am kind of a skincare fanatic.

"So..." Trish says as she crosses her arms over her chest and looks over the absolute disaster that is the toilet stalls. "I guess we should clean this up?"

I sigh and tug out my hair elastic so I can redo my bun, but I end up leaving the strands down so I can rub my fingers along my scalp in an attempt to ward off an oncoming headache.

"I guess that's all we can do. I just hope hearing about this is enough to get Dad out here to work on it tomorrow. I don't want to call in a plumber unless I've got absolutely no other choice. They always rip us off like crazy and charge a fortune to come all the way out here."

I sigh again as I start doing the financial calculations in my head. We pushed off a lot of repairs last year to recoup from having to shut the whole campground down in the middle of high season the year before that. I'm already paying more than I'd like to have a company come in to do some updates to our septic system, and it's too late to push that off another year. Even a few hundred bucks spent on a plumbing emergency would hit us hard.

"I guess I could call that old contractor guy over in Port Alberni," I say, my eyes unfocused as I stare down at the floor with numbers whirring around in my vision. "He's not really a plumber, but he installed all those pumps with Dad a few years ago, and he'd probably give us a better deal than someone we don't know. Oh, or maybe Scooter knows somebody. They must have to get stuff fixed at the bar. Then again, they might just be getting ripped off as bad as us. Maybe I could call—"

"Emily."

I only realize I've been speaking so fast I'm out of breath when Trish steps in front of me to grip both my shoulders. I pull in a deep gasp of air as she gives me a squeeze.

"There we go," she says. "Breathe."

She spins me around so she can start rubbing my back. I'm about to tell her I'm fine, but the pressure of her hands on my stress-tightened muscles cuts off all my protests.

Trish gives some of the best back rubs in the world. I think she gets her skills from spending pretty much every morning of her life kneading countless batches of dough in her bakery.

"Dad is going to come back soon, and once he realizes how much we need him, he's going to get the plumbing sorted out," she says in a firm but reassuring tone. "We're not going to have to spend a bunch of money on it. Everything is going to be fine."

My shoulders slump forward, and I groan as she works out a particularly vicious knot just under my neck.

"I hope so," I say. "There's just so much to do. We have a month until the start of the season, and the septic system guys are nowhere near done. They didn't even show up at all today. Plus, I've got that whole thing with the garbage collection to sort out, and—"

"*Emily.*"

The warning note in her tone is paired with a sharp dig of her thumbs.

"Okay, okay," I say so she'll continue with the massage. "I'll stop."

"It's always a crazy time of year, and we always get it all done. Clover will be here soon, and we'll get all our usual student workers for the summer too. It's all going to come together."

Our youngest sister, Clover, is doing her bachelor's degree down at the University of Victoria, but she comes home to work at the campground every summer. Even at twenty-one, she's way better at wrangling the college students we take on for seasonal positions than I am. She doesn't arrive for another few weeks, though, and most of the students don't get here until late April.

I have about half a million things to figure out before then. This season has to be our most profitable yet if we're going to recover from the shutdown two years ago.

I don't mention that part to Trish. She already knows we've only been scraping by, and after the day I've had, the last thing I want to do is get into a conversation that reminds us both we're just a couple months away from the two year anniversary of losing our mom.

"I just wish I had some kind of full-time, all-purpose handyman," I say instead, "like a jack of all trades who could reliably take on all the little things Dad usually does. I wonder if there's anyone local who could do that for a few weeks, just until we open. Maybe Scooter knows if—"

"Emily, enough!"

Paint the Moon

Trish gives me a whack to the back and then whirls me around to face her.

"I bet you haven't even eaten dinner. You've been running around this place all day. You're not gonna solve all our problems tonight, so just relax, okay?"

She stares me down with her warm brown eyes narrowed in challenge.

She has Dad's brown eyes and brown hair. So does Clover. I'm the only one who's blonde like Mom.

"Ha," I bark. "Relaxing. You're funny."

She plants her hands on her hips. "I'm serious. It's Friday night, and we've both been working like crazy all week. Let's have some fun. We'll get this mess mopped up, and I'll heat up some of that big batch of stew I made, and after we eat, we can drive up to the bar. I bet Scooter will give us free shots if we look sad enough."

She wags her eyebrows like she's just presented me with an offer I can't refuse, but I scoff and shake my head.

"Yes to the stew. No to the bar. Look at me, Trish. I am not fit to be in public this evening."

She waves my excuse off as we both head to the door so we can hunt around for mops in the cleaning supply room.

"The bar doesn't count as public. It's just going to be local old dudes there at this time of year. They'll call us dolls no matter what we look like. They'll probably even buy us beers. It'll be great."

I shake my head. "Yeah, no thanks. I think I'll stay in and enjoy my seven thousand dollars' worth of skincare products instead."

Trish has a way of getting what she wants. After guilt-tripping me about slaving over the stew we ate for dinner as well as her 'heroic efforts' with the toilet pipes, she convinced me to take a shower and reconsider her proposal about going to the bar.

I reminded her that she got paid to make that stew for the bakery, cafe, and pre-made meal shop she runs year-round at the campground, but I still got in the shower.

I finish wrapping my hair in a towel and then slip into my well-loved terrycloth robe before dabbing on some moisturizer and eye cream. My bathroom is on the smaller side, but I've maximized the storage space as much as I can to fit my extensive collection of bottles, jars, and canisters.

The huge picture window that is the bathroom's crowning jewel gives me a view of the last traces of soft evening light filtering through the thick fir tree forest that spans the property of Three Rivers Campground. I've always thought the window would be the perfect backdrop for a decadent soaker tub, but despite moving into the tiny A-frame next to the main house way back when I moved home after college, I still haven't gotten around to that particular renovation.

Once my face is hydrated and I've given myself a couple seconds to glare at the faint wrinkle I spotted earlier, I head out to the main room and find Trish sprawled on her stomach on my couch with one of my thick coffee table books about interior design propped in front of her face.

"There's some weird stuff in here," she says without looking up from the page. "I'm really glad you didn't come back from Vancouver and try to turn the whole campground into some ultra-modern alien house thing."

I chuckle at the admittedly apt description of the book

she's looking at and then head up the stairs to my lofted bedroom.

After high school, I did an interior design program in Vancouver and then worked in the city for a bit before making the move back out to the island. I still take design clients during the off-season, and my skills were put to good use turning what was once an outdated guest house into my little dream home here in the A-frame.

The wood panels of the walls are blended with the soothing beige and moss green tones of my bedroom decor. I wanted the whole A-frame to feel like the perfect midpoint between the cozy country charm I grew up with and the clean contemporary look I fell in love with at design school.

I toss my robe onto the bed and pull on a pair of underwear and my comfiest bra before I start hunting around for some loungewear. I may have said I'd consider going out, but after the soothing warmth of the shower, there's no way I'm leaving my nest tonight.

Trish comes stomping up the stairs before I have a chance to make my clothing selection.

"Knock much?" I ask as she heads over to my bed and flops onto her back.

"Your loft doesn't have a door," she shoots back. "Plus, I had to make sure you didn't sneak into pajamas. We are going to the bar tonight, whether you like it or not."

I glance between her and the fluffy pajama bottoms I was halfway to pulling out of my dresser drawer.

"But I'm all cozy," I whine.

She shakes her head. "No excuses. It's Friday, woman. The least you can do is have a beer with your poor sister so she doesn't have to face the sadness of being a twenty-six year-old woman alone at a bar."

She springs to her feet and heads for my closet. I watch

her spend a few seconds flipping through the hangers before she pulls a light grey sweater out and tosses it at my head.

"Wear that," she orders, "and some jeans, and then we're good to go."

She sits back down on the edge of my bed with her arms crossed, and the look in her eye tells me I won't get any peace tonight unless I submit to her will.

"Fine, but I'm only getting one drink."

Chapter 2

Kim

River's Bend was supposed to be a must-see attraction, but even on a Friday night, the supposedly 'vibrant and artistic community' halfway between Port Alberni and Tofino feels as ghostly and neglected as most of the tourist hotspots I've visited. Apparently early March was the wrong time of year to take a road trip around Vancouver Island.

I knew the open air theater that puts on low-budget plays and readings would probably be shut down for the season, but I was hoping to pull in here early enough in the day to visit the River's Bend Indigenous Arts Center and get a spot at the local campground to park my van for the night.

Turns out both those things are closed for the season too.

The only thing in town with any lights on—if you can call a collection of about ten buildings along a strip of highway a 'town'—was a bar, so I settled on French fries and an IPA for dinner.

"Where you headed, love?"

One of the old men who've been piled around a big round table in a corner of the room since I arrived props his elbow on the bar beside me and grins.

I jerk upright in my barstool. I'd been zoning out while sipping from my pint glass and didn't notice him walk over. He keeps beaming at me, and I can't tell if he's being creepy or just small town friendly. After so many years of living in Toronto, I'd forgotten that sometimes people really are just being nice when they walk up and say hello to you.

"Oh, uh, just doing the whole drive to Tofino thing," I answer as I set my glass back down on a coaster advertising a small British Columbia brewery.

"Not a popular time of year for that."

I notice him trying to catch the bartender's eye where he's polishing some glasses down at the other end of the bar, and my posture relaxes a little. This guy is probably just making conversation while he waits to order another drink.

That does make a lot more sense than him trying to shoot his shot. It only takes the faintest trace of gaydar for anyone to guess I'm a raging lesbian. If the undercut doesn't do it, the men's shirts and stacks of butch-tastic leather bracelets usually tip them off.

"Yeah, apparently not," I say. "I didn't realize there was this much of an off-season."

He nods. "We do get folks passing through year-round, but March is nothing like the summer. You wouldn't catch me in here on a Friday night in July even if you paid me. Too many city people. Too much of that noise Scooter has the audacity to call rock music."

He directs the last part at the bartender, who's set his polishing cloth down and wandered over to us.

Even I can tell he'd be hot to those interested in the men

folk, with his long, sleek black hair pulled up into a bun and tribal tattoos coating both his arms under a tight t-shirt.

Despite the bad boy look, he's got that same small town friendliness as the old guy beside me. He literally leaned over the bar when I walked in to shake my hand and introduce himself as Scooter Lee, manager of the establishment.

I still haven't figured out what 'the establishment' is actually called. There was no name outside, just a buzzing neon open sign in the window along with a few light-up logos for some of the beers they have on tap.

The interior is just as nondescript: a few strings of colourful flags adorning the walls, shelves of liquor illuminated by some tacky blue strip lights, and a collection of battered wooden tables arranged around the room, their surfaces rubbed to a glimmering sheen by years and years' worth of elbows and coasters. The air is tinged with the bitter tang of beer and musk, cut through with a faint wisp of the fresh fir tree scent that seems to cling to this entire island.

That's another thing Toronto made me forget: what it's like to step outside and fill your lungs with so much fresh air you get dizzy, to gulp the oxygen down again and again because it just tastes so damn good. I've spent almost my whole trip with the van windows cracked despite the March chill, my nose always seeking the next hit of those trees.

"It's alternative rock."

Scooter's voice pulls me back into the moment. I turn to watch the old man's reaction while Scooter pours his drink without needing to ask what his order is.

"Alternative, eh?" the man says. "Alternative to what? Good quality? Talent?"

Scooter shakes his head and chuckles as he flicks a

coaster off the top of a nearby stack and then plops the beer down to slide it across the bar, all in one smooth motion that makes my eyes widen.

"Ouch, Jerry. Way to bite the hand that fills your beer up."

The old man—who I can now presume is named Jerry—chuckles too as he takes his drink.

"Someone's got to knock you down a few pegs before the tourist girls start showing up and inflating your ego all summer." He turns to wink at me. "Watch out for that one's big head, love."

I press a fist to my mouth to stifle a laugh as he heads back to his table. I guess Jerry just has a respect for age-appropriate flirting and in fact possesses no gaydar at all.

"Sorry about him," Scooter says when I turn back to face him. "He's just chatty."

I shrug. "It's fine. He seems like quite the character."

Scooter laughs and heads back for his polishing cloth before bringing the tray of glasses he's working on closer so we can keep talking.

"That's an understatement. The guy has an opinion on everything. He's actually the reason they started calling me Scooter around here."

I dip a French fry into the glob of ketchup on my plate and ask, "Oh? Do I get to hear the story?"

Scooter leans against the edge of the bar and spins the cloth around the rim of a glass while he answers.

"So, I showed up in River's Bend on a holiday from the city. Same as you. Same as countless other people, and just like countless other people, I fell in love with it. Thought about it the whole time I was over in Tofino, so when I drove back through, I thought, why not look for a job here? Just something for the summer. I'm from Vancouver, and I needed a break from the whole big city life thing. The first place I started asking around for work was here at the bar."

I take a sip of my beer as I nod for him to go on. When I was first planning my trip to the west coast, the fact that Vancouver the *city* is over on the mainland and not here on Vancouver the *island* kept tripping me up, but I've got it sorted out in my head now.

"I was travelling on a motorcycle," Scooter continues, "and when I asked to talk to the owner, he came out and wanted to know if I was the one who pulled in on a bike. He happens to love motorcycles, which was lucky for me. Jerry, however, knows absolutely nothing about them, but he took one look at my bike through the window and then yelled to the whole bar, 'That's not a motorcycle! That's a damn scooter!'"

His Jerry impression is spot-on, and I have to force myself to swallow before I start laughing so I don't choke on my beer.

"I guess it wasn't big enough to impress him," Scooter continues. "Like I said, he's got opinions on everything, and he loves to share them. He started calling me Scooter after I got the job, and it just stuck. I'm pretty sure ninety percent of people in River's Bend don't even know that's not my legal name."

"Wow, that's some small town lore right there," I say through more laughter.

Scooter picks up the next glass and lets out a laugh of his own.

"Yeah, that's kind of how it goes around here. Things just...stick. So don't say I didn't warn you if you find yourself back in this bar in a few days looking for a job. It's not busy enough yet for us to hire anyone else on."

I shake my head. "I don't think that'll be a problem. I

only started travelling a couple weeks ago, and I'm trying to see as much of BC as I can."

He nods. "It's beautiful. Not just the island. The whole province is stunning."

"Yeah, it's—"

I cut myself off when the sound of the bar's door opening behind me is met by a chorus of greetings from the old boys club. Scooter looks past me and lifts his hand in a wave as his face splits into a wide grin.

I twist around and grip the back of my bar stool to get a look at whoever seems to have just made the day of everyone in this bar.

It only takes a split-second of staring before my whole day is made too.

There are two women standing in the doorway.

Two very attractive women who I would happily fight through an entire crowd of chatty old men just to get the chance to say hi to.

"Scooter!" one of them shouts. "My favourite bartender ever!"

Scooter lets out a fake groan from behind me. "You're trying to get me to give you free drinks, aren't you, Trish?"

The woman saunters over with an exaggerated innocent expression on her face. She's got thick brown hair with the slightest hint of red to it and curves for days under her cardigan and leggings.

"What? No! I just want you to know how great I think you are." She props her elbows on the bar next to me and beams at him. "Although now that you mentioned a free drink, I wouldn't say no."

He sets his features into a glare he can't quite manage to keep up. "This establishment is for paying customers only, ma'am."

She scowls. "Don't ma'am me."

A laugh bursts out of me as I watch their stare-down continue, and the woman turns and blinks like she's just noticed me sitting beside her.

Her eyes widen as she looks me up and down and then blurts, "Who the hell are you?"

"Trish!" Scooter scolds. "You can't come in here and say things like that to my customers."

She waves him off as she keeps staring at me, her surprise wearing off and shifting into an expression I can only describe as mischievous. "Oh, you know I didn't mean it like that. I just meant we don't usually see anyone new in here at this time of year. I think Emily is going to be *very* happy we came out tonight."

She glances over her shoulder, and I follow her line of sight to the other woman, who's still standing back at the door with her phone in her hands. Her head is bent over the screen. She's got her honey blonde hair up in a tight ponytail, but a few strands have slipped out to frame her face.

From what I can see of her face so far, it's a particularly gorgeous one, with rounded cheeks, a strong, almost regal-looking nose, and rosy pink lips pushed into a little pout as she frowns at whatever is on her phone.

That plush bottom lip is just begging for someone to bite it.

I whip my head back around to face the bar again as soon as the thought enters my mind.

I came to British Columbia to avoid this kind of thing: sitting in bars with pretty women I always end up feeling way too much for way too fast. The whole point of my road trip is to process the break-up with Steph in a healthy and mature way that does not involve jumping into bed with anyone new. I'm living in a campervan that barely *has* a bed to jump into. I've made it as easy as possible for myself to stick to my post-break-up, post-job-loss resolutions.

That doesn't stop the back of my neck from itching with the urge to turn around and get another look at the blonde woman.

"Emily!" the woman beside me snaps. She slaps one of her palms against the bar to emphasize her shout. "Stop working and get over here."

I keep myself busy taking another sip of beer as I listen to Emily's footsteps approach behind me.

"Hey, Scooter."

I watch from the corner of my eye as she slides up to the bar beside Trish.

"Hey, Emily." Scooter is back to his polishing now, and he waves his cloth in greeting. "How's it going?"

Emily props one of her elbows on the bar so she can lean forward and massage her temple. She's still got that little frustrated pout going, and I decide I've never seen anyone in my life who can make 'tired and slightly pissed off' such a sexy expression.

"Oh, you know, busy time of year for us," she says. "I was actually wondering who you use for your plum—"

She gets cut off by Trish clearing her throat and giving a pointed jerk of her chin towards me.

I figure this is the moment to stop side-eyeing Emily and turn to face her instead. I shift in my bar stool, and our eyes lock for the first time.

She's even prettier when I'm looking at her straight-on. It's hard to see exactly what colour her eyes are in the dim light of the bar, but I can tell they're some kind of blue-green. She blinks at me, the pout falling away as her bottom lip drops into a soft expression of surprise.

She's wearing a light grey sweater with a wide enough

neckline to show off a hint of her collarbones as well as a gold necklace with a tiny charm I can't quite make out from here. I think it might be some kind of bird.

I jerk my gaze back up to her face when I realize it's going to look like I'm ogling her chest, but I find her in the middle of giving me a full once-over. A rush of satisfaction runs through me, along with a few scattered pricks of heat that seem to spark against my skin wherever she looks at me.

I'm sure the whole exchange only takes a couple seconds, but when she meets my eyes again and then flicks her gaze away as soon as she realizes I've caught her staring, it feels like the whole room jumps back into action after grinding to a complete standstill.

"Sorry," she says, staring down at the bar for a moment as she adjusts her hair. "I didn't even see you there."

When she looks back up at me, her body language has shifted. All the openness of her surprise—and her subsequent checking me out—is gone, replaced by a calm and reserved sort of friendliness.

"Who, um, are you?" she asks.

Scooter groans.

"Seriously, you two, you've got to learn some manners if you're going to come in here and talk to my customers. People are going to think you live in the woods. Oh wait, you literally do."

He laughs at his own joke. My curiosity must show on my face because he tacks on an explanation for me.

"They run the campground down the road. They rarely see civilization."

Trish scoffs. "Oh, and you're *so* civilized up here. Freaking Michelin Star establishment you've got going on."

He shrugs. "I mean if anyone in River's Bend did get a Michelin Star, we all know it would be me."

Trish smacks the bar top again and leans forward like she's about to grab him by the collar and drag him into the street for a brawl. I've only known her for about five minutes, but I already believe she could manage that just fine.

"Oh, them's fighting words, boy," she says. "We all know the Riverview Cafe would get that star, even if there were more than two places in a forty kilometer radius that serve food around here. Your French fries just wouldn't cut it, my dude."

Scooter gasps and places a hand on his chest. "My French fries are incredible. Just ask our new friend here."

He sweeps his hand out towards me, and everyone turns to look at me. I glance down at the remnants of fries and smeared ketchup left on my plate.

"I wouldn't get involved in this if I were you," Emily says, coming to my rescue as I'm contemplating the most diplomatic response to make. "I've learned to just stay out of their rivalry."

I give her a grateful smile. "That's good advice, considering I don't even know what the rivalry is about."

Emily leans farther forward across the bar so we can see each other better.

"This one manages the bar, and this one manages the Riverview Cafe and Kitchen down at our campground," she says, pointing at each of them in turn. "You would think they could coexist peacefully considering the bar only opens an hour before the café closes, but you'd be wrong."

I nod. "I see, I see. So, uh, it's River's Bend...and the Riverview Cafe...and Three Rivers Campground. Is there anything within a forty kilometer radius not named after a river?"

I expected a couple chuckles, but as soon as I'm done

Paint the Moon

talking, all three of them burst out laughing hard enough they need a few seconds before they can speak.

"It's just funny when you say it all out loud like that," Emily explains after noticing my confused expression, "considering our last name is literally Rivers."

She motions between her and Trish.

"So you're sisters?" I ask. "Is the town named after your family or something?"

Trish slings an arm around Emily's shoulders.

"Yep, this is my big sis. We've got a little sister too, so everyone's always joking about us *being* the three Rivers, but the campground is named after three *actual* rivers nearby. Our grandpa just happened to decide his last name was a sign he should buy the campground way back before our dad was born."

I grin as I listen to the small town lore. That's turned out to be one of the perks of travelling at this time of year; almost every local person I've met has had time to share a few stories with me instead of being swamped by other tourists.

"But I can see why you'd believe these two own the whole town," Scooter adds with a fake glare at Trish. "They certainly act like they own my bar."

Trish smirks at him. "Speaking of, where's my drink?"

After a few more rounds of banter, Scooter pours the two of them pints of the same IPA I'm drinking. He also pours them a shot of whiskey each, which Trish demands over the sound of Emily's protests.

"It's Friday," she insists. "You said you'd come out and have fun."

"I said I'd have one drink," Emily counters.

"So pour the shot in your beer and drink them both at the same time."

Emily makes a face. "Sometimes I find it hard to believe Clover is the one still in college, not you."

I'm assuming Clover is the little sister. I'd place Trish and Emily in their late twenties like me. I'm about to ask where their sister is going to school when Scooter looks over at me after setting down two shot glasses filled with amber liquid.

"You want one too? I'll give it to you on the house to compensate for having to put up with these two."

Trish huffs. "Oh, *she* gets a free shot?"

Scooter shakes his head at her and then grabs another shot glass after I've given a shrug to show I'm game. The place I've booked to stay tonight isn't too much farther up the highway, so I can spare a couple hours before I start driving again.

A twinge of guilt hits when the responsible part of my brain tries to tell me I should be getting out of here as fast as I can, not hanging around to make more small talk with Emily, but really, that's all it is: small talk with some friendly locals. It's not like I'm trying to put the moves on her or anything.

"Be nice, Trish. Have you even asked for her name yet?" Scooter asks.

Emily gasps from around Trish's other side.

"Oh my god," she says as she slides off her bar stool and steps over to me. "We really are being rude. We didn't even introduce ourselves. I'm Emily Rivers."

She offers me her hand, and I twist around in my seat so I can reach for her.

Her palm is warm as it slides against mine. Her skin is soft and a bit slippery, like she put lotion on not too long ago, but I can feel a few calluses at the base of her fingers too. I imagine she must spend a lot of time working outside at the campground.

Something about her dainty necklace, soft skin, and carefully pinned back hair combined with the grit her palm hints at makes me keep clutching her hand for a little too long.

Femmes with a rough side are my weakness. My most recent ex, Steph, always had people asking for proof when she told them she works as a general contractor. Nobody believed a woman who made walking in heels look as effortless as she did could also install a washing machine and fix a leaking fridge with just as much ease.

It drove me crazy. She was always trying to teach me things around the house, but most of our lessons got interrupted by me grabbing her face to tell her how goddamn sexy she was.

But that's done now.

My longest relationship to date ended with zero warning just a couple weeks before I was let go at work with a similar level of warning.

I realize both Scooter and Trish are staring at me now as Emily's gaze continues to bore into mine. I force myself to swallow down the lump in my throat so I can answer her.

"Kim Jefferies. It's, um, nice to meet you."

I let go of her hand, and she stands there staring for another half a second before she moves back to her seat.

Scooter is now pretending to be extra busy with his polishing, but Trish does nothing to hide the smug look on her face as she glances between me and her sister.

"Do you two want to get your own table?" she asks.

Emily's too shielded behind Trish for me to see what kind of look she gives her, but I notice Trish's stool rock a little. I bite back a smile when I realize Emily must have kicked Trish's chair.

Trish turns to me and sticks out her hand. "I'm Trish Rivers. It is very nice to meet you, Kim. We thought the only company we were going to have tonight was Jerry and his million and one opinions on everything."

She nods over at the table of old guys.

"Oh, she's already met Jerry," Scooter says, "and he's already shared a few opinions."

I join in their laughter since I'm actually in the loop on this one. Trish grabs her shot glass and lifts it up.

"Let us raise a toast," she says, "to the arrival of Kim Jefferies, the mysterious off-season tourist who has appeared to give us a fun Friday night."

"To Kim," Scooter says, lifting the empty glass he's just finished polishing. "May she survive her first night with the Rivers sisters, or may God rest her soul."

I don't know why he says 'first night' when he already knows I'm just passing through.

"To Kim," Emily echoes.

I hold my breath as I wait to see if she'll add anything else. I'd be happy if all she did was say my name again.

I'd be happy if all she did was say my name all night.

No. Bad Kim.

I force myself to focus on my own shot glass before my gaze can dip to Emily's bottom lip again—the delicious, plump pink lip that I will absolutely *not* have between my teeth tonight.

That was my promise to myself before I flew out here: no vacation flings. No runaway romances. Not even any hook-up buddies.

I came to BC to focus on me. I came here to heal and sort my life out so I don't keep making the same damn mistakes again and again. I came here to walk in the mountains, run on the beaches, and listen to the whisperings of the earth resonate in my heart, or whatever the hell the tourism industry of British Columbia tries to convince people they can do here.

Right now, I'm just sharing a drink and some conversation.

Just one drink, and then I'll be gone.

Grab your copy at www.katiarose.com!